DEMANDING LOVE

"I am a woman, Jason. I am your wife. How long will you continue to ignore me?" Hannah demanded, then gasped as Jason stalked toward her furiously, his strong fingers closing painfully on the flesh of her shoulders.

"Hannah, you go too far!" he warned, shaking her for emphasis. Hannah grew silent, peering up at him with wide, misty eyes, her hair tumbling riotously about her shoulders, her bosom rising and falling, her face becomingly flushed. She ached for Jason's arms about her, yearned for his mouth on hers, and she leaned against him and closed her eyes, lifting her face for his kiss.

Jason stared down at her, fighting the desire that threatened to overwhelm him. Finally able to fight it no longer, he surrendered to his deepest urges and swept her against him, his strong arms closing about her trembling softness, his mouth swooping down upon her parted lips.

EXCITING BESTSELLERS FROM ZEBRA

PASSION'S REIGN by Karen Harper   (1177, $3.95)

Golden-haired Mary Bullen was wealthy, lovely and refined—and lusty King Henry VIII's prize gem! But her passion for the handsome Lord William Stafford put her at odds with the Royal Court. Mary and Stafford lived by a lovers' vow: one day they would be ruled by only the crown of PASSION'S REIGN.

HEIRLOOM by Eleanora Brownleigh   (1200, $3.95)

The surge of desire Thea felt for Charles was powerful enough to convince her that, even though they were strangers and their marriage was a fake, fate was playing a most subtle trick on them both: Were they on a mission for President Teddy Roosevelt—or on a crusade to realize their own passionate desire?

LOVESTONE by Deanna James   (1202, $3.50)

After just one night of torrid passion and tender need, the dark-haired, rugged lord could not deny that Moira, with her precious beauty, was born to be a princess. But how could he grant her freedom when he himself was a prisoner of her love?

DEBORAH'S LEGACY by Stephen Marlowe   (1153, $3.75)

Deborah was young and innocent. Benton was worldly and experienced. And while the world rumbled with the thunder of battle, together they rose on a whirlwind of passion—daring fate, fear and fury to keep them apart!

Available wherever paperbacks are sold, or order direct from the Publisher. Send cover price plus 50¢ per copy for mailing and handling to Zebra Books, 475 Park Avenue South, New York, N.Y. 10016 DO NOT SEND CASH.

Breathless Passion

BY CATHERINE CREEL

ZEBRA BOOKS
KENSINGTON PUBLISHING CORP.

ZEBRA BOOKS

are published by

KENSINGTON PUBLISHING CORP.
475 Park Avenue South
New York, N.Y. 10016

Printed in the United States of America

For the newest little love in my life—Caleb
James Creel; and for his Granny, too.

One

Hannah Fairfield gazed outward across the rolling white-capped water and thought back once again to the disturbing turn of events that had served to bring her to this particular moment in time, this moment when she stood alone in the cold, damp wind upon the creaking, pitching deck of the masted ship, now a few short hours' sailing time from their destination of Seattle. As she brought a slender, gloved hand up to sweep several escaping tendrils of the honey-blond hair from her flushed cheeks, she thought back to the day, some six months earlier, when she had, for better or for worse, she reminded herself ruefully, made her fateful decision to become a member of this group of "mail-order brides" bound for new lives and unseen husbands in the far Northwest, a rough-and-ready timber country still inhabited almost exclusively by woman-hungry men in this year of 1866.

She remembered vividly her determination to escape from her virtually uneventful life on her family's farm in upstate New York, to escape the increasingly harsh and cruel treatment of her new stepfather. When his unwarranted bullying and vile attentions had finally become too much to bear, she had fled and eventually found her way to the city.

Though she had saved the small amount of money which her late father had given her so long ago, money which had remained hidden beneath the mattress of her bed, she had been forced to seek employment the same week she arrived in the huge, unfamiliar city. She had been fortunate enough to locate a distant cousin of her mother's—a woman no more than ten years her senior—who worked at a local tavern. And, although Hannah certainly did not relish the idea, the cousin had persuaded her employer to hire Hannah.

It had taken her only two days in that raucous place to convince her that there must surely be a better way for a young woman to earn a living. Men were always pawing at her, making crude, suggestive remarks, and attempting to force their unwanted attentions on her. She had left the tavern and attempted to find more genteel employment, but to no avail. She had finally lapsed into such desperation that she was more than eager for an opportunity such as the one that presented itself.

Her cousin had shown her the unusual advertisement in the newspaper. Although there was a shortage of men in the East due to the recent war, there was certainly no shortage of them in the timberlands. Hannah read of the proposed voyage of brides with avid interest, then obtained the necessary details. She signed on for the voyage—in essence, signing a contract to marry a complete stranger. She hadn't paused to consider seriously what sort of new life she would find in that faraway land, what manner of man to whom she would be committing herself as a wife.

Now, as Hannah recalled making that momentous

8

decision, the very reasons for it came flooding back into her mind. She recalled the night she had left home—the night her mother had entered her only daughter's bedroom to find Hannah packing all her rather meager belongings hastily into one pitifully worn and faded carpetbag.

"Hannah, what are you doing?" her mother demanded anxiously, her once-beautiful face now marked by the ravages of time and stress.

"I'm leaving, Mother. I've got to get away now, tonight," Hannah replied, her proud chin lifting even higher as she whirled about to face the older woman, her beautiful green eyes sparkling with mingled defiance and unshed tears.

"But . . . why?" Her mother frowned, as if she didn't know, or couldn't easily guess, the reasons for Hannah's actions. "What has happened? What is all this foolish talk of leaving?"

"You know perfectly well what it is!" Hannah snapped, unwilling to engage in any further discussion about the matter. She had tried often to warn her mother about the man she had married nearly six months earlier, tried to force her mother to see the awful truth of the situation: that Joseph Greer both hated and lusted after his beautiful young stepdaughter. But Sally Fairfield Greer refused to believe the worst of her new husband and was ready to take his side against that of her own daughter. She was desperate to make her unsteady marriage work, no matter what the cost.

"But where are you going? You can't just go off without any money to help you get by," Sally Greer protested. Nevertheless, she felt a twinge of relief that her daughter was leaving, and hated herself for it, although she realized that it might be for the best if Hannah did leave. There would no longer be the temptation of her shapely young daughter to come between herself and Joseph, and perhaps after Hannah was gone, Joseph would be once more as he was in the very beginning of their marriage. Yes, she hated herself, despised these growing feelings of relief, but she knew that she was willing to let her daughter leave if it would help her keep her husband's attentions.

"I'll find a way. You needn't worry about me." Finishing with the packing, Hannah turned about to face her mother and added painfully, "I would have gone long before now, but for you. I stayed here after you married Joseph only because I promised Father that I would look after you, because I was foolish enough to believe that you needed me in some way. But you married Joseph anyway. You refused to listen to me, to heed any of my warnings about what sort of man he is. You've always been blind where he is concerned. Shall I tell you what he said to me tonight? Shall I tell you, Mother, what he tried to do to me?" she asked bitterly, the hot color rising to her face as she recalled the loathsome details of the encounter with her stepfather earlier that evening.

"No!" Sally Greer whispered hoarsely, her eyes wide and frightened in her lined face.

"I didn't think so. I've tried to tell you often enough before. I can no longer remain in the same house with that man, no matter what promise Father made me give before he died. I don't think he'd want me to stay here under such horrible conditions. I'm going to find a way to make a life for myself," Hannah announced, picking up the bag and marching toward the doorway.

"Hannah, please, try to understand!" her mother

pleaded tearfully, blocking her daughter's path.

"Understand? Mother, if you had only listened to me, if you had only taken my part, just once—but no, your own daughter, your own flesh and blood wasn't as important as that despicable man!" Hannah's immense hurt flashed in her green eyes.

"I just can't bear for you to leave this way!"

"There's no reason for me to remain here. I'm nearly twenty, and it's time I looked after myself, time I chose a new way of life for myself," Hannah stated quietly.

"But, Hannah, you're still my daughter, my only child!" her mother cried as an overwhelming wave of guilt washed over her suddenly, the tears coursing freely down her cheeks.

"Good-bye, Mother." Hannah relented enough to give her mother a brief hug before pushing firmly past her. Then, without a backward glance, she left the room swiftly and hurried out of the house, grateful that her stepfather wasn't there to confront her as well. He was probably getting drunk in the nearest tavern. Hannah knew that later, after the bitter pain had subsided, she would write to her mother. But now she was ready to leave her old life far behind.

"Hannah?" A soft voice spoke at her shoulder, startling her out of her silent reverie. She turned to face her friend, Molly Willis, whom she had met on that first day when the two of them and the other ninety-six brides had boarded the ship. She smiled as she saw that Molly's pleasantly round little face was almost completely hidden by the large hood of her heavy woolen cloak.

"Molly, you shouldn't be up here on deck," Hannah chastised her young friend gently. "This fierce wind will most certainly do you more harm than good!"

"I know. I can't understand what makes you brave this awful chill and damp so often," Molly replied with a heavy sigh as she drew the cloak more tightly about her petite form. "Why don't you come below with me now? Everyone is so busy making preparations, so excited that we're finally going to reach Seattle. I can hardly believe that we'll soon be meeting the men who will be our husbands, that our lives—our futures—will lie in the hands of these men we know only by their names. Oh, Hannah," she said with a sudden involuntary shiver, "I feel as if something terribly awesome and important is about to happen. I suppose it is like that with all brides. The only difference is that most other brides have already met their prospective husbands before the wedding!"

"Yes," Hannah answered quietly, turning her pensive gaze toward their long-awaited destination, "I only pray that we've done the right thing, that we haven't ruined our chance for happiness. I've dreamt about it often at night, about this uncivilized land which will soon be our home, about the unknown men who will take us to wife. I suppose, like all the other women on board this ship, I, too, have longed for adventure and romance. I only hope that we have journeyed to the right place to find whatever it is we're seeking," she commented a bit somberly, all her fears and doubts rising to the surface as they finally neared the end of the seemingly endless voyage.

"Oh, Hannah," her friend replied with an amused giggle, "I never thought I should hear such ominous words from you! Why, what have you to be concerned about? You are young and exceedingly attractive. You're bright and witty—much more so than most of the others.

I've never known anyone with as much determination and spirit as you."

Hannah faced her young friend with an answering laugh as she shook off all dismal thoughts. She linked her arm companionably with Molly's as they carefully made their way back across the unsteady deck and descended to the cabin they shared with two other young women.

Later, as Hannah returned to the small, stuffy cabin alone following a late breakfast with the other brides in the crowded dining room, she closed the door and sank down onto the hardness of her narrow bunk, lost in thought again as she unpinned her bright hair and shook its curly masses, allowing it to tumble freely about her shoulders in complete disarray and splendor. Taking up her hairbrush, she began methodically stroking the thick tresses.

Molly was right, she told herself; it really was difficult to believe that they'd be reaching Seattle within a few hours. Even now, the other brides were all chattering excitedly amongst themselves as they took their last meal together. Hannah smiled to herself as she thought of the other brides. They were women from all walks of life; most of them young, like herself, most of them seeking the very same things she was. Schoolteachers, farm girls, widows, seamstresses, and more—all willing to brave a long and relentless voyage over rough, treacherous seas for a chance at obtaining whatever it was they each wanted out of life.

The men who had sent for them—the lumbermen and shopkeepers—had all paid more than three hundred dollars each for their brides, women they themselves knew only by their names on a slip of paper. The men had chosen their prospective brides at random, or merely

13

permitted the voyage's organizer to find them the appropriate mate. Whatever the case, none of the ninety-eight brides knew anything about the men they were now expected to marry. All they knew was the fact that the men wanted decent, hard-working women to become their partners, their companions, to bear their children and hence to populate and civilize the still-untamed land.

Acting upon impulse, Hannah jumped up from her seat on the bunk and stepped across to the single cracked mirror hanging above the washstand near the lone window in the small cabin. She moved closer and scrutinized her reflection critically.

Yes, she mused, she supposed she was what one would call pretty, that a man would find her shining hair and flashing green eyes to his liking. Her healthy figure was well-rounded in all the right places and she was not overtall. She smiled faintly as she recalled Molly's words earlier up on deck.

It was true that she had received a much more extensive education than most other girls raised on a farm. But then, the education had been her father's idea. He had wanted his only child to have all the advantages he lacked. Hannah had read a good deal and studied diligently, had even been allowed to take lessons with the local schoolmaster. She had been a hard worker on the farm as well. Good, hard work was certainly no stranger to her. Hannah realized that she'd have need of such knowledge and experience in this new land, that she would be called upon to toil long and hard, just like other pioneer women she had read about. The prospect did not bother her, for she was anxious to have a home of her own, was determined to make it happy and comfortable. What was truly worrying her about her future was the

14

man she would soon be marrying.

She prayed only that he would be kind, that hopefully he would be able to read and write, that he would treat her with gentleness and respect. Whenever her thoughts wandered involuntarily to the more intimate relationship she would be sharing with the unknown man, she forced herself swiftly to think of other things, for that was surely her foremost concern about wedding a total stranger.

After all, she told herself, she was young and romantic enough to hope that she would fall in love with her husband, that he would grow to love her in return, that the two of them would share much more than a mere partnership. She blushed as several unmaidenly thoughts entered her head, and she whirled about from her post at the washstand as the cabin door swung open suddenly.

"Hannah! Hannah!" Molly cried as she burst into the cabin, her color high and her eyes shining with excitement. "I had to hurry down and tell you the news," she breathlessly spoke. She grasped Hannah's shoulders and announced happily, "The captain says we are to disembark as soon as we reach Seattle, that we'll actually be going ashore in less than two hours' time!"

"But"—Hannah's face was puzzled and apprehensive now that the moment was fast approaching—"I thought we were to remain on board ship for one last night and then go ashore first thing in the morning!"

"We were, we were!" Molly answered with a laugh. "But we're arriving sooner than the captain thought we would, and he said that there will be a large crowd awaiting our arrival impatiently. He said that he won't be able to keep us on board the ship without fear for his very life! Oh, isn't it wonderful? We are to meet our new

15

husbands in less than two hours now!" She gazed up at Hannah in expectation, waiting for her friend's reaction to the startling news.

Hannah hesitated for a moment, then glanced down into Molly's sparkling blue eyes and forced a smile to her own lips. Still, she felt an uncomfortable knot in the very pit of her stomach.

"Yes, it is very exciting, isn't it? Well," she remarked casually, turning away as she began repinning her thick hair atop her head with fingers that were not quite steady, "I suppose we had best prepare ourselves to meet our fate!" Dear Lord, she added frantically in a silent prayer, please give me the strength to endure what is ahead!

Two

Along with the other brides, Hannah and Molly gathered anxiously close beside the ship's weathered rail, all grateful for the warming sunshine as they faced the throng of cheering men assembled opposite them on the shore. The ship had docked just that moment, and the obviously appreciative crowd of male spectators roared even louder as they caught their first glimpse of the long-awaited "mail-order brides" from the East. There was an infectious air of mingled anticipation and intense excitement, and Hannah found herself clinging tremulously to Molly's equally unsteady arm as the two of them proceeded slowly to take their designated places in line, cautiously approaching the lowered wooden gangplank with the other women.

The voyage's organizer, who had also served as the caretaker and guardian of the group of brides, smiled broadly and waved his felt hat high in the air as he led the ninety-eight women ashore gallantly. He beamed with pleasure at the exuberant response to his ambitious venture.

Viewing the noisy, laughing crowd with more than a touch of awe, as well as a twinge of fear, Hannah leaned

17

closer to Molly in order to speak, but discovered that her words were soon lost in the earsplitting welcome she and the other young women were receiving. She glanced about quickly, noting with interest the great variety of men who were making their admiration known. There were men of all shapes and sizes, some clean-shaven but most bearded, men who looked as if they hadn't bathed in years. It was difficult for her to fasten her curious gaze on any one man. They were all moving about and shouting robust encouragement, almost as if they were but one large, animated being.

Glancing upward toward the almost cloudless blue sky, Hannah's gaze was drawn instantly to the splendid backdrop of the curious-looking town, the green foothills in the distance, and the one spectacular mountain that towered majestically above the smaller tree-spotted ones. The air smelled fresh and clean, especially after the long ocean voyage, and she closed her eyes momentarily and inhaled deeply. Then her eyes were drawn downward once more as she strained to see what she could of the town itself.

All that she could discern now were the many weathered rooftops of the buildings, and she finally abandoned any hope of surveying the town further at that moment; there were too many people blocking her already limited line of vision. However, she recalled with a faint smile of satisfaction, from what she had been able to observe from her vantage point on the deck of the ship as it neared the dock, Seattle was indeed as beautiful a place as she had heard, though still apparently just as wild and untamed as she had imagined.

She wondered if perhaps she would be living near the city, if the stranger she was to wed would be taking her

18

very far away, perhaps even up into those strangely inviting mountains which seemed to be reaching upward toward the magnificent blue sky with such admirable determination. Her thoughts were interrupted abruptly as she and Molly reached the end of the sloping gangplank, as the crowd of men quieted suddenly and stepped backward to clear a path for the ladies.

Hannah gasped aloud as she discovered that her legs were still shaky, unaccustomed to standing on solid ground these many months, after the long voyage around Cape Horn. She had grown so weary of the incessant rocking of the ship, and she was now surprised to find that its movement still affected her so much. She grasped Molly's arm once more for support, smiling in response as her friend did the same. The two of them paused for just a moment, seeming to draw courage from one another, then lifted their heads proudly as they were led through the now-hushed assembly, toward a clearing near the center of the town. They were still within sight of the ship which had brought them so far from their homes and families, the vessel which had transported them to this beautiful land which would now be theirs.

Clutching at her blue woolen cloak and pulling it more closely about her trembling form, Hannah felt a slight chill even beneath the sun's bright, warming rays. She lifted her heavy brown cotton skirts to avoid the swirling dust of the unpaved streets as she and the other silent women filed neatly in pairs toward the spot where a crude wooden platform had been erected, evidently for the sole purpose for which it was now to be used. She watched with widened eyes as Mr. Melton, the voyage's organizer, climbed the few steps to the top of the unpainted platform, his large hands stretched outward as a signal to

19

the waiting crowd that he was about to begin conducting the anticipated ceremony.

The brides themselves, the very objects of the solemn occasion, remained huddled closely together, each apparently lost in her own thoughts—or fears—as she realized that the time had finally arrived. They had come so far, had endured so much discomfort for this one instant in time, this moment when each would finally meet and marry the man who had sent for her. Everyone could see that the women were all overwhelmed by the finality of what was to occur. And, even though many of the women might now be having second thoughts, none of them spoke a word.

Hannah was pondering how the brides would be matched with their husbands, and she soon perceived that she and the other women were to be led up onto the platform to stand before the great number of staring male eyes. She and Molly turned wordlessly to one another with perplexed expressions on their young faces as they realized that they were preparing to allow their lives to be forever altered. But, after all, Hannah staunchly reminded herself as she managed to give Molly an encouraging smile, forcing herself to remain calm, wasn't this what they had all wanted, the very reason for which they had traveled so far, to find new lives with their new husbands?

"Gentlemen!" Mr. Melton announced in a booming voice, replacing his hat atop his thick brown hair, his serious mien bespeaking the great importance he felt this moment. "Gentlemen, this is a great day, a great day indeed! You see before you now the results of your many prayers and letters, your dreams and wishes. My only regret is that I was unable to escort an even greater number of these lovely young ladies to you; but, alas, these brave young females you see before you now are the sum total of delightful companions I was able to deliver," he said eloquently, then cleared his throat noisily and wiped his furrowed brow with a linen handkerchief before continuing with his speech.

"Now, as you all know, these young ladies have already been matched with the names of the gentlemen who have paid me in advance to deliver them. I must say that I was very pleased at the great response to my humble advertisement, at the vast amount of mail I received from so many of you who wished to enter into the holy bonds of matrimony with a decent young woman. However, I promise you here and now that I am, at this very moment, making plans to return to the East and escort more young ladies back here to you on my next voyage!"

His words were greeted with an outburst of cheers and encouragement from the men, and he smiled with even greater satisfaction as he gestured for quiet once again.

"I knew that my proposal would meet with your approval. However, I shall be more than happy to discuss the various details of my next voyage after we have taken care of the matter at hand. Now, on to the very reason these charming young females are so patiently and modestly standing here before you. It is my intention to have each of the ladies come up here beside me as I call the name of the gentleman who is destined to become her fortunate spouse. I have been informed that the parson is waiting just across the street in the Red Dog Saloon, ready to perform the marriage ceremony for you all as you make your way to him. I remind you that these young ladies are to become the lawfully wedded wives they were brought here to be, and nothing else," he remarked sternly, placing a special emphasis on the last three words, which drew a hoot of boisterous laughter from more than a few of the men. Mr. Melton ignored their rude laughter and stepped across the platform to escort the first young woman up beside him.

Hannah watched with increasing curiosity as the first one of the group, a rather girlish young woman of no more than seventeen or eighteen years, followed Mr. Melton blushingly up the steps to the platform, then stood with modestly downcast eyes as the name of her husband-to-be was announced. The man, a big, strapping fellow of perhaps twenty-five, with a mane of thick blond hair and a bushy beard and mustache to match, bounded up on to the platform amidst a round of applause and cheers to make the acquaintance of his bride—the woman for whom he had paid three hundred dollars so many months ago. After exchanging a few words with Mr. Melton, the young man, his face wearing a huge grin, grasped the hand of the shy creature and pulled her along with him across the crowded street to where the visiting parson would soon declare them man and wife. The entire procedure of pairing the two young people took less than three minutes' time.

There was much accompanying applause and many ribald comments as each bride and man were paired, and Hannah watched all of the rapid proceedings in a daze, gasping sharply as she suddenly felt Molly's elbow dig gently into her side and heard her friend whisper,

"Hannah, it's your turn now. Hannah! Hannah, are you listening? Mr. Melton is waiting for you!"

Hannah blinked rapidly, then nodded slowly to her friend to indicate that she had indeed understood. The two of them quickly exchanged one last frantic hug before Hannah took Mr. Melton's outstretched hand and stepped up beside him nervously. She found herself trembling once more as she viewed the hundreds of pairs of eyes upon her, the manner in which the crowd of men were gazing so avidly at her, the way in which they all observed her gracious movements as she took her place beside Melton in the center of the wooden platform.

Merciful heavens! she exclaimed silently as she stared outward toward the softly mumbling assembly of perhaps three or four hundred men. She felt as if their eyes were undressing her, rendering her naked and totally vulnerable to their unblinking stares!

Oh, dear Lord, she prayed frantically in silence as she took a deep breath and forced herself to focus her eyes at a point just above the heads of the crowd, please help me to endure this ordeal. Please help me to know that I have indeed done the right thing in coming here, the right thing in pledging myself to a strange man, who could very easily turn out to be harsh or cruel. Please God, please let him be kind, and if—if it's not too much to ask, she added hastily, let him also be fairly young and at least passingly attractive!

"Mr. Theodore Whitworth!" Mr. Melton announced loudly, then frowned in puzzlement as several seconds passed and no one came forward. "Mr. Theodore Whitworth, are you here?" he called impatiently, turning to Hannah, apparently at a loss about how to proceed. This was certainly not a prospect for which he was prepared! He hadn't even considered the possibility that one of the brides' intended would fail to come and claim her!

Where is he? Hannah asked herself with a sinking

feeling of dread as her eyes scanned the crowd for any sign of her future husband. As no one appeared to be making any move to come forward, she felt herself beginning to panic. Suppose he didn't come at all! Her eyes darted about nervously as she stood before the continuing stares of the men. Suppose this Theodore Whitworth had changed his mind, had decided that he didn't want to marry a complete stranger, perhaps didn't want the added responsibility of a wife?

Why in heaven's name have I traveled halfway around the world, only to be met by such a humiliating dilemma? Hannah chided herself furiously, becoming more than ever convinced that she had made a disastrous mistake in ever signing on for this voyage. As she felt the hot telltale color rising to her cheeks, standing there feeling terribly foolish and still on embarrassing display before the fascinated gazes of so many men, she suddenly raised her stricken eyes to the opposite end of the platform as she finally detected some movement. A man was now making his way easily through the crowd and climbing the steps, his boots proclaiming his arrival as they moved across the bare wooden platform.

The man approaching was tall—well over six feet— and lithely muscular, precisely as Hannah would have envisioned a lumberjack. He was the handsomest man she had ever seen, his chiseled features bronzed by the sun, his dark brown hair thick and wavy, his dark mustache neatly trimmed. He wore the same attire as most of the other men, and yet the coarse trousers and flannel shirt accentuated his rugged handsomeness, his masculinity, his obvious virility. He appeared to be about thirty years of age, and Hannah noted quickly that his eyes were the most vivid blue she had ever before seen.

Her prayers had been answered! she told herself breathlessly, her heart pounding wildly. He was so very much more than she would have ever dreamed possible. And to think that such a man was to be her husband!

Of course, she then cautioned herself sternly as she lowered her gaze once more, physical beauty was not the most important quality in a man. She prayed once more that despite his obvious muscular strength, he would prove to be a kind man, a gentle husband. She raised her eyes again as the man stood before Mr. Melton now, and she was unable to suppress a feeling of intense disappointment when she realized that her future husband hadn't yet so much as glanced in her direction.

"Ted Whitworth was my partner. He sent me in his place. The name's Caldwell, Jason Caldwell."

"But where is Mr. Whitworth? Why hasn't he come himself? Doesn't he realize that this young lady has come all the way from New York in order to become his wife?" Mr. Melton demanded pompously, frowning darkly with displeasure, lowering his voice in an effort to keep the rest of the discussion private.

"There was an accident." Jason Caldwell's voice was deep and resonant. "Ted won't be coming at all." He finally allowed his steely gaze to wander toward Hannah, who experienced a mild shock as her eyes met his.

She saw his eyes narrow almost imperceptibly, then return abruptly to Melton. His eyes had seemed so cold, so very impersonal, almost as if he were looking right through her, she thought in confusion. But what was it he had said? He wasn't the man who had sent for her; he was not the man who was to become her husband?

"My dear Miss Fairfield, I'm afraid something unforeseen has occurred. You see, this gentleman here has just informed me that your intended husband, Theodore Whitworth, has met with a most unfortunate—and fatal—accident. It seems that Mr. Caldwell has come in his place," Mr. Melton explained patiently, as if Hannah hadn't been standing beside him during Caldwell's grim explanation.

"Mr. Whitworth is dead. I see," Hannah replied quietly, glancing down at her feet as the full import of his words sank in. Her future husband—the man who had sent for her—was dead, was not coming at all. What was she to do now? This man standing so arrogantly before her claimed that Theodore Whitworth had authorized him to come instead. Very well, she told herself, but did that mean that Jason Caldwell was to marry her himself, then? Before she had any further time to ponder the situation, Caldwell's deep voice broke in on her thoughts.

"Mr. Melton," he said, the tone of his voice low and level, and, it seemed to Hannah's ears, full of deep displeasure, "I promised my partner that I'd look after his intended bride, that I'd take care of her for him." His handsome features mirrored his obvious reluctance. As he waited for the other man to consider his statement, he finally took a long moment to silently appraise the woman he had traveled so far to meet, the woman who had already caused him so much trouble, the woman who was to have been Ted's bride.

She was much prettier than he had imagined she would be; he had been fully prepared to meet a hawk-faced old maid. Instead, he saw a beautiful young woman with hair the color of ripened wheat and eyes so green that they rivaled the rich color of the pines. Her figure, from what he was able to see, was well shaped, and her face, turned toward him now as he stared deep into her eyes, was full

26

of feminine sweetness and charm. Damn! he swore to himself as he tore his gaze away from her inquisitive expression, what had Ted gotten him into? Why had he ever made him that fool promise? The last thing in the world he wanted was to get himself tied to a woman in this country—particularly such an attractive, desirable little bundle such as the one standing so bravely before him.

"Look after her?" Mr. Melton repeated, his brow clearing. "Oh, you mean that you promised your late partner that you would marry her! Well, it certainly seems that it is the only logical solution to the problem, doesn't it? Very well, I suppose that I must honor your promise as well. Of course, I assume that all of this meets with your approval, Miss Fairfield?" he inquired politely, turning to Hannah with a faint smile, making it perfectly clear to her that the entire matter was already settled. After all, he told himself, she really had very little say in the matter now.

Hannah hesitated before answering him, knowing that she had no choice. No, she reasoned with herself quickly, if Theodore Whitworth, the man who had originally sent for her, had paid her passage, was indeed dead, then what other choice did she have? Perhaps she could refuse to marry this Jason Caldwell and then choose a husband from one of the crowd of men before her. But no—she realized that such a prospect was not at all desirable, and that it was extremely unlikely that she would be able to do any better than Jason Caldwell! If only he didn't appear to be so cold, so unwilling to carry out his promise to his late partner. However, she decided as she raised her head and squared her shoulders, she was certainly in no position to find fault with the man. Hadn't she come all this way to marry a total stranger?

"Very well, Mr. Melton," Hannah replied with a determined nod, not trusting herself to say anything further.

"Miss Fairfield, I wish you every happiness," her benefactor remarked with a broad and much relieved smile, taking her small hand and placing it into the larger hand of Jason Caldwell.

Hannah couldn't refrain from shivering slightly as her hand touched the strong, calloused hand of her future husband, as his fingers closed almost painfully upon hers and pulled her along with him briskly, back across the platform and down the steps into the cheering crowd. She attempted to stop a moment in order to try and catch one last glimpse of Molly, but was unable to make Jason Caldwell pause as he pulled her none too gently along with him, across the street to the saloon where the marriages were being performed.

As the two of them stepped across the threshold into the dusty, crowded building, Hannah tugged on her hand to finally make the man stop. She allowed her eyes to adjust to the darkness inside the saloon after the bright sunlight outside. She felt her hand being released completely, then her arm taken in a firm grasp as she was led to stand beside four other waiting couples, Jason Caldwell moving to her right as they faced the parson, a man who was actually the visiting circuit rider and who was to remain in town only this one day. Before she knew what was happening, the four brief ceremonies were over, and it was her turn.

Why, she thought in a state of shock, here she was, being married to an absolute stranger, a silent giant of a man who hadn't even spoken a single word to her yet, who had propelled her impatiently into this dirty saloon where she was now standing mutely beside him as a man read the wedding ceremony in a droning, almost toneless voice. Well, she wouldn't stand for it! She had long ago resigned herself to the fact that her wedding in this new land wouldn't be the sort of grand affair she had always dreamed of, but neither had she for one moment believed it would be such a farce as this!

"Mr. Caldwell!" she whispered furiously, oblivious to the words which the thin-nosed parson was pronouncing in such apparent disinterest.

"Keep quiet!" Jason nearly growled in response, his tone low and angry.

Hannah's mouth flew open in surprise, and she was about to call a halt to the whole thing and flee, when she heard the parson pronounce them lawfully married. She realized with a gasp of dismay that she was now legally bound to this disagreeable, handsome man standing silently beside her, that she hadn't even been given the opportunity to respond during the brief, hurried ceremony.

"But—but, you didn't even ask me if I would consent to take this man as my husband," she protested feebly to the parson.

"Didn't have to. You're here for that reason, aren't you? You've been married, legal and proper," the small black-haired man replied in a voice still devoid of emotion. He appeared to dismiss her, abruptly turning aside now to a man standing near them.

"It's time we got moving. Come on," Jason commanded, not too unkindly. Hannah peered up at him in horror, unable to believe that her wedding had just taken place, that she was indeed now married.

Oh, she wailed silently, she had no idea that it would be

like this! What had she done? she asked herself as tears started to her eyes, tears she fought back with a valiant effort. Why had she ever left New York?

Without another word, she clamped her mouth shut tightly and numbly allowed her own husband to lead her outside into the blinding glare of the sunshine. She passed her friend Molly with an unseeing stare.

Three

Wearily and almost painfully, Hannah slid from the saddle, maintaining her tight hold on the smooth leather for extra support as her feet met the solid ground. She and her new husband had been riding for several hours before finally stopping to make camp for the approaching night. She peered upward suddenly, gazing thoughtfully at the darkening twilight and the bright flecks of light which dotted the deep blue of the sky. Sighing heavily, she moved away from the horse and readjusted her long skirts, glancing now and then at the silent stranger to whom she now belonged.

He had not spoken so much as a single word to her since leaving the outreaches of the town. Instead he merely led her high into the mountains to the east of Seattle, setting a hurried and arduous pace for her to follow. Upon several occasions throughout their ride, she had determinedly attempted conversation with her new husband, but had finally abandoned her efforts when she perceived that the man obviously had no intention of talking to her until *he* felt the necessity arose. Now, standing in the partial clearing of the thick cluster of trees, Hannah vowed to herself that she would endeavor to make him speak somehow, that she would force him to acknowledge her existence!

More than once she had contemplated her decision to come to Seattle, the humiliating and disturbing circumstances which had subsequently met her there, and then her rushed and emotionless wedding to this bewildering man. It all seemed as if it were merely a dream, as if it were some strange unreality from which she would soon awaken. But no, she thought as she turned to the rushing stream of water several yards away, she was now Jason Caldwell's wife, and she must learn to make the best of it.

"I'll build a fire as soon as I tend to the horses. You can wash up." His voice startled her. She whirled about to face him from where she had bent down to the cool, inviting water, preparing to dampen her handkerchief and wash at least a little of the journey's dust from her face.

"Very well," she answered with a brief, hesitant smile. But her smile changed quickly into a frown as he turned his back abruptly on her once more and led the horses away. Why did he persist in treating her in such a manner? Why was he so reluctant to even glance in her direction?

Kneeling beside the water, she stared downward at her reflection; the light of the setting sun was fading quickly now. Surely the man would unbend eventually enough to speak with her, would begin to treat her with more respect and regard. Why had he ever consented to marry her if he did not want a wife? Why had his partner—the man who was to have been her husband—demanded that Jason Caldwell agree to such a promise?

Hannah dipped her handkerchief into the stream, distorting the contours of her image for a moment.

Perhaps he's simply a difficult man to know, she told herself with a sigh.

"Take care or you'll fall in," Jason warned her. He was returning from seeing to their mounts, his muscular arms full of wood for the fire.

"You needn't worry, I can swim," Hannah responded tartly, attempting to inject a bit of humor into her voice in an effort to hide her nervousness. She averted her face from his suddenly probing eyes.

"The last thing I need on my hands is a woman with pneumonia," he answered tightly, dumping the wood unceremoniously on the forest floor, his broad back toward Hannah so that she couldn't see the brooding expression on his handsome features, the strange glint which now appeared in his steely blue eyes.

Damn! he swore savagely in silence, taking some of the pieces of wood and arranging them expertly for the fire. It was hard enough being saddled with a wife he didn't want, but why in thunder did she have to be so blasted pretty? He cursed the day when Ted had told him of his plans to get himself a mail-order bride. As much as Jason had thought of Ted, treating him more like a brother than a business partner, he found his blood boiling at what he had been forced to promise. He realized that he was probably being too harsh and unfair to the young woman who now bore his name, but he also knew that he couldn't seem to help himself. He wanted no part of being bound to any woman!

Not, of course, that he didn't believe women weren't good for something. Quite the contrary, he mused with a sardonic grin as he quickly fanned the budding fire which now flickered beneath his skillful hands. He had found women to be very enjoyable companions, at times, only not on any permanent basis. That was something he'd solemnly sworn to himself many years ago; that he would avoid marriage at all costs, avoid it like the plague!

Jason's attention was drawn suddenly to where Hannah was still kneeling at the water's edge. She had unpinned her bright hair and was running a comb meticulously through its silky tresses, wincing slightly as she encountered a particularly stubborn tangle. She had removed the jacket of her traveling suit, and Jason's intense gaze was drawn irrevocably to the curve of her full breasts which pressed against the softness of her cotton blouse. He watched, immobile, as she raised her arms to her hair, completely unaware of his smoldering gaze upon her, oblivious to the turmoil she was creating deep within him.

Hannah pinned her thick hair atop her head once more, then shivered involuntarily as a slight breeze struck a chill in her body. She gathered up her heavy cotton skirts and prepared to stand when her ankle turned beneath her suddenly and she toppled headlong into the cold water, unable to stifle a tiny piercing shriek as she fell.

Jason had leaped to his feet immediately the moment he saw what was happening and was there beside her in an instant, plucking her easily from the chilling water of the mountain stream, his strong arms lifting her effortlessly and placing her quickly upon her feet once more. She stood there, mouth agape, her drenched clothing clinging to her body, molding its beautiful curves, wisps of hair streaming about her pale face as she caught her breath in small gasps. She was surprised to discover how very cold she was, not realizing that the combined effects of the water and the evening breeze could prove very

34

dangerous to her health. She raised her eyes in dismay, meeting Jason's eyes with another gasp.

He stood silently before her, his deep blue eyes boring into her green ones as she forced herself to meet his gaze without wavering. It seemed as if there were some unexplainable heat radiating between them in that instant, and the two of them stood in total silence, staring at one another for several long seconds, until Jason's angry words destroyed the momentary spell.

"I told you to take care not to fall in!" he muttered with a dark frown, his eyes sweeping up and down her drenched and shivering form in stern disapproval.

"I'm sorry, I didn't mean to, I . . . well, I—" she murmured quietly, her teeth beginning to chatter uncontrollably as the breeze swept across her again. She felt like a naughty child, furious with herself for having been so careless, yet still believing his angry chastisement of her to be unwarranted.

"You'll have to get out of those wet things at once," he commanded, his tone only a trifle less harsh than before as he gestured toward the thick cluster of trees nearest the fire. "Get in there and change into some dry clothes." He turned upon his heel and strode away, leaving Hannah standing there with a hot blush rising to her face.

Marching over to her carpetbag, she took out some dry things quickly and followed her husband's instructions. She picked her way into the thick shelter of trees and underbrush and removed her wet things, hanging the various articles of clothing over some low limbs while she donned fresh undergarments, then a simple woolen dress she had taken from her bag. She gathered up her wet clothes and carried them with her to the fire, which was now blazing brightly against the semidarkness of the clearing. She arranged the clothing on several bushes near the fire's heat, then took a seat on a flat rock close to the fire.

"You'll feel warmer in a minute or two. I'll fix our meal for tonight," Jason offered, though his features were stony and expressionless. The tone of his voice made him seem as unapproachable as before.

Hannah merely nodded in agreement, taking the pins from her hair and running her slender fingers through its wet strands, trying to keep from shivering as she waited to get warm.

"I really am sorry for being so careless, especially after you had warned me," she said, controlling the chattering of her teeth successfully now.

"Don't talk. Just sit there and get warm," Jason ground out, his chiseled features almost savage. Hannah clamped her mouth shut tightly again, totally exasperated at the brusque manner in which he always cut off any conversation she attempted. Was he never going to talk to her? she wondered angrily, moving a few inches closer to the heat of the dancing flames.

After the space of nearly half an hour, Jason handed Hannah a plate of fried salt pork and beans. She took the plate with a polite response, then began to eat, amazed to discover that she had suddenly developed a voracious appetite. Nothing had ever tasted quite so delicious before, and she didn't look at Jason again throughout the course of their first meal together.

When she had finished, Hannah rose to her feet and said, "Thank you. The food was very good. I'll be happy to wash the dishes now." She took the plate he held up in silence, ignoring the frown he gave her as his eyes were drawn to her loose, flowing hair which curled softly about her shoulders, the way her woolen dress clung to her womanly curves. She turned away and quickly carried the dishes to the stream a few yards away.

Scooping up a handful of sand from beneath the water, she scrubbed and then rinsed everything well before she returned to the fire. She was surprised to discover that she was suddenly feeling quite apprehensive. She had given barely any thought to the fact that this was her wedding night, that she was now the wife of this man who was still nothing more than a stranger. It occurred to her now that he might demand his husbandly rights, and she abruptly sat back down upon the rock, averting her anxious eyes as she drew her feet up under her long skirts, her manner tense as she focused her gaze on the colorful flames of the fire.

What am I do to? she asked herself, feeling panic creeping up on her as she waited for him to either speak or move. True, she had thought many times of her wedding night, knowing full well that she would be required to perform her wifely duties; and yet, now that the fateful moment was actually at hand, she was becoming increasingly fearful. She was honest enough to admit to herself that she was attracted to her new husband, even though the admission of such was considered unseemly for a young woman. However, she refused to admit that she was more than merely attracted to him, that she felt something for him which already ran far deeper than physical attraction.

Jason's thoughts were similarly preoccupied as he stared across the flames at his new wife. He knew he'd be a fool to deny the growing desire he felt for her, the powerful, nearly overwhelming impulse to consummate his so-called marriage. But he knew that by doing so, he'd

37

be stepping even deeper into a trap, that it would only serve to ensnare him further. Damn it, he didn't want a wife hanging like a noose around his neck!

His thoughts and desires warred with one another for several more moments, before he finally rose to his feet and stated tersely, "It's time we got some sleep. We've got a full day's ride ahead of us tomorrow, and I want to get an early start."

"Yes, but—" Hannah attempted to reply, but was cut off.

He continued, "You can bed down here by the fire. I'll get you a blanket." He strode away toward the horses, leaving Hannah to watch him with widened eyes, a very puzzled expression on her beautiful young face. Was he not planning on exercising his rights? she asked herself. Or did he really mean "we" when he had said "you"?

Hannah's questions were soon answered as Jason returned carrying the blankets, and she stood up, her knees feeling suddenly very weak. She opened her mouth in surprise as he merely handed her one of the heavy woolen blankets and took the other one back across to the spot where he had been sitting a few moments earlier. Without another word, he threw the blanket down on the hard ground, placed his rifle beside it, then lay down and rolled over on his side, presenting his back to his new wife.

Hannah heaved a sigh of relief. For whatever reason, her new husband obviously was not going to demand anything of her just yet—at least not for tonight. She followed his example and spread the blanket upon the ground, then lay down and drew it up over her as she peered overhead at the twinkling stars, grateful for the flickering fire's warmth.

Before Hannah finally drifted off into a troubled sleep, her last waking thought was that she was certainly relieved her new husband had stayed away from her. But, she felt something else as well, something strangely akin to disappointment. Scoffing at her ridiculous notions, she shifted her position in an effort to make herself more comfortable and went to sleep.

Four

Hannah awoke shortly after dawn the following morning, her green eyes sweeping open and focusing slowly on the bright panorama of the cloudless sky as the sun's golden rays streaked the horizon. The tall, fragrant pines gently swayed with the soft morning wind, and Hannah smiled to herself as she inhaled deeply of the fresh mountain air. She lazily stretched and allowed her gaze to wander across to the spot where Jason had made his bed, her beautiful face registering first surprise, then dismay as she saw that he was no longer there.

Surely he hadn't already gone, hadn't left her alone in this wilderness? she wondered frantically, throwing off the heavy blanket with a twinge of panic as she rose unsteadily to her feet, her head spinning from the abruptness of her movements. She quickly glanced left and right, scanning the clearing and the nearby forest for any sign of her missing husband, when he appeared suddenly, casually leading the two saddled horses, apparently ready to begin the day's journey.

"Thought I'd let you sleep in a bit longer just this once," he said by way of explanation as she continued to stand as if rooted to the spot.

40

"You should have awakened me sooner," she replied, a trifle angry with him for causing her such concern. She bent down and retrieved the blanket, folding it into a neat bundle as she approached Jason and the horses. "I can see that you're ready to leave, but aren't we at least going to have our breakfast first?"

"No. We'll stop for a quick bite later when we rest the horses. You can have a cup of coffee if you want it. I left some there for you near the fire," he offered generously enough, though the tone of his voice was clear indication that he believed he had already waited long enough.

Hannah didn't answer him. Instead she snatched up the clothes she had left to dry on the bushes the night before and packed them hastily into her carpetbag, then poured herself a cup of the aromatic brew and sat upon a rock as she sipped the hot liquid. Jason finished loading their baggage and other provisions onto the horses, then sauntered over to the stream nonchalantly and scooped up a handful of the cool, sparkling water to drink. When Hannah had finished her coffee, burning the tip of her tongue in her efforts to hurry, she turned toward her husband to speak, frowning slightly as she saw that he appeared to be lost in his own thoughts as he knelt beside the stream. Grasping her skirts, she marched into the same cluster of trees where she had changed her wet clothing the night before. When she emerged a few moments later, she found her husband standing impatiently beside the pawing horses, the fire already extinguished with the remainder of the coffee, everything ready to go.

Hannah was bruised and aching from the hours spent in the saddle the day before, as well as from sleeping on the hard ground all night. She mounted her horse painfully, without assistance, since none had been offered, and the two of them slowly made their way from the clearing, riding back into the enveloping thickness of the mountain forest. She couldn't refrain from taking one last, lingering look at the small clearing and the rushing stream of water, musing to herself that she would certainly never forget the spot where she had spent her most unusual wedding night. If yesterday had been any indication at all, what on earth would her future married life be like?

They rode along for several hours, plodding through forests and brush, up and down the narrow mountain trails, before pausing to rest the tiring horses. They drew rein beside another mountain stream, a bit smaller than the one from the night before. Hannah was relieved when Jason said they would be eating, for she found herself to be quite hungry, definitely ready for something a bit more nourishing and filling than a mere cup of coffee. She had always possessed a healthy appetite, and her mother had chided her about it on more than one occasion, cautioning her daughter that she would surely become fat as a milk cow if she didn't change her foolish ways. However, no matter how much food Hannah managed to consume, her shapely figure had always remained the same. Thinking briefly of her mother, she forced herself once more to try to forget the painful past—at least for the moment—and to concentrate on her life in this new country.

"I'll make us something to eat," she offered with a determined smile, taking the provisions from Jason's hands, noting with pleasure the barely concealed look of surprise in his blue eyes. Did he think she didn't know how to cook over an open fire? Well, there were quite a number of things Jason Caldwell would learn about his new bride! If only she could get him to talk to her, she reflected with a sigh as she set about preparing the simple meal.

Soon the fire was blazing and the food cooking; the salt pork sizzling in one hot iron skillet, the johnnycake baking in another, the coffee boiling in the pot. Hannah piled a plate high with the food and offered it to her husband, unable to suppress an impish grin as he viewed the plate's contents with another surprised expression on his handsome face. She waited a moment, watching intently as he hesitantly sampled a bite of the johnnycake, then took another bite, and then another. She prepared a plate for herself then, pleased that at least she had apparently passed the first real test of her new married life.

After the meal and a short rest, they were on their way once more. Hannah was growing increasingly weary with the silence of the tedious ride, and she decided to try once more to engage her husband in something that would at least resemble a conversation between the two of them.

"Would you tell me, please, just where it is we're going?" she inquired in a friendly voice, edging her mount a bit closer to his.

"It's another full day's ride from here. My cabin's a few miles from a town called Red Creek, a lumber town," Jason answered readily enough, prompting Hannah to continue.

"I see. Do you work in the town, then?"

"No. I own a timber camp up near my cabin. Been there nearly six years now."

"Were you born out here?" Hannah asked, curious to know more about this stranger she had married. She was

43

more than a bit surprised that he was actually beginning to talk to her, to answer her questions so willingly. Perhaps he was finally beginning to accept the fact of their marriage, had finally decided that she was at least worth getting to know.

"My folks came here from Missouri, some fifteen years back."

"Do they still live here, then? Do you have other family here as well?"

"No. My folks are dead. The only brother I had was killed about five years ago." Why was he suddenly revealing so much to her? Jason asked himself scornfully. He had sworn to keep his distance from her, and yet, here he was, jabbering away like some foolish boy!

On the other hand, he attempted to reason with himself, glancing toward Hannah, why shouldn't he try and make the best of a bad situation? After all, this woman was his wife now, whether he liked it or not. Simply talking to her didn't mean he was going to get all tied up with her, did it?

"You must have been very young when your family came here. How did you happen to become involved with lumbering?"

"Seemed like the natural thing to do. I worked a lot of camps before getting together enough money to open an operation of my own. I've got a pretty good-sized camp now, other loggers working for me, and a fine cabin. I guess you could say I've got just about everything I ever set out to get," he added with a tight frown. A wife hadn't been one of his goals.

"But what about Mr. Whitworth, your partner? How did you meet him?" Hannah probed, anxious now to hear something about the man she was supposed to have

44

married, the man who had answered the advertisement for a wife from back East. She vaguely wondered if he had been anything at all like Jason.

"Ted and I had been friends since we were boys. He helped me to get the camp started."

"I suppose you must have been very good friends. How did he die?"

"It was what we call a 'widowmaker.' He was crushed by a falling limb, one that was nearly three times the size of a man. There wasn't anything anyone could do about it."

"Oh, how horrible," she murmured quietly. She bit pensively at her lower lip, then decided to ask, "Why did Mr. Whitworth demand such a thing of you—that is, the promise to take care of his unknown bride?"

"He'd already made me promise a few days before he was killed, just in case anything ever happened to him. I guess he must have had a premonition, must have somehow sensed something," Jason told her, his usually stony expression replaced now by a softer, more vulnerable one as he spoke of the loss of his friend.

To Hannah, Jason suddenly seemed much more human, and she longed to comfort him in some way. But she hesitated. Hadn't he made it clear that he didn't want her comfort, her companionship? If only he would allow her to at least become his friend, if not his partner in a more intimate relationship.

"I'm sorry about your partner. I'm also sorry about the promise he exacted from you. You see, I've been wanting to ask you, Mr. Caldwell, precisely why it is you didn't just go away and leave me standing up there on that platform in Seattle yesterday?" she demanded bravely, wanting nothing more at that moment than to clear the air between them once and for all. "Why did you proceed to marry me? Surely your friend wouldn't have wanted you to marry me when you didn't desire a wife," she asked in a rush.

"I told you before. I gave Ted my word. If a man isn't true to his word, he isn't a man at all. I did what Ted would have wanted me to do, what he would have expected from me," he responded curtly, the steely light in his narrowed eyes telling her that he was finished with their brief conversation, that she had gone too far.

It still doesn't truly explain why you went so far as to marry me, Jason Caldwell, Hannah insisted defiantly to herself. Surely you could have "taken care" of me without resorting to such drastic tactics. After all, she told herself, Jason could have undertaken the task of finding her another suitable bridegroom, since there were only several hundred men staring up at her on that platform yesterday!

She still wasn't certain why she had gone along with him, either, why she had allowed herself to be swept away and bound legally to this strange man for life. Though she was undeniably attracted to him, she was also completely perplexed by his behavior toward her.

Several hours later, following a hard day's ride with only a few pauses to rest, Hannah and Jason made camp for the night, choosing another clearing which was only a bit smaller than the one of the night before, but which was also conveniently located near water. Hannah was grateful that Jason had stopped before dark; for she wanted nothing more than to go to the stream and wash some of the dust and dirt from her hair and body. Her husband had finally informed her that they would reach his cabin by late afternoon of the following day, and she was determined to try and look her best when she finally gazed upon her new home.

"I would like to wash up a bit, if you have no objections," Hannah said as she dismounted, frowning as she discovered that she was even sorer than the night before. These long hours in the hard saddle have certainly taken their toll, she reflected, wincing as she swung down and straightened her skirts about her.

"All right, but don't be too long. It's going to be dark soon," Jason agreed reluctantly, unsaddling his mount.

Hannah pulled her bag from where it was fastened securely behind her saddle, opened it and withdrew the things she needed, then made her way through the dense forest to the nearby water, choosing a spot only a few steps away from the clearing, yet out of sight of where Jason was now building the fire. She neared the water's edge and sat down upon the bank to remove the pins from her hair.

That done, she drew off her woolen dress, then removed the several layers of petticoats, her boots, and her stockings. She reflected that it was certainly fortunate that she and the other brides had been advised by Mr. Melton that they would be forced out of necessity to abandon the customary elaborate hoops and corsets which were considered proper attire back home, that they would have to adapt themselves to their new country by wearing more serviceable attire. Hannah was also fortunate that she had never needed the assistance of a corset to make her figure more shapely; and, after all, she had always despised the deplorable custom of wearing those silly hoops! But, ever since the end of the war, fewer and fewer women were advocating the wearing of such ridiculous contraptions, although they still steadfastly refused to abandon the uncomfortable custom of being bound in corsets in an effort to improve their figures.

Clad now in only a thin cotton chemise and drawers, Hannah stepped forward and knelt carefully beside the sparkling stream. With the cake of soap she had drawn from her bag, she began to soap and scrub at all the exposed parts of her body, knowing that she'd be truly satisfied only when she was finally able to take a real bath, to soak for hours in a hot tub. She finished washing her face and neck, arms and legs, then gave her full attention to her flowing blond hair, kneeling farther downward and forward so that its long tresses were immersed in the rushing water.

The water was very cool, but Hannah felt good to know that she was attempting to remain as clean as possible. However, after several minutes of trying to get her hair clean by leaning precariously over the water, she decided to abandon her rather primitive efforts and remove all of her clothing for a bath. It might not be a proper bathtub, but it was certainly better than nothing!

Stripping herself quickly of her chemise and drawers, Hannah glanced about, then waded out into the cool depths of the stream, the water coming up no farther than her shapely hips. Resigning herself to the fact that she would have to sit upon the rocky bottom of the stream in order to bathe, she took a deep breath as she bent her knees and immersed herself slowly, resolutely, in the cold water, up to her shoulders.

Meanwhile, Jason had built a fire and was lounging beside its warmth. He was becoming increasingly concerned as minutes went by and Hannah did not return. Evidently she was just like all other women; it took her much too long to perform even the simplest tasks. Only a woman would take so long to wash and primp herself.

Muttering a curse, he rose to his feet and stalked across the clearing, telling himself that he'd never be able to understand the ways of a woman. He'd best go and fetch her before she came to some harm, he thought with a fierce scowl as he grasped his rifle and set off through the woods to the place where Hannah had left her clothing folded neatly on the bank, just within the protection of the thick trees.

Hannah, of course, heard Jason crashing through the forest just as she rose dripping from the water, and she sat back down quickly with a stifled shriek, wincing as her saddle-sore derrière made contact with the hard surface of the rocks on the sandy bottom of the stream once more. She opened her eyes wide in astonishment and breathless anticipation, not knowing what to expect as she saw Jason standing there on the bank beside her discarded pile of clothing, his handsome face registering shock and disapproval at finding her stark naked in the stream.

They stared speechlessly at one another for several long seconds, before Jason, with a deepening frown on his features, said in a voice full of anger, "What in blazes do you think you're doing, woman?"

"As you can see, I am taking a bath," Hannah responded calmly, though the water's coolness was making her very anxious to get out and dry off. Just for an instant, she had thought that Jason was going to come in after her, but she now chided herself for her foolishness. He always seemed so stern, so disapproving of her. What had she done that was so reprehensible?

"Well, you can damn well get yourself out of there right this minute! Don't you know how dangerous it is to go gallivanting around here, naked as the day you were born? Hell, anyone could have seen you!" he shouted, the scowl deepening as his gaze was irresistibly drawn to the white curve of her round breasts which were just visible above the water's surface.

"I certainly didn't think that anyone else would be up here in the mountains, in the middle of nowhere, watching me!" she retorted with spirit, then asked, "What could possibly have happened to me?"

"Surely you've heard of wild animals. And what about other men who might be up here? Don't you have sense enough to know better than to go parading yourself about in a country where you can count the number of white women on one hand?" he demanded hotly, his eyes glowing strangely as he clutched his rifle in one hand and his hat in the other.

"Animals?" Hannah repeated, unable to suppress a sudden shiver which ran up her spine at the very thought. Well, of course she knew about wild animals, but she hadn't really thought much about them since arriving in Seattle. She and the other brides had often talked about the wilderness and the hardships they would have to contend with. As for the possibility of another man seeing her, wasn't it unlikely? After all, here they were, miles from the nearest evidence of civilization. It certainly hadn't occurred to her to worry about someone's watching her bathe.

"I would like to get out now. The water is quite cold," she said, ignoring Jason's angry demeanor.

"I'd have thought last night's little 'bath' would have been enough for you!" he responded with biting sarcasm, before ordering her tightly, "Get out of the blasted water and get yourself dressed."

Once he had disappeared into the forest again, Hannah tentatively emerged from the rushing stream, continuing to cast a wary eye about for Jason, as well as for any of the other men he had warned her about a minute ago. She donned her clothing quickly, then repinned her bright hair hastily as she hurried back through the trees to the small clearing.

"Mr. Caldwell," she began, her eyes shining with unshed tears as she halted a few feet away from where her husband was setting the coffee on to boil, "Mr. Caldwell, I wish to say something to you. I did not think of myself as being in any real danger while indulging in a hurried bath." He turned toward her, his steely gaze fastened on her flushed face. She held herself stiffly erect as she continued, "I am truly sorry if I have behaved foolishly once again; but, I must remind you, I was not raised in this country as you were. I was raised on what you would consider to be a rather genteel farm in the state of New York, where a woman was able to bathe properly in a tub, where she did not have to be anxious about someone spying on her. We did not live under the constant threat of wild animals there, Mr. Caldwell, so it really isn't fair of you to blame me for not being aware of the vastly different circumstances of life in this wilderness. I will learn in time, I can assure you, only you must give me the time to learn," she said, seeking to make him show her at least a little understanding and patience.

"Furthermore," she continued, growing uncomfortable beneath his unwavering gaze, "I wish that you would stop treating me like a child! I am your wife, I wish to be treated with the respect due me as such. I will cook for

51

you, clean for you, mend your torn shirts, do your dirty laundry—everything you would naturally expect from your wife. All I am asking from you in return is a bit more patience, a bit more tolerance in your behavior toward me." Her speech finished, she stood in silence and waited for his response.

Jason's eyes moved from Hannah to the fire. Understanding and patience! he muttered beneath his breath, refusing to answer her. Naturally he had been angry when he'd seen her standing naked in the water! If he was going to keep to his vow to stay away from her . . . he still recalled the way she had looked when their eyes met, when he had first discovered her taking that bath. That, coupled with the fact that she truly could have been in danger because of her foolish actions.

It didn't dawn on him that he truly cared what happened to her. Several years ago, he had taken a solemn oath that he'd never care for a woman again, that he would never allow himself to become emotionally involved with any woman.

"You'll learn, all right," he replied finally, poking savagely at the fire with a long stick. "You'll have to learn if you're going to stay alive in this country."

"I have said that I will learn, and I shall. This is my adopted homeland, now, Mr. Caldwell. It is now my home as much as it is yours. I would never have dreamed of coming so far, of traveling to this untamed land, if I had not intended to make it my own," she told him, sensing that, once again, he was in no mood for further discussion on the subject. She moved away to prepare for the coming night, unable to forget the strange, un-fathomable expression which had been on Jason Caldwell's face when he had come crashing through those trees.

It was going to be extremely difficult to make a life for herself here, Hannah realized, ready tears starting to her eyes once more as she turned her back rigidly on Jason. If only her husband could like her, at least a little. She was so close to being overcome by complete and utter desperation, but the spirit and determination Molly had noticed in her would not allow her to surrender!

Five

By the time Hannah and Jason arrived at his cabin, the sun was sinking low in the sky, casting a magnificent glow over the timbered, mountainous landscape. Although very tired and aching in almost every part of her body, Hannah was still afforded a good view of her new home as she and Jason pulled up before the log buildings. Her first impression was that the cabin was much larger than she might have expected, and she dismounted with a secret smile of mingled relief and satisfaction as Jason took her bag wordlessly and led the way toward the cabin.

The buildings were situated conveniently in a sizable clearing near the very top of the mountain, surrounded by immense, fragrant trees which formed a shelter of awesome splendor. To the left and slightly downhill from the cabin were the stable and a small corral; to the right was a narrow path leading to the necessary outhouse. Myriad wild flowers were sprinkled everywhere about the landscape. Though Hannah would be able to peer outward from the windows of her new home, would be able to feel the warm, comforting sunlight streaming in through the paned glass, she would be able to see nothing but those huge trees. Unable to suppress a slight shudder

54

which quickly traveled the length of her spine, she gazed slowly upward to the very tops of the timber which belonged to her new husband.

"You'll get used to the trees in time," Jason commented with a slight frown as he noted the brief look of trepidation which passed across his wife's lovely features. He said nothing further as he swung open the cabin's heavy wooden door and stepped inside, setting Hannah's bag on the table near the doorway. Moving to light a lamp, he turned to face his new bride.

"Well, this is it. I expect you'll want to look over the place. I'll leave you alone for a spell to settle in," he announced. His eyes suddenly seemed very cold as Hannah looked across at him from where she stood framed in the doorway, her eyes striving to adjust to the dim light from within.

"But where are you going?"

"I've got to get up to the camp for a while," he answered, setting the oil lamp down upon the rough surface of the table. "It's just a few hundred yards on up the mountain. Don't worry, I'll be back in a couple of hours. You stay here inside the cabin. I'm leaving you the rifle, though you won't need it. I'm close enough to hear you if you need anything."

"But . . . you aren't really going to go off and leave me here alone!" Hannah demanded in disbelief. She stared across at him, all her emotions frayed by the difficult journey they had just completed. She had expected things to be different once they had arrived at Jason's cabin, her new home. She now realized with growing dismay that nothing had changed; no miracle had occurred to make her husband want her as his true wife.

"I told you there's nothing to worry about," Jason

replied sternly, obviously displeased by her questioning. "You'll be perfectly safe till I return. Just stay inside the cabin and bolt the door until I get back." Then, without another word, he moved past her and strode away.

Hannah turned and watched him as he led the weary horses into the stable, continuing to watch as several minutes later he disappeared into the dense forest, stepping lithely along a trail which had been cut through the trees. She could feel hot, angry tears welling up in her eyes, and she grabbed hold of the door and closed it with considerable force, then shot the bolt and leaned against the door, her bosom heaving with indignation.

Ever since she had left Seattle with this strange man who was now her husband, she had been trying her best to reach him in some way, at least to persuade him to treat her with courtesy and respect. His chilly indifference made her wish she had never met Jason Caldwell, had never traveled halfway around the world to this wilderness. Everything was going all wrong, she reflected with a choked sob, and she sank down slowly upon the bare wooden floor, the tears slipping unheeded down her cheeks as she surrendered to her misery.

Hannah wept for several long minutes, all the disappointments and fears and worries feeding her tears as she sat there alone in the cabin, her knees drawn up to her chin, her head cradled upon her crossed arms. When she had finally spent herself with crying, she discovered, with a small degree of surprise, that she felt renewed. She rose resolutely from the dusty floor and surveyed the interior of her new home for the first time.

She took up the lamp and, holding it high, moved slowly from room to room to critically inspect the cabin.

There was one large bedroom, the middle room, which served as the main living area, a storage room, and a spacious kitchen. The cabin had apparently been well planned, she mused, and she was surprised to discover that the rooms were relatively neat and clean as well. The furnishings, all rather rough-hewn, were obviously handmade, but appeared to be very serviceable and sturdy. All in all, she decided as a determined gleam appeared in her green eyes, she knew that she could have done much worse. Still, she thought, taking off her cloak, and lighting several lamps around the cabin, there were many things that needed a woman's touch!

Hannah became so absorbed in her work as she swept and rearranged, that she failed to notice when darkness fell. When she had finished all she had set herself to do that first evening, she moved into the kitchen to cook the evening meal. She was occupied with that particular task when she heard a loud knock at the front door.

Expecting that it was her ungrateful, decidedly unappreciative husband returning, she proudly lifted her chin and crossed the newly swept floor to answer the second knock at the door.

Sliding back the heavy bolt, she opened the door, her mouth already forming the name of her husband, when she was startled to see that it was not Jason, but a complete stranger who stood upon the doorstep.

"Who are you?" she asked, her eyes growing round and anxious. She noticed then that it was quite dark outside, but the light given off by the lamps provided her with enough illumination to see the man clearly. He was nearly as tall as Jason, and about the same age, but was of a slighter build. His tailored clothing was that worn by a townsman and not a lumberman, she thought. He was not unattractive, she noted quickly, though he was a trifle too dark for her tastes, with his raven-black hair and golden eyes. Suddenly she grew embarrassed as she realized that she was staring rudely at the man, and she blushed when she saw the admiring look he was bestowing upon her as his eyes swept openly up and down her form.

"I'm sorry, but I certainly wasn't expecting such a beautiful young lady to answer the door," the man remarked pleasantly as he removed his hat gallantly and smiled down at Hannah. His voice was deep and he sounded well educated—not at all the sort of man she expected to find on her doorstep in this wilderness.

Hannah remembered suddenly that the rifle was standing upright behind the door, then wondered vaguely why she thought she might possibly need it.

"Who are you?" she demanded again, refusing to return the man's smile. She was growing increasingly uneasy as she stood there before him, and she inched backward unconsciously behind the protection of the door.

"This is where Jason Caldwell lives, isn't it?" the man asked, ignoring her question once more. His eyes were roaming over what he could see of her, and Hannah grew angry at being ogled so blatantly by the man.

"I am Mrs. Caldwell," she announced, striving to remain calm. She recalled what Jason had said about being within earshot if she should need him.

"I didn't mean to frighten you, Mrs. Caldwell," the man said with another smile, though Hannah noticed that the smile didn't quite reach his unusual golden eyes, "but I had no idea Caldwell had gone and gotten himself such a pretty little bride. My name is Lewis Harland. I'm a friend of your husband's."

"Well, I'm afraid my husband isn't at home at the moment, Mr. Harland. But, he did say that he'd be back any moment now," she informed him quickly. For all his politeness and apparent charm, there was definitely something about the man that continued to make her feel uneasy.

"I see," the man murmured, almost to himself. "If you'll please inform your husband that I came by, Mrs. Caldwell, I'd be grateful. He and I have some rather urgent business to discuss," he said with a sudden frown. Then, with another smile, he inclined his head briefly toward Hannah, replaced his hat upon his head, and bid her good-bye. She watched as he mounted his horse and rode off into the enveloping darkness.

She quickly closed the door and returned to the kitchen, where she had left a large iron pot of beans cooking. She was unable to shake the vivid recollection of Lewis Harland's golden eyes moving boldly over her, and she was still disturbed by her brief encounter with the man. Telling herself that she was merely being foolish again, that the man was a friend of her husband's, she sighed and set out preparing the rest of the meal.

She whirled about as she suddenly heard the front door open, realizing with a sinking feeling of utter dismay that she had forgotten to draw the bolt after Mr. Harland had gone. She hurried out from the kitchen, vastly relieved when she saw that it was Jason, then drew up abruptly as a huge dog bounded playfully into the room.

"What on earth is that?" she uttered as she stood in the doorway to the kitchen, clutching a wooden spoon to her breast. She stared apprehensively at the unruly beast, who was now growling deep in his throat, his ears laid back menacingly as he eyed her warily.

"That's enough, Thor!" Jason commanded sharply. The animal cowered and tucked his tail between his legs as he sank down onto the floor at his master's feet. He was very large, his coat a grayish-brown mixture of coarse hair, his paws nearly as big as Hannah's hands, his tail long and bushy. Hannah couldn't help thinking that he looked more like a wolf than a dog.

"Is that animal yours?" she asked, her heart pounding. She had never been around many dogs, and she certainly didn't like the looks of this one!

"Why didn't you have the door bolted?" Jason angrily demanded, ignoring her question.

"Oh . . . I'm sorry, but I—I forgot," she faltered beneath his furious gaze, then gathered courage again and faced him squarely. "I know I should have bolted it again after Mr. Harland left, but I simply forgot. I can assure you that it won't happen again. I'm usually not so careless." Why did he persist in trying to make her feel like a child? How was she ever going to succeed in her determination to make him a good wife if he continued treating her this way?

"Harland? Lewis Harland was here?" he demanded brusquely, the scowl deepening on his ruggedly handsome features as he stepped closer and peered angrily down into Hannah's widening eyes.

"Why, yes. I was a bit frightened of him, at first, but he said he was a friend of yours. He said he had come to discuss some urgent business with you. He told me to tell you that," she explained hurriedly, puzzled by the intense light which appeared in his steely blue eyes, and she gasped aloud as his large hands closed upon

60

her shoulders.

He spoke in a rigidly controlled voice, "Don't you ever let that man in here again, do you hear?" He shook her slightly for emphasis.

"But why not? He said he was a friend of yours," Hannah insisted, taken aback by his violent reaction to the news that the man had been there. "He didn't come inside; he only stayed at the door for a moment," she went on, her eyes very round and fearful as they met his unflinchingly.

"Lewis Harland is no friend of mine!" he stated savagely, his face suddenly growing impassive. Just when Hannah was going to speak again, he released her shoulders and moved abruptly away from her.

Hannah stared at his broad back as he turned away to remove his jacket. She was totally bewildered by his irascible behavior, and she wanted nothing more than to question him further about the visitor, but she deemed it wiser to avoid the risk of angering him again. She marched back into the kitchen and began serving their supper.

Jason ate in silence, glancing at Hannah only a few times as she offered him more beans and cornbread. After they had both eaten, Jason and Thor left the cabin while Hannah cleared the table and washed the tin plates and mugs, then scoured the pots. When she had finally finished her chores, she was feeling very close to exhaustion and she slowly stepped from the kitchen into the center room, wondering what she was to do next.

Since Jason had not come back inside, she decided to go into the bedroom and change her clothes. She closed the bedroom door behind her and proceeded to remove her travel-stained and dusty attire. Pouring water from a pitcher into a matching washbowl, she washed herself all over as best she could, then donned a clean cotton nightgown. Feeling refreshed, she removed the many pins from her thick hair and began brushing out its golden tresses, thoughtfully taking a seat upon the newly made bed and wondering what the night would hold for her.

After all, she told herself, Jason Caldwell didn't want a wife, hadn't made any indication that he considered her to be anything more than an absolute nuisance. He hadn't made any real demands on her, hadn't even attempted to claim his rights as her husband. But, would things possibly be different now that they were here in his cabin, in what was now to be their home together? Whether he wanted to acknowledge the fact or not, she was his lawful wife, would remain so until death parted them.

Shivering suddenly, she put aside the hairbrush and scurried beneath the covers of the bed in order to wait for her husband. She left the lamp burning, not certain when Jason would return, and she lay with her arms crossed beneath her head as she stared at the ceiling.

It seemed as though hours had passed by the time she detected the sound of Jason entering the cabin again. She could hear Thor padding about noisily on the bare wooden floor, then finally settling down for the night. She lay very still as she listened, waiting for Jason to open the door to the bedroom. Almost afraid to breathe, she pulled the covers up to her shoulders and glanced anxiously toward the doorway, but was puzzled when Jason did not appear.

She could still hear him moving about in the next room, but she was even more confused when she heard his movements cease. Wasn't he coming? she asked herself. Couldn't he even bear to sleep in the same room with his new wife? She was close to tears again when she waited for several more minutes and her husband still did not enter the bedroom. She lay there a moment longer, then decided to discover for herself what had become of Jason.

Flinging off the covers, she tied a wrapper on over her nightgown and eased the bedroom door open. Her eyes, traveling swiftly about the room, perceived the form of Jason sleeping on the floor near the fireplace, Thor peacefully snoozing at his master's feet. Hannah hesitated then, not knowing what to do, not knowing whether she should return to her bed, or should be so bold as to approach her husband. Reminding herself of her staunch resolve and firm determination to make this marriage of hers work, she decided that it might be for the best if she swallowed her pride, forgot her maidenly modesty, and took matters into her own hands.

"Mr. Caldwell? Mr. Caldwell, I think it's time we had a talk," she began quietly, startled when Jason leaped up from the floor at the first sound of her voice. He stood fully dressed, apparently poised for battle, surprised when he saw that it was Hannah who stood there before him.

His handsome face grew perceptibly aloof as he demanded, "What is it? What do you want?"

The only light in the room was given off by the fire, which still crackled in the stone fireplace. Thor, who had also grown immediately alert when Hannah first spoke, now settled back down with a soft groan, to return to his dreams.

"I think it's time we had a talk," Hannah repeated,

nervously clearing her throat as she averted her eyes from Jason's piercing gaze. She stared deeply into the flames of the dying fire. "I don't really know how to put it, but—" she started, her eyes meeting Jason's once more.

"Well?" he demanded impatiently, glaring down at her. He was torn between an irrational anger toward her, and a begrudging admiration. She looked so very young and innocent, standing there with the fire casting pale shadows across her beautiful face. Her bright hair was cascading riotously about her face and shoulders, and Jason forced himself to remain unmoved by her sweet beauty as he looked at her.

"I . . . that is"—Hannah faltered again, then finished in a rush—"I am your wife now, Jason Caldwell. I think there's still much to be said between us." It was so very difficult to remain courageous and determined when his eyes were so cold and inscrutable. The expression on his face grew harsh and he grimly answered,

"I don't think there's anything to be said between us. I didn't ask for a wife," he reminded her in a low, steady voice. "I give you my word that I'll provide for you, that you'll never have any cause to worry on that score. But that's all." He turned away from her and prepared to lie back down upon the blanket on the floor, obviously dismissing her for the night.

"Mr. Caldwell, I insist that we talk about this!" Hannah persisted stubbornly, refusing to back down. Her own temper was beginning to flare now, for she believed that she had reached the limit of her tolerance for this maddening man, of his insulting, bewildering manner toward her. She reached out quickly and put a hand on his muscular arm, thinking to force him to turn back and face her.

She was totally unprepared for his reaction. Jason jerked about abruptly, his blue eyes blazing. As Hannah stood wide-eyed and trembling, he muttered a curse and pulled her roughly to him, his well-muscled arms holding her prisoner as she cried out in alarm and struggled to escape. His actions had taken her completely off guard, and she realized that she was more than a little frightened by the intense gleam in his smoldering eyes as he bent his head slightly to hers and captured her soft lips with his own hard, demanding ones.

Hannah's struggles ceased just as suddenly as they had begun. She felt a warming, unfamiliar sensation burning deep within her as Jason's lips moved roughly over hers. Those bruising lips became more gentle, more tender, as Hannah surrendered against Jason's lean, muscular body. She found it difficult to breathe as she gave herself up to his kiss, her arms creeping up about Jason's neck as he pulled her even closer against him, until their bodies were molded together in perfection. His hands began to roam caressingly down her back, until they grasped Hannah's softness below the hips and she could feel his masculine hardness pressing into her. She moaned unconsciously deep in her throat, a sound which was barely audible to her own ears, but which caused Jason to draw his lips away from hers and gaze deep into her shining eyes.

She experienced a deep disappointment as he released her suddenly. While she gazed up at him in bewilderment, her face flushed, he ground out another curse and stalked from the cabin, Thor padding along in his wake. Hannah stood forlornly before the fire, striving to regain her composure as she watched him go. She discovered that the unfamiliar yearning had overtaken her completely, an intense yearning which still remained unfulfilled as she sank down onto the floor and stared unseeingly into the fire.

What had just passed between herself and Jason had caused her to feel more vibrant, more alive than ever before in her young life. His kisses, his passionate embrace had made her forget all else but the two of them together. She had never been kissed before, not truly. She was still amazed that such a strong man could be so gentle and loving, that he could make her feel this yearning which still burned within her. Why had he stopped? she asked herself in confusion, her face still bright and flushed. Why had he left her that way?

She waited a long time, sitting there until the fire had dwindled to a few glowing embers. Finally she rose to her feet and walked slowly to the bedroom. She removed her wrapper and crawled beneath the covers of the bed once more, her thoughts still in a whirl as she snuggled deeper into the softness of the bed, hugging one of the pillows to her breast. She smiled to herself then, pleased with what had occurred that night. She fell asleep long before Jason returned to his own bed before the fireplace, her dreams sweet and undisturbed, dreams of herself and Jason and the happy life she envisioned for them. She was unaware that her husband was still awake in the other room, the expression on his face dark and brooding.

Jason silently berated himself for losing control. It had taken all his firm resolve to turn away from his beautiful young wife. But when she had touched him, he had felt his skin burn, even through the protection of his flannel shirt. What had happened then had not been planned, should have been avoided, he reflected moodily. She had looked so incredibly desirable, her bright green eyes pleading with him for understanding. But no, he reminded himself sternly as he yanked the blanket up over him with a vengeance, it was better for them both if he kept his distance.

Keeping his distance would be a hell of a lot harder than he ever could have imagined! he thought, his arms crossed beneath his head. He could still feel Hannah's yielding softness against him, could feel her sweet, curving lips returning his kisses, tentatively, her soft arms twining themselves about his neck. He had lost himself for a few moments, until Hannah's soft moan had brought him to his senses again. He knew that if he hadn't torn himself away when he had, hadn't left the cabin, his resolve would have been shattered completely. And that, he told himself with a ferocious scowl, was something that must not happen.

Still, a tiny voice at the back of his mind persisted obstinately as Jason finally drifted off into a troubled sleep, Hannah was so young and lovely, so eager to please him, so determined to make him a good wife. Why was he allowing the past to rob him of any future happiness he might find?

The following morning, Hannah was awakened by the bright sunlight filtering in through the bedroom windows. She jumped from the bed and washed and dressed quickly, pinning up her hair deftly and smoothing down her printed cotton dress. Opening the bedroom door, she stepped into the other room with a smile on her face. But her smile faded as she noticed the empty space on the floor where Jason had slept the night before. Then she was pleasantly surprised when Jason strolled out of the kitchen, a steaming mug of coffee in his hand.

"Good morning," Hannah spoke with a smile, though she was feeling a bit shy before him. She couldn't help thinking that he was the handsomest man she had ever seen, and she was glad he seemed to find her attractive as well.

"Morning," Jason muttered quietly in response, glancing briefly at her. "There's coffee on the stove."

"I'm sorry I wasn't up before now. I'll have your breakfast ready soon," she told him, moving toward the kitchen.

"I won't have time for that today," he said, glancing away again. "I've got to get on up to the camp. There's a lot of timber to be cut, and I've been away long enough as it is." His tone was gruff, but Hannah refused to be offended by his coolness this particular morning.

"Very well. I have an awful lot to do here at the cabin, too. Will you be home for the noon meal?" She was determined to remain even-tempered with him, to make him like her. She knew that he found her desirable; she knew that much after last night, even if he had gone off the way he had. As she stood there looking across at the man she had married only a few days earlier, she suddenly realized that it mattered very much to her that he like her, that he respect her. She knew that she wanted him to like her more than anything else in the world. This was no romantic dream, she thought; this was real. She knew that she had come to care for Jason a great deal.

"I'll get something to eat up at the camp," Jason remarked as he set the mug of coffee down on the table and donned his jacket and hat. Hannah watched him in secret wonderment, hugging to herself the realization of the depth of her feelings for him after so short a time. "Remember, if you need anything, I'm just a short way up the mountain, right up the path."

"I'd like to come up and see your camp," Hannah offered, wanting to be near him that day, to see where he worked, to meet the men who worked for him.

"No," he responded curtly, a frown creasing his brow at her words.

"But why not? After all, since I'm to be living here now, as your wife, it's only natural that I should want to see my husband's business," she reasoned.

"It's not a good idea. Those men up there don't see many white women in these parts."

"But isn't there a town nearby? Surely there are women there."

"The town's a few miles south of here. There are women there, all right, but only a handful of them are what you'd call decent. It's best if you stay here around the cabin. I'm leaving Thor here, and the rifle as well. We've not had any trouble with bears or wolves for quite a while, so there's no real need to worry about them. But," he cautioned her, "don't let anyone inside the cabin, and keep an eye out for strangers."

"But when will you be back?"

"Not until nightfall." He opened the door and started outside, then turned suddenly and faced Hannah, who stood expectantly, watching him. He appeared to be planning to say something else, his expression unreadable, but then he apparently changed his mind and set off at a brisk pace, up the trail through the tall trees.

Once again Hannah was left alone with her thoughts. She closed and bolted the heavy front door, then took a seat at the table, resting her chin in her hands. She could hear Thor moving about, and, realizing that she had forgotten momentarily about the dog, she hurried out to the kitchen to fetch him something to eat.

Thor eyed her suspiciously as she approached him with the food, but began wagging his immense tail when she set the bowl of food before him. She backed away cautiously, still not quite certain about the dog, but telling herself that she would have to get used to him sooner or later. So she slowly extended a hand toward him and patted him softly on the head, pleased when the dog responded with another enthusiastic wag of his tail. While he continued eating noisily, Hannah stroked his head gently and murmured a few conversational words to him.

When Thor finished eating, he gazed up at Hannah with his large brown eyes and whimpered, pressing his wet nose against her hand and wagging his tail with even more exuberance. She laughed aloud as he pranced about her, and found herself thinking that it might not be so bad after all to have a dog around the cabin. She petted and spoke to him a few moments longer, then moved away thoughtfully.

Her thoughts returned to her husband as she began her work for the day. She intended to give the cabin a thorough cleaning, and, since it was apparently going to be a clear and pleasantly warm day, she decided to open all the windows to air out the rather musty cabin.

It still amazed her that she had come to care for her new husband so quickly. Perhaps all her dreams about love and romance were going to come true, she mused as she scrubbed the kitchen floor. Though Jason was not yet ready to accept her fully as his wife, she sensed that the time might not be very distant now, especially given what had happened between them the night before. The memory of their shared embrace caused her to feel an enveloping warmth again, and she smiled to herself, feeling optimistic. She was startled when she suddenly heard Thor growling, then barking ferociously in the next room.

"Thor? What is it, boy?" she called anxiously, getting up off her hands and knees and rubbing her hands on her apron. She stepped through the doorway and looked about, but saw nothing. Perplexed by the fact that the dog continued to bark, she felt a tremor of growing fear. She whirled about and reached for the rifle which Jason had left for her near the front door, but she was unable to reach it before someone came from behind and grabbed her, pinning her arms to her sides, pressing a rough hand across her open mouth.

"Be still!" Hannah heard a deep voice rasping close to her ear. She struggled wildly to escape the unknown intruder, intent only upon freeing herself and screaming for help.

"I said to be still!" the voice repeated angrily. Thor was still growling and barking, and he lunged forward suddenly toward Hannah and her assailant, the man who held her in his iron grip. He released Hannah for a fraction of a second as the dog moved, long enough for her to scream, a scream that was abruptly cut off when a shot rang out. She gazed down in horror to see that the man had shot Thor, but she had no more time to think about the poor animal when the man, whose face she hadn't yet been able to see, grabbed her once more and dragged her roughly toward the front door. He held her with one bruising arm as he opened the door, then lifted her up, her feet helplessly flailing, a cruel hand still clamped across her mouth, and rushed outside. Hannah continued to struggle, though her strength was quickly waning. She could feel panic threatening to overtake her, and she forced herself to try and keep a clear head.

"Come on, let's get out of here!" she heard another masculine voice shout, and she saw another man waiting on horseback. She couldn't see his face very well, either, since his hat was pulled down low upon his head. The man who held her lifted her quickly up to the rider, who positioned her in front of him and swiftly tied a strip of cloth about her mouth, then bound her hands behind her back. Then the other man mounted up and they kicked their horses into action, galloping away from the cabin and into the thick forest.

Six

Hannah still had no idea who had abducted her, nor their reason for doing so. She could only lean helplessly against the man behind her as they traveled at a breakneck speed, as her captor kept one arm clamped about her midsection, almost cutting off her breath, and guided the horse along a well-worn trail through the surrounding trees. She thought again of poor Thor, who had tried to protect her, who now lay dead on the cabin floor. She thought of Jason, who might or might not have heard her scream or heard that single shot. She prayed that someone at the camp had heard, that they would be coming after her.

It seemed as though they traveled for hours without stopping. Hannah was aware only of the trees as they rode on and on, taking her farther and farther away from the cabin, from Jason. She again prayed that Jason would be able to come after her, would be able to follow them before nightfall. She forced herself to refrain from thinking about why these men had done such a thing, what purpose had prompted them to spirit her away in such a manner. She closed her eyes and choked back a sob as the overwhelming fear returned, her only comfort

73

in the fervent hope that Jason would follow.

When the two men finally pulled their exhausted mounts to a halt, Hannah noticed that they had drawn up before a small cabin, still deep within the forest. She renewed her struggles as the man behind her dismounted and dragged her unceremoniously from the horse's back. He easily lifted her and carried her inside the darkened cabin, then set her on her feet. She blinked rapidly as a lamp was lit, striving to see where she was, who the men standing before her were.

"I'm sorry about the way we had to do this, Mrs. Caldwell," Lewis Harland spoke in a mocking voice, his dark features very sinister in the dim light. "You see, I didn't think you'd come along very willingly."

Hannah's green eyes widened in stunned astonishment, then flashed with indignant fury. Lewis Harland merely laughed, then moved forward and drew a knife slowly from a sheath at his belt. Hannah's eyes grew round with terror, but Harland laughed again and cut the strips of cloth that bound her hands and then the gag about her mouth.

"Why have you done this, Mr. Harland?" Hannah demanded as she rubbed her wrists vigorously where they had been tied. "What possible reason could you have to do such a treacherous thing?" She was perilously close to tears, but she was determined that these men would not see her cry. She refused to give any sign of weakness before Lewis Harland or his accomplice.

"For a very simple reason," Harland replied lazily, the mocking grin flashing across his face once more. He turned to the other man, a small, wiry man who was very repulsive to Hannah's eyes, and said, "That's all, Lem. Now go on, get out of here."

"But, Lewis, you told me—" the man called Lem started to argue, only to be silenced by Harland's next words.

"Get out of here, damn you! You've been paid. Now go on! And don't come back; don't breathe a word of this to anyone. Do you understand?" He spoke with a menacing light in his golden eyes, causing Lem to back down. The smaller man hesitated a moment longer, giving Hannah one last leering glance, before leaving the small cabin.

Hannah's eyes darted about the room, trying to discover some avenue of escape. Lewis Harland chuckled when he looked at her again, guessing correctly where her thoughts were leading her.

"I wouldn't try anything, Mrs. Caldwell. You see, we're all alone up here now. No one else knows that we're here. You can scream all you like. There's no one about to hear you." He seemed to take a cruel delight as he watched her beautiful face, as he detected the unmistakable fear in her shining green eyes.

"Why . . . why are you doing this?" Hannah demanded again, striving to maintain her composure. She must think of some way to escape this horrible man! Jason might not be able to find her, might not even be aware of her disappearance. She must get away before . . .

"For one simple reason," Harland replied mockingly, slowly edging closer to her. "I haven't seen a woman like you since I left the East, and I usually take what I want. Besides, I have a certain score to settle with your husband."

"You mean that you abducted me as some sort of revenge against Jason?" Hannah asked breathlessly. She inched backward as Harland advanced upon her.

"That was only part of it," he answered with another derisive snort of laughter. "I must admit, this is certainly a very sweet revenge! I had no idea that you'd turn out to be so young and lovely, so incredibly fresh and innocent. I've been searching for a way to get even with Jason Caldwell for a long time, and I knew that I'd finally found the means when I saw you there at his cabin yesterday. Yes, sir, this is going to be sweet revenge indeed!" he repeated with another evil laugh. He was within a foot of Hannah now, his hands reaching out for her, an ugly expression on his dark, hawkish face, a dangerous light emanating from his golden eyes.

"No!" Hannah screamed in desperation, jerking away from him. She flew toward the doorway in desperation, but Harland caught her easily and pulled her back against him.

"Now, now, Mrs. Caldwell, it's not going to do you any good to fight me," he remarked sarcastically, his brutal hands closing in a painful grip on her upper arms as she twisted and turned in his grasp.

"Let go of me!" Hannah retorted spiritedly, refusing to surrender. She managed to twist away, kicking out at the man with her feet, then escaping to the other side of the room. She stood facing him, her bosom heaving, her hair streaming about her flushed face as her mind still searched desperately for the means to get away.

"You're only going to make this harder on yourself," Harland ground out, his expression turning even uglier now. He approached her again, the menacing light in his eyes causing Hannah to nearly bolt in panic, until she suddenly felt the stone fireplace behind her. Her hand moved behind her full skirts, and she nearly fainted with profound relief when she discovered the iron poker

76

hanging beside the mantel. She only prayed that Harland hadn't noticed it as well, that he wouldn't see her grasping it and hiding it behind her skirts.

"It's been a long time since I beheld such a delectable little morsel," Harland muttered, his eyes filled with cruel lust as he moved closer and closer. "Jason Caldwell's not going to be very pleased that I had his sweet little wife," he added, lunging forward suddenly, his hands closing about Hannah's slim waist.

Hannah didn't remember screaming as she raised the poker and struck him. She noticed a sudden, arrested expression in those cruel golden eyes before she once again brought the heavy iron poker crashing down onto Lewis Harland's head. He swayed toward her for a brief second, his eyes wide and confused, then collapsed in a heap on the floor at her feet.

She stared down at him in horror, transfixed. She didn't move for several long moments, then abruptly dropped the bloody tool, which clattered to the wooden floor. She clutched her skirts and ran toward the door of the small cabin, a hysterical shriek escaping her lips. The door burst open before she could reach it, and a man rushed inside.

"Jason!" she exclaimed, then threw herself into his arms and burst into tears, silently thanking God that it was her husband who had come through that door, and not the man Harland had called Lem.

"Hannah! Hannah, are you all right?" Jason demanded anxiously, glancing only briefly toward Lewis Harland's unconscious form on the floor. His strong arms held her tight against him, so tight she could barely breathe. She couldn't see the expression on his handsome face, couldn't see his eyes close for a moment

77

as he hugged her gratefully to him.

"I'm all right. I—I think Harland is dead. I hit him with the poker. He had another man with him, a man called Lem. I don't know where he went. Oh, Jason, how did you find me so soon?" she poured out, the tears coursing freely down her cheeks as she allowed herself to be cradled against his muscular chest.

"We heard the shot at the cabin. Someone said he thought he heard a scream as well. They'd never have gotten close to the cabin if they hadn't knocked out the man I had watching it," he explained, still unable to believe that he'd managed to find her in time, that she was safe, that she had even been able to take care of that damned snake Harland on her own. He recalled the terrible feeling he had felt in the very pit of his stomach when he'd heard that shot. He and some of the other men had rushed down the trail, but they had been too late. Thor had been shot, but was still alive, and Jason remembered the overwhelming rage that had taken hold of him when he realized that Hannah had been abducted. That rage had been coupled with another intense emotion as well—an emotion which he still did not want to face.

"You had someone watching the cabin?" Hannah asked in wonderment, raising her tear-streaked face to gaze up at him, her shining eyes asking another, silent question. Jason didn't answer; he simply led her through the doorway and outside to his waiting horse. Hannah saw that there were a handful of men standing around, and she could feel them all staring at her as Jason easily lifted her up onto the horse's back.

"We'll talk about all this later. Right now I'm going to

78

take care of Harland," he informed her tersely, his expression grim.

"No, please!" Hannah pleaded. "Please, just leave him be. I don't even know if I killed him or not—but please, let's just go home."

"Leave him be?" Jason asked, his face incredulous at her request. "After what he tried to do with you? That's not the way things are done out here, Hannah. A man can't get away with making off with another man's wife." He turned away from her, and the other men, at a curt gesture from Jason, mounted up again.

"You can't just go in there and kill a man!" Hannah insisted tearfully, jumping down from the horse and racing toward her husband. "Please, please, for my sake, just take me home!"

"You hit him with a poker, didn't you?" Jason reminded her harshly. "Didn't you intend to kill him yourself?"

"I did only what I had to do, to defend myself," she cried, the tears spilling from her eyes.

Jason turned back to her, intent upon commanding her to get back to the horse, but suddenly he was drawn up short by the sight of her beautiful face, the tears glistening on her flushed cheeks, her hair wildly streaming about her face and shoulders, her bright green eyes silently pleading with him. He glanced uncomfortably toward the other men, who shifted in their saddles and seemed to be avoiding his eyes.

He looked down at Hannah and said, "All right. I'll leave him be, for now. If he's still alive, I'll settle the score with him later. That is," he added with a savage scowl, "if he's still in these parts after this." He led Hannah to the horse and lifted her up again, then

79

mounted behind her. He knew he'd probably regret not going inside and finishing off Lewis Harland, but also knew that it was going to be easier in the long run if he appeased his wife for the moment. She had already been through so much.

He didn't pause to consider that this was the first time in his life he hadn't immediately sought to even the score with an enemy; that it was because of this spirited, beautiful young woman seated before him, her head resting securely on his broad chest. He wouldn't admit to himself—at least not yet—that Hannah had touched his heart, more than it had been touched by anyone in the past six years. He simply tried to ignore the long-dormant stirring deep within his breast as he took Hannah home.

Seven

Jason thanked the other men for their assistance as they reached his cabin once more. The men rode on up the trail to their own quarters at the timber camp, leaving Jason to lift Hannah down from the horse, his strong arms supporting her weary body. It was early evening, Hannah noted, surprised to discover that she had been gone for so long, realizing that she had apparently lost all track of time. The stress of the terrible events of the day was just now crowding in on her, and she was silently grateful for Jason's comforting strength.

"How did you manage to find me so quickly?" she asked, her voice giving evidence of her weariness.

"You didn't have a very long lead on us. It wasn't very difficult to follow Harland's tracks. In fact, I'm amazed that he even thought he could get away with something like this."

"What about Thor? He tried to save my life, you know," Hannah told him sadly.

"He's still alive, or at least he was," Jason replied not unkindly, his features softening. When they stepped inside the cabin, they saw a man waiting for them by the fireplace. "How's he doing, Tom?" Jason asked, indi-

81

cating the injured dog on the floor before the blazing fire.

"I think he's going to make it. I dug the bullet out of him. He lost a lot of blood, but I think that if you can just keep him quiet for a few days, he'll soon be good as new." He smiled shyly as he turned to Hannah, who responded with a smile of her own. "I'm glad to see you're safe, ma'am. I'm Tom Reynolds," he announced politely with a nod in her direction.

"Thank you. I'm pleased to make your acquaintance, Mr. Reynolds. And thank you for seeing to Thor. I'm so very glad he didn't die," she softly spoke, moving across the room to kneel beside the sleeping dog.

"Thanks, Tom. I'll see you in the morning," Jason said to his friend. The two men spoke quietly together for a few moments as they stood in the doorway. And then Tom left. Jason closed and bolted the door after him, then turned back to Hannah with a faint smile, remarking, "Old Thor there is a pretty tough rascal. This isn't the first time he's been hurt."

Hannah glanced up at him, then rose to her feet. "Why did Lewis Harland do this? He talked about some kind of revenge, but for what?" She was almost too exhausted to question him, to stand there and face him, but she believed that she must ask him now, while the unpleasant incident was still so vivid in their minds.

"It concerns a personal matter between Harland and myself," Jason responded curtly, his expression growing unfathomable. He averted his gaze from her and stared intently into the fire.

"But what is it? I'm involved in it now, whatever it is," she insisted, raising a tired hand to sweep the thick curls away from her face. Her clothing was torn and dusty, and she felt as if she could never be clean again—not after those two horrible men had touched her. She had felt much the same way when she had worked at that tavern for a brief time, and she now wanted nothing more than a hot, cleansing bath. But, not until after she and Jason had talked.

Hannah could still recall the absolute joy she had experienced when he had come bursting into that cabin. He had been so gentle, so comforting while she had wept, holding her close and making her feel so safe and secure. He must care about me to some degree, at least a little, she told herself. She watched as Jason knelt beside Thor and reached out a large hand to caress the dog's fur.

"It's not anything that concerns you," he repeated quietly, still staring into the dancing flames with that inscrutable expression in his steely eyes.

"But, it does concern me! Lewis Harland kidnapped me, he planned to . . . to dishonor me, all because I am your wife, because he spoke of his thirst for revenge. Please," she asked, "won't you tell me what it is?"

"Lewis Harland is a no-account bastard!" Jason ground out, rising abruptly to his feet and glaring down into Hannah's upturned face. "I'm sorry you were hurt because of the bad blood between us, but it still doesn't concern you!" His steely eyes held some secret fury. Obviously it was something still very painful for him to think about, Hannah realized. She deemed it wiser to capitulate; she did not have the strength to argue with him about it any longer. She swept past him slowly, heading toward the sanctuary of the bedroom.

"I'd like a bath, a real bath," she remarked wearily, her back to Jason's piercing gaze.

"Hannah," she heard him murmur quietly behind her. She was startled to hear him speak, not really expecting a response to her comment, and she turned back to face him with a slight frown.

"Yes?"

He stared across at her, not speaking, the silence hanging heavily in the air between them. Finally he cleared his throat gently and said, "I'll set the water to heating."

She watched as he marched from the room, disappearing into the kitchen. Totally bewildered by his behavior, she reflected that he was impossible to understand. One moment he was holding and comforting her; the next he was angrily refusing to tell her why she had been abducted. And just now there was his kindness about the water. Her face grew very pensive as she entered the bedroom and sank down onto the bed, forgetting to light the lamp as she sat there alone in the semidarkness.

Jason remained outside while she took her bath. The water's soothing warmth helped take some of the soreness from her body. And, although the tub was really only a large wooden barrel that had been sawed in half, she didn't mind as she washed the dust from her body, then washed her long, thick hair. When she had finished, she donned her nightgown and wrapper, then went to the front door and called to Jason.

"Feeling better?" he asked as he entered the room, his arms laden with firewood. He took the logs to the fireplace and stacked them neatly beside the hearth.

"Yes, much better, thank you. I'm afraid I'll have to ask you to empty the tub for me."

"I'll take care of it. I expect you're pretty hungry by now." He removed his jacket and hung it negligently on a peg behind the door.

"Yes, I suppose I am," she replied thoughtfully,

realizing that she hadn't eaten anything since early that morning. "I'll get supper right away."

"No, I'll fix us something to eat tonight. You just go over there by the fire and keep Thor company," he suggested, his manner rather gruff, as if he were uncomfortable about his offer.

"Thank you," Hannah murmured softly. She took a seat on one of the wooden chairs before the fireplace. Glancing down at Thor, she was pleased to discover that he was still sleeping soundly. Sighing, she leaned forward toward the fire, holding her hands out to its blazing warmth, losing herself in her thoughts once more.

When Jason stepped from the kitchen several minutes later, he found that his wife had fallen asleep, still sitting upright in the chair. Smiling to himself, he moved forward quietly and took her gently in his arms, carrying her effortlessly into the bedroom and placing her on the bed. He stood staring down at her, noting the way her bosom rose and fell softly with the evenness of her breathing, the way her thick curtain of hair fanned out across the pillow. Her face appeared so very young and vulnerable there in the darkness of the bedroom, with the light from the other room streaming in faintly through the doorway. He reached out and touched her cheek tenderly, then withdrew his hand swiftly and strode from the room, closing the door quietly behind him.

It was much later when Jason heard Hannah calling out to him. He jumped to his feet and rushed into the bedroom, only to find that she was having a dream. She twisted her head feverishly from side to side, crying aloud and calling his name over and over again, her eyes closed tightly. Jason hesitated for a brief moment, then approached her. "Hannah! Hannah, it's all right, you're

85

safe now," he reassured her, shaking her as his hands closed upon her trembling shoulders.

Her eyes immediately swept open at the sound of his deep voice, and she blinked rapidly, seeking to reassure herself that it was really Jason who knelt beside the bed, who was rescuing her from her terrible nightmare, just as he had rescued her earlier from the terrible reality of Lewis Harland.

"I . . . I'm sorry. I guess I was dreaming," she explained drowsily, sitting upright in the bed and sweeping the hair from her flushed face. She saw Jason's intense gaze lingering on her face, then moving slowly down to her body. She was dismayed to see that her wrapper had come untied, that her nightgown had become bunched up above her knees. She drew in her breath sharply as Jason's blue eyes traveled slowly upward and met her green ones. She continued hurriedly, "I'm sorry if I disturbed you. I was dreaming that Lewis Harland had captured me again, that—" Her words were cut off when he suddenly sat down beside her, drawing her into his arms with a muttered curse.

She gasped as his demanding lips touched her hotly at her throat, and she grew frightened as his hands grasped her hair and he buried his face in its thick masses. She was uncertain what to do, but she turned her face instinctively to meet his, rewarded when his lips moved on her own. His arms tightened about her as he pushed her backwards gently, stretching his full length out on the bed beside her, and she moaned softly when his warm mouth nuzzled her ear, her slender neck, her face. She sensed that he would not be stopping this time, and she knew that she didn't want him to.

Jason continued kissing her as one of his hands drew

the nightgown even farther upward, until Hannah's entire body was exposed and the garment had been discarded, floating downward to lie forgotten on the floor. As Jason's eyes roamed over her naked body, she flushed and waited with downcast eyes as he stood and shed his own clothing quickly. She gasped again as his firm masculine flesh pressed her farther into the softness of the bed, but she moaned in growing ecstasy as his passionate, demanding lips trailed downward to tease lovingly at one of her rounded breasts. She closed her eyes tightly and entwined her slender fingers in his thick hair, as his kisses and caresses brought on the deep yearning she had experienced that other time, the yearning which blazed within her like a smoldering flame bursting to life.

"Hannah," she heard him whisper her name hoarsely, his deep voice barely audible to her ears. His lips returned to capture hers once more, his mouth moving upon hers with increasing urgency. She strained upward, her eyes flying open in surprise when one of his hands touched her gently between her thighs, as his long, warm fingers stroked her tenderly. The dizzying sensation she was feeling seemed to build and build, until she felt consumed with overwhelming wonder.

At that moment, however, Jason eased himself carefully into her, causing her to cry aloud at the sudden, sharp pain. Her cry was silenced quickly by the pressure of his seeking lips on her mouth again, and she gasped as he plunged fully into her moist warmth, then began slowly and gently moving back and forth, her body responding quickly to the rhythm of his loving. Jason expertly brought them both to a shattering sense of fulfillment, then moved away from her slowly and lay breathless at her side, leaving one of his muscular arms relaxed across her soft, quivering curves.

Though only moments had passed, Hannah hugged the sweet bliss to herself. She knew that she was a complete woman now, that she was truly Jason Caldwell's wife in every sense. As she lay there nestled beside him, still striving to regain her own breath, she knew something else as well. She was in love with Jason. She had given herself to him gladly for that very reason, because she loved him. This sudden revelation caused her eyes to grow very round with dawning amazement. She glanced up at him shyly, her green eyes silently bespeaking her love for him.

But Jason didn't return her gaze; instead he lay with his eyes closed. He remained still a few seconds longer, before he rose quickly from the bed and gathered up his discarded clothing. He glanced down at Hannah's revealed beauty once more, then stalked from the room, leaving her to stare after him in hurt confusion.

"Jason?" she called out to him hesitantly. But she was sorely disappointed to hear the front door to the cabin opening, then slamming shut.

Why had he been in such a hurry to get away like that? she asked herself in bewilderment, drawing the covers upward unconsciously to hide her nakedness. After what had just passed between them, what possible cause could he have to leave like that?

She wasn't sorry he had made love to her. No, she now admitted to herself, it was what she had wanted almost from the first moment she had met Jason Caldwell, had been bound to him in marriage. Was *he* sorry, she then wondered. Was he displeased with her for some reason?

Hannah lay there thinking of the many ways she loved

Jason, loved him in every possible way. She loved his rugged handsomeness, his strength and his sense of honor, his kindness to her in times of trouble. She even loved his brooding silence, and was ecstatic that she had become a part of him in a way that nothing could ever change. She belonged to him now, her heart captured forever by her elusive husband.

Still perplexed by his disturbing actions, she tried to concentrate on what had just happened to her. From the rather limited knowledge she possessed, she hadn't really expected to find such pleasure when her husband had finally claimed his rights. But she had indeed found pleasure, even with the brief pain. Her body still tingled all over from their passion. She savored the memory of his burning kisses, his loving, yet demanding caresses. She knew that it had been made truly beautiful for her because she loved him, because she wanted to please him. Did he love her as well? Though he obviously found her physically attractive, desirable, did he care for her as she had come to care for him?

Hannah lay there alone in the darkness, yearning for Jason to come back. But he did not return. She waited for what seemed like hours, drifting off finally into a dream-filled sleep in the early hours of the dawn. When she awakened once more, it was very quiet, and she arose, washed, and dressed quickly, hoping to find Jason still inside the cabin.

But she found only Thor, who still lay beside the fireplace, though he was now fully awake. His huge tail thumped noisily on the floor when he saw Hannah, and she smiled at him and commanded him to remain still, then added an affectionate pat to his head as she inspected his wound anxiously, before setting about to find Jason. She searched in the kitchen, then the storage room, then opened the door and stepped outside, frowning to herself when she saw that it was raining softly, on this gray and overcast day. She was relieved to see Jason, and she ignored the small drops of cool rain that fell on her as she crossed the short distance to the corral, where her husband was saddling two horses. He glanced up as Hannah approached.

"Good morning, Jason," she spoke in a pleasant voice, inwardly surprised that she was feeling no real shyness with him after last night.

"Morning," he responded coolly, continuing with his task.

"Are we going somewhere today?" she asked, flashing him a winsome smile, her heart nearly bursting with her love for him.

"We're going to town."

"Just the two of us? Oh, I'm so glad! I've been wanting to see what the town is like. Perhaps I can get a few provisions we need while we're there," she said, her eyes glowing with excitement. She also wanted to purchase some dress goods, for she felt her wardrobe to be sadly lacking. She reflected that she was fortunate to have managed to bring as much as she had, since the brides had been unable to bring anything more than the barest necessities on the voyage. Anyway, she thought, she needed another pair of shoes—a good, sturdy pair that would serve her better for walking. She hoped that Jason wouldn't mind her spending the money for such items. She hated to ask him, but she wanted to look her best for him, wanted him to be proud of her appearance.

"You can buy whatever you need," he replied with a shrug, almost as if he could read her mind. He pulled the cinch tighter, refusing to meet her shining eyes as he kept busy. He was ashamed of himself for having taken advantage of her the night before, for breaking a solemn promise he had made to himself. Although he couldn't deny that he had enjoyed their lovemaking, that it had meant something special to him, had affected him so intensely that he knew they couldn't go on this way, he believed it would only lead to disaster if he allowed Hannah to think that things had really changed between them. Not pausing to consider the true reasons for the decision he had made in the early hours of the morning, he finished saddling their mounts, then looked up at Hannah.

"You'd best go inside and get all your things together."

"What do you mean?" Her beautiful face became puzzled.

"Get all your things together. I'm taking you down to the town," Jason responded in a low, even tone of voice, still unable to meet her gaze for very long.

"But why?" Hannah demanded, a sudden, foreboding sensation assailing her. "Why are you taking me there? What has happened?"

"You're simply going to live down in town for a while. You'll be staying with a good friend of mine, a widow woman by the name of Maggie Clancy. She'll look after you."

"But I don't want to leave!"

"You're going to leave, and that's all there is to it," he told her, his blue eyes appearing colder than ever, his manner even more aloof.

"Why? Why are you doing this? Why are you sending me away?" she asked tearfully, not at all understanding

91

what could have gone wrong. Just when she thought they had a real chance for happiness together, when he had finally made her his true wife . . .

"It's too dangerous to leave you alone here at the cabin all day. I can't be watching out for you all the time. I've got a lot of work to do up at the camp. We've got a lot of timber to cut and start moving. It's best if you live in town for a while." He couldn't tell her that the question of her safety was only partly the reason he was sending her away. He couldn't tell her he was afraid their involvement would only deepen if she stayed, and that it was something he didn't want to have to face.

"I can't believe you're doing this!" Hannah cried, fighting back the tears. "After what happened last night, after the two of us—"

"I said you're going, and that's that!" Jason cut her off angrily. His wet hair was plastered closely to his head, and his face appeared very grim in the gray morning light.

Hannah was oblivious to the fact that she herself was becoming quite soaked. She didn't know what was happening, couldn't understand why Jason was sending her away to live in the town. If it was because he was concerned about her safety, surely she could make him see that she would be more careful, that she could learn to take care of herself while he was away at the timber camp during the day. Surely she could somehow convince him that there was no need to take such drastic measures!

"Jason, please, listen to me!" she pleaded, moving forward to clutch his arm. He turned and stared deep into her glistening eyes, and she was certain that he wavered, if only for a moment. But the aloof mask returned, and he strode away from her, back toward the cabin. Hannah stood there in the rain a moment longer, then plodded after him, still desperately trying to think of some way to make him abandon this plan.

"Jason, I don't want to leave! I want to stay here, to be your wife, to keep the cabin for you, to cook for you, to take care of you and Thor. Please don't send me away like this!"

"Hannah," he said, his hands closing upon her shoulders as he whirled about to face her, "I've already made up my mind, so there's no use arguing with me about it. I'm taking you down to the town, right now, so get your things together and let's get going." The expression on his handsome face told her that he would brook no further resistance, and she did as he ordered listlessly, stepping into the bedroom and packing her things slowly, feeling as if her heart was breaking.

She could resist; she could flatly refuse to go, Hannah thought, but then realized that such foolish behavior would do her no good. Jason would only force her if she resisted, she told herself with a heavy sigh. So, her carpetbag in one hand, she bade a tearful farewell to Thor, then preceded a silent Jason from the cabin. Again she felt as if her heart was breaking as she mounted up, Jason riding beside her as the two of them left the cabin far behind, the light rain soon turning into a veritable downpour.

Eight

By the time Hannah and Jason approached the town of Red Creek, it had stopped raining. They had barely spoken to one another throughout the five-mile ride. Jason's eyes and ears, alert as always, were constantly scouting the surrounding terrain, while Hannah merely hung her head in misery against the onslaught of the rain, trying to keep dry beneath her woolen cloak. Now, as her horse followed Jason's obediently toward the muddy streets of the small settlement, she raised her head to peer about at the strange surroundings.

It certainly wasn't much of a town. Hannah took quick note of the unpainted wooden buildings which lined the single main road. There were many men milling about, but no women. A rough boardwalk ran in front of the stores and old buildings, but the planks didn't appear to help much. The men plodded along the muddy street, their boots clumping noisily on the equally filthy boardwalk as they went about their business.

Hannah suddenly noticed that the buildings they were now approaching were painted brightly, in sharp contrast to the others she had seen, and she looked up in avid curiosity when she perceived that they were saloons. She was fascinated as her eyes were drawn to the women who appeared at the upstairs uncurtained windows of the saloons.

Most of the women's faces were bright with paint as well. But it was their strange attire—or, rather, their lack of it—that drew her attention. Hannah could feel herself blushing hotly as some of the women now opened the windows and proceeded to call out gaily to Jason as they rode past, their laughter and rather ribald comments making Hannah's ears burn. She couldn't help wondering how the women knew her husband's name, and she glanced ahead to observe how he was reacting to the women's colorful remarks.

"Jason!" one of the women sang out, laughing all the while. "What's that you got there?"

"You ain't gone and got yourself a permanent woman, have you, Jason?" another chimed in, leaning far outward so that Hannah could see the woman was wearing nothing but a thin chemise.

"We ain't seen you around here in a long time, Jason!" a third woman shouted. "When are you coming back to pay us a visit?"

Hannah could feel herself growing alternately angry and jealous at their immodest, insulting behavior. She attempted to ignore them as it appeared Jason was determined to do, but she still wondered why it was that the women appeared to know her husband so well.

"This is it," Jason spoke finally, reining in before a two-story building near the outer limits of the town. "Maggie Clancy runs a boardinghouse and small restaurant here." He swung down and took Hannah's carpetbag from behind her saddle, then extended a hand to assist her in dismounting.

"How did those women know your name? Are they friends of yours?" Hannah couldn't refrain from asking him, her face still flaming from the incident.

"It's not important," he responded evasively, leading her up the muddy walk to the front door of the fading whitewashed house. Although Hannah wanted to question him further about those scantily clad females, she was forced to desist when the door swung open to reveal a tall, sturdily built woman of about fifty.

"Jason! How nice it is to see you again, my boy!" the woman said with a broad, welcoming smile, her voice colored with an unmistakable brogue.

"Maggie, this is my wife, Hannah," Jason told the woman, returning her smile with a faint one of his own. "I've brought her here to stay with you for a while. I hope that's all right with you." It was obvious to Hannah that he had already presumed it would be.

"Of course, Jason, of course! Hannah, I'm very glad to meet you! You two come on inside and take off those wet things!" Maggie Clancy insisted with a motherly air, not appearing to be at all surprised at the news that Jason Caldwell had a wife. Hannah stepped across the threshold, allowing the older woman to take control of her sodden, dripping cloak.

"I'm afraid I won't be staying, Maggie. I've got to get back up to the camp. I want you to know I appreciate your letting Hannah stay with you," Jason remarked stiffly, then turned toward Hannah. She stared up at him, her eyes brimming with tears again as he prepared to leave, the unhappy expression on her lovely face almost causing him to change his mind.

"Jason, please," she pleaded softly one last time, unaware that Maggie had moved away to allow the two

96

young people a moment of privacy.

"I'll be back to look in on you in a week or two," he said, schooling his rugged features to hide the turmoil he was experiencing when he looked at her. "Maggie's a good woman, a kind woman. She'll take good care of you. I'm leaving you some money. You'll be able to get anything you need."

Hannah knew it was useless to say anything else. She merely nodded in response, her face looking very grave, hating herself for having displayed such emotional weakness, yet hating even more to see him go. Still not fully understanding why he was leaving her there, she watched as he strode away purposefully, back down the muddy walk to the waiting horses. Soon he was out of sight.

"Don't worry, dear, I'm sure he'll be back for you soon," Maggie murmured quietly, seeking to comfort the young woman who was so obviously in love with Jason Caldwell, so obviously unhappy at being left behind. She hadn't bothered to ask Jason the reason he had brought his young wife to her, but she didn't really need to ask. She trusted him enough to know that it must have been for a good reason. Funny, though, she thought as she examined Hannah with a quizzical smile, she didn't know Jason had married, didn't even know he had a sweetheart. She was nearly bursting with unspoken curiosity, but she decided to put all her questions aside—at least until the poor thing standing so forlornly before her had been given a chance to rest and compose herself a bit.

"You're being very kind," Hannah murmured softly in response, giving Maggie a watery smile.

"Why don't you come with me now? I'll show you upstairs to your room. I'm certain you'd like to be alone for a spell," the older woman suggested knowingly. She led the way up the staircase as Hannah followed silently. Maggie suddenly reflected that her own graying brown hair looked downright mousy next to this young woman's beautiful golden tresses, and she stole a quick glance at Hannah as the two of them reached the top of the stairs. Jason Caldwell had certainly gotten himself a beauty for a wife, even if there was some reason he felt the need to leave her in town for a while.

Hannah liked the older woman, yet she was feeling too drained to carry on a conversation as she was shown into a small, comfortable room just to the right of the staircase. She noticed the calico curtains hanging at the single window, the iron bedstead covered with a patchwork quilt, an oak wardrobe and washstand. Her thoughts, however, were still on Jason, and she wondered when she would see him again. She would find it difficult to bear their separation.

"This is very nice, thank you," she told Maggie politely. "Mrs. Clancy, I suppose you can tell that I'm not pleased about my husband leaving me here—" she started to explain, but was interrupted quickly.

"Now, now, Hannah, dear, you don't have to explain anything to me. I have eyes, and I can plainly see that you don't really want to be here. But I'll do my best to make you comfortable while you're here. To tell the truth, I think it's going to be great fun having you about for a spell. I don't get the chance to visit with any other 'decent' womenfolk very often. And," she added with a warm smile, "you're to call me 'Maggie,' all right?" She reached out and patted Hannah's arm gently, then left her alone in the room.

It was more than an hour later before Hannah

ventured downstairs again. She had washed, changed her dress, tidied her hair, and had also succumbed to even more anguished tears. Finally, she had commanded herself to stop being so childish, washed her face once more, and descended the stairs with determination, her head lifted proudly. She could hear voices coming from somewhere, but she decided to take advantage of the moment alone and strolled about downstairs, telling herself that she might as well become familiar with her current surroundings, even if they were not of her choosing.

The parlor, which served as the main living room, was bright and cheerful, even on this rainy day. The furnishings were simple, yet appeared to be comfortable, and there were gingham curtains hanging at the windows. The wooden floors were clean and polished, and several cheerful braided rugs added to the feeling of comfort. She moved into the dining room, taking note of the long trestle table and benches. She still heard the voices—a man and woman's—and she directed her steps toward what she surmised to be the kitchen, judging from the delectable aroma which drifted outward.

"Oh, Hannah, I'm glad to see you're up and about and feeling better," Maggie Clancy commented with an Irish lilt, wiping her floury hands on her white apron as she bustled forward to greet her new charge.

"I thought I'd come down and take a look around," Hannah said by way of explanation, suddenly growing aware of the man who stood watching her a few feet away. He was fairly tall and muscular, his hair a light golden brown, his eyes very blue. He was very attractive, she thought, and didn't look much older than herself. She also noticed the unmistakable resemblance between the smiling, frankly admiring young man and the woman who stood before her.

"This is my son, Hannah, my one and only child, who's been giving his poor mother nothing but trouble ever since the day he was born!" Maggie joked, pointing a thumb in the man's direction and giving him a mockingly stern look.

"The name's Rob," the young man announced, his voice lilting with the same brogue as his mother's. "I guess you're the bride of Jason Caldwell's my mother's been telling me about." His eyes crinkled pleasantly when he smiled, and Hannah couldn't help warming to him and his friendly manner.

"Yes, I'm Hannah Caldwell. I'm very pleased to meet you, Mr. Clancy." She could feel herself flushing slightly as he continued to gaze at her in unabashed appreciation.

Finally his mother clapped him on the shoulder and said, "Now, there, Rob, there's no use in making the girl feel uncomfortable! Besides, you have work to do, remember?" Again she frowned quite severely, but her son merely chuckled in response.

"I remember, I remember." He sauntered off toward the doorway, passing Hannah and bestowing another charming smile upon her, then turning and blowing a kiss to his mother before he left.

"That rascal!" Maggie muttered to herself, though she was unable to suppress a soft chuckle. "I don't see him that often, mind you, so it's nice to have him about. His own timber camp's up on the other side of the mountain from your husband's." She continued with her bread-making as she talked, adding more flour and kneading the soft dough. The kitchen was much the same as the rest of the large house, simple and yet homey.

Hannah asked, "Is there anything I can help you with?"

"No, thanks, not just now. I've got to get this bread in to bake before it gets any later. The cook at the restaurant next door didn't have time to do his baking, so I've got to do double today," Maggie replied as she punched and rolled the white dough, then sprinkled more flour on top.

"Jason told me you had the boardinghouse and restaurant. I don't see how you have the time to take care of both," Hannah commented, watching the older woman work, leaning back against the door frame.

"It's not easy. It wasn't so bad until my husband died, nearly eight years ago now. He was in the restaurant business back home in Boston."

"So you've been here in Red Creek since then?"

"No, not quite that long. But, we've been in this country now for almost fifteen years. Things haven't been that bad, all in all. Not until my Tim caught the fever and passed away when we were heading west. It's a good thing Rob was already grown by then. He's been a lot of help."

"I didn't think he was much older than myself," Hannah remarked thoughtfully.

"He's always looked younger than his years," his mother answered as she began shaping the dough to put into the pans. "He and Jason are about the same age. They've been friends for years, even before I came to Red Creek."

"Jason's never mentioned him to me," Hannah said, half to herself, musing that Jason hadn't ever mentioned much about himself, his friends, or his life out here. There were still so many things she wanted and needed to know about the man she had married, the man she

101

now loved.

"I'm not surprised," Maggie replied cryptically, glancing up from her task to look directly at Hannah, her features growing rather solemn. "Rob and Jason aren't exactly on what you'd call friendly terms at the moment. Seems the two of them had a falling-out over some lumber deal a couple of years ago. They've hardly spoken to one another since then."

"But," Hannah said, hesitated, then continued, "you and Jason are apparently such good friends. Why, he brought me here because he seems to think so much of you."

"That's right. What's happened between him and Rob hasn't affected our friendship. Neither one of us would ever let it. I know it's hard to understand, but that's the way it is," she added, smiling at Hannah's bemused expression. "I love my son more than anything in this world, but Jason's been like another son to me almost ever since I met him. I try not to get involved in their affairs, since it's really none of my business."

"There's so very much I'd like to ask you about Jason, Maggie, but I don't know where to begin. I'm afraid the man I married is still a stranger to me," Hannah confided with a sigh.

"I'll be glad to tell you anything I can, but I don't think I can tell you much. Jason Caldwell is a very private sort of man. He's a good man, a fair man, but he doesn't allow anyone to get too close, though I don't really know why. Rob knows, I think, but he doesn't talk about it." She positioned the dough in the pans, then set it aside to rise. "Anyway, there's a lot about yourself I'm curious to know. That is, if you'd like to tell me." She was so friendly, so motherly, that Hannah found herself telling

Maggie all about her earlier life, her voyage to Seattle, even about her marriage to Jason. It was such a relief to be able to confide in another woman, especially one who seemed as wise as Maggie Clancy, and the two of them talked together for nearly two hours, long after the bread dough had doubled in height.

Hannah reluctantly rose to her feet and prepared to return upstairs to freshen up before the evening meal, then paused to ask, "Maggie, how many other people live here?"

"We've got nearly a full house at the moment, which is to say there are four others beside yourself. All men, of course, except for you and me."

"Oh, I see," Hannah murmured, evidently uneasy at the thought of residing in a house full of strange men.

As if reading her thoughts, Maggie sought to reassure her. "Don't trouble yourself about the men. They're all good sorts. Most of the men around here have wives and families of their own back home someplace. There aren't many white women out here yet. The rough life this country offers isn't likely to persuade these men to be bringing their women out here in the near future. That's why I'm so glad Jason brought you, even if only for a brief time. The other women in this town are the sort who live above the saloons, and I'm sure I don't have to tell you about them!" she remarked with a grimace of distaste.

"I saw some of those women when Jason and I rode into town today," Hannah admitted, still experiencing a twinge of jealousy at the memory. "They called out to us as we passed them. It seems that they even know my husband's name."

"Oh, now, don't let that bother you. They know all of

103

the men, whether they're regular customers or not. This town isn't very big, Hannah, and talk travels fast. I can tell you that Jason isn't the kind of man who'd spend much time with women such as those."

"I hope you're right," Hannah spoke only half-aloud, then turned and slowly climbed the staircase to her room.

Maggie Clancy gazed up after her, shaking her head. She hated to see the poor young thing so miserable. Well, she'd do all she could to make things easier on her.

She told herself that it had been for the best—her not telling Hannah the entire truth just now, about Jason's connection with those women at the saloons. But, after all, what she had said had been *almost* the total truth. Jason hadn't spent any time to speak of with those girls, she knew, but she didn't have either the heart or the inclination to confide to her new young friend the talk she'd heard about Jason and one particular female. It had been nearly a year ago, and even if there had been some truth to the gossip she'd heard, it was all over and done with now.

Now Jason Caldwell had himself a new young wife, a beautiful and sensitive and apparently courageous woman. Maggie prayed that the man knew how very fortunate he was.

Nine

Hannah slept a great deal more than she had expected to that first night at Maggie Clancy's boardinghouse. Following a pleasant supper, during which the other boarders talked wistfully of their own families, she had insisted on helping Maggie with the dishes. By the time she had finally trudged upstairs to her bed, she was feeling extremely tired, her thoughts still never far away from Jason. She wondered if he was perhaps thinking of her as well. But then her thoughts drifted peacefully as she undressed and climbed wearily into bed, sleep overtaking her quickly as soon as she closed her eyes.

After breakfast the next morning, Maggie suggested that she and Hannah venture outside for a walk about the town. They could buy the few things they needed as well, she added. Hannah agreed willingly, wanting another view of the town under more favorable circumstances than those of the previous day. The day had dawned bright and clear, and she and Maggie stepped out onto the front porch and inhaled the crisp, cool air deeply.

"It looks like it's going to be a really nice day, Hannah," Maggie remarked with a bright smile. "Just the sort of day that can't help but lift your spirits." She threw a knitted shawl about her shoulders and tied a serviceable bonnet on her head.

"I don't believe it can be any worse than yesterday, can it?" Hannah spoke with a heavy sigh, then smiled in response. Making their way carefully down the board-walk, she and Maggie took pains to lift the hems of their full skirts, keeping them safely away from the dark mud which seemed to be everywhere. Hannah was conscious of the many male heads that turned as she and her new friend strolled toward the other end of town. Maggie had already warned her that she would be the object of a good many curious stares, as well as outright amazement, since the town had seldom seen such a beautiful young woman as Hannah.

"I thought we'd go on down to the mercantile first. I was thinking that you could probably use a few new dress goods, and I guess I could really use a new dress or two while we're at it," Maggie declared, suddenly beginning to walk a bit more briskly. Though puzzled, Hannah quickened her pace as well, then noticed the reason for Maggie's hurry. They were just passing in front of the saloons.

"Are the saloons open all day?" Hannah asked curiously. She couldn't resist peering inside one of the buildings as they passed. She glimpsed several men inside, even at this early hour, but she observed none of the women such as those she had seen the day before.

"The blasted things never close!" Maggie frowned darkly. "I guess it gives the men a place to go. There really isn't any other 'entertainment' for them around here," she added with another frown.

"But," Hannah questioned, "doesn't the town have a church, or a school?" She continued to glance through

106

the open doorways as they walked.

"There are a few of us who meet for services whenever the circuit rider comes through town. There isn't any school. But then, there aren't many children up here in these parts."

Suddenly Hannah's interested gaze was drawn to a woman just stepping out of one of the saloons. The woman, she noted quickly, was rather small and petite, yet very shapely, her gleaming black hair piled high atop her head in an elaborate style that seemed totally out of place in the town's rough surroundings. The dress she wore was of bright yellow satin, and was extremely tight-fitting, and Hannah mused to herself that it wasn't at all suitable attire for the middle of the morning.

"Who is she?" she asked Maggie, nodding briefly in the brunette's direction.

"Who?" Maggie responded, then saw where Hannah's curious gaze was fastened. Maggie's eyes grew round for a brief instant before she hesitated visibly, seeming to be searching for words.

"She doesn't look quite like the other women from the saloons I've seen," Hannah thoughtfully commented.

"That's Colette," Maggie finally answered, a tiny frown creasing her brow. "She owns the Timber Saloon."

"She looks much too young to be the owner," Hannah remarked, continuing to stare curiously until the woman disappeared into one of the doorways ahead.

"She's not nearly as young as you think," Maggie replied with a derisive snort. "She's been here in Red Creek for more than two years now. I heard that she'd been around quite a bit before she came here, if you catch my meaning."

"I thought you said there weren't any other white women living here in town."

"Colette's not white," Maggie answered with a brief shake of her head. "That is, not entirely. She's half Indian and half French. Her skin's a bit lighter than that of the other girls', and because of that, she likes to put on airs, to think she's better than the others of her kind. But, as far as I'm concerned, she's no better at all!" she finished with an emphatic nod.

"How is it that you seem to know so much about her?" Hannah asked with a faint smile. "I wouldn't have thought you to be very friendly with those other women."

"Like I told you before, talk travels fast in a town as small as this one. Since there isn't really much of an opportunity to talk with other women—at least, other women besides those like Colette—I can assure you that we take full advantage of it whenever we do have the chance!"

Hannah merely smiled in response as they paused before the doorway of the town's only mercantile store. She had all but forgotten about the men who continued to stare at her, the dumbfounded expressions on their faces appearing almost comical. When she and Maggie stepped inside the cluttered building, she saw immediately that Colette was also there.

Apparently, Maggie didn't notice, saying, "Why don't you go on over there and see what you can find? I've got to get a few things for the restaurant, too. MacDonald carries quite a few things for his female customers, even though they are sort of rare," she added in a preoccupied manner, absorbed now in studying the list she'd pulled from her pocket. Hannah took her advice and strolled across the wooden floor, toward the table where the clerk and the dark-haired woman named Colette were standing.

"I'm sorry, Miss Colette," the man said in a voice heavy with a Scottish burr, "but I can't get any more of that for at least four months." He nodded, indicating the bright red printed fabric which the woman was fingering.

"All right, then," she answered with a pout, obviously much displeased. "Just give me what you have of it. I suppose this will have to do." Her voice bespoke her French heritage, and Hannah told herself that the woman did indeed appear older when seen up close. She was wearing lip rouge and face powder, and her yellow dress was cut immodestly low across her full, swelling bosom. She turned toward Hannah abruptly, and her brown eyes narrowed as they swept rather disdainfully up and down the younger woman's form. Hannah gazed steadily back at her, the corners of her mouth curving up into a smile. The smile faded quickly as Colette fixed her with a cold stare. Hannah was relieved when Maggie spoke behind her.

"Have you found anything yet?" Maggie's own smile disappeared when she perceived Colette, who was now eyeing her defiantly, her small chin held high.

"Well, good morning to you, Mrs. Clancy," Colette almost purred. Her brown eyes glinted coldly, though she smiled very sweetly. "Who is your friend here?" she asked, fluttering a small, delicate hand toward Hannah.

"Come on, Hannah, let's go," Maggie spoke in a low, even voice. It was obvious that she was doing her best to ignore Colette.

"Are you really so cowardly that you cannot even face me, Mrs. Clancy?" Colette remarked with a contemptuous little laugh. She placed one hand on her hip, the other moving languidly upward to pat unnecessarily at a dark curl. Her whole demeanor gave evidence to the fact that she took pleasure in taunting Maggie, and when she turned back to Hannah, she appeared to be awaiting an answer.

"I am Hannah Caldwell," Hannah announced coolly, facing her squarely. "Mrs. Jason Caldwell," she added. She wondered why there appeared to be such animosity between Maggie and this Colette, then decided she'd ask Maggie about it later.

At Hannah's words, the smile froze on Colette's painted face. Her brown eyes widened briefly in surprise, before narrowing again. It seemed to Hannah that the woman's eyes literally blazed at her for a moment, before she murmured in an undertone, "I did not know that Jason had taken a wife!"

"Well, he most certainly has!" Maggie couldn't refrain from uttering triumphantly, placing a protective hand on Hannah's arm. "And I'd say that he's gone and married himself the prettiest woman he could ever hope to find!" Again she urged Hannah to leave with her, but Hannah stood her ground, suddenly curious about Colette's apparent familiarity with Jason.

"Do you know my husband?" she calmly inquired.

"But of course!" Colette answered with a delighted little laugh. She had recovered her poise now and smiled broadly. "Jason and I are very old, very dear friends. You must be sure to ask him about Colette sometime!" Then, with a low, meaningful laugh, she turned and left them, her high heels clicking across the wooden floor. Hannah and Maggie stared after her.

"You didn't tell me Colette knew Jason," Hannah remarked quietly, feeling unaccountably upset by the brief encounter.

"There was nothing to tell," Maggie reassured her quickly, studying the younger woman's face. "Just about everyone in town knows Jason Caldwell, or at least knows of him."

"So it seems," Hannah replied with an ironic smile. She appeared to shrug it off for the moment, turning to the rather bemused clerk and inquiring about some dress goods. But her thoughts still drifted occasionally to Colette, and her implied familiarity with Jason. Such thoughts were definitely not pleasant.

Maggie and Hannah completed their business at the mercantile, and again raised their skirts and retraced their steps carefully along the muddy boardwalk to the boardinghouse, their arms laden with their purchases. It was nearing noon by now, and Maggie asked Hannah for her assistance in the kitchen. Hannah agreed readily, hurrying upstairs to toss her packages on the bed in her room, then returning downstairs to help prepare the meal.

Rob Clancy surprised his mother by appearing for supper that evening. He hadn't been present in the dining room the night before, though his mother refrained wisely from questioning her son about his whereabouts.

During the meal, Rob's blue eyes twinkled irrepressibly whenever he glanced across at Hannah. She was pleased by his charming attentiveness, his infectious humor, and she was more than a little surprised to discover that she was actually enjoying herself. She was, however, unaware of the fact that she mentally compared Rob to Jason every so often, comparing Rob's easygoing nature to Jason's silent moodiness, Rob's boyish good looks to Jason's rugged handsomeness. She wasn't in the

111

least bit attracted to Rob Clancy in a romantic way, though it was undeniably pleasant to pass the time with him. As an only child who lived quite some distance from the nearest town, she had never really possessed a male friend before, so she enjoyed his company all the more, treating him more like a brother than an older man who admired her, who flirted shamelessly with her right before his mother's watchful eyes.

"Rob, my boy," Maggie told him, long after the other boarders had left and only he and Hannah remained with her at the table, "I don't think Jason would take too kindly to the way you're trying to turn the head of his young bride!" Though she was teasing, she was more than half-serious. She knew that there really was no danger of Hannah's head being turned, but she also knew what a ladies' man her scamp of a son had turned out to be!

"Now, Mother, you know I'm only trying to keep Jason's young bride entertained while she's here," Rob retorted with a mocking grin.

Hannah attempted to suppress an amused smile. "It's all right, Maggie. Rob is really a very welcome change after the men I've met out here so far." She hadn't forgotten about Lewis Harland, but she resolved to do just that. However, Maggie's mention of Jason served to sober her thoughts. She missed Jason terribly, and not even Rob Clancy's charm and wit could erase the emptiness she felt inside. She rose to her feet and said, "If you'll please excuse me, I'd like to go upstairs to my room for a while. I'll be back down to help with the dishes a little later, if that's all right with you, Maggie."

"Don't you worry your head over that, dear," Maggie replied kindly, standing up beside Hannah. "I'm sure

112

that Rob here will be more than happy to help his old mother out." She cast a meaningful glance in his direction, satisfied when he agreed laughingly. Hannah bid them both goodnight and climbed the stairs to seek the privacy of her room.

"It's such a pity, the way she tries to keep from showing how much she misses her husband," Maggie murmured, starting to gather up the dishes.

"I don't understand why he left her here with you in the first place," Rob remarked, his expression growing serious. "If she were my wife—"

"But she's not!" his mother pointed out quickly, gazing at him with a stern eye. "Before you start to judge the way you'd treat Jason Caldwell's wife if she were yours, why don't you instead start thinking about taking a wife yourself?"

"Am I never going to have peace on that subject when I'm with you?" Rob demanded with a soulful expression, his eyes twinkling merrily. His mother couldn't help laughing at him, and together the two of them cleared away the table.

Hannah found it difficult to sleep on that second night away from Jason. She lay wide awake, her eyes frequently darting over to the single window in her small room, then back up toward the shadows on the ceiling as she wondered what Jason was doing, whether he missed her at all. She remembered their last night together, the night he had made her his wife in the truest sense of the word.

She recalled awakening to find him bending over her, the way his eyes had gleamed, the way he had stared down at her in the darkness of the bedroom. She could still feel his strong arms about her, his hands lovingly, passionately caressing her, his warm lips moving on her own. She sensed that their loving could be even more wondrous than that first time, and she yearned for his powerful, yet gentle, embrace as she lay there alone in the darkness, her heart crying out to him silently.

Jason was also unable to sleep. He sat staring into the blazing fire, the faithful Thor lying at his feet. The dog was beginning to mend, though he still couldn't follow his master about as he was accustomed to doing. Jason reached down and stroked the big dog's fur softly, then stretched out his long legs as he shifted uncomfortably in the chair again.

He wouldn't acknowledge—even to himself—that his thoughts constantly strayed to Hannah, that he actually missed her presence about the cabin. He had kept himself totally occupied up at the camp, driven himself to near-exhaustion since he had taken Hannah down to the town the day before. Unbidden images of her lovely face drifted into his mind on all-too-numerous occasions.

He rose to his feet abruptly, startling Thor. He leaned one powerful arm against the mantel, moving closer to gaze even more deeply into the flames of the crackling warmth below. Thoughts of Hannah persisted, and he finally ground out a savage curse and took himself off to bed, there to toss and turn restlessly for the remainder of the night.

The following day was cool and cloudy, and Jason strode up the trail to his timber camp in the early morning, the expression on his face appearing almost brutal in the morning light as he marched along the path cut through the trees. When he reached the camp, he was greeted by Tom Reynolds.

"Morning, Jason. Looks like it might just rain again."

Jason didn't answer, didn't even seem to hear the man,

114

who stared after him in confusion. Jason strode forward, halting his steps before the bunkhouse where the timberjacks he employed slept every night.

"Let's get things moving, damn it!" he ordered loudly, picking up an ax and striding deep into the forest. Soon the sound of that single ax fiercely chopping away at one of the huge spruces could be heard by the men who had just finished their hearty breakfast and were appearing outside to begin the day's work.

Some of the men took up the large axes, while others chose to use the two-man saws. A couple of the men strapped on the climbing irons, which they used to scale the tall trees in order to top them off. After these high climbers had done their work, the trees would then be felled by the cutting crews and hauled to the flumes, runways which would then carry them down to the river. It was hard and dangerous work, there was good money to be had in lumber, and Jason Caldwell's operation was well known to be just about the best to work for, as well as one of the safest.

Not that accidents didn't occur. Invariably trees would fall in the wrong direction, huge limbs could fall and injure or even kill a man on the ground below, logjams at the river had to be broken up with hazardous explosives, and there was always a threat from rival timber camps who would do whatever they felt was necessary to sabotage the competition. So far, there had been relatively few such disasters at Jason's camp, although he was always on the lookout for the unexpected. A forest fire had burned out several thousand acres of good timber just a couple of years earlier, but his camp had been spared. Things had been going along pretty evenly—that is, until Ted was killed and Jason had gone to Seattle to keep that promise.

Thinking of Hannah again, Jason plied the ax even faster and with more vigor. He couldn't let himself think of her; he had too much work to do. The logs had to be moved down the river to the port by the end of the month. He didn't have the time to waste on worrying about a woman!

"Jason!" Tom Reynolds called out. Jason whirled about to face Reynolds. "Jason, we've got a problem."

"What is it?" Jason demanded tersely.

"It's Cal Williamson. Seems he's ripped up his leg pretty bad on account of those climbing irons of his," Tom told him somberly.

"Just how bad is it?" Jason asked as he set off with Tom to see about the injured man.

"It looks like he's definitely going to need stitching up. The leg's been torn up almost to the bone."

Jason finally reached the spot where the man lay. Quickly examining the unfortunate man's injuries, he agreed with Tom's diagnosis and instructed him to see that the man was taken down to the town right away. One of the other men quickly saddled a couple of horses and was preparing to mount, when Jason suddenly announced that he would be the one taking Cal down to Red Creek.

"But, Jason, what about—" Tom started to question, then grew silent as Jason fixed him with an angry glare.

"You just see to things up here till I get back. I should be back before nightfall," Jason told him curtly. The injured man was helped into the saddle, slumping forward with the terrible pain that shot through him, trying to keep his injured leg, which had been bandaged now, across the saddle horn. Jason took the reins of Cal's

116

horse and led it along behind his own, his concern for the man tempting him to hurry, but wisdom forcing him to keep the pace moderate and his eyes wary.

He didn't stop to ask himself why he had insisted on taking the man down to town. It was something he usually left to one of the other men. He concentrated on guiding the horses down the mountain path and toward Red Creek, glancing upward and scowling darkly when the first drops of rain began to fall.

Ten

By the time Jason and Cal arrived in town, the rain had started coming down in blowing sheets of chilling moisture. Jason delivered the injured, barely conscious man to the only doctor in Red Creek; a middle-aged man known only as Sam, with a graying head of red hair and a rather large frame. The building which housed the doctor's office also served as the local barbershop. Doc Sam assured Jason that Cal would recover in due time, and Jason thanked him, before leaving his employee to the doctor's care. He stepped outside onto the muddy boardwalk and surveyed the wet scene before his eyes.

His booted steps had turned in the direction of the opposite end of town even before he would admit to himself where he was headed. He pulled his hat down lower on his head and strode toward the building where he had deposited his wife a couple of days earlier, telling himself with a deep scowl on his handsome face that the least he could do since he was already in town was to check up on Hannah and see how she was faring. It was the least he could do, his mind repeated defiantly.

He acknowledged greetings by several acquaintances and friends, though he didn't seem to be too aware of them. But he was unable to ignore a familiar feminine voice that called out to him from one of the open doorways as he was striding past.

"Jason! Jason Caldwell!" Colette's voice sang out as she happened to glance up in time to see him outside her saloon. She rose to her feet and flew outside, satisfied that her voice had served to make Jason pause. "I haven't seen you in a very long time," she spoke now in a low, seductive voice. A suggestive smile played about her painted lips as she gazed up at him, her brown eyes sparkling with obvious pleasure.

"I don't get into town much," Jason muttered, no answering smile on his face. He didn't appear happy to see her, and Colette bristled at his coolness.

"What is the matter, Jason Caldwell? Is Colette no longer good enough to consort with now that you have gone and married that prim little wife of yours?" Colette taunted, her face flushing in jealous anger. "She does not look like your type at all, you know. She seems much too stiff and proper to satisfy a man such as you! And who better to say such a thing than I?" she added with a derisive smirk, her hands on her hips as she swayed toward him.

Jason's blue eyes hardened at her words. He controlled his temper quite admirably, merely stating, "My wife is none of your concern. In fact, nothing about me is any of your business any longer. I've already made that clear, Colette," he reminded her grimly, turning to be on his way again.

Colette's clutching hand on his arm stopped him. "That was not my choice and you know it!" she hissed up at him, reveling in the attention they were beginning to attract from the surrounding spectators.

"It's been a long time," Jason ground out, tiring of the dramatic little scene. He shook off her hand easily and stepped away. "You'd do best to find yourself another man, Colette. One who isn't wise to vipers like you!" With that parting shot, he was gone, leaving Colette to glare murderously at his retreating back.

Jason soon forgot all about Colette as he reached Maggie's house and climbed the front steps, his boots clumping noisily on the porch. He raised an arm and knocked loudly on the front door. No one answered, and he told himself that Maggie must be busy out in the kitchen, or perhaps was next door at the restaurant, so he opened the door and stepped quietly inside. He took an extra second to wipe his muddy boots at the threshold, smiling faintly to himself as he recalled how particular his friend Maggie was about her clean floors.

"Maggie!" he called out. "Hannah!" soon followed. Still, receiving no answer, he turned his steps toward the kitchen. Detecting the faint sound of voices, he swung open the door, expecting to find Maggie and Hannah inside. Instead, he stood in the doorway with his drenched hat in his hands, his eyes widening with surprise, then narrowing with a violent, unfamiliar emotion. He could feel himself growing almost rigid with fury as he stared at the two people in the room.

Their backs were toward him, and they were apparently still unaware of his presence. Rob's arm was clamped tightly about Hannah's waist, and the two of them were laughing gaily together as Rob attempted to show her the next step in an Irish jig he had been demonstrating. Maggie was nowhere in sight.

"Rob, you're holding me much too tight!" Hannah chided laughingly, trying to draw away. "I can't possibly learn the step with you trying to squeeze the breath out of me like that!" Her hair was drawn back away from her flushed and smiling face with a blue ribbon, and her green eyes were glowing with delight. She was wearing a simple gingham dress with a white apron tied about her slender waist, and Jason thought she had never looked so beautiful. But the thought crossed his mind only for an instant, for he heard Rob's answering laugh and saw the way the other man—the man who had been his friend for a good many years—looked at his wife, saw the way he hugged her and refused to relinquish his hold on her squirming form.

Hannah finally managed to pull away from Rob, and she was about to admonish him for doing such a thing again, when she happened to glimpse Jason in the doorway, standing as if turned to stone. His tall, wide-shouldered frame filled the space, and she opened her eyes wide in happy surprise and started forward to throw herself impulsively into his arms, when the savage look on his face and the dangerous light in his steely eyes abruptly halted her movement.

"Jason!" she breathed, hardly able to believe that he was really standing there before her. She wondered why he appeared to be so angry, but she didn't have time to question him, since Rob had turned at the sound of her saying her husband's name.

"What the hell do you think you're doing?" Jason demanded harshly of Rob.

"Hello, Jason," Rob spoke with maddening nonchalance, a grin tugging at the corners of his mouth. "What are you doing here?"

"Oh, Jason, I didn't expect you to come today!" Hannah declared in a rush, sensing that she'd better intervene. Jason was behaving so strangely. He seemed to be angry at finding her and Rob alone together in the kitchen. But why?

"Hannah, go upstairs and get your things," Jason ordered curtly, not even bothering to look at her. His eyes still glowered at Rob, who merely lounged back against a table and met Jason's eyes with infuriating calm. Rob had a pretty good idea of why Jason was so furious.

"Are you taking me home with you?" Hannah asked in bewilderment, her eyes wide and questioning as she moved closer to her husband and peered up at him. Her heart was pounding in her breast. She was so overjoyed to see this man she loved, and she prayed that he had indeed come to take her back with him to his cabin, to their cabin.

"I told you to get upstairs. *Now!*" Jason thundered, glaring down at her. He was torn between the desire to gather her tightly against him and carry her forcefully from the house, and the desire to shake her until her teeth rattled!

Hannah started to question him further, but was put off by the look on his face, by the darkening scowl. She turned and shot Rob a puzzled glance, then hurried past her husband and up the stairs to her room.

"There's no need to be treating the little woman that way," Rob remarked, still grinning slightly, though now his own eyes were beginning to flash.

"It's none of your business how I treat my wife!" Jason muttered wrathfully, facing Rob across several feet of space. "And you've also got no damned business laying your filthy hands on another man's wife!"

"An innocent little dance is no hanging matter," Rob

122

retorted, rising to his full height now and moving closer. "If you don't want other men dancing with your pretty new wife, then you'd best not go off and leave her alone the way you did!"

"I should have expected as much from someone like you, Rob Clancy," Jason spoke from between tightly clenched teeth. Suddenly a muscle twitched in his cheek. He had restrained himself almost to his limit, and it took only Rob's next remarks to push him over the edge.

"Wake up, man! Don't you have any sense at all? Don't you see that you can't go treating that sweet, beautiful girl you've married as if she was nothing more than a mere possession, something you can put away and then take up anytime you please? I never would have believed you to be so unfeeling, Jason Caldwell! You weren't such a black-hearted, moody devil a few years ago, back when we first met. There's no reason to take out what's happened in your past, to make Hannah suffer because—"

Jason ground out a curse and moved forward with lightning speed, taking hold of the front of Rob's flannel shirt and twisting it in one of his large hands, literally lifting Rob off his feet as he drew back his fist to smash it into Rob's face. But Rob dodged the coming blow and struggled free, quickly moving away and preparing himself for the fight he knew was coming.

"You don't have any reason to be jealous of Hannah!" Rob declared angrily. "She's not the sort of woman who would play you false—can't you get that through that thick skull of yours?"

"Shut up, Clancy!" Jason countered furiously. Though he wanted to believe Rob's assurances about Hannah, he couldn't forget the fact that he had seen his wife laughing and standing with Rob's arm about her waist when he had come in. No matter how things stood between himself and his wife, he would allow no man to make a fool of him!

Jason lunged forward, this time catching Rob off guard. He planted his fist in Rob's face and knocked him to the floor. Rob shook his head in stunned silence as Jason turned on his heel and strode from the kitchen. As he stalked to the front door, he remembered Hannah, and, as if on cue, she appeared at the top of the staircase, clutching her bag in her hand. She hurried down the stairs, a look of anxious concern on her lovely young face.

"Jason, what is it?" she asked breathlessly. "What's happened?"

"We're leaving," Jason muttered, then lapsed into stony silence. He grabbed hold of her bag, snatching it from her hand, then took a firm grip on her upper arm and propelled her forcefully to the door.

"But, I haven't said good-bye to Maggie yet!" Hannah protested, holding back.

"I've already said all the good-byes that are needed!" Jason pulled her along with him out of the house and down the front steps. It was still raining, though it had begun to let up a bit, and Hannah attempted to free her arm from Jason's grasp long enough to lift the hood of her cloak up over her head. But he refused to let go, and he pulled her with him relentlessly, all the way back down the boardwalk to the doctor's, where he had left the two horses tied to a hitching post. Hannah was relieved when they finally stopped, for she couldn't help but notice the curious, amused glances directed their way.

"But where are we going?" she ventured to ask. She

still wanted to know what had happened back in the kitchen at Maggie's, but she sensed that Jason was in no mood to answer her questions.

"A man can't allow himself to be made a fool of," Jason replied tightly, taking hold of her wrist and lifting her effortlessly up into the saddle. He mounted the other impatiently pawing steed, and, leading Hannah's horse behind his, set off at a brisk pace.

"Jason?" Hannah attempted conversation with him again, but he remained stubbornly silent. It had been unfortunate that Jason had happened to come today, that he'd seen her innocently laughing and dancing with Rob in Maggie's kitchen, she reflected with an inward sigh. Judging from the way he was behaving, he must believe there was more than mere friendship between herself and Rob.

But, she asked herself, gazing ahead at Jason's broad, muscular back from her vantage point a few feet behind him, why had he become so angry? She drew her cloak more closely about her body, trying to shield herself from the misting rain. Could it possibly be that Jason was actually jealous of Rob Clancy? Her heart sang at such a thought! For, if Jason was jealous, then he surely must care for her—care more than he had led her to believe. She cautioned herself to hold back such a conclusion—at least until she'd had the opportunity to talk to him. But all the same, Hannah mused with a secret smile, Jason's behavior *did* seem like a good sign. And, for whatever reason he had come for her that day, she was glad. She would be with the man she loved once more, back where she belonged. Perhaps now she would have the chance to persuade him to love her in return.

Jason told himself that he'd been a downright idiot to

react that way back at Maggie's. What the devil had possessed him? he berated himself silently. It was true that he and Rob Clancy were no longer on the best of terms, but there hadn't been any real call for such violence, he reflected angrily.

Of course, the vivid recollection of Hannah with Rob still served to make his blood boil. And the memory of Rob's taunting words certainly hadn't helped his explosive temper. He didn't want to examine his motives, his reasons. But, damnation! he swore to himself with a vengeance. He hadn't acted like such a silly, lovesick fool for a long, long time.

Suddenly Jason heard a twig snap a few yards ahead of where he and Hannah were riding through the forest. Knowing instinctively that the sound hadn't been caused by either the soft rain or the wind, he reached behind his saddle and felt for his rifle, then pulled his horse to an abrupt halt.

"Why are we stopping here?" Hannah asked, puzzled when Jason merely signaled her to remain quiet and handed her the reins. Her eyes widened in growing anxiety as she watched Jason dismount slowly, then creep forward, his footsteps making very little noise on the wet ground. She felt a tremor of fear when she too heard a shuffling sound up ahead, and she tightened her grip on the reins, staring at Jason in breathless silence, suddenly praying that the danger he sensed would not materialize.

Jason crept along the path more slowly now, his blue eyes glancing about warily as he held his rifle in readiness. He had caught the scent of a wild animal and was prepared when suddenly a large brown bear, growling menacingly, came charging from the cover of the thick

126

brush a short distance away.

"Jason!" Hannah screamed in frantic warning, then flinched as a shot rang out. It took all her strength and determination to hold onto the frightened horses, and her eyes widened in horror as she saw that the bear was still advancing upon Jason. With terrified dismay, she realized that her husband wouldn't have time to reload.

Jason moved into action as the bear drew closer. He slid a large, glinting knife from a sheath at his belt and clutched it in one hand. The bear's immense fangs were bared, his huge claws reaching out to swipe at Jason's head.

Hannah screamed again as Jason's shoulder was raked by the razor-sharp claws, fortunately it was merely grazed, and Jason's blood flowed very slowly from the wound. Using all his might, Jason swung the knife in a powerful arc, driving it to the hilt, burying it deep in the bear's massive chest. The animal screamed loudly, then staggered forward, before finally collapsing almost at Jason's feet.

Hannah slid from the saddle and tied the reins to a tree branch, then hurried toward her husband. He was breathing heavily and was covered with blood, both his and the bear's.

"Are you all right?" Hannah asked anxiously. She felt close to tears with overwhelming relief, but she remained calm as she examined Jason's shoulder wound. "It doesn't look very serious, though I'm certain it's paining you terribly," she murmured.

"It's nothing," Jason said in a low voice, trying to dismiss the injury as inconsequential. But Hannah stepped back and lifted her skirts to tear a strip of fabric from her white petticoat. She folded the cotton into a

127

bandage, then applied it firmly to the bleeding flesh. Jason watched her intently, not saying a word, yet inwardly pleased that she hadn't grown either hysterical or weepy because of what had just happened. He remembered that she had reacted with the same resourcefulness as when Lewis Harland abducted her, and a persistent voice at the back of his mind told him that she was some woman, that she was better suited to the life in this country than he would ever have believed.

"I'm afraid it will continue to bleed for a while," Hannah stated quietly, her hand still holding the bandage in place with gentle pressure. Then she glanced up into Jason's face, drawing in her breath sharply when she met his gaze. His steely eyes seemed to pierce her to the very depths of her soul, and she was tempted to tell him how much she loved him, how desperately she wanted his love in return. But Jason broke the spell by retrieving his knife from the bear's body.

By now the rain had soaked them both to the skin. Jason said, "We'd better get up to the cabin before we catch a chill." He helped Hannah mount up before swinging up into his own saddle, his injured shoulder not even appearing to bother him. The horses were still skittish, and they rode a wide path around the spot where the dead bear lay.

"What about the bear?" Hannah asked, shivering as she looked at the glazed eyes that stared unseeingly up toward the gray sky.

"Normally, I'd skin him and take the meat, but I don't want to take the time for that now. Don't worry," he added a bit ruefully, "the wolves will appreciate the meal."

Hannah shivered again. She was beginning to feel

128

tired, and they still had quite a distance to travel. She could still feel Jason's piercing gaze, and now she gave silent thanks that he was safe. She realized that Jason Caldwell meant more to her than life itself.

Thor was awaiting them impatiently when they reached the cabin and swung open the door. The dog's immense tail wagged with great enthusiasm when he caught sight of Hannah entering the cabin, and he bounded forward to greet her.

"Thor! How are you doing?" Hannah murmured, chuckling softly as she knelt to hug him, pleased by his display of affection. "He looks almost himself again," she remarked to Jason, who had come in behind her and closed the door.

"He'll be good as new in a couple of days," Jason commented with a faint smile as he set her bag on the floor. He appeared to be on the verge of saying something else, but apparently changed his mind and strode forward to stand before the fireplace. "I'll get a fire started," he stated quietly.

Hannah stood up, one hand still reaching downward to scratch beneath Thor's furry chin. She watched as Jason positioned the split kindling in the fireplace, then piled the wood on top. He struck a match and waited patiently for the kindling to catch fire.

She noted with loving eyes the way Jason knelt on the floor, the way the muscles in his broad back moved beneath his wet, clinging shirt. His hair was plastered to his head, his trousers molded to his powerful, muscular thighs and buttocks. She thought once more that he was the most handsome man she had ever seen, his masculine virility striking a fire deep within her as she watched him.

"That ought to catch all right," Jason said, rising to his feet and gazing down at the smoking wood. He turned and faced Hannah. The rain beat against the roof of the cabin as the kindling crackled in the stone fireplace. "You'd better get out of those wet things," he told her, his eyes meeting hers, then glancing away. He turned and put out a hand to brace himself as he leaned toward the fire.

"Jason, why did you bring me back so soon?" Hannah asked softly as she moved toward him, pausing just behind him. Thor curled up on the floor in front of the fireplace, sighing contentedly.

"I wasn't planning to. I wouldn't have, if it hadn't been for the simple fact that you and Rob Clancy seemed determined to make a fool of me!" Jason muttered angrily, his back still toward her.

"There is nothing between Rob and me," Hannah insisted. "He was merely teaching me a dance step, that's all." He was jealous, she told herself. Jason was jealous!

"It damn sure looked like you were doing more than dancing!" Jason replied, his voice dangerously low. He didn't want to talk about this. He didn't even want to think about it anymore. He couldn't bring himself to turn around and face Hannah, though her face was before his eyes.

Why was it, these past few days, that he kept seeing her the way she had looked when he had burst into the bedroom the other night? What was it that made it impossible for him to forget the silken texture of her skin beneath his hands, the fresh fragrance of her beautiful hair as he'd buried his face in it? Why couldn't he get the memory of that night out of his mind?

"But, you were already there in town," Hannah pointed out, stepping even closer. "Why were you there, Jason?"

"A man was hurt. I had to take him to the doctor," Jason stated dully, fighting the terrible urge to yell that he wished he'd never set eyes on her, that she'd been nothing but trouble to him from the very beginning. But, he couldn't say that. In all honesty, he just couldn't say those words. Again, that stirring deep within his breast made itself known. He could no longer deny that he felt something for Hannah, that he'd been almost ready to kill Rob Clancy for laying a hand on her! He tried telling himself that it was simply because he had been alone for so long—that Hannah was nothing more than just another woman—but he failed to convince himself. He knew that it wasn't true.

"Jason, why were you so angry when you saw me in Maggie's kitchen with Rob? Was it because you were jealous?" Hannah asked obstinately. She was rewarded when Jason spun about to face her. His eyes gleamed with a savage light, his lips formed a thin line below his mustache. His face blanched as he faced her, as he glared down at her and denied her accusation vehemently.

"No!" You're a liar, Jason Caldwell, his mind told him. She hit the nail squarely on the head, and you're too proud to admit it! His fists clenched tightly at his sides as he stood there, towering above her. A flash of lightning and the accompanying thunder rang out, causing Thor to awaken momentarily and then settle back down with a groan.

"I think that's what made you so angry," Hannah insisted. "What did you do after I went upstairs? What happened between you and Rob?"

Jason knew she wanted him to admit his jealousy, that she wanted him to say that she mattered to him more than he'd ever cared to admit. He told himself that he wouldn't give her that satisfaction, that he wouldn't let her know how jealous he really was. He couldn't tell her that he'd been unable to get her out of his mind, that he had missed her. No, he thought, he wasn't ready to tell her the things she wanted to hear.

"I've got to get some more wood in and feed the horses," he announced, abruptly moving away, leaving Hannah to stamp her foot in frustration. She was certain that she had almost succeeded in getting him to admit that he was jealous of Rob. She whirled about and marched into the bedroom to change her wet clothing, vowing that, before the night was through, she would force Jason Caldwell to own up to the fact that he wanted and needed her!

Eleven

"Supper's ready," Hannah announced less than an hour after she and Jason had arrived at the cabin. She carried the bacon, corncakes, and pot of hot coffee to the table.

Jason left his seat by the fire, his shoulder already cleaned and bandaged by Hannah and his wet clothing exchanged for a dry shirt and pair of trousers. He sauntered across the room to the table, and he and Hannah ate their meal with few comments to one another, though Hannah glanced from beneath her eyelashes at her husband's face several times throughout the meal, trying to guess what he was thinking. Afterward, she cleared away the dishes and hurried to clean up, anxious to finish and be able to sit before the fire with Jason, anxious to try to talk to him again.

"I hope you don't mind, but I bought a few things while I was in town." Hannah rejoined Jason after her work in the kitchen was done, sank down into a chair beside him, and spread her fingers out to the fire's comforting warmth. The storm had passed and it was dark now, the only light in the room provided by the blazing fire.

"That's why I left you the money," Jason reminded

133

her quietly, glancing in her direction. His handsome, rugged features were an impassive mask, and Hannah prayed silently that she'd somehow be able to break through his reserve.

"Well, I bought some fabric to make a few dresses, and I also purchased a pair of more suitable boots. I'm afraid I didn't come very well prepared for the climate or the terrain here. We weren't allowed to take much on board the ship," she remarked, striving to keep her tone casual. She was relieved when Jason appeared willing to talk.

"It must have been a difficult trip," he commented thoughtfully, his anger apparently forgotten for the moment. He folded his sun-bronzed arms across his muscular chest and stared into the flames.

"It was. I had never even set foot on a ship before this voyage. A good many of the women became quite seasick. I think the most difficult thing about it was the fact that we were all living in such close quarters for so long. The steady diet of salt pork and beans certainly didn't help matters, either," she stated with a slight grimace, following his example and gazing toward the fire. "Jason, what about the man you took to the doctor's? I hope he wasn't seriously injured."

"Cal? No, he'll be all right."

"So that really is the reason you came to town?" she ventured, her eyes wide and questioning as he turned his head to look at her.

"I don't see that it really matters," Jason replied evasively, his eyes very blue in the firelight. "I thought I might as well see how you were doing while I was there. You are my responsibility, you know. Of course, I had no idea I was going to find you doing so well!" he added sarcastically, an angry glint returning to his eyes.

134

"Oh, Jason!" Hannah sighed, meeting his look with an earnest expression on her face. "I missed you so very much! I didn't want to leave here in the first place, remember? I still don't understand why you made me leave. I'm not any less safe here with you than I was in town. And, as far as Rob Clancy is concerned," her green eyes flashed with annoyance, "I've already told you that he means nothing to me! I am your wife. I certainly wouldn't go about flirting or carrying on with other men." She crossed her arms against her bosom and stared at him, her eyes searching his face.

"I know Rob Clancy better than you do," he replied grimly, drawing his gaze away from Hannah. He was acutely conscious of her there beside him. He could smell the fresh lavender scent of the soap she had used. Her bright hair shone in the firelight, and he was all too aware of her soft, rounded curves in the fitted dress she wore. He could feel the fury building up inside of him again at the mention of Rob, as he again saw Hannah in Rob's arms. He knew it wasn't right for him to blame his wife, for he knew in his heart that she was innocent—and yet he couldn't seem to help feeling this rage toward her.

"Rob Clancy has been a good friend to me these past few days. He and Maggie were both very kind to me," Hannah informed him.

"I could see for myself just how kind Rob's been to you," Jason countered mockingly.

"Yes, he was!" she retorted. "But, that doesn't mean there was anything but friendship between us. I am your wife," she repeated, rising to her feet now and facing him with her hands on her hips.

"You're my wife, all right, whether I like it or not!" Jason muttered angrily, standing up as well and scowling

135

down at her, mere inches away. "And since you are my wife, you'll behave in a proper manner!" he commanded harshly.

"I *was* behaving in a proper manner!" Hannah insisted, her own temper rising. She felt so frustrated whenever she tried to talk to this exasperating, impossible man! She loved him so desperately, and yet she always seemed unable to reach him.

Jason started to say something, then clamped his mouth shut and spun about, making for the door. He knew that he had to get out of here. He didn't trust himself when he felt such burning anger, and he knew he was likely to do something that he'd later regret.

"You come back here, Jason Caldwell!" Hannah demanded imperiously, then grew shocked at her own boldness. Well, I don't care! she told herself defiantly. Something had to give, something had to happen to change her relationship with Jason! She was so tired of trying to please a man who didn't want to be pleased. Why had she gone and fallen in love with a man who didn't seem to want her love?

Jason halted abruptly and then slowly, very slowly, turned around, his blue eyes now glinting like cold steel. It was obvious that he was striving mightily to keep his raging temper in check.

"I won't put up with that, Hannah," he ground out, his voice very low and vibrant. "I take orders from no one, especially not from my own wife!" He stood perfectly still, staring across at her, his eyes narrowing wrathfully.

"Why is it, Jason Caldwell, that you will never listen to me? Why will you not even finish a conversation? Ever since you married me, you've done your best to try and

136

ignore me, haven't you? I am a woman, Jason. I am your wife! You certainly weren't able to ignore me that night before you took me down to Red Creek, were you?" she threw at him, then gasped as Jason stalked toward her furiously, his strong fingers closing painfully on the flesh of her shoulders.

"Hannah, you go too far!" he warned tightly, shaking her for emphasis. Hannah grew silent, peering up at him with wide, misty eyes, her hair tumbling riotously about her shoulders, her bosom rising and falling, her face becomingly flushed. She ached for Jason's arms about her, yearned for his mouth on hers, and she leaned against him and closed her eyes, lifting her face for his kiss.

Jason stared down at her, fighting the desire that threatened to overwhelm him. Finally able to fight it no longer, he surrendered to his deepest urges and swept her against him, his strong arms closing about her trembling softness, his mouth swooping down upon her parted lips.

Hannah's arms crept upward and wound themselves about Jason's neck, and she pressed herself even closer against him, rewarded when Jason groaned deep in his throat and suddenly lifted her high in his arms, carrying her swiftly into the darkened bedroom.

Hannah soon discovered that this time would not be like the other. Jason took his time as he lay her down upon the bed and unbuttoned her bodice, then slowly stripped her of her dress. She felt the rush of cool air on her bare arms and legs as she lay there clad only in her chemise and drawers. She averted her gaze shyly as Jason divested himself of his own clothing, and she gasped as his fingers expertly untied the ribbons of her chemise and drawers, removing them and rendering her naked to his intense gaze.

A shaft of silver moonlight streamed in through the window, casting a pale glow on the two occupants of the room. Jason stared down at Hannah's beautiful moon-drenched form for several long moments before lowering himself to the bed. Hannah tilted her head to look at him with loving eyes as he lay down beside her. She shivered suddenly, but not from the cold. She was breathless as Jason gathered her against his warm masculine body, as his hands began stroking, gently caressing down her back, his fingers cupping her rounded hips. His lips captured hers again, his mouth moving on her own with increasing fervor and growing passion.

"Jason!" Hannah whispered as his lips now roamed down her throat, his mustache softly brushing as his mouth closed about the tip of her firm breast. Her fingers wound into his thick hair, hair that smelled pleasantly of wood smoke and pine, and her eyes swept closed as his warm lips pleasured her breasts, as his hands moved lower, trailing softly along her hips to her thighs. She gasped again as his searching fingers touched her delicate flesh, as his mouth teased first one rounded breast, then the other.

Timidly at first, her own hands moved to caress Jason's muscular back as his lips returned to her mouth. Her slender fingers moved in gentle patterns on his hard flesh as his tongue plunged within the warm moistness of her parted lips. She could feel the burning sensation she remembered building again, only it was even more intense this time. She found it difficult to breathe as Jason's lips moved from her mouth to nibble at her ear, and she whispered his name again, then was surprised when she heard her own name spoken as well.

Just when she was certain she could bear it no longer, could no longer suffer the delightful, exquisite torture he was inflicting upon her, Jason's body covered hers and he entered her welcoming warmth, thrusting slowly, gently at first, then faster and faster as Hannah moved in sensual abandon, urging him onward with her soft cries and moans. Soon the two of them attained the ultimate satisfaction, then lay breathless in the darkness, their two hearts beating as one.

In the soft afterglow of loving, Hannah reached up tenderly to smooth a lock of damp hair from Jason's forehead. He raised his head and gazed down at her, a confused expression in his eyes. He moved away gently and lay beside her, neither of them saying a word. Soon he turned upon his side and drew the covers up over them both.

Hannah looked at him, experiencing a rush of intense love for her husband. She wanted to tell him how much she loved him, how much he had pleased her. She was certain now that things could never be the same between them again.

"Jason?" she whispered softly, her hand lightly touching his bare shoulder.

Jason heard her, but pretended that he had fallen asleep. He was thinking that he didn't want to talk about what had happened. He could no longer deny to himself that he cared for Hannah, but he wasn't ready to admit it to her yet. It crossed his mind that he was falling in love, just the way he had vowed he would never do again. Love? His mind repeated, surprising him.

"Jason?" Hannah whispered again. Still she received no answer, and she lay back upon her pillow with a tiny sigh. Thank you, Lord, she prayed in silence. Thank you for allowing this to happen. It was so good and right for them to be together, she thought. Finally she turned on her side, too, though she snuggled closer to Jason before falling asleep.

The trilling music of a bird, welcoming the first blush of dawn, awakened Hannah the next morning. She was pleasantly surprised to discover that Jason was still sleeping beside her, and she nestled down beneath the covers, moving to warm herself against her husband's body. She felt happier and more contented than ever before, and she smiled to herself as she felt Jason's bare flesh against hers.

Jason's eyes flared open as Hannah's body made contact with his. He turned abruptly on his back, startling his wife. He looked at her, forgetting at first that he had slept beside her all night. He was nonplused when Hannah smiled shyly up at him, flushing slightly as she drew the covers higher over her naked form.

"Good morning, husband," she said, gazing up at him with all the love in her heart reflected in her green eyes.

Jason appeared to awaken suddenly from a trance, and he flung back the covers as he left the bed. Hannah watched in bewilderment as he snatched up his clothes and dressed swiftly. He shot her one last, unfathomable look before leaving the room and closing the door behind him.

Hannah sighed, musing that he had acted in a similar, puzzling manner after that first time, but she refused to become discouraged again. She hugged herself with absolute joy, and soon climbed from the bed as well.

When she came out of the bedroom a few minutes later, she found Jason already tending the fire. She

140

smiled to herself as she glimpsed Thor running about outside the open door of the cabin, and she noticed that it looked like a much nicer day than the one before. Fastening the last button of her bodice, she asked Jason, "How is your shoulder this morning?"

"It's fine," he answered. He soon had the fire going again, and he stood up to face his wife. "Hannah, about last night—" he started to explain, then broke off. He appeared to be searching for the right words.

Hannah hurried to say, "There's no need to explain anything, Jason. You are my husband, and it's your right to share my bed whenever you wish."

Jason stared at her a moment longer, before clearing his throat gently and remarking, "I'm hungry. How about some breakfast?" He watched as she smiled in agreement and disappeared into the kitchen. He strode outside to gather more wood for the fire, his thoughts totally preoccupied as he went about his task.

After they had eaten and Jason had gone for the day, Hannah sat down for a few minutes to contemplate all that had happened to her in so short a time. She didn't feel like the same girl who had stepped off that ship back in Seattle little more than a week ago. But then, she reminded herself, she was no longer a girl. She was a woman now, a wife. She loved with all the depth of feeling as only a woman could do.

Finally realizing that she couldn't spend the entire day daydreaming, she went about her morning chores with a light heart, humming softly to herself as she cleaned the cabin and prepared to do the washing.

She found the washtub and washboard in the kitchen, along with some lye soap, and she carried everything outside into the fresh mountain air and sunshine. She gazed about in awe at the colorful wild flowers that continued to burst forth in the meadow surrounding the cabin, and she looked up to notice the huge tree limbs swaying in the gentle breeze as the morning wore on. She washed the clothing, then hung it up to dry on a length of rope that ran from one side of the cabin to a large tree.

That accomplished, she went inside and searched in her carpetbag for the fabric she had purchased in town. She was determined to make herself some pretty new dresses so she could look her best for Jason. She spent the remainder of the day plying the scissors, needle, and thread. Pleased with her day's efforts, she set aside her sewing and brought the dry clothing inside as the sun began to set.

Hannah greeted Jason with a sweet, welcoming smile as he entered the cabin later that evening. She informed him that supper was nearly ready, then remarked, "I hope your work went well today."

"Well enough," Jason replied. He took a seat at the table and watched as Hannah carried out a large iron pot of stew. She had arranged her shining curls in a most becoming style, pinning them high atop her head, and she had donned a freshly laundered dress and apron, tying on her new boots as well.

"I don't know very much about timber," she commented casually, serving herself some of the stew. "Do you cut a great many trees?"

"Yes. We've got enough logs in the river now to make the trip downstream. If nothing happens, we'll be ready to move them out by the end of the week," he told her, apparently willing to enlighten her—at least a bit—about his business.

"Where will you be moving them?" Hannah continued with interest. She knew that she'd have to try and convince him to allow her to pay a visit to the timber camp one day soon.

"Downstream to one of the shipping ports. Oh, it's not as big as Seattle, but from there they'll take the timber and load it on the ships to make the voyage to San Francisco. It's not an easy task," he said, breaking off a piece of fresh bread from the loaf she had baked.

"Will you be going then?"

"Of course," he replied with a slight frown.

"I see," she murmured thoughtfully, not at all pleased at the prospect of Jason being gone. "How long will you be away?"

"A few days. Hannah," he said, looking at her squarely now, "you needn't worry. I'm not about to leave you up here alone while I'm away. You'll be going back down to Red Creek to stay with Maggie."

"With Maggie?" Hannah repeated in surprise. Before she had thought about her next words, she asked, "But won't you mind? I mean, after what happened yesterday . . . well, what about Rob?" She could have cut her tongue out for bringing up Rob's name again, and she stared at Jason after she'd said it, watching his face nervously for any signs of renewed anger.

"Rob won't be there by then," he stated simply. "He's got his own camp to run. If he wasn't such a lazy, reckless—" He stared, then paused before continuing, "All the camps will be moving their timber by the end of the week, or thereabouts."

"But couldn't I come along with you?" Hannah braved, not wanting to be parted from him again so soon. They needed time alone together, she thought. The last thing they needed was another separation!

"Don't be silly," he uttered gruffly. "I've told you before that I don't want you around the men. You'll go down and stay with Maggie," he told her again. It was obvious to Hannah that his decision was final.

She lapsed into silence again, but her thoughts were spinning about in her head. There must be some way, she mused, some way I can get him to change his mind. The expression on her face grew pensive as she took another bite of the stew. She didn't see the way Jason watched her from the corner of his eye.

Twelve

Hannah remained busy throughout the following two days, cooking and cleaning and sewing, while Jason toiled up at the logging camp from dawn till dusk. He would return to the cabin in the evening with a weary step, and Hannah endeavored to remain both cheerful and patient with him. As a result, Jason began talking to her a bit more as they sat together before the fire after supper. Thor lay near the two of them as they spoke, always lulled to sleep by the peaceful murmur of their voices.

Though Hannah was pleased that Jason continued to sleep beside her in the bed every night now, she was sorely disappointed by the fact that he didn't make a move to touch her again. She could hear him breathing evenly, mere inches away, wanting more than anything to reach out and touch him, to prompt him to show her any sign of affection. She was unaware of the tremendous struggle he was undergoing beside her.

Hannah couldn't know how much his turbulent thoughts were centered on her, how very much he wanted to make love to her again. But, he wasn't accustomed to sharing himself or his life with anyone, and he cautioned himself against complicating things even further between them until he'd sorted out his true feelings for this wife of his. But, just the same, it was becoming increasingly difficult to sleep beside her without touching her, without giving in to the burning desire that threatened to overwhelm all his caution.

One night, however, toward the end of the week, Jason and Hannah sat together as usual following the evening meal. Hannah was sewing busily as she added the finishing touches to the dress she had been working on all week. Suddenly she turned her head and smiled sweetly at Jason, who sat on the chair beside her. He met her gaze, then averted his eyes hastily and looked toward the fire once more.

"You know, Jason," Hannah remarked with a faint smile and a chuckle, "this is exactly how I've always pictured married life. My husband sitting in front of the fire beside me, myself here with sewing in my lap."

"I guess that's something women think of," Jason replied with a brief smile of his own. He was thinking how very lovely she looked, how tranquil his life had begun to seem as he watched her out of the corner of his eye, the expression on his chiseled features appearing unusually softened. He reflected that he had even begun to smile more than usual of late.

"I suppose it's something every girl dreams of," Hannah spoke wistfully. "I'm sure my mother was much the same before she married my father." At the thought of her mother, Hannah's face grew sad, a fact that did not escape Jason's notice.

"Where are your parents now?" he asked her, frowning when he saw the glistening tears that started to her eyes.

"My mother is in upstate New York," she answered

146

with a catch in her voice. "My father is dead. My mother and stepfather live on the farm where I was born." She was surprised to discover that the bitterness and resentment she had been harboring against her mother was already fading, and she knew that it must be because of Jason. She could now better understand how unbearable it must have been for her mother to lose her husband. Not, she reminded herself, that it was any excuse for allowing her second husband to mistreat his stepdaughter. No, she sighed inwardly, but after all these months, after so much had happened to her, it was best that she try at last to forgive her mother.

Jason watched the changing emotions playing across Hannah's young face, and he experienced a sharp twist of his heart. He discovered that it disturbed him greatly to see her looking so melancholy, and he wondered what had happened to cause such sadness.

"I take it that you don't care much for your stepfather," he said, his voice deep and low.

"How did you guess that?" Hannah asked him in surprise, her expression now turning to puzzlement.

"I think it was something in your voice. Maybe it was just the way you looked when you mentioned him."

"It seems that you already know me better than I would have thought," she responded with a faint smile, fighting back the tears that had sprung so readily to her eyes.

"Why did you leave home?"

"Because I was so unhappy there," she stated simply. She didn't want to tell Jason the entire truth about her stepfather, didn't want him to know that she had worked in a tavern for a brief time. She was uncertain as to how he would receive such news about his wife, so she was hesitant to enlighten him too much about her past.

"And did your stepfather cause that unhappiness?" he persisted. He realized that he wanted to know more about this woman beside him. He wanted to know what had occurred back home to cause her to leave, why she had journeyed all the way to Seattle, why she had been willing to give herself in marriage to a perfect stranger.

"Yes," she admitted, glancing up to meet his steady gaze. "He and I did not get along. He's a cruel man. I couldn't understand why my mother married him. I suppose it's because she was never the same after the death of my father. I don't know really, but she was never very strong, you see." Her features looked very somber in the dim light of the cabin. She glanced back down at the sewing in her lap. "I left home and went to the city. I lived with a cousin for a short time, but I wasn't satisfied with the kind of life I found there. It seemed like the answer to my problems when I read of the voyage of brides. And, I must say, Mr. Melton made it all sound so exciting, so very romantic. I think all of us hoped to find the answer to our dreams out here," she said, her eyes lifting to meet his as she smiled again.

Hannah's smile faded slowly as she and Jason stared at one another, the firelight playing across their faces. It was raining again—not unusual for that time of year—and they could hear the raindrops beating steadily down on the cabin roof.

In that simple moment, Jason realized how much Hannah had begun to mean to him. It had happened against his will. He never would have believed that he could care for a woman this way again. He discovered that he no longer resented his marriage to this beautiful young woman gazing up at him, her green eyes wide and

148

waiting. He knew that there could be a new beginning for him with Hannah, something that could be nourished, could grow and blossom into something deeper. He knew that it could change his life for the better, and change it forever.

Hannah looked at him with all the love in her heart, waiting for him to speak, to make some move toward her. She knew that things had been going much better between them, that they were slowly beginning to know one another. She now prayed that Jason would give her the chance to show him the depth of her feelings for him.

Suddenly Jason frowned and tore his gaze away from Hannah's. He glanced downward, then back at the fire, then back at his wife. He rose to his feet, staring down at her. She grew breathless as she waited, not knowing whether to sit still or rise and stand before him. Then a loud knock at the cabin door shattered the stillness and quiet in the room.

"What is it?" Jason demanded as Tom Reynolds flung open the door.

"I'm sorry to bother you, Jason, but some of the men want to talk to you right away. It's about the—"

"All right, all right," Jason interrupted gruffly. He turned back to Hannah. "I'll be back as soon as I can." He stared at her a second longer, then turned and was gone.

Hannah hurried to the door and watched as Jason and Tom disappeared up the trail. She was barely able to make them out in the darkening twilight. Closing and bolting the door, she strolled back across the floor to take a seat in front of the fireplace again and took up her sewing once more. A thoughtful look descended on her face.

After she had sat waiting for at least half an hour, she

put aside her sewing impatiently and marched into the kitchen as an idea suddenly occurred to her. She'd been unable to take a bath in the tub since the day before yesterday, and she decided that now, while she was waiting for Jason's return, now would be the perfect time. She dragged the wooden tub across the floor to position it near the fire, then hurried back to the kitchen to put the water on to heat.

Discovering that she needed more wood for the stove, she marched to the front door and drew back the bolt, scurrying outside to fetch an armful of wood. She soon had the fire built up in the stove, and it wasn't much longer before she was pouring water into the tub.

Peeling off all her clothes and pinning up her hair deftly, she stepped into the soothing water and eased herself downward, the water's warmth surrounding her up to her chest. She leaned back and closed her eyes for a few blissful moments, then took up the cake of soap and began lathering her skin, smiling indulgently at Thor as he was awakened by the splashing sounds she made as she bathed.

Jason expertly soothed the brewing discontent among the handful of his employees, then began striding back down the trail to the cabin, the pale moonlight that filtered through the receding rainclouds illuminating his path. He could feel a sense of urgency—a sensation that something was about to happen—and he opened the door to the cabin without bothering to knock, then immediately grew angry as he realized that his wife had once more forgotten to bolt the door.

"Hannah!" he called out, stopping short when he saw her, the raindrops that had clung to his clothing now dripping quietly to the floor.

She was just rising from the tub, the cooling water cascading in tiny droplets down her white skin, her face flushed and glowing from her bath. She gasped as Jason burst in, and she whirled about to face him, nearly losing her balance as her feet slipped in the tub of water. She could feel Jason's eyes moving slowly up and down her naked form, and she blushed furiously as she snatched up a towel from the chair and attempted to shield her nakedness.

Jason continued to stand as if turned to stone, though his gaze was riveted now on Hannah's face. It was the first time he had been afforded such a clear view of his wife's charms, and he thought her absolutely beautiful. He reflected that her body was superbly fashioned, that her soft, rounded curves were even more lovely than he had imagined. His desire for her now returned to hit him with full force, as well as his newly awakened feelings of tenderness toward her, and he approached her slowly as she stood in the tub.

"Jason, I—I didn't expect you back so soon," Hannah murmured, a sudden shiver running the length of her spine. She was experiencing no small degree of embarrassment at having been caught in such a vulnerable position, but she also felt an unaccountable thrill that Jason had seen her this way. She stepped from the tub now, her wet feet and legs dripping on the bare wooden floor as she held the towel about her body. She blushed rosily again, then made a move toward the sanctuary of the bedroom, intent upon retrieving her clothing.

"Hannah, don't," Jason commanded quietly. His smoldering gaze drew her eyes upward to his as he halted

151

her flight with his words. "You're so beautiful," he whispered, so quietly she could barely hear him.

She didn't know what to say, so she simply stood there before him, her eyes wide and her breathing unsteady as he reached for her, his powerful arms closing about her and his lips descended on hers. Her arms came up to surround his neck, the towel soon forgotten as it fell unheeded to the floor.

Hannah moaned softly, deep in her throat, as Jason's warm hands trailed a fiery path down her naked back, his fingers now softly kneading the firm mounds of her bottom. His lips moved demandingly on hers, and she strained upward to surrender even more of herself to his burning kiss. She was bewildered when he drew away, and she blushed again as he stepped back, his hands still on her arms, as his eyes drank in the sight of her naked white body in the light from the blazing fire.

Jason could no longer resist the beauty of his wife's charms, and he scooped her up in his arms to spirit her away to the bedroom. Swiftly removing his wet clothing, he lowered the length of his hard, lithe body next to hers. His lips teased at her breasts, his caressing hands seemed to be everywhere as he made love to her again. This time, however, he knew that it would be different, that *he* was different. He had discovered that his heart was coming to life once more, that Hannah had been able to pierce through his icy reserve and make him feel again.

Hannah, too, sensed the difference as she whispered his name in passion. She could sense that he was giving more of himself than ever before, and she responded in kind, allowing all the love in her heart to shine through whenever their eyes met.

152

"Hannah, Hannah," she heard him murmur, before his lips captured hers once more. One of his large hands was reaching downward to her hips, the other moving gently on one of her breasts. She gasped as his warm mouth left her lips to tease at her nipples, his moist tongue circling and tenderly sucking until she thought she could bear it no longer. Now his hand was between her trembling thighs. Her fingers entwined themselves in his thick, damp hair, her eyes closed tightly as he drove her onward.

"Oh, Jason, I—" she began, abruptly breaking off as his lips trailed downward from her breasts to her belly, as his tongue teased at her navel, before returning to capture a rosy nipple once more. She gasped aloud as his fingers continued to caress her at the secret place between her thighs, and she grew emboldened enough to reach downward and grasp him with loving hands, soon driving him to a fever pitch as he drove her.

She cried his name aloud when he took her, as he plunged into her warmth and moved with increasing fervor. Afterward, he did not move away as was his usual custom, but remained as if still one with her, his warm lips now bestowing a gentle, feathery kiss on her forehead.

"Oh, Jason," Hannah whispered, a soft smile on her lips. Her arms clung to him as he finally eased himself off her and stretched out beside her on the bed. They did not speak again, though Jason allowed her to snuggle up against him, his strong arm beneath her head as the two of them drifted off to sleep.

The next day was rather warm and clear, and Hannah felt a certain peaceful contentment as she went about her chores. She looked forward to that evening, when she would make herself beautiful for Jason, and she found it difficult to concentrate as she baked bread that day, nearly forgetting to remove the bread from the oven before it burned.

When the long-awaited darkness began to fall, Hannah hurried into the bedroom and took up the dress she had carefully laid out upon the bed. It was fashioned of a soft green wool. The fitted bodice was cut square across Hannah's swelling bosom, the skirt gathered softly at the waist. The bodice and long sleeves were edged with a delicate white lace, and she was satisfied with the result as she turned before a mirror hanging in the bedroom. She removed the pins from her thick hair, allowing its shining tresses to flow about her shoulders. Brushing it with gentle strokes, she decided on impulse to leave it unbound.

Strolling back into the other room to wait for her husband, she smiled to herself. It seemed that her determination was finally going to be rewarded. Jason was beginning to care for her. She knew it was so, and she knew the day would soon come when she would be able to profess her love for him and know that he would be glad. She mused that she was one of the luckiest women in the world, to have such a handsome, virile husband such as Jason Caldwell. The memory of their loving the night before brought a pink flush to her cheeks.

She turned as Jason opened the door a few minutes later. Smoothing her skirts one last time, and with a quick pat at her loose curls, she smiled and said, "Good evening, Jason." She stood before the fireplace, waiting for him to notice her new dress.

He hung his jacket on the peg behind the door, then turned to face Hannah. His blue eyes widened briefly as he caught sight of her, and he, too, smiled as he remarked, "You're looking very well tonight, Hannah." It was only the second time she had known him to pay her such a compliment, and she flushed with pleasure at his approval.

"I was hoping you'd like it. I know it's not quite as practical as it should be, but I couldn't resist making it. I've never had anything quite as pretty," she said with another bright smile.

Jason realized that he was even more pleased that Hannah had apparently gone to such trouble to make herself even more beautiful for him. But, he then mused, he thought her to be much more beautiful the way he'd seen her last night, rising from that water in all her delectable splendor. He found that his eyes were drawn irrevocably to her lovely, smiling face, and suddenly he grew impatient for the evening to wear on, his mind drifting to the time when they would be together again in the bedroom. He had been unable to get the memory of last night out of his thoughts all day long.

"I have supper ready and waiting," she announced, her eyes shining. "I'll put it on the table right away." She glided across the floor into the kitchen, her heart singing.

The evening passed very pleasantly. Following a delicious meal, Hannah and Jason sat together and talked of many things, though of nothing in particular. They were both eager for the time when they would be close again, and that time, they knew, was not far off. Jason opened the cabin door to allow Thor outside to run a bit later in the evening, then turned back to where Hannah was standing a few feet behind him.

"I—I hope you didn't have too tiring a day up at the camp," she remarked, then blushed as she realized how such a statement could be easily misinterpreted. She averted her face as Jason approached.

"The logs will be ready to move out by the next day or so," he told her, his hands reaching out for her. She came into his embrace with already quickened pulses, her parted lips ready as Jason's head bent silently to hers. They kissed with sweet passion, losing themselves in their growing desire, when a knock abruptly sounded at the door.

"Damnation!" Jason swore savagely, tearing himself away from Hannah. He stalked over to the door and jerked it open to reveal Tom.

Hannah gazed curiously toward them, and she moved to pause just within earshot of the two men. She heard them speaking in very low voices, and she grew impatient to know what was going on.

"Jason, what is it? What has happened now?" she asked.

"All right, Tom," Jason said, his back still to Hannah. "You stay here at the cabin with Hannah in case they come this way!" he ordered grimly, turning aside now to take up his gun.

"Jason, what is going on?" Hannah demanded, beginning to grow frightened.

"You stay here with Tom. There's some trouble up at the camp, but you'll be safe if you just stay here," he commanded, before hurrying out the door and up the trail toward the camp.

"Tom, what is it? What's happening?" Hannah

questioned anxiously, whirling to confront him.

"It's one of the other logging gangs from around here. Seems they're going to try and keep our logs from getting through to port. Things like this happen pretty often out here," he told her, his own face showing his concern. He put out a hand to stop Hannah as she started for the door. "You heard what Jason said, ma'am. You and me are to stay right here. There's nothing you can do up there." It was obvious to Hannah that he didn't like the orders he had received from Jason, that he was torn between obeying and bolting after Jason toward the camp.

"I'm not going to stay here and wait while my husband is in danger!" Hannah exclaimed defiantly, breaking away from him and running out the door into the moonlit night.

Tom muttered a curse beneath his breath and took off after her, telling himself that Jason Caldwell would probably have his head if anything happened to Hannah. He followed her as she reached the beginning of the trail, finally catching up with her and grasping her arm as he pulled her to a halt.

"You'll not be helping your husband any if you go up there and put yourself in danger!" he insisted, wondering whether he was going to have to use force to get her to stay at the cabin. He was reluctant to lay a hand on Jason's wife.

"Don't tell me, Tom Reynolds, that you don't want to be up there as well!" Hannah retorted, twisting in his grasp. "I'm going up to that camp, and you are not going to stop me!" Her green eyes blazed at him.

Tom was forced to admit the truth of her words. He didn't see how he was going to be able to sit down there at that damned cabin while Jason and the others were fighting off the intruders. He finally gave in, smiling briefly, then led Hannah cautiously up the trail toward the camp. As they quickened their pace through the trees, they could now make out the unmistakable sound of gunfire.

Thirteen

Hannah was continually hampered by the long, full skirts of her new dress as she and Tom hurried up the trail that was strewn with pine needles and thick underbrush. She stumbled more than once, grateful for Tom's supporting hand on her arm as they moved along urgently. They could still hear a spattering of occasional gunfire, and sudden fear clutched at Hannah's heart— fear that something terrible might happen to her husband. She made her way along the trail as swiftly as she could, breathless when she and Tom finally broke through the shelter of tall trees to halt just within the spacious clearing where the logging camp was situated. The full, glowing moon hovered peacefully over the chaotic scene.

Time seemed to stand still as Hannah's widened eyes took in the noisy commotion before her. She watched as men seemed to be running everywhere, and she gasped aloud as she spied the bunkhouse where the loggers had been sleeping earlier now being put to the torch. She gazed in horror as the log structure caught fire and was soon almost consumed by the leaping flames. She could hear men noisily shouting and cursing, could make out the frantic whinnying of the terrified horses, and she winced involuntarily as several more shots rang out in the night air. Silently praying that Jason's life would be spared amidst all the dangerous confusion she surveyed, Hannah nearly fainted with relief when she spied her husband standing off to one side of the burning log bunkhouse, a rifle clutched in his hand. He was shouting orders to men around him, still unaware of Hannah's presence.

"Jason!" she called out, escaping Tom's restraining hand as she sped forward, oblivious to the men scurrying about. Tom muttered another curse and took off after her again.

"What the devil are you doing here?" Jason demanded furiously, reaching out to her as he raised his voice even higher to be heard above the din. "I told you to stay put with her down at the cabin!" he then thundered as Tom appeared.

"Damn it, Jason, there wasn't any way on God's green earth I was going to be able to keep her there!" Tom countered, then asked abruptly, "What the hell's going on? Who is it?" He and Jason could only stand by and watch helplessly, the expression on their faces very grim, as the bunkhouse continued to burn, the bright flames dancing higher and higher.

"It's Dugan's gang. You can damn sure bet they're already heading down to the river!" Jason ground out, his blue eyes suffused with a savage light.

"But why are they doing this?" Hannah asked anxiously, clutching at her husband's arm. "Surely they didn't come here to kill anyone!"

"They'll do whatever they think they have to do to keep us from moving our timber downriver!" Jason

160

answered, then suddenly grasped her arm and pulled her protectively behind him as he raised his rifle. A man on hoseback galloped past them at a furious pace and fired once in their direction, the bullet missing Jason by mere inches. Jason returned the fire, but the lone rider had already disappeared into the forest.

"I'm going on down to the river," Jason announced, turning to Tom again. "You keep Hannah up here with you. Get out of sight and wait till I get back. And that's an order!"

"What are you going to do?" Hannah demanded, refusing to relinquish her hold on his arm.

He wrenched his arm away, then took hold of her shoulders in a painful grip. "You're going to do what I say this time—is that clear?" His eyes were gleaming dangerously. "I don't want to have to worry about you! You shouldn't even be here in the middle of this mess. Now, do as I say, Hannah, and stay here with Tom!" He glared meaningfully down at her a moment longer, angered when she raised her chin defiantly, her green eyes flashing in response. She opened her mouth to speak, but Jason muttered a curse and dragged her along with him unceremoniously, forcing her almost roughly down to the hard ground to take shelter behind a felled tree. "Stay here!" he ordered angrily, then turned on his heel and stalked away, soon disappearing into the darkened forest at the far edge of the clearing.

Hannah watched him go, her eyes filling with tears. Tom took a seat on the ground beside her, though his eyes remained watchful as he held his gun in protective readiness. The two of them could discern the faint sounds of more shots ringing out on the other side of the mountain top now, but they could only sit and wait as

Jason had commanded. Hannah stared unseeingly toward the bunkhouse, now well on its way to becoming nothing more than a pile of smoldering rubble.

It had been unfair of Jason to treat her that way, Hannah reflected miserably. True, he was worried about his timber and his men, but she was equally concerned about him! She wanted to be with him, to be by his side in times of trouble, for she knew that was where she belonged. Just when she thought their marriage was beginning to show signs of improvement, Jason had made it clear once again that she was nothing more than a troublesome burden to him.

"You all right, ma'am?" Tom inquired in a voice barely above a whisper, glancing at her from the corner of his eye.

"I'm fine," she answered in a low voice, averting her face from his gaze. She stared now toward the spot where she had seen Jason disappear into the trees, soon forgetting her anger with him as she began to pray once more for his safety.

Nearly an hour later, though it had seemed to Hannah to be more like an eternity, she and Tom saw three men moving slowly into their line of vision. Hannah immediately noticed that one of the three was Jason, and she jumped to her feet and ran forward, gasping aloud as she observed the dark red stain spreading outward on the trouser leg just above his left knee.

"Jason, you're hurt!" Hannah cried, moving to his side. The two men helped him over to the felled tree, easing him down onto it while Hannah stood with her heart pounding in her breast.

"What happened?" Tom asked quietly, his own features worried.

"I took a bullet in the leg just as I reached the river." Jason grimaced as the pain shot through his leg like fiery arrows. "Get down there, Tom. Someone's got to take charge and see to it that those thieving bastards don't—"

"I'm on my way," Tom interrupted, anxious to be off. The other men went along with him, leaving Hannah alone in the clearing with her injured husband.

"We've got to get you to a doctor right away," she said, inspecting the wound as best she could in the moonlight. She could definitely make out the bullet hole just above Jason's knee, and her lovely features reflected her growing concern as she raised her face to his.

"There'll be no need for that. I'm sure it went clean through." Jason was still breathing heavily from his exertions. There had been no horse to carry him back up to the clearing, since Dugan's gang had scattered the stock all over the mountain by that time.

"We've at least got to get you down to the cabin so I can see to you," she told him, her mind still set on a doctor. "Do you think you can make it that far?"

"Damn it, woman, I'm not entirely helpless!" he spoke between clenched teeth as he pushed himself up and stood unsteadily. He set off toward the trail which led back down to the cabin, making his way as best he could on the injured leg. Hannah followed swiftly, relieved that he at least didn't protest when she placed a supporting arm about his waist.

Jason was beginning to lean more heavily on his wife by the time they finally reached the cabin. Once inside, he collapsed into a chair before the dwindling fire as Hannah flew about to fetch medicine and bandages for his wound. Thor gently nudged his master's hand, and Jason took a brief moment to administer a reassuring pat on the animal's furry head before Hannah returned.

"That bullet might have done more damage than you seem to think," Hannah frowned, bringing a lamp closer as she bent to the task of inspecting the wound again. "It might possibly have shattered some of the bone," she murmured quietly, hesitating when she glanced up to catch the tight-lipped expression on Jason's face. She touched the torn flesh carefully. "Jason, we've got to have a doctor look at this as soon as possible!" she insisted, applying a wad of the cotton bandaging to try to stem the flow of blood.

"A doctor won't be needed," Jason replied, wincing when she touched him again. He lapsed into silence as she worked, staring toward the fireplace, until he suddenly muttered, half to himself, "If only I knew what was going on down at that river!" Having to hand over the responsibility to Tom galled him mightily, bullet wound in the leg or not.

"I'm sure Tom and the others will be able to take care of things," Hannah assured him, inwardly grateful that he wasn't down there at the river helping his men fight off the rival gang. She knew that there was a good chance that he might have been more seriously injured, or perhaps even killed, if he had remained in the middle of the night's trouble. Though she hoped his timber would be saved, he was the foremost thing on her mind. The bullet wound in his leg looked bad, but how in the world was she going to manage to persuade him to have a doctor tend to it?

"At least you must rest for a while," Hannah insisted, finishing her task. "There's nothing more I can do for this now. We'll simply have to wait and see if any infection sets in."

"You did well, Hannah," Jason stated quietly, his eyes meeting hers now as he rose slowly. "Many women would have fainted at the mere sight of this wound." He praised her partly out of a feeling of guilt, and he knew it. He realized that he had been pretty harsh with her back up at the camp, but it was just that he'd been so afraid something might happen to her. He was still more than a little bewildered about how much she had come to mean to him, but he didn't say anything else. He simply moved away and made his way into the bedroom, deciding to take her advice about resting his leg.

Hannah was disappointed when he left without speaking again. She had been almost certain that there was something else on his mind, something that she sensed might be very important to her. But, she thought as she sank down onto the chair, she was pleased that her husband thought she had done well at something!

Sighing softly, Hannah's face grew pensive as she stared down at the dark red stains on her new dress, the dress she had worked so hard to make in order to impress Jason. She smiled ruefully to herself, realizing that the rest of her must also look quite a sight. She raised a hand to her hair, not at all surprised to discover that it was tumbling riotously about her shoulders. The evening had certainly ended far from the way she had expected.

Some time later, Hannah heard a knocking at the front door. Having dozed off a few minutes earlier as she sat before the fire, she was awake instantly, and now hurried to open the door to admit Tom.

"What happened?" the two of them heard Jason ask from the doorway of the bedroom. He limped stiffly into the room with a pained expression on his handsome face, his eyes very bloodshot.

165

"Everything's all right, Jason," Tom answered with a heavy sigh. His own features looked tired and drawn, and Hannah went to fetch him some hot coffee as he and Jason sat down.

"Did they get to the timber?"

"Yeah, but we managed to drive them off before they were able to do much damage. They were trying to set off some explosives, but luckily we got to them before they'd had time. The timber's safe."

"What about the men? How many injured?" Jason asked grimly.

"Eight in all, counting yourself. Two of them are hurt pretty bad, but I think they'll pull through. We've already sent for Doc Sam. Maybe you should let me have him stop by and take a look at that leg of yours," Tom suggested, though he already knew what the answer would be.

"The doc's going to be needed a hell of a lot more for the others than for me. I'll be good as new in a couple of days," Jason replied stubbornly, unable to suppress another grimace as his leg pained him again.

"Sure you will," Tom agreed, though his voice lacked conviction. "But, just the same, I don't think that little wife of yours will be willing to let it rest until Doc Sam sees to you," he added with a faint smile. He smiled again at Jason's answering grunt and stood up, waving away the coffee Hannah was just carrying out from the kitchen. "Sorry, ma'am, but I'd better be getting back up to the camp. We've got a lot of cleaning up to do." He nodded politely in her direction, then started to leave.

"Tom, I couldn't help overhearing you say that there were other men injured. Why don't you have them brought down here, and I'll try to make them as comfortable as I can until the doctor arrives," she said as she followed him to the door.

"That's very nice of you, Mrs. Caldwell, but I think it would be better if we left them up at the camp until Doc Sam gets here. You're going to have enough on your hands with the one patient you've already got!" he remarked with a tired grin before he left.

Hannah stole a quick glance back at Jason before going outside as well. She returned in a matter of seconds, closing the door softly behind her, then poured a cup of the steaming coffee and held it out to him, saying, "I'm glad they didn't get to your timber, Jason. I don't understand how or why this man Dugan would want to do such a terrible thing in the first place." She took a seat beside him, raising a cup of the black liquid to her own lips.

"Greed." Jason's eyes met hers for an instant. "Just plain greed. He knows he'll get a higher price for his own timber if he can keep mine from getting through. Some men don't stop to think about whether they're doing wrong or right, Hannah, they just do what they feel driven to do. Dugan's a no-account bastard. You can bet he's not going to waste any time feeling any sort of remorse for tonight's trouble."

"I'm only thankful no one was killed, particularly with all that shooting going on up there. That's why I had to come up to the camp tonight," Hannah attempted to explain, meeting his unblinking gaze with softly pleading eyes. "I couldn't simply sit here and wait to find out if you were alive or dead! Don't you see that?"

"I told you to stay here," he answered, his voice low and even. "It's as simple as that." Damn her! he swore inwardly. She had put him through hell, worrying about

167

her being hurt up there tonight.

"No, it was *not* that simple!" she retorted stubbornly.

"From now on, you're to do as I say, regardless of what you think!" he commanded harshly. He moved toward her in the chair, then halted just as quickly as the pain shot through his leg.

Hannah was instantly contrite as she viewed the pain in his eyes. She smiled sweetly across at him, causing him to eye her suspiciously, wondering to himself what had caused her unexpected capitulation.

"It's time you were back in bed," she told him, cutting short their conversation as she stood ready to help him back into the bedroom.

"Just remember what I said, Hannah." He gazed relentlessly into her soft and shining eyes. "If I tell you to do something, I damn sure mean for you to obey me! You're the one who's always been reminding me that we're husband and wife. Well, then," he said, starting toward the bedroom with a set look on his face, "a wife is supposed to obey her husband in all things!" Hannah went after him, slipping beneath his arm to lend her support.

"Yes, Jason," she murmured in agreement, though with a secret smile to herself. "I'll try to remember." But the humor in her eyes faded, however, as Jason stumbled a bit, leaning heavily upon her before they finally made it to the bed. She waited until he had eased himself down, then gently placed a pillow beneath his injured leg, arranging the covers over him.

"I'm afraid you've lost a lot of blood," she said, then put a hand to his forehead. "And it feels like you're already beginning to run a fever." She left the room for a few minutes, returning with some cloths and a bowl of cool water. She drew up a chair and began applying the wet compresses to his head.

"You might as well get some sleep, too," Jason muttered in a deep voice, his eyes closing in weariness. "It's not going to do you any good to sit there all night!"

"Hush," Hannah soothed, "just go to sleep." She was satisfied when he didn't argue any further, and she sighed with relief when he went to sleep a few minutes later. She stood and went around to the other side of the bed, removed her dress, and quickly brushed through her tangled curls. She lay down beside her husband and closed her eyes, but the sleep she sought eluded her. She was unable to keep from worrying about Jason. She was glad she had gone ahead and talked to Tom, but she knew Jason would be mad as a hornet that she had disobeyed him again.

It doesn't matter, she mused, her chin lifting defiantly. It doesn't matter if he's angry or not! She loved him more than life itself, and she would do anything to ensure that he was soon well so that she could start convincing him again that she was just the sort of wife he needed.

Hannah rose before Jason was awake the next morning, shortly after sunrise. She set about her various chores, stepping outside into the early morning light before returning to the cabin and sweeping out the other rooms as quietly as possible. She looked in on Jason periodically, frowning whenever she put a hand to his forehead and discovered it very warm to the touch. She glanced out the window several times as she worked, and she was making breakfast when she heard the sound of riders approaching. Quickly wiping her hands on her apron, she hurried to open the cabin door.

"Morning, ma'am. Sorry it took us so long to get here.

Doc Sam was up all night, riding up from town and then seeing to the more seriously injured men up at the camp," Tom Reynolds explained hastily, dismounting and moving forward with the doctor.

"Thank you for coming," Hannah greeted them politely.

"Where is he?" the doctor inquired briskly, apparently too tired to bother with the usual amenities.

"In bed," Hannah replied, leading the way inside the cabin. "He's still sleeping. I don't think he stirred all night. He still has a fever, but he doesn't appear to be very restless. Perhaps that's a good sign," she remarked hopefully.

"Could be. Maybe not. Let's have a look at him," the weary doctor replied brusquely.

Jason was awakened by the sound of their voices, and he blinked rapidly as Hannah, instructed by the doctor, brought a lamp to provide extra light.

"Doc Sam? What are you doing here?" Jason demanded hoarsely, confused and drugged by the lingering fever. His gaze then flew toward Hannah, who faced him with an anxious expression on her face.

"I've come to have a look at that leg of yours," the doctor stated, drawing back the covers. He paused a moment to withdraw a bottle from his bag, uncorked it, and offered it to Jason. "Take a good swig or two of that. You'll probably need it while I work." He bent and started removing the bandages.

Jason did as he was bid, taking a long drink of the whiskey, then glared at his wife. "Hannah!" he ground out, suddenly putting out a hand to grip the doctor's arm as he exclaimed, "I don't need a doctor! There are plenty of others for you to see to!" he declared obstinately as he turned his gaze on the doctor.

"Jason, you've got to let him take a look at your wound," Hannah attempted to reason with him.

"I'll tend to you later!" he shot back at her, causing the color to flood her face as the doctor glanced back and forth at the two of them, one eyebrow raised sardonically.

"Don't be a damn fool, man," Doc Sam remarked, frowning down at the angry man on the bed. "From what I can see"—he examined the wound more closely now—"it's a good thing your wife here didn't listen to you. This leg doesn't look good, not good at all. But," he announced, taking a few more things from his bag, "I don't think you're really in any danger. That is, if we're lucky and a bad infection doesn't set in. You'll have to keep off this leg for at least a week or so."

"A week? You're mad!" Jason thundered, wincing suddenly and stifling a curse as the doctor probed his torn flesh again. "I've got a timber camp to run! I can't lie here like some damn invalid for a whole week!"

"You can and you will," countered the older man, finishing with his work and bandaging the wound again. Then, he turned a stern eye on his patient and cautioned, "You'll do as I say, Jason Caldwell, or you'll suffer the consequence of possibly losing that leg!" He left the room, leaving Hannah to glance worriedly toward her husband before turning about and following the doctor.

"Will he suffer much pain?" she asked, not failing to notice that the poor doctor was striving to keep awake.

"Off and on, but I've left a bottle of medicine beside the bed that he's to have whenever the pain gets too much to bear. I've really done all I can for him at this time. I don't believe he'll suffer any lasting complications, though. He should be just fine if he'll stay off that leg."

"I'm afraid you don't know my husband," Hannah murmured with a faint smile. "But I'll certainly do my best to make sure he follows your instructions."

"I don't envy you that job," the doctor replied with a sudden grin. "That leg is going to start stiffening up a lot more by the end of the day. I don't think you'll have much trouble in persuading him to take it easy—at least for a few days."

"Thank you so much for coming. Would you like something to eat before you go? Or perhaps some coffee?" Hannah offered.

"No, thanks. I've got to get back up to the camp. We've got to take a couple of the men down to town so I can keep a closer watch on them for a while. These logging wars are mighty good for business, but I'd just as soon not have this kind of business," he commented softly, almost to himself. He nodded his head briefly in her direction, then was soon on his way up the trail to the logging camp.

Hannah stood and watched him for a moment, leaning back against the door with a sigh. She dreaded facing Jason, knowing that he would be quite furious with her for having sent for the doctor. Well, she told herself, raising her chin higher as she closed the door and started back to the bedroom, she didn't care how angry he was. She knew she'd done what was necessary, and she would face him with confidence in that fact.

"How are you feeling?" she asked him brightly, forcing a note of lightness into her voice as she smiled upon entering the room. She moved to pick up the lamp she had left burning beside the bed.

"Hannah!" His anger was still quite visible. "Hannah Caldwell, you deliberately disobeyed me again!"

"It was for your own good!" she retorted, busying herself about the room. "I was afraid your wound might not heal properly without a doctor's care. I was only thinking of my husband's welfare."

"I've had just about enough of your defiance, woman!" He raised the bottle to his lips again.

"I know," she replied innocently, smiling at him as she started arranging the covers once more. "I'm truly sorry about having to go against your wishes again, but what's done is done, and there's no use in arguing about it any longer. The doctor said you should be just fine if you'll take it easy for a week or so."

"I don't give a damn what he said!" Jason snapped irritably, then collapsed against the pillow as the combined effects of the whiskey and the fever began to take hold. "I'm not about to stay here in this bed for a week! I'll be going back up to the camp by tomorrow and—"

"You most certainly will not!" Hannah interrupted, hands on hips as she faced him with a severe frown, her color heightened by the confrontation. "You're going to stay right there in that bed, just like the doctor said. And I'm going to see to it that you do, if I have to tie you down!"

"Hannah," Jason scowled at her, "if I didn't feel like hell right now, I'd tan your hide but good!"

"I don't know why you're being so childish about this," Hannah answered quietly. "All you have to do is to follow the doctor's orders for a few days, and then you can get well and carry on as before."

"That's just fine!" he roared. "And have you forgotten

that I still have a logging camp to run?"

"No, I haven't forgotten about that at all. But you needn't worry about that. I'm sure Tom will see to it that your timber gets downriver in time. I'll do all I can to help with any problems that might arise here."

"You don't even know the first thing about logging! And, besides that, I sure as hell don't need some fool woman trying to run things while I lay here on my backside!"

"I've already thought of someone who might be able to help," Hannah remarked, pleased that the notion had entered her head just seconds earlier. "I'm going to send word to Rob Clancy, to ask him to help out until you're up and around again."

"Rob Clancy?" Jason repeated in disbelief, then glared at her again. "You're not going to send word to him or anyone else, do you understand? I don't need his help, and I damn sure don't want him around here!" He threw back the covers with a flourish, a decidedly menacing look on his face, then suddenly fell back again as his leg began to throb and his head began to spin.

"Oh, Jason," Hannah spoke with a sigh, hurrying to his side and easing the covers over him again. "Now you just lie there and rest. We'll talk about it later."

"There's no need for any further discussion on the subject, Hannah," he said threateningly, reaching up to take her wrist in an iron grip and staring deep into her eyes. "You'll either do as I say, or—" He broke off abruptly, breathing heavily as a spasm of pain crossed his face and he closed his eyes tightly.

"Don't worry about it now," Hannah whispered soothingly, placing another cool compress on his forehead. "You need to get some sleep. I'll have some

174

broth ready for you when you wake up." He didn't answer. Apparently he had already lapsed into unconsciousness.

Hannah hated to disobey him again, but once more, she deemed it necessary. She would prove to him that she was dependable, that she was precisely the sort of wife he needed. She'd see to it that he stayed in bed, and she would also see to it that his business didn't suffer because of his absence. It was a difficult task she had set for herself, she mused as she left the bedroom and directed her steps toward the kitchen.

Fourteen

Jason continued to lapse in and out of consciousness throughout the night. Though he remained feverish and in pain, Hannah was vastly relieved to see that no dangerous infection set in. Indeed, Jason was much improved the next day, and she proceeded to nurse him with loving care. She applied cool compresses to his head, held a glass of water to his lips, fed him broth despite his very vocal objections that he required something more substantial to eat. He was not exactly an ideal patient, remaining alternately silent and irascible, but she did not mind. Tom had come by to check on Jason again, and Hannah had secretly given him a message to carry back to the doctor before Doc Sam departed for town once more.

Rob Clancy arrived at the cabin that afternoon; he had received Hannah's request for help via the doctor. She smiled warmly as she swung open the cabin door to admit him, giving a silent prayer of gratitude that Jason was asleep at the moment.

"Rob! How nice to see you again. Thank you for coming," she greeted him warmly. "I'm sorry I had to ask you for help, but—"

"There's no need to explain, Hannah," he interrupted

176

with a charming grin of his own, sweeping his hat from his head in a theatrical gesture. Stepping inside, he said, "You know I'll be glad to come whenever you need me. Jason and I are old friends, remember? And you and I are new friends, aren't we? So, enough of that! I'm here to do whatever I can. By the way, how is the patient today?" he asked with a look of genuine concern.

"He's doing much better today. But the doctor did say that he was to stay off his leg for a week. That's why I sent for you, Rob. Jason's timber is ready to be taken downriver, and Tom is the only one he'll trust with that. But that leaves no one in charge up at the camp, and they've got so much to do, what with the bunkhouse having to be rebuilt and all."

"Does Jason know you sent for me?" Rob asked with a sudden, searching glance in her direction, his eyes never leaving her face as she indicated a chair for him. She was looking as beautiful and desirable as ever, he told himself. Jason Caldwell held a priceless jewel in his hands and didn't even have the good sense to realize it!

"I told him I was going to ask for your help," she replied evasively, beginning to feel guilty once more for having disobeyed her husband so blatantly. She mused that she seemed to be making a habit of defying Jason.

"I see. I didn't think he'd be wanting me here!" Rob remarked with another broad grin, his brogue quite pronounced. "But here I am, and here I'll stay as long as you need me. Now, I'd best quit my gabbing and get on with my work. Do the men up there know I'm coming?"

"I've already told Tom and he's explained everything to them. But Rob, I hope this isn't going to cause you much inconvenience. What about your own camp?"

"Fear not," he assured her quickly. He walked to the

177

door with her again. "I've been away for quite a while as it is. A few more days certainly won't matter. My own men are used to my coming and going at will. Alas," he spoke with a heavy sigh and an accompanying wink, "I'm afraid I'm just not as devoted to my work as your husband, Mrs. Caldwell! Well, good day to you. I'll be back down for supper when the sun sets."

"Supper?" Hannah repeated, hesitant to agree. After all, she'd like nothing better than to be able to keep Rob's presence secret from Jason a little longer. But she simply couldn't turn him away, not with him doing her such a favor. "All right," she said finally with a quick smile. He tipped his hat to her and was off, striding jauntily across the clearing to the trail. She closed the door, her smile fading. Knowing full well how Jason would react, she had placed herself in a most uncomfortable predicament.

"Hannah!" she heard his deep voice rumbling from the bedroom. Her heart was pounding heavily in her breast as she turned her steps in his direction, dreading the confrontation she knew to be inevitable, realizing that he must have overheard her conversation with Rob.

"Yes, Jason? What is it?" she asked innocently, pausing in the doorway. The sunlight filtered faintly through the curtains at the windows, and Jason couldn't help noticing that the worn gray dress she was wearing did nothing to diminish her fresh beauty as she gazed at him with bright green eyes.

"Was that Rob Clancy's voice I heard?" he demanded, sitting up in the bed. He scowled darkly, looking even more threatening due to the growth of beard on his face. "Answer me, Hannah!" he insisted when she hesitated.

"Yes, it was," she answered calmly, though there was a defiant gleam in her eyes. "And before you start yelling

178

at me, Jason Caldwell, I'd like to say that you should be grateful to Rob. It was extremely generous of him to come all this way to help us." She swept into the room and approached the bed. "He's going to be here only a few days, until you're up and about again. I certainly don't see any harm in that!"

"You knew how I felt about it. We talked about it again last night, didn't we? You knew damn well that I didn't want him here!" Jason thundered, the anger shooting like sparks from his steely eyes. His temper was fueled by the fact that his leg still pained him considerably whenever he moved, and also because he couldn't seem to hold back the jealousy he despised himself for feeling.

"Oh, Jason, please try to be reasonable," Hannah pleaded, weary of having the man she loved so angry with her. She stood above him, then sank down into the chair beside the bed as she reached out to grasp his arm with both of her hands. "I'm sorry if you're angry with me again. I'm sorry if it seems as if I enjoy disobeying you, but I truly only want what's best for you."

"Rob Clancy isn't needed here!" he declared stubbornly, though some of his wrath began to melt away at her nearness, at the sight of her beautiful young face, her lavender-scented soft curves so close to him. What the devil was happening to him? he asked himself irritably. Was he really so weak that he was going to let a woman— his own wife—run roughshod over him? "Hannah," he began again sternly, only to be silenced as she suddenly leaned over and placed a tender kiss on his lips. He reached out for her, but she was already starting toward the doorway.

"Don't be too angry with me, Jason. I'll be back with some broth in a while," she said, scurrying from the room and closing the door swiftly behind her.

"Hannah! Get back here!" she heard him demanding, but she went blithely on about her chores. She sighed again as she reflected that she'd probably pay dearly for her defiance of him once he had recovered.

She wondered if it was just his pride that caused him to be angry about Rob, or if he was feeling jealous as well. She remembered the way he had exploded at Maggie's when he had come upon her and Rob in the kitchen. As she set about making a fresh pot of coffee, she decided that she honestly wouldn't mind if Jason were to become a bit jealous again. Not that she wanted his temper to explode, but it would be gratifying to have him prompted to declare his love for her.

Better put such nonsense out of your mind! she chastised herself firmly, setting the black pot on the iron stove. Purposely seeking to make her husband jealous was a wicked temptation. Nevertheless, there was a faint smile on her lips as she went on with her work.

It was some time later before she returned to the bedroom to take Jason his meal. She had already offered to shave him, but he had declined her offer with a curt shake of his head. He spoke very little to her for the remainder of the day, and his lips compressed into a thin line of extreme displeasure when they heard a knock at the front door.

"Well, here I am!" Rob announced cheerfully, sauntering inside as he swept off his hat. "I've been looking forward to this meal all day. Where's Jason?" he asked, glancing around with a nonchalant look on his face.

"In bed, of course," Hannah replied with a welcoming smile. She had donned a freshly laundered calico dress and a clean white apron, her shining tresses pulled away from her face in a simple but most becoming style. "But Rob, I know he'll want to speak with you. I'm afraid to say he's not been in the best of tempers about your being here," she added with a slight frown.

"Don't worry, I'm well aware of Jason's moods, Hannah." He shrugged off her warning with a laugh. "I've known him a good many years now. You needn't be afraid he's going to be able to scare me off so easily." His eyes moved quickly up and down her form and he spoke in a softer voice, "You look quite lovely tonight."

"Thank you," Hannah answered with a rather nervous smile. She realized then and there that she couldn't go through with it—she couldn't use Rob to make Jason jealous. She wanted only Jason's admiration, and she realized that she would feel too uncomfortable trying to flirt and pretend with Rob. "I'll get our supper."

"You'd best wait until I've had a word with your husband. I have a feeling we'll have no peace during the meal if I don't!" he said with a rueful grin. He stepped over to the bedroom door and knocked briskly, then entered without waiting for a response. He found Jason sitting up in bed, obviously waiting for him. "Well, well, how's the old leg feeling, Jason?"

"Why aren't you up at the camp?" Jason countered, striving to keep control of his temper, yet wanting nothing more than to wipe the smile off his old friend's face.

"If you must know," Rob answered with a chuckle, "it's because I knew I'd prefer your charming little wife's cooking to the sort of inedible grub they serve up at the camp."

"Look," Jason gritted, moving forward a bit and then

clutching his leg in pain. He clenched his teeth and continued, "I know Hannah asked you for help, but *I* did not! Now that you're here, you might as well get a few things straight. I can't very well throw you off the place, but you can keep away from this cabin—and from my wife! If you insist on helping out, then your place is back up at the camp with the other men!"

"What's the matter, Jason? Are you by any chance afraid I might try to steal your wife while you're lying helpless in here?" Rob taunted, a certain edge creeping into his voice. He remembered all too well another argument over a woman—though a woman much different from Hannah.

"Clancy, you and I have been needing to have things out for a long time now," Jason responded in a low, steady voice, his expression tightening. "You're not welcome here, so get the hell out!"

"Not until I've had my supper," Rob answered with a cocky grin, heading for the door. "By the way," he added, turning back for a moment, "in the event that you're at all interested, the bunkhouse should be rebuilt within the week. There isn't much cutting going on, but at least your timber's headed downriver. I know all about your personal feelings toward me, but I'm honestly going to do my best." With that, he was gone, leaving behind a frowning but thoughtful Jason.

Hannah couldn't help overhearing the two men talking as she carried the food from the kitchen to the table. But she said nothing about what she had heard as Rob took a seat across from her and the two of them began to eat. He entertained her with humorous tales of his exploits as a boy and young man, and she listened politely, but with only half an ear, and she ate very little. In truth, she was

182

thinking about Jason, lying in bed on the other side of the bedroom door, probably listening to every word that was said between herself and Rob. And so it was with great surprise that she and Rob turned to see Jason making his way out of the bedroom and toward them at the table. He was limping badly on his injured leg, but he wore a grim look of determination on his face.

"Jason! What are you doing out of bed?" Hannah exclaimed, rising so abruptly to her feet that her chair toppled backward noisily to the floor.

"What does it look like I'm doing?" he retorted ill-naturedly, finally grabbing hold of a chair for support.

"The doctor said you were to keep off that leg. And you're likely to start your wound bleeding again!" she protested, trying to pull him back toward the bedroom.

"Don't you think you're behaving childishly?" Rob asked mockingly, leaning nonchalantly back in his chair and gazing almost challengingly up into Jason's smoldering eyes.

"Get out of here, Rob Clancy, or I'll personally beat the hell out of you!" Jason spoke through clenched teeth. "No man can sit by and allow himself to be made a fool of in his own cabin!"

"What are you talking about?" Hannah demanded in puzzlement. "No one is trying to make a fool of you, Jason!"

"I mean it, Rob," Jason threatened again. "Get out of here or I'll throw you out!"

"Now, Jason, you yourself admitted a short while ago that you're not capable of throwing me out right now," Rob replied with a sarcastic gleam in his eyes, still sitting in the chair.

"Let me help you back to bed," Hannah insisted once

more, tugging on Jason's arm.

She looked helplessly from her husband to Rob and back again, and bestowed upon Rob a look of immense gratitude when he stood and said, "Never mind, Hannah. I was about to be on my way before we were so rudely interrupted. Thank you again for the delicious meal and for your pleasant company. Good night to you," he added with an unabashed grin and a mock bow, then turned to Jason. "Good night, Jason." He sauntered to the cabin door, opened it, and was gone without another word.

"Jason, please, get back to bed now," Hannah spoke soothingly, her hands grasping one of his muscular arms in a firm grip. She gasped in dismay when she glanced downward to see that his wound had indeed begun bleeding again.

"You shouldn't have done it, Hannah. You shouldn't have let him come in here!" he said, obviously still seething. There was a decidedly grim expression on his handsome features as he turned his gaze on her, adding ominously, "Don't play me for a fool, Hannah. If I ever believed that you were encouraging him, that you were even thinking of being unfaithful—" He broke off, passing a hand wearily over his face and leaning more heavily on the chair for support.

"Don't talk that way," Hannah answered softly. "You know I'd never think of doing such a thing. You're my husband; you're all the man I could ever need or want." She placed an arm about his waist, pleased when he didn't resist, and the two of them started back toward the bedroom. She felt a sudden sadness as she realized that she still had so far to go to convince him of her true love and devotion. Why couldn't he trust her? What had happened to him to make him think she could ever be tempted to play him false?

After bandaging his wound once more, Hannah started closing up the cabin for the night. Opening the door to admit Thor, she bolted it again and watched as the dog curled up before the dwindling fire in the fireplace. Blowing out all the lamps in the other rooms, she returned to the bedroom and began undressing, the single lamp still burning beside the bed.

Jason watched her as she presented her back to him and pulled her dress carefully up over her head, then drew off her petticoat and took the ribbon from her hair. Now clad only in her thin cotton chemise, she took up her hairbrush and gave her long tresses a few quick strokes, before taking off the chemise and putting on a cotton nightgown. She turned and pulled the covers back on her side of the bed, easing herself in and being careful not to jostle the bed too much. As she leaned over to blow out the lamp, Jason's hand on her arm stopped her, and she looked at him with a questioning expression on her face.

"Do you want something else, Jason?" she asked, thinking him to be either thirsty or in pain.

"Hannah, I . . . well, I'm sorry about the way I acted tonight." He was obviously uncomfortable with the admission. Yes, he was sorry for making it seem as if he doubted her, but he wasn't sorry for doubting Rob Clancy! He released her arm and lay back against the pillow, staring down toward the foot of the bed as he crossed his arms beneath his head.

Hannah was at a loss for words for several moments. She was pleased that he cared enough to be jealous of her, and yet she wanted him to be able to trust her, to confide in her, to look upon her as his one true companion in life.

"I suppose it was partly my fault," she confessed with just the hint of a smile tugging at the corners of her mouth as she extinguished the lamp and lay down. "Rob Clancy may delight in flirting and carrying on, Jason, but he's absolutely harmless where I'm concerned. But, to please you, I promise I'll not invite him to supper again."

"It would have pleased me even more if you had obeyed me and never sent word to him to come here!" he replied gruffly, though he was secretly pleased when she professed to have no interest in Rob's attentions.

"Let's not begin arguing again just now," she spoke with a soft sigh, snuggling farther beneath the covers and pressing her soft, warm curves against him. She suddenly drew back, her face registering concern when he moaned deep in his throat. "What is it? Oh, Jason, did I hurt your leg?" she asked, trying to see his face in the darkness.

"No," he answered hoarsely, sounding as if he was in pain. He cursed his leg, still so stiff and sore. He wanted to make long, leisurely love to his wife, and instead was forced to settle for merely sleeping next to her in the same bed.

Hannah lay back down and eased herself next to him again, closing her eyes in sleepy contentment. She soon drifted off to sleep, unaware of the fact that her husband lay wide awake beside her.

She was startled to discover him out of bed again the following day as he limped from the bedroom and took his place at the table while she poured him a cup of coffee. Knowing that it was entirely useless to demand that he take himself back to bed, she set about preparing their meal, relieved when Rob didn't put in an appearance at the cabin again.

Jason's leg continued to improve as he exercised it

186

about the cabin for the next couple of days. He was growing increasingly restless and impatient to return to his work, but was forced to admit to himself that he'd be no good at the camp until he could get around better. Hannah did her best to please him, but she realized that she, too, would be glad when Jason returned to work. He did finally confess to her that, whatever else he thought of Rob, he knew that the man was taking good care of things up at the camp. Beyond that, the two of them didn't speak of Rob again, each wishing to avoid the subject altogether.

One night, long after they had finished supper, Hannah and Jason sat before the fire, she with her sewing and he with his hand stroking Thor's head idly. It had been five days since the raid on Jason's camp. His leg was healing more rapidly than they had expected, and he announced that he would be returning to work the next day.

"But Jason, I don't think you're ready yet," Hannah protested, glancing up from the sewing in her lap. "Why, your leg has only now begun to stop paining you, hasn't it? I think it would be better if you waited the full week, as Doc Sam suggested."

"I'm sure I can make it up the trail by now," he replied, rubbing his hand lightly across his leg. "And it doesn't pain me much at all any longer," he insisted stubbornly. Yes, he thought, it was time. But, he had come to realize something these past few days while shut up inside the cabin. He knew how much Hannah had come to mean to him, how fortunate he was to have her as his wife. She had done his bidding without once complaining, had kept him company and tried to ease away his pain. Nevertheless, he knew he needed to get back up to the logging camp. This life of lazing about was certainly not for him, even if it did carry with it the compensation of Hannah's company. It would also mean that Rob Clancy would be leaving, could return to his own business. Though he knew Hannah hadn't even spoken to Rob these past few days, he still didn't want the man around. He'd have to think of some way to repay Rob for his help. Jason Caldwell always repaid his debts.

"I don't suppose there's any use in my trying to dissuade you," Hannah commented ruefully, smiling up at him. Her breath caught in her throat as she met his gaze, and the smile faded from her lips. He was staring at her in a disturbing manner, suddenly making her feel lightheaded, and she averted her eyes nervously as she tried to focus on the fabric she had been stitching.

"Hannah." He spoke her name in a voice barely above a whisper, rising slowly to his feet and reaching down to draw her up before him. The sewing in her lap fell unheeded to the floor. Jason told himself to proceed slowly, to woo her gently, but it seemed an eternity since he had held her in his arms, since he had loved her the way he now longed to do.

Hannah felt increasingly breathless when his arms came around her, when he pulled her unresistingly toward him, moving with tantalizing unhaste. Her eyes were still inexorably locked with his, and she raised her arms to entwine them about his neck as his head came down and his lips touched hers, at first tentative and gentle, then harder and more demanding. She, too, felt as if it had been ages since he had embraced her in such a fashion, and she found herself yearning impatiently for what she knew was to come.

They were standing so close together they seemed as if

one, until Jason finally raised his head, his hands moving commandingly to the bodice of Hannah's dress, his fingers undoing the buttons deftly as the firelight played across them. One by one the buttons were unfastened, until Hannah stood trembling, every nerve in her body tingling, as Jason eased the dress from her, allowing it to float downward until it lay in a heap at her ankles.

Shocked at her own boldness, Hannah gazed up at him seductively as she untied the strings of her petticoat, which soon joined her dress on the floor. Jason worked swiftly to remove his own clothing, then grew impatient and tugged Hannah's chemise from her body, leaving her totally bare to his searing gaze. Their eyes each adored the other's body, until Jason muttered something unintelligible and swept her up against him again, his warm lips seeking hers as his hands began roving masterfully across her sweet curves. She gasped aloud at the delicious sensations she was experiencing, and her fingers clutched almost convulsively at his hair when his lips wandered lower to her firm, rounded breasts. She nearly cried out as his tongue lazily circled the nipples, as his strong hands traveled lovingly down her back to clasp her rounded buttocks and mold her perfectly against his masculine hardness.

"Hannah, you're so beautiful," he whispered feverishly, his lips trailing hotly from her breasts to her arched neck, then up once more to her waiting lips. She, too, was swept away by the tide of their mutual passion as he finally lifted her high in his arms and carried her to the bedroom, depositing her on the bed and covering her waiting flesh quickly with his own.

"Oh, Jason!" Hannah gasped, breathless as he continued his rapturous assault on her body. He seemed intent on kissing every inch of her quivering form, and she was nearly driven wild as he commenced to bring her toward a burning peak of desire. When his fingers caressed her tenderly between her thighs, she moaned softly, and she opened to him as he entered her, her legs seeming to have a will of their own as they wrapped about his muscular waist. He moved slowly at first, then began thrusting deeper, faster, until she thought she would die with the exquisite torture.

Afterward, she lay contentedly in his arms, his hand gently stroking the damp curls from her flushed face. She smiled to herself, cuddling against him.

"Jason, I love you." It was a simple statement of fact for her, and she waited in anticipation for him to respond. But, after several long moments of silence on his part, she asked, "Don't you believe me?" She drew away from him a bit, raising herself on one elbow in order to see his face, her eyes already well accustomed to the room's darkness.

"I'd like to believe you," he answered finally, a decidedly grim expression on his face, his steely eyes suddenly holding a strange light.

"But, how can you doubt me? After what we've just shared, after everything that has happened—" she pleaded, breaking off as he looked at her, his eyes holding hers with an intense look. She grew uncomfortable beneath that gaze, fearful of the pain and doubt she glimpsed there.

"If I ever truly thought you had played me false, Hannah, if you were ever tempted to betray me—" he spoke tightly, silenced when she placed a caressing hand across his lips.

"Don't say such a thing, Jason," she chided softly, her

eyes sparkling with her love for him. "I love you. I'll never betray you." Though she was tempted to ask the reason for his difficulty in trusting her, in accepting her love and loving in return, she did not, knowing in her heart that he would tell her only when he was ready to do so.

"I'd like to believe you, Hannah," he repeated in a low voice, glancing away now.

"Then simply allow yourself to. Simply trust me and believe me. I'll never give you any reason to doubt me." She leaned over and placed a tender kiss on his lips, satisfied when he returned the kiss and pulled her toward him once more. Soon they were once more safely within their own special world, all doubts and fears and worries forgotten for a few precious moments in time.

Fifteen

By the time Hannah awakened the following morning, Jason was already gone. She sat bolt upright in the bed when she discovered the empty place next to her, immediately feeling guilty that she had allowed him to leave without breakfast. But, smiling to herself, she then settled back with a contented sigh and stretched lazily beneath the warm covers. Rolling onto her stomach, she pushed aside the curtains at the window above the bed to peer outside, musing to herself that, no matter what the unpredictable weather chose to do, it would be a gloriously beautiful day to her. However, she was pleased to see that it did not look a bit like rain—at least not yet—and she finally eased herself out of the bed, unable to suppress a fiery blush as she viewed her clothing strewn unceremoniously about the floor in the other room.

Last night had been the most wonderful of her life, she thought as she moved about the room. She believed Jason was beginning to trust her, and she also believed that he would be able to admit his love for her in the very near future. She knew he had been close to giving all of himself to her last night, but she also realized that he still held a tiny part back. Well, whatever had caused him to be so fearful of allowing himself to love and trust her, he was definitely beginning to overcome it! She knew it would not be long until her patience would be rewarded.

After enjoying the luxury of a morning bath, Hannah dressed in a blue-sprigged cotton dress and pinned her hair more elaborately than usual. As she stepped into the kitchen, her mind was already formulating a plan. She would climb the trail to the logging camp and take Jason his lunch. She knew he didn't approve of her presence at his camp, but she didn't believe he'd be too angry with her—particularly since he had gone off without eating anything that morning. And, she reflected as she knelt to build a fire in the iron cookstove, it was one more way—albeit a small one—that she could show her devotion to him.

The clouds were beginning to build in the sky as Hannah climbed the trail toward the logging camp, a basket of food in one hand, her other hand clutching her full skirts to sweep them up out of the dirt. She suddenly began to experience a twinge of trepidation as she walked, uncertainty about the wisdom of her plan beginning to plague her as she drew nearer to the camp. She firmly told herself that it was nothing more than nonsense. After all, she was merely taking the noon meal to her husband, and what could there possibly be in that to cause her this sudden sense of foreboding? Nevertheless, she couldn't say exactly why she was beginning to have misgivings about such a simple thing.

As Hannah reached the top of the trail and stepped out onto the edge of the clearing, she scanned the group of men she saw working there for any sign of Jason. Disappointed when she didn't see him anywhere, she was uncertain about what to do next. She knew that he would most definitely disapprove if she attempted to go in search of him amongst his men. As she stood there, just within the shelter of tall trees now, she spied Rob coming toward her, and she smiled with relief.

"Hannah! What are you doing here?" he asked, smiling broadly as he grasped her arm in greeting. His boyishly attractive face reflected his obvious delight in seeing her again.

"I was looking for Jason. But I might ask you the same thing. I thought that with Jason back, you'd be well on your way back to your own place by now."

"I decided to stay on a bit longer, at least until this afternoon. I'll be heading back down to town for a few days before returning to my camp."

"I see," she murmured, then said, "Rob, I can't begin to tell you how grateful I am that you came. Your friendship means a great deal to me, and, I'm sure, to Jason as well. You must not take offense at his treatment of you the other evening. I'm afraid he's impossibly jealous. Of course, I know the friendship between the two of you has been strained for other reasons, and I do wish one of you would choose to enlighten me on that score!"

"It's nothing of any great importance," he evaded, unwilling to disclose the unknown event. "But you don't have to try and explain Jason to me. For your friendship, however, I am truly thankful," he spoke lightly. "And it might surprise you to know that your husband has already expressed his own gratitude to me. Oh, not in so many words, of course, and most certainly not as prettily as yourself, but he has informed me that he intends to repay me in some manner. But tell me, Mrs. Caldwell, what have you got hiding in that basket there?" he asked, gazing curiously down toward the basket of food.

"I've brought Jason his lunch. Have you seen him?" she explained, feeling rather foolish again.

"The last I saw of him, he was heading down to the river with some of the men. I don't think he'll be back for some time. But, since I'd hate to see your efforts go to waste—your *considerable* efforts, if my sense of smell is any judge—why don't you and I share the meal?" he suggested, taking hold of the basket and tugging lightly on it, frowning with mock severity when she refused to let go.

"I don't think Jason would like it very much if I allowed you to steal his lunch!" she laughed. "I think there's enough trouble between the two of you as it is."

"Then a little more certainly won't matter, will it?" Rob grinned unabashedly, successfully capturing the basket as he inched closer and snaked out an arm to clasp her unsuspectingly about the waist. Then, despite her shocked protests, he whirled her about playfully, moving the two of them a bit farther into the shelter of the forest. When she continued to berate him for his outrageous behavior, he laughed, and she couldn't help but laugh along with him, though she continued her struggles to free herself from his surprisingly strong grasp. But her laughter died abruptly when he pressed his lips upon hers, leaving her too overwhelmed with surprise to struggle any longer—at least for the moment.

When Hannah finally recovered from the considerable shock of his actions, she pushed against him again in earnest. But he was suddenly torn violently away from her and spun about to face an obviously furious Jason, who smashed his fist into Rob's face without a word of warning.

"Jason!" Hannah whispered in horror, gazing almost unseeingly downward toward Rob. That unfortunate young man picked himself up off the ground and shook his head as if to clear it, while Jason turned his rage on Hannah.

"I should have known!" His eyes were suffused with a fiery glow, the expression on his face more savage than she had ever seen before. "I should have known better than to trust you, to believe you when you so innocently denied you could ever think of being unfaithful! What a fool I've been! How long has this been going on, Hannah? Just how long have you been giving your body to two men at the same time?" he sneered, laughing derisively and without a trace of humor. By now Rob had recovered enough to stand, and he made the mistake of grabbing hold of Jason's arm as he said, "You're a bloody fool, all right! Your wife had no part in what you think you saw! It was my fault. I was only playing a silly game—" The words were barely out of his mouth when Jason hit him again, and Rob's own temper exploded as he responded in kind.

Hannah watched numbly, hot tears gathering unnoticed in her widened eyes. She watched in horror as Jason knocked Rob to the ground once more, saw Rob grasp Jason's legs and wrestle him down as well. She wanted to scream at them to stop, to scream at Jason that she and Rob were not lovers, as he had assumed, but she couldn't seem to find her voice. Finally Jason stood alone before her. Rob was lying unconscious, his face bruised and bloodied, and Jason's own face showed visible signs of their battle.

"Jason, it isn't what you think," Hannah now found

196

voice enough to declare. "I love you! There has never been anything between Rob and myself—you must believe me!"

"Believe you?" he repeated sarcastically, his voice sounding bitter and strained. "Oh, I believe you, all right, I believe you love to deceive; you love to use your beautiful face and tempting body to get what you want! How many others have been taken in by that innocence you affect so well? How many other men have made love to you—been ready to love you—only to discover what kind of lying, conniving little witch you really are?" he taunted cruelly, beyond all reason now as his jealousy and pain overpowered him. He didn't notice the stricken, ashen look on Hannah's face, the expression of heartbreak in her eyes. He continued relentlessly, mercilessly. "It's my own fault for ever being tempted to trust a damned female! It isn't as if I shouldn't have had better sense. Oh, no, I knew better, but I didn't want to trust my own instincts. I let you worm your way into my life, and almost—almost into my heart. But I didn't let you get that far!" he added furiously, knowing full well that he was lying, that he was reacting so violently for the simple reason that she *had* made a place for herself in his heart. He was too hurt to listen, too hurt to give her the chance to explain.

"Jason, I love you. What you saw was nothing more than Rob Clancy's idea of a silly, childish little prank! You must believe me! You must surely know by now that I'm not at all what you're accusing me to be!" The tears were coursing freely down her flushed cheeks now, and she didn't even try to stop them as she pleaded with him to believe her. What was happening didn't seem real to her, she thought suddenly. Jason couldn't really be

197

saying those terrible things to her, couldn't be gazing so murderously at her!

"Get the hell out of my life!" he ordered finally, his fury still all too evident. "I don't need you—I don't need anyone! You can bet I won't be foolish enough to make the same mistake again! Go on, go back to town with your lover! I want you out of my cabin, out of my life!" he thundered before spinning about on his heel and limping away as quickly as he could.

Hannah felt as if her heart was indeed breaking in two as she watched him leave. She knew that she would die at that moment if only she could. But Rob's moan as he began to regain consciousness forced her back to reality, and she flew to kneel beside him on the hard ground, her arm supporting his shoulders as he struggled to a sitting position.

"I'm sorry, Hannah," he gasped, still breathless from having the wind knocked out of him. "If I had had any idea that Jason was there, that he had seen or heard us—"

"It doesn't matter now," she said dully, appearing very pale. "None of it matters now—" Her voice trailed off as she choked back the tears, but she managed to ask, "Are you all right, Rob? Can you stand?" She dashed the tears from her eyes impatiently.

"I think so," he answered, staggering to his feet, waving away her offer of assistance. "Don't worry," he told her with a quick, reassuring smile. "I'll talk to Jason once he's had time to cool down a bit. I'll manage to straighten things out."

"You can't," she replied sadly, shaking her head slowly. "You didn't hear the things he said to me, didn't see the way he looked at me. He looked as if he hated the

198

very sight of me. He'll never listen to reason, Rob. He'll never believe there's nothing between us. Oh, Rob, why did you do it?" she asked in a pained tone of voice, gazing up at him with her tear-streaked face.

"I don't know, Hannah. I honestly don't know. I was carried away, I guess. I'm truly sorry."

"What am I going to do?" she asked in desperation, sobbing wretchedly now. "He told me to get out of his life. He even told me to go down to the town with you." She did not resist when his arms came around her as he sought to give her a small measure of comfort. She allowed him to lead her back down the trail to the cabin, though her tears nearly blinded her as she stumbled along. He was forced to move slowly as well, his body sore and aching from the fight with Jason.

"I'll help you gather up your things, if you like," he offered once they had reached the cabin.

"Perhaps I shouldn't leave," Hannah said in confusion. "What if he should change his mind? But he won't," she said dejectedly, answering her own hopeful question. "He meant every hateful thing he said to me, Rob."

"Not at all," Rob disagreed, one arm still protectively about her shoulders as they entered the cabin. "Just give him a few days and he'll listen to reason. Come down to Red Creek with me, stay at Maggie's, and he'll probably be there to beg your forgiveness in less than three or four days' time."

"Do you really think so?" Hannah asked, some small glimmer of hope returning. She had no idea how forlorn, yet beautiful, she looked as she gazed up at Rob. He hesitated for an instant before trying to inject some confidence into his voice.

"Of course. Jason's a hothead, Hannah. He has a short fuse, but give him a while to cool down, and I'm sure he'll be more reasonable." He smiled encouragingly at her as she went into the kitchen, then returned with a bowl of cool water and some cloths. She started gently cleansing the blood and dirt from his face as she gestured for him to take a seat at the table.

"I do hope you're right, Rob. I love him so much. I can't bear the thought of our marriage ending this way," she spoke with a heavy sigh, trying to stem the new onslaught of tears that was threatening her once more.

She and Rob rode down to Red Creek that same afternoon, reaching Maggie's house just before the cold, chilling rain began to beat down upon the waiting earth. She had been reluctant to leave at the last moment, but Rob had convinced her that it was for the best, that Jason would indeed be more ready and willing to listen to her after a brief separation in which to think things over.

"Rob! Hannah! What are the two of you doing here?" Maggie exclaimed in surprise when they unexpectedly crossed her threshold. She immediately wrapped her ample arms about Hannah and hugged the younger woman, then drew away a bit with a look of concern on her kindly features when she detected the tears on Hannah's face. "What is it, child? What has happened?"

"Maggie, I—Jason—he asked me to leave," she replied brokenly, looking every bit as miserable as she felt. "But no," she amended hastily, "he *told* me to leave!"

"Told you to leave?" Maggie repeated in bewilderment and disbelief, her arm still about Hannah's shoulders. "Why would the fool man be doing such a thing as that?" she demanded in exasperation.

"Because he believed I've been unfaithful," Hannah

200

admitted, a bitter smile on her face now. "And he wouldn't even listen to me when I tried to tell him it wasn't true, that I'd never even think of betraying him. I love him, Maggie. I'll always love him."

"Of course you do! And I don't believe for a minute that you're guilty. But Hannah, where did that husband of yours get such a notion in the first place?" she asked quietly, her kindly eyes still searching Hannah's face.

"I'll explain everything to you later," Rob interrupted at this point, propelling an unresisting Hannah toward the stairs. Turning back to his puzzled mother, he asked, "Is the room at the end of the landing still vacant?" When she nodded, he said to Hannah, "You go on up and rest a bit. I'll be here when you come down again." She cast him a grateful look, then ran up the staircase. Once she had disappeared inside the room and closed the door, Rob faced his mother and began relating the entire story.

Maggie listened avidly as her son talked. When he reached the part of the tale that involved his disgraceful action toward Hannah, Maggie fixed him with sternly disapproving eyes, and he did at least have the grace to squirm uncomfortably beneath that accusing stare as he finished the story. Afterwards, he was forced to endure a severe tongue-lashing from his outraged mother, as if he were not a grown man but a mere boy once more.

Meanwhile, Hannah lay upon the bed in the darkened room upstairs, the only sound in the room coming from outside her window where the steady rain beat softly against the roof of the house. She felt so very weary, but her mind refused to grant her the rest she sought. She could still vividly see Jason's twisted, wrathful features, could still hear his cruel, taunting words to her. Though she knew herself to be entirely innocent of what he had accused, she also realized that her husband was almost uncontrollably jealous, and it had appeared to him that she was indeed enjoying a lover's playful romp with Rob. But, jealous or not, she told herself with a heavy sigh, he should have listened to her, should have allowed her to explain.

Oh, Jason, she pleaded silently, willing him to listen. Don't cast me aside like this, don't discard my love for you so easily. It simply couldn't end like this. He'd have to listen sooner or later, wouldn't he? Surely, following a few days apart—time in which he could ponder what had happened—he would be willing to listen to reason.

But, she asked herself, moving an arm across her eyes as she lay there alone in the darkness, what am I going to do if he won't ever listen? What am I to do if he never believes me? Soon she slept the sleep of utter exhaustion, though her dreams were haunted by Jason's savage, accusing glare.

Sixteen

"Now, Hannah, there's no use in worrying yourself sick over this," Maggie Clancy scolded gently. The two of them were seated at the small wooden table in the kitchen of the boardinghouse, Maggie occupied with her day's breadmaking, Hannah peeling potatoes for the evening meal.

"I know," Hannah agreed with a sigh. She appeared a trifle thinner, and there were telltale circles beneath her eyes, but she was still quite lovely as she sat there in her simple cotton dress and apron, her hair pulled away from her face to cascade down her back. "But I can't seem to help myself, Maggie. I don't know what I'm going to do if something doesn't happen soon." Jason still had not either come or sent word, and it had now been three days. She was not only distressed by that fact, but also by the fact that she was forced to take advantage of Maggie's good nature and warm hospitality. She hated having to impose upon that good woman, but, in truth, she realized she had nowhere else to turn. She was forced to wait until she heard from Jason, and she grew angry with the delay, though she was still aching terribly in her heart.

"Give him time, child. Jason Caldwell is the sort of

man who feels things deeply, though I grant you he'd never admit it. It seems to me that he's so much in love with you he doesn't quite know what to do."

"In love with me?" Hannah repeated in disbelief. "He's certainly never said so. I've told him how much I love him, but he's never said as much to me in return."

"Well, it's plain to see the man's burning up with jealousy, isn't it? You know yourself he wouldn't be jealous unless he cared an awful lot," the older woman pointed out with an emphatic nod. "But, whatever the case, none of this sitting about and worrying is going to help! I wish I knew of something to take your mind off your troubles for a spell."

"There isn't anything to do that, Maggie," Hannah replied with a sad little smile. Though Rob had done his utmost to lift her spirits, and Maggie was kindness itself, she yearned for Jason more and more with each passing day. She knew she appeared childish and rather spineless, moping about as she was, but she couldn't seem to help herself. She loved him, she wanted and needed him, and she could only remain here in town and wait impatiently as the time slowly passed. Her hopes were beginning to dwindle, though both Rob and Maggie assured her constantly that Jason would come soon.

"Why don't you go on upstairs and rest a bit now?" Maggie suggested, dusting her hands generously with the flour as she prepared to knead the dough. "You've been working about here all day."

"I have to do something to keep my mind occupied," Hannah answered with a brief smile. "But I think I will go into the parlor. I noticed earlier that the furniture in there needs dusting pretty badly."

"I was suggesting that you rest, not work!" Maggie

protested, but merely shook her head as Hannah left the kitchen with another quick smile.

Hannah climbed the stairs to her room and emerged with a white kerchief, returning downstairs to the parlor as she wrapped the fabric about her head, tucking her thick curls upward beneath its cover. She drew another cloth from the pocket of her apron and set to work, determined to have the entire room finished before it was time to help Maggie serve the evening meal. There were only two men staying in the boardinghouse at the moment, and she saw them only once a day, at supper.

She was in the process of kneeling on the floor in the parlor in order to reach the spindled legs of a table when she heard a knock sound at the front door. Quickly putting aside her work, she hurried to answer it, swinging open the door with an expectant smile on her face, hoping within her heart that Jason had finally come for her.

"Yes?" she said, staring at the woman on the doorstep, disappointment at not finding Jason there causing her to frown. The woman looked familiar, Hannah mused, though she couldn't recall where she had seen her before. The dark eyes that met her gaze coolly hardened almost imperceptibly as the petite black-haired woman remarked, "Well, so we meet again, Mrs. Caldwell." Her voice held an umistakable French accent, and her startling attire, which consisted of a bright scarlet dress and matching plumed hat, finally prompted Hannah to remember.

"You're Colette, aren't you?" she asked, recalling now the rather odd incident in the general store some time ago. "I'm sorry I didn't remember you right away. Won't you please come inside?" she offered politely, standing aside as the smaller woman swept almost haughtily past her and headed straight for the parlor without waiting to be shown the way. "I'll fetch Mrs. Clancy for you," Hannah announced.

But Colette replied quickly, "No! It is you with whom I've come to speak." She raised her chin in what Hannah perceived to be a faintly defiant, challenging gesture, then sank down onto the settee and settled her skirts about her. It was obvious that she had something on her mind, and she gazed coolly at Hannah.

"Very well," Hannah responded calmly, taking a seat opposite her. "What is it you wished to speak to me about?" She suddenly reached up to remove the kerchief tied about her head, her gloriously bright hair falling like a shining cloud about her shoulders. She didn't know why, but she felt the need to appear a bit more presentable in the presence of this dark beauty.

Colette stiffened visibly. "I find it surprising that you are here once more. I have been told that you have been here for several days now."

"Why should you find that surprising?" What was it the woman wanted? Hannah asked herself in puzzlement.

"I would not have thought Jason to be the kind of man to allow his wife to be so—shall we say, independent," Colette remarked, her mouth curving into a smile which did not quite reach her eyes. "I would say he is the kind of man who appreciates a more unselfish nature." Again, that smile that appeared almost feline. Hannah again wondered why the woman had come to see her, why she was talking about Jason in such a personal manner.

"I wasn't aware that you were so well acquainted with my husband's likes and dislikes." Hannah was unable to prevent a certain edge from creeping into her voice. She was striving to be polite to the woman, but it was becoming increasingly apparent to her that for some reason this Colette seemed determined to provoke her.

"Acquainted! But, of course! Jason and I are very old, very dear friends. Surely you must have heard about that."

"About what?"

"I'm very surprised that your husband never mentioned me to you," Colette purred, quite pleased with the way things were going. "I have known many men, but none such as your husband! He knows how to please a woman. But you do not need for me to tell you that, do you?" she insinuated crudely.

"Just what are you trying to say? Why are you here?" Hannah demanded curtly, a slight flush on her face.

"Jason Caldwell and I were lovers. We were once, and we shall very soon be so again!" Colette smirked triumphantly, her brown eyes flashing.

It couldn't be true! Hannah told herself in shocked disbelief. Jason and this woman? Colette operated a saloon, was obviously the sort of woman who was popular with all the men. It simply couldn't be true that Jason had ever become involved with someone like her!

But why not? asked a tiny voice at the back of her mind. Jason had not wanted a wife, had led a life she knew nothing about before she came. Whatever he had done in the past was a mystery to her. But she was certain that Colette's bold statement that she and Jason would be lovers again in the near future was a lie!

"Well," Colette said, growing impatient, "aren't you going to say anything? I have just told you that your husband and I were lovers, that once you are gone he will return to me. Doesn't that bother you?"

"I don't even know if you're telling me the truth," Hannah answered finally, keeping her voice steady, "but if you and my husband were indeed involved before he married me, there is certainly nothing I can do about that now." Except feel this dull ache in my heart, she added silently. "As for your assumption that I am going to leave Jason, that he'll then resume his so-called relationship with you, I'm afraid you are very sadly mistaken!"

"Oh? And what makes you so certain?" Colette sneered contemptuously, her face turning ugly. She knew she was taking a risk in being here—in confronting Jason's wife like this—but she was desperate and had to do something. No other man had satisfied her like Jason Caldwell, and she would never give him up!

"Because I know my husband!" Hannah retorted angrily.

"If you know him so well, then what are you doing here? Why are you not with him now?" Colette demanded with a malicious smile. "I think it is because he does not want you with him!"

"You cannot possibly know what you are talking about!" But—she cried inwardly, feeling quite wretched—it's true. Jason told me to leave. He hasn't come for me, hasn't sent for me. Could it really be because of this spiteful woman? No! She wouldn't believe it! "I don't know what purpose you had in coming here and saying these insulting things to me, but I am not going to leave my husband, and I am not going to give you the satisfaction of believing anything you have said!" Hannah announced defiantly, a determined light in her bright green eyes. She couldn't let this awful woman know how much she had been affected, how very hurt and confused she was.

208

"It's very simple to discover if I am telling the truth," Colette responded with a throaty laugh. "Just ask your husband the next time you see him. That is, if you see him again." She rose to her feet and swept gracefully from the room, though she turned back at the doorway. "You are not his type of woman, you know. The proof of that is right before your eyes. Look at how very different the two of us are. Jason preferred me long before he even met you, and he will definitely come back to me!" She turned then and was gone, closing the front door rather forcefully behind her.

Hannah was stunned by the force of the anger and pain and jealousy she was feeling. Although she still didn't want to believe Colette's startling claims, she realized that at least part of them could very well be true. But she knew deep in her heart that Jason wasn't being unfaithful to her; he couldn't be carrying on with Colette after the way he had reacted upon seeing her with Rob the other day.

"Hannah?" Maggie called, appearing in the doorway now. "I heard you talking to someone. Mind if I ask who it was?" It had been a woman's voice she had heard, and she was nearly bursting with curiosity, particularly since there were so few women in town.

"It was that woman called Colette," Hannah replied miserably.

"Colette!" Maggie exclaimed. "What did that she-devil want with you?"

"She wanted to tell me that she and Jason were lovers. She wanted me to believe that Jason wants me out of the way, that he's going to go back to her once I'm gone."

"That's the most ridiculous thing I ever heard!" Maggie cried, looking totally outraged. "If I had known she was here, I'd have thrown her out on her disgraceful little ear! You can't believe anything a woman like that says!"

"But what if it is true? That would certainly explain why Jason hasn't come for me, wouldn't it?" Hannah asked bitterly.

"You know good and well that doesn't have anything to do with it!" Maggie insisted emphatically. "That little troublemaker. She's caused enough commotion around here without doing something like this!" She appeared quite angry, and Hannah glanced at her suddenly with a searching look.

"What do you mean? What sort of commotion has she caused?" She watched as Maggie hesitated, evidently at a momentary loss for words. "Do you know something you're not telling me? You do, don't you! Colette was telling me the truth, wasn't she? She and Jason were involved with one another before I came, weren't they?" she insisted.

"Even if they were," Maggie answered evasively, "it doesn't mean a thing now. It has no bearing on the way things are now."

"Please, Maggie," Hannah entreated, crossing the room to grasp hold of the older woman's arms. "Please tell me the truth. I need to know whether those horrible things she said were true!"

"What difference does it make?" Maggie demanded, wanting to avoid answering her. "It won't change how you feel about Jason, will it? It won't change a thing."

"It will if he does indeed have intentions of taking up with her again!"

"Taking up with her again? Why, Jason Caldwell's not that big of a fool, no matter what else he's done!" Maggie snapped, then realized she had admitted the very thing she had sought to keep hidden. With a resigned sigh, she looked Hannah straight in the eye and said, "All right. It's true that Jason and Colette were once involved with each other. She was involved with a good many men around here! In fact, though I know I'll probably be made to regret telling you, that no-account female is the main reason my son and your husband are no longer the good friends they once were."

"So that's the reason!" Hannah repeated in wonderment, surprised that she hadn't thought of such a thing before. "I suppose that's why Rob wouldn't tell me himself—because it concerned another woman. And Jason had never told me much of anything about his past."

"Colette wasn't important enough to mention! Everyone in these parts knows what she is, including Rob and Jason. But it was a long time ago, and the two of them were young and hotheaded. When Colette made it all too plain that she preferred Jason to Rob, my Rob went nearly mad with envy and jealousy and the two of them fought. After that, there was something to do with some sort of business deal between them that also went sour. I've never been able to understand how they could let something as insignificant as Colette ruin their friendship," she remarked with an expression of utter distaste. "But there, now you know. Colette never meant anything to Jason, not really. She was simply a woman— a painted slut, if you will. There's nothing to worry about as far as she's concerned, especially since it was Jason himself who once told me that she didn't mean a thing to him."

"I hope you're right," Hannah murmured, digesting

the startling news she had just heard. It disturbed her greatly, knowing that Jason and that woman were . . . but, as Maggie had said, that was long ago and in the past. Surely she was right about Jason's feelings toward Colette now as well. If only he would come for her! She was convinced the two of them could still somehow work things out between them, that she could make him believe she was innocent. She was as different as she could be from Colette. She loved Jason with all her heart, and he was the only man in the world she would ever want. "I'm glad you told me, Maggie. At least now I can perhaps understand a few things better. But why did Colette come here today? What did she hope to gain by telling me those things?"

"She's a jealous, spiteful little cat! She probably thinks she's spotted the perfect opportunity to move in and take advantage of your separation from Jason. She doesn't have the sense to know she doesn't stand a chance!" Maggie said with a vigorous shake of her head. "I think you should forget all about her. She doesn't have anything to do with you and Jason. In fact, I don't think you should ever mention her to him. When he comes for you, just be prepared to show him how much you really love him."

"Do you really still believe he'll come?" Hannah asked wistfully.

"Of course he will. He just may need a little more time. But, you mark my words, he'll come for you. He's too much in love with you to stay away forever."

Hannah hugged her friend in gratitude, and the two of them walked arm-in-arm back into the kitchen. Later that evening, Hannah felt compelled to confess to Rob that she knew the truth about Colette. Though he was less than pleased that his mother had told her, he agreed with Maggie that Jason wouldn't ever think of returning to Colette. Why, he himself was no longer attracted to Colette, he assured Hannah with a broad grin, adding with a teasing wink that beautiful young blondes were now more to his liking. Hannah laughed at him, refusing to take him seriously, while his mother sternly reminded him that such flirtatious behavior was what had caused the trouble between Hannah and Jason in the first place.

Later that same evening, Hannah slipped quietly out of the boardinghouse, hoping to remain unobserved by Maggie. She knew her friend would insist upon sending Rob along as an escort, and Hannah desired nothing more than to be alone. She wanted to walk out into the fresh, cool night air, wanted to escape from the stifling confines of the house. She hadn't been outside much since coming to town, and she sorely missed the time she spent outdoors up at the cabin. She believed she would be safe enough if she remained near the house, and she set off along the boardwalk with a quick glance over her shoulder as she descended the front steps.

It wasn't long before she decided she had made a mistake in venturing out alone. Two men, obviously quite drunk, stepped in front of her path as she tried to sweep past them. She clutched her woolen shawl tightly about her body and attempted to ignore them, but they would not allow her to do so. One of them reached out and grabbed hold of her arm, and Hannah wrenched it from his grasp and began running along the boardwalk, slowing her steps to a walk once more when she ascertained that the men were not going to give chase.

They were probably too drunk to be able to run, she told herself with a grimace. By now she was accustomed to the rough ways of Red Creek, though she hoped it would someday be quite different. As she passed in front of one of the saloons, the lights from within illuminating her path, she curiously turned her head and glanced inside, her eyes widening in shock at what they beheld.

Jason was seated at a table inside the noisy, smoke-filled room, clutching an empty glass in one hand and a half-full bottle in the other. There was an unfathomable expression on his face as he poured himself another drink, swallowing the whiskey in a single gulp. As Hannah stood just within the shadows of the doorway, her heart pounding in her breast, she saw Colette sidle up to Jason and settle herself upon his lap, flinging an arm nonchalantly about his broad shoulders as she laughed loudly at something he had just said. But, Hannah noted, Jason wasn't laughing. No, he appeared unsmiling and very grim, even when Colette laughed again and pressed a kiss to his cheek. There were several other men in the saloon, but Colette was giving her attention exclusively to Jason.

Hannah drew in her breath sharply, hot tears starting to her eyes. She realized with a feeling of painful dismay that Colette must have been speaking the truth. Jason was in town—but not to fetch his wife, she reflected bitterly. Oh, no, he was here to see his paramour! As she felt certain her heart was breaking, the pain began to give way to absolute fury.

How dare he! she raged silently. Her eyes narrowed as she continued to watch Jason and Colette. How dare he publicly flaunt his adulterous relationship with that woman, all the while knowing that his wife waited for him here in town! Colette must have known he was coming, must have known she had already won, Hannah thought as her mouth twisted. What enjoyment the two of them must have received to know that Jason's devoted wife was still waiting for him, waiting in vain.

Hannah thought she would explode with the tumult of emotions warring within her, and she entered the saloon without thinking, moving forward until she stood directly before Jason and Colette, her hands on her hips, the angry tears shining in her flashing green eyes.

"Jason!" Several heads in the room turned curiously their way.

His eyes were bloodshot, his handsome face darkened by several days' growth of beard. He looked very tired, Hannah noticed vaguely as he turned toward her in surprise, his lips compressing into a thin line of anger.

"What in thunder do you think you're doing here?" he demanded harshly, his whole body tightening as he glared at her.

"Well, well, if it isn't the little wife!" Colette mockingly remarked, her own eyes full of gloating triumph. She remained draped intimately across Jason, her arm clasping him even more tightly against her as her eyes also mocked Hannah. However, Hannah ignored her and addressed her wrathful remarks to Jason.

"I might ask you the same question!" she retorted hotly. "How dare you! How dare you accuse me of betraying you, when I have only to see right before my very eyes the evidence of your own betrayal!" she accused him bitterly. "Oh, Jason, how could you?" she cried, her features wearing a pained expression.

"Why don't you go back where you belong?" Colette broke in, climbing off Jason's lap and facing Hannah as if preparing to do battle. "You're not wanted in here!"

"You stay out of this!" Jason roared unexpectedly,

causing Colette to whirl about and cast him a startled look.

"She told me what was between the two of you, what is apparently still between you, but I didn't want to believe her!" Hannah exclaimed tearfully, casting aside her pride as she felt complete despair. "I loved you, Jason! I would have given my very life for you. No one could ever love you more than I, but you have destroyed that love!"

"Hannah," Jason spoke in a low, slurred voice, rising unsteadily to his feet as he faced her with a severe frown. But she refused to listen, instead continuing with the torrent of emotion that had been released.

"You have destroyed something beautiful with your accusations, your own hypocrisy! There was never anything between Rob and myself. There's never been any man in my life except you. But you couldn't accept that simple fact, couldn't allow yourself to trust and believe me!" The tears were flowing down her flushed cheeks now, but she paid them no heed. Nor did she seem to notice the curious onlookers who had gathered around them, the unnatural quiet that had settled over the place. "To think that I was always striving to please you, that I was so determined to make you a good wife, to make you love me as I loved you. I didn't know that such a thing was impossible, did I? It was always impossible, because you have no heart, Jason Caldwell!"

"Hannah," Jason was grim as he moved forward and took a firm grip on her shoulders. "Hannah, listen to me!" he ordered.

"Why?" she lashed out bitterly. "There's nothing further you can say or do to hurt me. You're everything you accused me of being! You're a liar and a cheat, and you're not worthy of the love I had for you!" she flung at him, raising her arms and pounding on his broad chest with clenched fists. "I hate you! Go back to your trollop! The two of you deserve one another!" She managed to pull away from him then, turning on her heel and running from the saloon, her face giving evidence of all the pain and humiliation she was experiencing.

Jason started to go after her, but Colette clutched at his arm and demanded, "What good do you think that will do? She's had her say, hasn't she? Let her go, Jason!" She gasped aloud as he rounded on her abruptly, jerking his arm free of her grasp, a murderous look in his blue eyes. She backed away from him, a look of fear on her face, expecting some outburst of violence from him. She was surprised when he did nothing, instead sinking back down into the chair at the table and raising the bottle to his lips. He said nothing, his expression inscrutable, and Colette decided wisely to leave him alone.

Meanwhile Hannah ran back along the boardwalk to Maggie's, bursting inside the house and blindly making her way up the stairs to the sanctuary of her room. She threw herself face down upon the bed and sobbed in anguish, feeling as though a part of her had just died.

Seventeen

"I shall go alone if you won't take me," Hannah declared stubbornly, facing Rob with a very determined expression on her lovely features. She had slept little the night before, making her fateful decision in the early hours of the dawn. There was nothing left for her here, she had told herself, nothing to hold her any longer. She experienced an overwhelming need to get away as quickly as possible, and the only destination she could consider seriously was Seattle.

"All right, all right!" Rob capitulated finally, a heavy sigh of resignation escaping his lips. "You know what Maggie will say, don't you?" Perhaps his mother could persuade her to stay, to abandon this irrational, impulsive course of action she was so set upon. He had certainly done his best to try and make her see reason, but to no avail.

"I know. I've already spoken to her. But it doesn't matter, Rob. I'm going to leave this very morning, with or without your help." She recalled the conversation between herself and Maggie which had taken place less than an hour earlier, remembered how adamant Maggie had been in her opinion that Hannah was doing the

218

wrong thing, that she should wait at least a few days and attempt to settle things with Jason first. But Hannah had been unwavering in her decision to return to Seattle. She had insisted that it was the only true recourse open to her now that her marriage to Jason had deteriorated so tragically.

It was as if she had been married to a total stranger these past few weeks, she reflected bitterly. Though they had begun married life as strangers, she had honestly believed that she had come to know Jason Caldwell. Oh, she told herself as her mouth twisted into a frown, not as well as she had hoped or wanted, but she never would have believed him to be the sort of scoundrel he had shown himself to be. Even now, her eyes stung with hot tears at the memory of his betrayal.

Hannah had waited in nervous anticipation for him to come, for him to appear at Maggie's and demand to speak to her. She had nurtured the faint hope that he would at least have the decency to try and explain his disgusting behavior with Colette, would at least have attempted to reconcile with her in some way. But no, he hadn't come. He had been with Colette, she reminded herself with another wrenching sob. It was Colette's arms that held him, Colette's lips that touched his in passion. There was nothing she could do to change things. That was when she had hit upon the notion of returning to Seattle. She didn't know what she expected to do once she had arrived there, but she didn't care. She simply had to get away; to put as much distance as possible between herself and the man she still so desperately loved, the man she would always love, the man who had stolen her heart and then so cruelly trampled on it.

Rob stared across at her, taking note of the pensive

look on her face as she appeared to be lost in another world. He gazed at her in bemusement, as if seeing someone else, as if seeing her for the first time. There was something quite different about her this morning, a deep sadness in her beautiful green eyes, a new strength of will. He knew that she had been crushed by Jason's unwarranted treatment of her, and he silently cursed the man who had caused her such heartbreaking distress. If he believed it would do any good at all, he mused, he'd confront Jason Caldwell himself. He would never be able to understand why his old friend would jeopardize his relationship with a woman such as Hannah by having anything to do with that little vixen Colette. But what was done was done.

"You know I'll help you," Rob stated earnestly, finally breaking in on her silent reverie, knowing full well that he could deny her nothing. "You're not really foolish enough to believe that you could possibly have made it alone, are you?"

"I would have tried," Hannah answered him with a faint smile.

Later, as she and Rob were making their final preparations to leave, Hannah walked with Maggie outside to the hitching post in front of the boarding-house. It was obvious to Hannah that her friend still firmly believed the journey to be a disastrous mistake, and she steeled herself when Maggie decided to try once more to dissuade her young friend from running away.

"Hannah, please don't go," she pleaded, gazing deeply into the younger woman's eyes. "I know things look pretty bad. I'll grant you that, but you don't know that they're beyond repair! You must wait until you've had a chance to talk to your husband again. Believe me, child, you'll always regret it if you leave like this!"

"No!" Hannah was vehement. "There's nothing more to be said between Jason and myself, Maggie. Not after last night. He isn't the man I thought him to be. He accused me of unfaithfulness with your son, while shamelessly flaunting his adulterous relationship with that woman. Surely you must see that there is no longer any hope for me." She demanded, looked at Maggie miserably with pain-filled eyes. She was dressed in a dark wool dress and cloak, her shining curls swept upward most severely. Indeed, Maggie reflected, Hannah appeared as if in mourning, particularly with that look of unhappy despair on her face, the dull light in her green eyes.

"But you still love him, don't you?" Maggie asked quietly, placing her hands on Hannah's shoulders and facing her with a searching look in her own eyes. "You still love the man, don't you?"

Hannah's gaze fell before that look, hot color flooding her face as she was obviously reluctant to answer. It surprised her that the tears still came so readily to her eyes, since she had believed it virtually impossible to cry any more than she already had. But she finally glanced up at Maggie and murmured in a barely audible voice, "Yes. Yes, I still love him."

"Then what in heaven's name are you doing? You can't go away now, don't you see that? You have to stay and talk to your husband," Maggie commanded sternly.

"No, Maggie. I can't face him again. Not now, not ever again! I love him, but my love is not enough. He doesn't love me. And, because of that, I can no longer remain. I cannot face the prospect of living with a man who doesn't really care for me, who doesn't even have the decency to respect our marriage vows. I'm going to Seattle."

"And just what are you planning to do there? What is waiting for you there, if you don't mind my asking?" Maggie inquired heatedly, growing quite angry now. She hated seeing two young people she truly loved destroying the rest of their lives so easily!

"I don't know!" Hannah cried in response. "I don't know what I'm hoping to find there, but I certainly know what I'm leaving here. I've been a fool, Maggie, an absolute fool! I was childish enough to believe that I could actually marry a man I didn't know, that we could find happiness together. Well, evidently I was quite mistaken, despite all my girlish hopes and dreams." She turned and went back inside the house. Several minutes later, she emerged, clutching her carpetbag in one hand. Rob walked beside her, but he left her alone with his mother on the front steps as he moved forward to see to the horses.

Hannah hesitated before glancing up into Maggie's disapproving features. She suddenly reached out and hugged the older woman, then descended the steps swiftly and allowed Rob to assist her in mounting. She turned back to Maggie for an instant.

"Good-bye, Maggie. Thank you for all you've done for me. I'll never forget your friendship or your kindness. I hope we see one another again someday."

"That's not very likely, now, is it?" Maggie responded, then relented enough to add, her own eyes brimming with tears, "Since there's no way you're going to listen to reason, I wish you luck. I've grown very fond of you, Hannah. I'll have you know that I intend to pray that you'll return." With that, she whirled about and disappeared inside the house, closing the door firmly behind her.

"You know she's only upset because you're leaving," Rob explained gently, smiling encouragingly across at her.

"I know," Hannah reassured him with a brief smile of her own, unable to prevent a tiny sigh as well. The two of them turned their mounts and rode away from the boardinghouse, the gray light of the cloudy morning matching Hannah's mood. It took all her resolve to keep from looking back, and she felt as if she were in some sort of trance as she and Rob soon left Red Creek far behind.

Almost exactly twenty-four hours later, Jason appeared on Maggie's doorstep. She answered his loud knock, then stood staring up at him in stunned astonishment when he announced that he had come to speak with his wife. As she remained speechless, he demanded irritably, "Tell her that I want to talk to her. I know what you must have heard, Maggie, but I'm not going to leave until I've spoken with my wife!" He appeared very tired, but he was clean-shaven and clad in freshly laundered shirt and trousers as well. "I'm warning you, Maggie, I'm not leaving here until I've seen Hannah!" he growled.

"Well!" Maggie spoke finally, crossing her arms against her ample chest and striking a post of righteous indignation. "So you've finally come to inquire about your wife, have you? Well, let me tell you, Jason Caldwell, you're an even bigger fool than I ever thought you to be!"

"What the hell are you talking about? All I want to do is talk to her, Maggie," he replied, striving to control his temper. "I know it's been a couple of days since . . . well, I'm sure you've heard everything by now. But I came as soon as I was able!"

"And what do you mean by that?" she demanded, allowing his entry into the house now. He strode inside and hastily scanned the interior for any sign of Hannah.

"I couldn't come here before now because I was dead drunk!" he answered between clenched teeth. "I was drunker than I've ever been in my entire life, Maggie Clancy, and I've been literally out of my head! Now, are you going to tell Hannah that I'm here, or am I going to have to go and find her for myself?"

"Were you with that little whore all this time?" Maggie asked rudely. "Because, if you were, I've got a few choice words to say to you!"

"I wasn't with Colette at all!" Jason thundered, growing impatient with the woman's persistent questioning. "I told you, I've been drunk for two days now. Not that it's any of your business, but I haven't even laid eyes on Colette since the night Hannah—"

"She isn't here," Maggie interrupted.

"What do you mean by that?"

"Just what I said. She isn't here. If only you had had the good sense to come after her that night, you might have been able to work things out. But, it's too late now. She's gone."

"Where is she?" he demanded, a gnawing fear growing in the pit of his stomach. It couldn't be true! he told himself. He couldn't be too late! Not when he had finally come to his senses, not when he had finally come to realize what a damned idiot he had been about Hannah and Rob! He knew she was innocent. It had hit him the other night. He would never be able to forget the pain and disappointment in her green eyes, the look of utter

224

despair on her beautiful face. No, and he'd never forgive himself for causing her such grief, for ever doubting her.

It had taken these past few miserable days and nights to make him see things more clearly, to make him realize that he was in love with his own wife! He loved her more than he ever believed possible. He knew she could never play him false. And he now silently prayed that he wasn't too late to tell her so. He had vowed that he would spend the rest of his life making it up to her if only he could persuade her to come back to him. He had to make her believe what had happened to him, that he had changed, that her love had finally broken through all the barriers he had erected so long ago.

"She's gone back to Seattle."

"Alone?" he asked in amazement, fear clutching at his heart.

"No, of course not!" she quickly retorted. "Rob agreed to take her. She asked him to, Jason," she added meaningfully.

"Rob again! Your son is going to pay dearly this time for his damned interference!" So, he thought, his lips compressing into a thin line of fury, Hannah and Rob had gone to Seattle. Together. Just the two of them alone out there somewhere right now. It was enough to make his blood boil, and his jealousy now raged unrestrainedly within him once more.

"It wasn't his fault!" Maggie answered hotly. "If you hadn't accused your wife of betraying you, if you hadn't made it a point of seeing that painted hussy again, none of this would have happened! All of this is your own fault, and you know it. You have only yourself to blame," she remarked with a brisk nod in his direction. "And why are you here now? Did you come to hurt that poor little girl again, to twist her heart some more?" she demanded furiously.

"I came to beg her forgiveness!" he responded with a short, humorless laugh, a savage look on his handsome face, his blue eyes turning cold. "I came to tell her that I've come to realize how much I love her. Isn't that amusing, Maggie? I've finally come to love a woman again, and for what? So she can betray me, so she can grind my heart into the dirt?" he raged.

"You know Hannah would never do that! She loves you. She told me so herself. Even after she believed you had been carrying on with Colette again, she could still stand there and admit that she loves you. First you accused her of being unfaithful; then you turned right around and made it seem as if you were guilty of the very thing you accused her of. She had been waiting for you to come, waiting and worrying and fretting these past several days. And, then what happens? She finds you in a saloon with a painted slut on your lap!" she spoke accusingly, confronting him with flashing eyes and an anger to match his.

"Colette means nothing to me, and you damn well know it. I was only having a few drinks that night. There's not been anything between Colette and me for a long time now. I was planning on coming here to see my wife that night," he attempted to explain, though he cursed himself silently for doing so. Maggie was making him feel like a naughty schoolboy! Added to that was the uncomfortable sensation of the jealousy still raging within him at the thought that Hannah was with Rob at that very moment, that she had left town without even bothering to tell him. He had forgotten what sheer, hellish torture loving someone could be!

"And you had to bolster up your courage with whiskey, is that it?" Maggie demanded with a mocking look, breaking in on his turbulent thoughts. "You should never have let her go in the first place! You should never have allowed your jealousy and suspicions to run away with you. I don't know what's made you this way, Jason, but you've broken that poor girl's heart. And, what's more, you've let her leave here thinking that you don't give a damn about her!"

"And whom did my wife leave here with?" Jason countered, the truth of Maggie's words stinging him more than he cared to admit. "With your son, that's who! I'm telling you now, Maggie, he's going to pay mightily for his interference between Hannah and me once I catch up with them!"

"Oh, and so you're going after them? Why?" she shot at him.

"Because . . . because—" he angrily searched for words.

"Because you love your wife. Because you cannot live without her and you know it! Forget those foolish notions that there just might be something between her and Rob. Wake up, man! The girl loves you with all her heart! My son is nothing more than a friend to her. That's all he ever could be. It's you she loves. And, if you love her as you say, you'll not let that jealousy of yours ruin things again!"

"Friend or not, there's going to be hell to pay for them both when I find them!" Jason spun about on his booted heel and stalked from the house. He couldn't know that Maggie's mouth twitched after he had gone, that the corners turned up into a broad smile.

227

Jason mounted his horse and set off after Hannah and Rob, knowing well the route they would be taking to reach Seattle. There would be hell to pay, all right! he repeated to himself in silence as he spurred the animal onward at a furious pace. Rob Clancy would be made to realize that he couldn't get away with taking off with another man's wife!

And, as for Hannah, he thought with a ferocious scowl, he wanted to wring her beautiful little neck for the hell she was putting him through! He loved her—loved her more than life itself—but he was furious with her for running away without a word. Oh, yes, he reflected grimly, the two of them—both Rob and Hannah—were in for a few surprises when he found them!

Eighteen

Before the end of the first day of her journey, Hannah had already begun to regret her impulsive decision to leave Red Creek. She missed Jason more with each passing minute, realizing that she was traveling farther and farther away from him with each mile she and Rob traversed. But, whenever she was tempted to entertain the notion of returning, Colette's detestable image would flash unbidden into her mind, and she would press on grimly toward Seattle.

It rained frequently throughout the first two days, but it had been a miserable trip for Hannah for other reasons than the drizzling, soaking rain that dampened her spirits as well as her clothing. She and Rob spoke little to one another, though Rob did cheerfully attempt conversation on several occasions. However, his traveling companion was in no mood to respond to his inconsequential chatter. When it came time to make camp that first evening, the two of them were both drooping with exhaustion, and even Rob was given to uncharacteristic silence as they managed to build a fire and cook their meal of salt pork and beans.

However, something quite unexpected occurred on

the last evening before they were to reach their proposed destination. They had made camp for the night, and Hannah was seated on the ground before the glowing warmth of the fire, her eyes fixed unseeingly on the flickering light as darkness fell about them. Rob was lounging a few feet away, his own gaze fastened on Hannah's lovely face. When she raised her eyes suddenly to his, she caught her breath involuntarily at what she saw there, unprepared for the unabashed desire in his intense gaze. She looked hastily to the fire again, but Rob covered the short distance between them quickly and drew her into his arms.

"Rob!" Hannah exclaimed in breathless surprise, squirming to free herself from his embrace. "Rob, what do you think you're doing?"

"Hannah, I've been biding my time for so long now, I cannot wait any longer!" he declared passionately, easily maintaining his tight hold on her. Her hair came tumbling out of its pins in the midst of their struggle, and its luxuriant, flowing tresses fanned about Hannah's face and shoulders as she pushed against Rob, her bosom heaving and her cheeks flaming with bright color.

"Rob, you can't do this!" she protested vigorously, her struggles intensifying as his lips now roamed feverishly across her face, his arms pressing her intimately against his masculine form. She could feel the panic rising deep within her, and she frantically sought to reason with him. "Rob, you are my friend! I trusted you! Don't do this!" she cried breathlessly, twisting her head from side to side in a futile attempt to escape the lips now ruthlessly descending upon hers. She screamed deep in her throat, his surprisingly strong arms like bands of steel about her softness as his lips moved demandingly upon her unwilling mouth.

"Oh, Hannah, if you only knew what torture it has been—" He whispered against her lips. When one of his hands moved to clutch at her breast, Hannah reacted violently, pushing against him with all her might, causing him to lose his precarious balance and tumble backward toward the fire.

"Rob!" she squealed in stunned horror as she watched him roll directly into the path of the flames. But he was miraculously unscathed when he regained his footing on the other side of the fire, his damp clothing fortunately providing a protective shield against the burning heat.

"What did you do that for?" he demanded angrily, rising to his feet and glaring at her as he hastily dusted the dirt and ashes from his shirt and trousers. His attractive countenance wore a rather childish expression of displeasure.

"You're very fortunate that I didn't do even more!" Hannah retorted, her green eyes flashing. "How dare you attack me that way!"

"I wasn't attacking you," he denied mulishly, though his gaze fell before hers. In all actuality, he was beginning to feel more than a trifle ashamed for his rough actions.

"Well, I don't know precisely what you would call it, but you certainly had no right to manhandle me in that fashion!" She had regained her composure and was trying valiantly to bring some semblance of order to her unruly curls. Suddenly she felt laughter welling up within her as it struck her how perfectly ludicrous the situation was, but she stifled any outburst of amusement as she demanded sternly, "Why did you do it?"

"I guess I just lost my head," Rob mumbled, taking a seat on the ground once more and running his fingers

231

distractedly through his hair.

"I've heard that rather lame explanation once before, remember?" Hannah sat down across from him, deciding it wiser to keep the blazing fire between them. "Oh, Rob," she remarked with a heavy sigh, all anger evaporating as she viewed his obvious embarrassment, "let's just try and forget that it ever happened."

"I can't do that!" he replied feelingly, raising his eyes to hers as the firelight played across his face. "I know you find it difficult to take me seriously, Hannah. After all, I'm not exactly the solemn type of man you've been living with, am I? But, believe it or not, I think I've fallen in love with you!" He gazed at her with a lopsided grin, though his glowing eyes bespoke the gravity of his emotions.

"Don't be absurd!" Hannah admonished firmly. "You know I'm a married woman. And you know how I feel about Jason." Yes, she thought, how she would always feel about him. Nothing could ever truly destroy the love she held for him.

"But you won't be a married woman much longer, will you? Besides, that doesn't keep me from feeling the way I do about you." He seemed so much younger than Jason, Hannah mused suddenly, though they were about the same age.

She didn't want to take him seriously, so she said sternly, "I don't want to talk about this! I don't want to hear another word about it."

"You'll have to, sooner or later," Rob remarked with another disarming grin. "You'll have to face the facts once we reach Seattle. I'll give you until then to think about it. But, once we're there, I won't be put off so easily."

"Things won't change simply because we reach Seattle," Hannah insisted with a quelling frown. "Now, please, let's just forget any of this happened!" She had enough on her mind without having to think about Rob's foolish notions. It was easy enough for him to talk of falling in love, when he could have no true understanding of her own feelings for Jason. No, Rob couldn't possibly know what he was talking about. It was as he said, she reasoned with herself; he had simply lost his head for a brief instant. The two of them were alone together—completely alone in the middle of nowhere—and he had lost his head. It really didn't bear thinking of any longer, she now told herself with an air of dismissal, and she would attempt to put it entirely out of her mind.

They reached Seattle the following afternoon. Although Hannah was endeavoring to behave normally toward Rob, she could feel the tension mounting between them as they rode into the bustling center of activity. She reflected that Seattle was certainly worlds apart from the small town of Red Creek. There were people milling about everywhere, horses and wagons moving down the wide streets which were lined with wooden buildings on either side. The sun had broken through the cover of clouds less than an hour earlier, warming Hannah's face as she gazed about her with avid curiosity. Rob finally motioned for them to stop, and she pulled her horse to a halt beside his, raising her eyes to see that they were before a building with a sign that read "Hotel."

"Why are we stopping here?" Hannah asked, grateful to climb down from the saddle after so long. She glanced about at the people around them, noticing a few women amongst the predominantly male population. One or two of them seemed vaguely familiar to her, but she had no time to hail them as Rob took hold of her arm and propelled her up the steps and into the hotel.

"We're going to get some rooms first. Then we'll consider our future," Rob informed her with a quick smile. Hannah glanced up at him in suspicion, but she kept silent.

The desk clerk informed them that there was only a single room available, and that every other hotel in town was full up to the hilt. Rob paid for the room and told Hannah that he'd sleep at one of the bunkhouses farther down the street, then escorted her up the narrow, creaking staircase to the second floor of the hotel.

"Rob, if you don't mind, I think I'd like to try and get some rest now," Hannah announced wearily, pausing in the doorway of the room.

"Not until we've had a certain discussion," Rob answered with a slight shake of his head. He stepped inside the room, past a visibly disapproving Hannah, and turned back as he waited for her to enter.

"Rob, there's nothing to be said. I told you last night; I'm a married woman. This ridiculous idea of yours doesn't bear discussing!" she insisted, entering the room and closing the door behind her. "I'm too tired to talk about it now, anyway." She moved across the rather dusty, bare wooden floor and sank down onto the bed, the rusting springs squeaking noisily beneath her weight. There was only the iron bedstead, a chair, and a washstand in the small, airless room, and Hannah suddenly longed for the large, comfortable cabin she had been living in as Jason's wife.

"I've come to a decision," Rob continued relentlessly, taking a seat in the chair and facing her with a very somber expression on his usually smiling features. "I think we ought to get married."

"I'm already married!" Hannah pointedly reminded him, striving to keep control of her temper, tempted to scream at him. "But it wouldn't make any difference if I weren't. I still love Jason. I love him, no matter what he has done or will do."

"You can't really mean that, not after running away from him," Rob argued. "You know I've been attracted to you from the very beginning. It ought to flatter you that I've never before seriously contemplated the bonds of matrimony with any other woman," he commented ruefully, a twinkle of ironic amusement in his eyes. "Of course, we'll wait until you're free of Jason; then we can marry and return home. Or, if you prefer, we'll go someplace else. It doesn't really matter to me," he added with a shrug of his shoulders.

"Rob!" Hannah cried in total exasperation. "Haven't you heard anything I've said? I am married to Jason Caldwell. I love him. I left Red Creek for reasons you probably will never be able to understand. I am indeed quite honored by your proposal, but I really can't take you seriously. After all, can you honestly sit there and tell me that you love me with all your heart?"

"I think so," he responded evasively. "I'm almost certain that I do. Anyway, I think we'd suit one another very well. My mother adores you, you know!" he remarked with a broad grin, then sobered quickly. "Hannah, I think it's about time I started thinking about settling down with someone, and you're the first woman I've ever met who could possibly deal with me as a husband. I realize you're still suffering under the delusion that you're in love with Jason, but you'll get over it in time. And I'm convinced that we'll come to care for one another even more as time passes. All in all, I think it's an admirable solution to all our problems!" he concluded, much pleased with himself.

"I'm truly sorry, Rob," Hannah told him in a low, quiet voice as she met his gaze squarely, "but it simply won't work. I don't love you. You don't love me. Though I didn't marry for love, I came to love my husband very much. Whether you believe it or not, I shall always love him. He'll always be the only man in the world for me."

"Then why did you leave Red Creek? Why did you insist that I bring you here to Seattle?"

"Because . . . because I couldn't bear the possibility of remaining a burden to a man who didn't return my love! I know it doesn't make any sense—it doesn't really make sense to me—but that's all I could think of after I saw him with Colette that night. He doesn't love me," she repeated sadly. "He doesn't even trust me. I couldn't bear to live like that for the rest of my life. So I felt I had to leave right away."

"What are you going to do now? You can't just sit here and brood about Jason Caldwell for the rest of your life!" Rob commented harshly. In truth, he was more than a little hurt by her refusal, though not quite as devastated as he had expected to be. Everything he had told her was the truth. He couldn't honestly say he loved her the way she wanted him to, but he was very fond of her—even liked her. He considered that more than enough basis on which to begin a marriage. All this talk of hers about undying love and devotion seemed utter nonsense to him!

"I'm going to have to find work first," she said, the determined gleam returning to her eyes. "Then I'll decide what to do once I've managed to put aside enough money to go somewhere else. Or, I might even decide to stay here. I don't know just yet, but I'm going to be independent!''

"And what about that husband you're so fond of?" he asked sarcastically. "Are you going to stay legally bound to him for the rest of your life, to remain his wife in name only? Are you really going to deny yourself any sort of happiness with someone else?"

"Jason will always be my husband," Hannah murmured. Closing her eyes for an instant, she leaned back against the iron bedpost. "If only he had trusted me, if only he hadn't gone running back to Colette. I don't think I'll ever be able to understand why he behaved the way he did. I suppose I'll never really know what turned him against women," she spoke with another sigh.

Rob stared at her with a strange look in his eyes for several long moments. He appeared to be hesitating about something, and the silence in the room grew increasingly heavy before he finally opened his mouth to speak.

"Hannah, there's something I think you should know." Her eyes flew open at his words, and she gazed at him with a puzzled expression on her face.

"What is it?" she asked.

"It's about Jason," he replied, then paused to take a deep breath before continuing. "I promised him I'd never tell a living soul what I'm about to tell you. Whatever else I may seem to be, I don't take lightly breaking a promise such as that. But, since it appears you won't be giving me the opportunity to make you forget him," he said with a twisted smile, "I may as well tell you. Maybe it will help you to stop torturing yourself, maybe not. But, nevertheless, I believe Jason is the way he is because of something that happened several years ago, when he was much younger and quite vulnerable. He was really quite an idealistic romantic then, you see. He strongly believed in love and marriage and the like. Until something occurred to tear apart all his hopes and dreams."

"It was a woman, wasn't it?" Hannah already felt certain of the answer.

"It most certainly was," he answered with a nod. "A very beautiful woman, according to Jason. He was in San Francisco when he met her. Seems that he was there on some kind of lumber deal. Anyway, her name was Elizabeth Lewis. At least, that's what she was calling herself at the time. I don't recall precisely how she and Jason first encountered one another, but he fell head-over-heels in love with her right away. She assured him that she returned his regard, and they were soon engaged to be married. She told him some story about being of a respectable family who had fallen on hard times, that her poor old mother was ailing, that she was forced to work for meager wages to support them. She said she was working in a dress shop. Jason believed everything she told him," he remarked with a deep frown.

"Were they married?" Hannah asked him.

"No. Thank goodness it never came to that. You see, Jason, being the proud sort he is, told Elizabeth he wouldn't marry her until he had built her a fine cabin, until he had made a bigger success of his timber business first. He left San Francisco and returned home, promising to send his betrothed a sum of money every month in order to help her care for her mother. He intended to return in a year's time and claim her as his bride. He worked very hard, built the cabin, and sent her every bit of money he could spare. Several months passed, until the end of the year was nearing. But, totally besotted as he was, he decided impulsively to return to San Francisco a few weeks early and surprise Elizabeth. He went to her house—a boardinghouse where she had been living with her mother—to find her." He paused for a moment.

Hannah asked quietly, "And did he find her?"

"Yes. He found her, all right, but she wasn't alone. And it wasn't her dear old mother with her. It seems that his beautiful, supposedly innocent young fiancée was in bed with another man. Jason couldn't believe his eyes at first; but, when he realized that he wasn't mistaken, he exploded and dragged her lover from her arms and proceeded to beat the fellow. The man managed to gasp out that Elizabeth Lewis was nothing more than a whore, a confidence trickster who had led Jason on in order to get his money. She had planned to be gone by the time he returned. She herself admitted it to Jason, laughing at his shock and pain. She cruelly taunted him, driving him to further violence. He nearly killed the man, but Elizabeth pulled a gun on Jason. Jason was nearly out of his mind with pain and rage by this time, and he lunged for her, knocked the gun from her hand, then was attacked from behind by her lover. Somehow the fellow managed to free himself from Jason long enough to retrieve the gun, but the thing went off and the bullet struck Elizabeth instead. She died, cursing Jason to the very end as he and the other man watched in horror, shocked into immobility. Immediately after that, Jason became a madman. He caught her lover as the man was trying to escape, and he all but killed the man with his bare hands. The fellow was still alive, but only barely so."

"Oh, Rob!" Hannah murmured, her eyes brimming

with tears. "How horrible! How terrible it must have been for him." To think that the man she loved had been betrayed so cruelly. She could feel the pain he must have felt, and it was almost more than she could bear.

"Jason was forced to flee before there was any further trouble. He came home, but he wasn't the same after that, as you can well imagine. He was very embittered by the experience, and I remembered that he vowed never again to love anyone. He said he'd never lay himself open to being hurt like that again."

"Yes, I can imagine how he must have felt," Hannah whispered, half to herself. "No wonder he was unable to trust me, to allow me to get close to him. He's been haunted by that tragedy all these years."

"So now you can perhaps begin to understand why it's been so difficult for him to behave in what you believe to be normal fashion." Rob rose to his feet and stared out the single window.

"I can understand how he was so reluctant to trust me, but not why he betrayed me himself!"

"You mean Colette?"

"You know perfectly well that's who I mean!"

"In all honesty, my dear, I think you've placed far too much importance on that distasteful little scene. You really don't know whether Jason is guilty of much beyond a little dalliance with her, do you? And, even if he were, he might simply have lost his head for a moment, the way I nearly did last night," he attempted to reason, glancing across at her with a faint smile on his lips.

"That doesn't excuse it," Hannah said severely. She was still quite stunned by what Rob had told her. So many things began to be clear to her now. She had been fighting against a dead woman, a woman in Jason's past, a foe she realized to be the most difficult of all to combat. But, she thought, she knew she had reached Jason's heart, had at least started to make him forget his bitterness! She was convinced that she could have managed to bury the past if she had only been afforded more time. If only Jason hadn't gone running back to Colette. She knew things would have been entirely different if only fate had been a little kinder!

"I've told you all I know about it. I don't think it will change things," Rob remarked, heading for the door. "But I'll give you some time to rest and think things over. I'll be back in about an hour to take you to supper."

Hannah merely nodded in response, watching in silence as he left, closing the door softly behind him. She felt dazed by what Rob had told her, and she did need time to think. She closed her eyes again and lay back upon the lumpy mattress of the bed, a vision of Jason's handsome face as it must have looked those many years ago floating unbidden into her mind.

Rob returned an hour later, just as he had promised. He had washed the journey's dust away and changed into clean clothing, pleased when he saw the transformation Hannah had also managed to achieve in such a brief time. She had bathed herself as best she could, making use of the porcelain washbowl and sponge she had found on the washstand, then had donned a fresh cotton dress. She had brushed the tangles from her shining hair and pulled it back from her freshly scrubbed face with a blue ribbon. She still wore a look of preoccupation, but Rob took her arm and the two of them headed for the restaurant located next door.

It was very crowded in the noisy interior of the small building, and Rob was forced to make a path for them as he escorted Hannah to a vacant table in the far corner of the room. Smoke and the aroma of various foods mingled together to fill the air, and Hannah didn't fail to notice the heads that turned her way as she took a seat opposite Rob.

"I don't think we have much of a choice, but I was told that the food is quite edible here," Rob commented with a smile as his eyes hastily scanned the handwritten menu on the table.

"I'm really not very hungry," Hannah confessed. She was still rather distracted, but she nonetheless agreed to eat something, and Rob stared across at her, a worried frown creasing his brow. Neither of them saw the person who had come to stand beside their table until Rob happened to glance up and notice a young, decidedly attractive woman who was apparently waiting to take their order.

"What will it be, sir?" her soft, pleasant voice asked. She had yet to really look at either Rob or Hannah, and she experienced a mild shock as she finally raised her eyes to Rob's openly admiring ones. Meanwhile, Hannah immediately recognized the young woman's voice and she jumped to her feet with an exclamation of joy.

"Molly!"

"Hannah! Oh, Hannah, I can't believe it's you!" Molly cried, clasping her friend to her, her own face alight with pleasure. "What are you doing here? I thought you had gone!" The two young women were the objects of much attention, for they made quite a striking picture together. Rob was certainly unable to take his eyes off them while they alternately laughed and chatted.

"I've just arrived in Seattle again," Hannah told Molly, her smile fading.

"Oh?" Molly asked in confusion, her gaze drawn back to Rob. "Is this your husband, then?" She reflected that he didn't look at all like the man she had remembered seeing Hannah with all those weeks ago. He was still staring up at her in a most disturbing manner, and she admitted to herself that she was immensely flattered by his attention.

She was even more pleased when Hannah hastened to answer, "No, this is not my husband. This is a friend of mine, Rob Clancy." Rob rose to his feet and smiled broadly down into the upturned face of the petite Molly, who was dismayed to feel herself blushing beneath his scrutiny.

"I'm very pleased to make your acquaintance, Miss—" Rob's voice trailed off as he looked to Hannah with a question in his eyes.

"What is your last name now, Molly?" Hannah asked. The three of them sat down, though Molly cast a wary glance toward her employer. But, she was so overwhelmingly happy to see her friend once more that she decided to brave the consequences.

"Braden. Mrs. Jack Braden," Molly replied, a deep frown accompanying the admission. "Though I don't like to own up to the name. You see, I'm a widow now."

"Oh, Molly, I'm sorry!" Hannah declared, her eyes full of sympathetic concern. She stole a quick glance in Rob's direction, bemused when she spotted a rather odd expression on his face as he stared at Molly.

"There's nothing to be sorry about. I was taught not to speak ill of the dead, but—well, Jack Braden was nothing more than a no-account drunk! We were only married a week before he was killed in a tavern brawl."

"How terrible it must have been for you," Hannah

murmured. The thought crossed her mind that whatever else Jason Caldwell had done, he had never taken to drink.

"I didn't grieve for him, Hannah," Molly said, her glance shifting to Rob now and then. "But I'll tell you all about it later. If you don't mind my asking, where is your own husband?"

"Well, I . . . that is—" Hannah faltered, obviously uneasy about answering.

"Hannah's husband is not with us," Rob explained for her. "I imagine he's at his logging camp. We've only just arrived from Red Creek. I escorted Hannah here." He grinned disarmingly as Molly stared at him in confusion.

"What has happened?" Molly demanded gently as she turned back to Hannah, her eyes searching the other woman's face as she put a consoling hand on Hannah's arm. "Why are you here without him?"

"It's a very long, very complicated tale," Hannah replied with a catch in her voice.

"Nevertheless, I want to know. After all, we're friends, aren't we? But I suppose I'd best be getting back to work right now," Molly announced, rising to her feet. "I'll meet you later, at nine o'clock, out front. We've got a lot of catching up to do!" she added with a bright smile. Again, her gaze was drawn involuntarily to Rob, and he favored her with a slow, puzzling smile of his own.

At that moment, Molly's arm was gripped abruptly and she was spun roughly about to face her employer, a large, burly man well over six feet tall. His features were very coarse, his black hair and unkempt beard lending him a decidedly evil appearance as he glared down into Molly's startled face.

"I ain't paying you to sit and talk all night with the

customers!" he roared, administering a head-snapping shake to her shoulders. "Now, get back to work!" At least two of the men in the restaurant jumped to their feet, ready to come to Molly's defense, but Rob was there first, his hand reaching out to grasp the man's shirt front and pull him away from a frightened Molly.

"I don't think there's any reason to treat Mrs. Braden that way!" Rob declared courageously. The man was several inches taller and outweighed Rob by at least sixty pounds.

"Please, Mr. Clancy, it's all right!" Molly whispered frantically, trying to prevent what she was certain would be a dangerous situation for Rob.

"No, it damn sure ain't all right!" Molly's employer snorted angrily, knocking Rob's hand down and glaring menacingly into the younger man's casually smiling features. "You ain't got no right to interfere!" He'd seen the way Molly had been gawking at the fellow, and his jealousy spurred him onward. Since she'd have none of him, she'd certainly not get away with making eyes at this young stripling!

"Aw, come on, Slade!" one of the other men in the crowded room called out. "You ain't got no call to treat little Molly that way. Why, not a one of us would be eating in this danged-fool place of yours if it wasn't for her being here!" His statement was accompanied by laughter from several of the others, which only served to further infuriate the man known as Slade.

"Get the hell out of my place and don't show your face around here again!" Slade bellowed as Rob stood his ground. "We don't need your kind in here!" He glanced down at Hannah, who had been watching with widened eyes and breathless dismay. "And take your little trollop here with you!"

Molly gasped aloud at Slade's insulting words, and she stifled a scream as Rob's fist shot out and caught Slade on the jaw, causing him to stagger backward. Slade recovered quickly, returning with a bellow of rage, obviously ready to do battle. Hannah and Molly hastily moved into the corner out of the way, clinging to one another as they watched the two men struggle with one another. The other men in the room leaped to their feet in visible excitement, forming a ring around the two combatants, shouting encouragement to Rob as he sought to defend himself against the larger man.

"Oh, Hannah, Slade will surely kill him!" Molly cried desperately, wincing as she saw Rob endure a vicious jab to his chin.

"I wouldn't be so sure about that," Hannah sought to reassure her. "The man is obviously a lot slower on his feet than Rob, and Rob's much younger." She prayed that she was right, that Rob would manage to emerge the victor. Then she stifled a scream of her own as Rob was knocked to the floor. But he stood again and faced Slade with a determined light in his eyes. It was obvious that Slade was indeed beginning to tire, and Rob wisely took advantage as he suddenly lunged forward and landed a punch square in Slade's midsection, catching him totally by surprise. Slade collapsed, gasping loudly for breath, to the floor, unable to move. The onlookers cheered Rob for his victory, and he acknowledged their congratulations with a lopsided but painful grin. Hannah and Molly rushed forward simultaneously and assisted him from the restaurant as quickly as possible, fearing that Slade would soon recover and be ready to fight again.

"You were wonderful, Mr. Clancy!" Molly exclaimed

in wonder, gazing up into Rob's rather battered face with eyes round as saucers.

"That was a very foolish thing to do!" Hannah chided him.

"I couldn't very well allow that blustering idiot to treat your friend that way," Rob countered. "And I certainly couldn't allow him to call you a trollop, could I?" he asked with a mockingly raised eyebrow.

Hannah opened her mouth to reply, but abruptly clamped her mouth shut instead. Molly, on the other hand, continued to praise Rob for his courage and skill, and it was apparent to Hannah that he was enjoying every minute of it as the three of them made their way into the hotel and up the stairs to Hannah's room. After having his cuts and bruises tended to most solicitously by the two women, Rob took his leave, vowing to return early the next morning and treat them to breakfast.

Closing the door after him, Hannah turned back to Molly and said, "I want us to talk now, Molly. It seems like ages since I saw you last! So much has happened—to both of us, it seems." She sank down upon the bed, gesturing for Molly to sit beside her. The two of them talked far into the night. Molly told Hannah everything about the miserable, unhappy life she had led since coming to Seattle, the cruelty of her late husband, the many proposals she had received since being widowed, and her firm resolve never to marry again, except for love. Hannah, in turn, confided her own troubles, her own desperate situation.

Molly listened intently, and when Hannah had finished, advised her friend with heartfelt sincerity, "You must go back to him. You have to go back and face Jason."

"I can't do that!" Hannah protested vigorously. "He doesn't love me, Molly. If only he had been able to say he loved me, I might have been able to bear anything."

"I don't think you realize how much better off you are than the other brides I've seen or heard about. Most of them are happy enough, I suppose, but some of them have found only misery and unhappiness here. Believe me, Hannah, considering all you've told me, you ought to count yourself fortunate. And, since there is still a tiny shred of doubt in your mind about Jason and that Colette woman, you've got to give the man a chance to explain."

"He had plenty of time to explain. He could have come after me that night when I found him in the saloon with her, but he didn't," Hannah replied bitterly.

"You've still got to go back. I think you know it, too. You're still married to him. It isn't fair of you to run away without talking to him. You'll regret it the rest of your life if you don't go back." Molly climbed off the bed and strolled across the floor to gaze out the window. "As much as you say you love him, you have to try and work things out. From what you've told me about his past, your running away as you did might just seem like further betrayal to him. I think you can make him believe in love and happiness again, Hannah. Don't ruin that opportunity with your pride. I wish I'd had a chance to try and make some man happy. I didn't even have two weeks. And, it really wouldn't have mattered if I'd had more time," she remarked with a heavy sigh, her eyes full of sadness. "Jack wasn't at all like your husband. He said he sent away for a bride only because he was lonely, because he wanted a woman. He didn't know the first thing about kindness or gentleness or love."

Hannah looked at her friend, Molly's words affecting

her more than she cared to admit. The two of them finally went to sleep after that, awakened the following morning by Rob's insistent knock on the door. He waited rather impatiently for the two women to dress, then gallantly escorted them to breakfast at a restaurant farther down the street. When they had finished the meal, Molly pressed her friend once more to make a decision, urging her to return to Red Creek.

Rob startled them by adding, "Yes, and I think you should come along with us, Mrs. Braden."

"You can't be serious, Mr. Clancy! What on earth would I do there?" Molly exclaimed with a disbelieving laugh. However her heart beat a little faster at his suggestion.

"Why, that's an excellent idea!" Hannah agreed enthusiastically. "I'm sure Molly can work for Maggie at the boardinghouse. Maggie will definitely welcome the female company."

"Of course she will," Rob stated with a brisk nod. "And, besides," he added with a rueful grin, "I don't think your job at Slade's will be waiting for you after last night." He grinned again in that disarming manner of his, causing Molly's heart to flutter. After that, it didn't require much persuasion to finally convince her to accompany them. It was only after they had settled that particular matter that Hannah realized she had just committed herself to returning to Red Creek, to returning to face Jason. The prospect frightened her, but it was also a relief. She knew she couldn't truly rest until things had been settled between them, one way or the other. It had taken these past few days to convince her of that.

As the three of them left the restaurant, Rob turned to

Hannah and informed her that he was escorting Molly to her boardinghouse to fetch her things. Hannah told them she would wait for them in her room at the hotel, and she continued in that direction alone.

She was just passing the building located next to the hotel when someone took hold of her unexpectedly and forced her bodily into the narrow space between the two buildings, out of sight of the other people moving about the streets. She opened her mouth to scream, but a large hand was clamped across her lips, and she gasped in rising terror as the unknown man pulled her far back into the shadows.

Nineteen

"I've been waiting all morning for you! Where the hell have you been?" A deep, familiar voice close to her ear caused Hannah's eyes to fly wide open in astonishment, her struggles ceasing abruptly. The hand was removed from her mouth, and she was turned about roughly to face the scowling countenance of her husband, his blue eyes smoldering down at her.

"Jason!" she breathed in mingled relief and joy, unable to believe her eyes. "What are you doing here?" When he didn't answer immediately, she demanded, "Why did you find it necessary to frighten me that way?" She pulled away from him in angry indignation, but his arm remained like a band of steel about her waist. Her thoughts were a veritable tumult in her mind as she asked herself how he could be here in Seattle when she had left Red Creek only a few short days ago, why he had come, why he was obviously so angry with her.

But she had no further time to try and sort out such questions. Jason lowered his head until his face was mere inches from her own, his steely gaze boring into her green eyes, his voice demanding furiously, "Why did you do it, Hannah? You didn't even bother to tell me you were leaving! I've been looking for you all over this blasted town, after tracking you and Rob for days now. And I discover that you and Rob Clancy are sharing a room here at the hotel!" he shouted, jerking his head toward the building a few feet away. His eyes narrowed in suppressed fury, while Hannah gasped aloud at his words.

"Sharing a room? We most certainly are not! Where on earth did you get such a ridiculous idea?"

"The man there told me that you and Rob had come in together, that Rob signed his name to the register. Did you really believe I wasn't going to find out about this? Did you really think I was a big enough fool not to be able to figure out what was going on after the two of you spent these past few days and nights alone together out there?" he lashed out, his voice low and scathing.

"I wouldn't expect you to be able to understand, but Rob Clancy has been a perfect gentleman to me these past few days!" Hannah declared, dismayed to feel herself blushing as she suddenly recalled Rob's momentary madness that last night before they reached Seattle. She raised her chin defiantly when Jason studied her with a visibly relentless suspicion. "You're always prepared to jump to the wrong conclusions, aren't you? Well, for your information, Rob is spending his nights in a bunkhouse down the street. The room is for my use alone!"

"I expected you to deny everything!" Jason replied caustically.

"I deny it because it isn't true! And just who are you, Jason Caldwell, to be standing here accusing me of anything? When last I saw you, you were being very well entertained by a certain woman named Colette!" Hannah was grateful that he had come after her, yet still very hurt that he was still refusing to believe her innocence. Her heart cried out to him to say something—anything—in his own defense, and for him to believe her denial concerning Rob.

Jason removed his arm from about her waist and took a step backward, though he kept a firm hand on her upper arm. She hung back, not at all certain what he intended to do next, and she protested when he began pulling her forcibly along with him, out of the shadows and into the light once more.

"What are you doing? Where are we going?" she demanded angrily.

"This isn't the sort of thing I want to talk about here in the streets. We're going up to your room—the room you claim is yours alone—and have this out between us!" His boots clumped noisily on the wooden boardwalk as he pulled her inside the hotel and up the stairs, finally halting before the door to her room. Hannah eyed him in obstinate defiance for a moment, before drawing out the key and unlocking the door with hands that were not quite steady. She found herself being pushed inside unceremoniously while Jason slammed the door behind them.

"Now," he began, tossing his hat on the bed and frowning as Hannah presented her back to him as she took up a rigid stance at the window, "I want some answers, and I want them to be the truth!"

"I have never lied to you about anything!" Hannah insisted furiously, whirling about to face him, her green eyes flashing. "Which is certainly more than I can say for you!"

"I never lie," he spoke between clenched teeth, his

handsome face suffused with a dull color, his own eyes gleaming dangerously. "I've never pretended to be anything other than what I am!"

"Then I suppose it's simply in your nature to spend your evenings sitting in a saloon with a—a creature like Colette on your lap, while your own wife is worrying herself sick because she hasn't even heard from you in days!" Hannah snapped accusingly, confronting him with heightened color in her own face.

"I don't want to get into that just yet!" Jason thundered, striding forward to tower above her at the window. "I want to know why the hell you left Red Creek, why you ran away without even bothering to tell me that you were leaving, or where in blazes you were headed!"

"I should think that would be quite clear to you by now! How could I stay there after you had humiliated me that way? I waited for you," she told him, her eyes filling with tears. "I stayed there at Maggie's and waited for word from you—any indication that you still cared about me. I received an entirely opposite indication when I spotted you with Colette that night!"

"You had no right to run away. You are my wife. You don't have any right to take off like you did whenever you feel like it, no matter what the reason!" Jason actually felt ashamed when he realized what he must have put Hannah through because of that inconsequential incident with Colette—an incident which Hannah apparently believed to hold far more importance. He finally relented enough to add, "There wasn't anything going on between Colette and me. I was having a few drinks in the saloon when you happened by. There was absolutely nothing for you to get so all-fired upset about!"

"It certainly looked like something to me!"

"Well, whether it did or not, you shouldn't have run away. And you shouldn't have gone off with Rob, of all people! Damn it, Hannah! Don't you have any better sense than to take off with another man, particularly that man? What was I supposed to think when I found out the two of you had run off together, headed for Seattle?" He glared down into her upturned face.

"You could have trusted me as far as Rob was concerned! That day up at the logging camp, you could have listened to me. I've never given you any reason to doubt me, Jason. And, after all those terrible things you said to me, the hateful way you accused me, I found you sitting with another woman on your knee in a saloon!"

"I told you Colette doesn't enter into any of this!"

"And neither does Rob!"

"He was kissing you, damn it!" Jason growled, his hands moving to her shoulders, gripping her soft flesh with bruising intensity. "How was I supposed to react when I found another man kissing my wife?"

"You might have tried believing me when I told you there was nothing for you to be jealous about. You might have tried listening to Rob when he told you that I had nothing to do with his foolish actions! The man grabbed me and kissed me before I even knew what was happening!" she declared passionately, one hand moving to her face to dash away the angry tears.

"And just why would he feel compelled to do something like that in the first place? You're telling me that you never offered him any encouragement?" Jason asked, his eyes narrowing again as his fingers clutched painfully at her shoulders.

"Of course not! I don't know why he did it. He claimed

he had simply lost his head for a moment. Whatever his reasons, I most certainly did not encourage him!" She attempted to pull away, but he held fast to her, and she gazed up at him with a pained expression on her lovely face. "Why did you say those things to me, Jason? How could you have doubted me? I loved you—I tried my best to make you a good wife. Why couldn't you have tried to believe me? Why did you have to allow your jealousy and anger to blind you to the truth?" The tears coursed silently down her flushed cheeks now, but she ignored them as she looked at him, as he stared back at her in silence. He suddenly dropped his hands from her and moved away, presenting his back to her as he stepped slowly across to the bed. He put a hand out to the iron bedpost, gripping it with clenched fingers before replying, his voice sounding strained and distant,

"I don't know, Hannah. God help me, but I don't know why." He allowed his hand to drop to his side once more, and his face wore an unfathomable expression. It was as if his fury had run its course, as if he were suddenly drained and weary.

Hannah sighed heavily, staring out the window with unseeing eyes. She hesitated only a moment before moving to pause behind Jason, her gaze softening as she put a hand to his arm, touching him gently as she spoke very quietly.

"I think I know why. I think I began to understand—at least a little—when Rob told me about Elizabeth." She was startled when he spun around to face her, his features tightening in anger again.

"Rob? What did he tell you?"

"As much as he knew, I suppose. About how she betrayed you. About how very much you loved her.

About how young and—"

"He swore never to tell anyone!" Jason interrupted, his fury with Rob quite evident.

"He told me because he knew how heartsick I was over the way you had treated me!" Hannah retorted defensively. "He knew I couldn't understand why you didn't trust me, why you were so bitter. He was right to tell me." She gazed up into his face with softly pleading eyes, asking him silently to put aside his anger and speak to her about what she had learned from Rob.

"I didn't want you to know about her," Jason murmured gruffly, his voice barely audible as he hastily averted his eyes.

"I'm glad I know. Oh, Jason!" Hannah breathed, sounding rather forlorn, "I love you! I'll always love you! I might as well admit that here and now. It doesn't matter about anyone else. I know I can help you forget about all the pain and bitterness if only you'll allow me to. I know I can free you of this thing that has haunted you for so long!" She was looking at him with shining eyes, her expression loving and earnest. Jason responded by reaching out and drawing her against him, burying his face in her hair. Hannah clasped him tightly about the waist, her face snuggling against his muscular chest.

They remained like that for several long seconds, before Jason said, "Hannah, I didn't realize how much you really meant to me until I thought I had lost you. That night in the saloon, I was there having a few drinks to bolster up my courage, that's all. I was coming to see you, to try and beg your forgiveness for the stupid way I acted up at the camp about you and Rob. You see, the more I thought about it, the more I realized that you couldn't be guilty of those things I accused you of. I realized something else, too," he told her, drawing away a bit and staring deep into her eyes.

"What, Jason?" Hannah whispered expectantly, a tremulous smile on her lips.

"I realized that I love you. I thought I'd never love again, but I do. I love you more than I could ever have loved Elizabeth or anyone else, more than I ever believed possible!" he declared huskily, his head descending swiftly as he took her lips with his own. When he raised his head reluctantly, crushing her tightly against him, he murmured in a shaken voice, "I didn't want to love you. I never wanted to allow anyone to become so important to me again. But, from the first moment I set eyes on you, I fought against it in vain!"

"Oh, Jason, I know I shouldn't have run away!" Hannah exclaimed, her eyes shining with her love for him. "I didn't want to go, not really. But I was so hurt by what I believed to be your involvement with that woman. And, well, after she came to see me that day and told me what the two of you had once meant to one another—"

"What are you talking about?" he broke in with a puzzled frown.

"Colette came to see me at Maggie's earlier that day. She told me you and she had been lovers, that you would soon be lovers again. What else was I to believe when I saw the two of you together in her saloon that same night? It appeared to me as if she had won, as if she had indeed been telling me the truth about everything. I'm sorry I doubted you, sorry I didn't wait for you to explain; but all I could think about was the two of you together. And then, when you didn't come after me that night, I thought it was hopeless for us."

"I didn't come because I was too damned ashamed!"

Jason admitted with a short laugh. "I knew you were right. Everything you said to me cut me right to the core. I knew I'd been a fool about you and Rob. I couldn't bear the way you looked at me. I stayed there at the saloon and drank myself into a stupor. I went to Maggie's as soon as I sobered up again, but you had already gone. I went nearly mad with worry and jealousy when I discovered you had left with Rob and headed for Seattle!"

"But Jason, I asked him to take me. He didn't really want to," Hannah hastened to explain. "Truly, Rob isn't to blame for any of this. Unless, of course, you count that harmless little kiss he forced on me up at the camp that day. It certainly didn't mean anything to me. He's a good friend, and that's all he could ever be. But—" her expression grew somber again—"about Elizabeth—"

"I think I've allowed her to ruin enough of my life," he remarked grimly, placing a finger upon Hannah's parted lips. "The past needs to be buried, Hannah, once and for all. I have you now. I love you—love you with all my heart. I'm going to try my best to make things up to you, you know. I'm going to try and put aside all that pain and bitterness and distrust I've been holding onto all these years."

"We've both been too ready to believe the worst of one another," Hannah told him after a short, thoughtful silence. "I'm sorry I ran away, but I had already made the decision to return. In fact, we were planning to leave for Red Creek tomorrow morning."

"We?" Jason asked disapprovingly.

"Yes, Rob and myself," she replied with a twinkle of mischief in her eyes, then smiled at his fierce expression, "and Molly."

"And who is Molly?"

"A very dear friend of mine from the ship. She's agreed to come to Red Creek with us. But I'll tell you all about her later. For now, I'd like to concentrate on my reunion with my husband!" Hannah declared with a saucy smile. She was rewarded when Jason kissed her again, his strong arms tightening about her until they were molded perfectly against one another. He protested when she pulled away suddenly, glancing up at him with an expression of utter dismay on her face.

"Oh, Jason, I forget all about Molly and Rob! They'll be returning here before much longer!"

"Then we'll simply have to lock the door," he replied masterfully, releasing her long enough to stride to the door and turn the key.

"But, they'll become worried if they return and I don't answer—" He faced her again with a certain gleam in his blue eyes that caused all further thought of Molly and Rob to flee her mind, and she welcomed him back into her arms as his lips captured hers and he bore her backward to the bed.

Several minutes later, the two of them had divested themselves of the last remaining barriers of clothing, and Hannah gloried in the words of loving endearment Jason whispered in her ear, the rapturous way his hands moved demandingly upon her soft, trembling curves. Her slender fingers entwined in his thick hair when his warm lips moved to her round breasts, and she moaned softly as his fingers touched her gently between her thighs, tenderly stroking. She grew emboldened enough to return his caresses, and her hand closed around his throbbing manhood, prompting him to groan aloud at the delicious torture. She gasped when she suddenly felt Jason rolling over on his side, his strong arms clasping her securely against him until he lay upon his back and she was atop him.

"Jason!" she breathed in laughing surprise. "What are you doing?" She was a little embarrassed by the position in which she found herself, and she tried to move, but he held her fast.

"Be quiet, woman!" he growled in mock sternness, silencing her protests with his mouth. She ceased to struggle as she felt the flaming passion building to a fever pitch within her again, as she and Jason became one, their bodies and their spirits joined together as they soared higher and higher.

When the storm of desire had passed, Hannah lay warm and contented in her husband's arms. He spoke quietly to her, telling her more about his mysterious past, baring his soul to her as never before. She listened intently, laughing softly when she finally came to the part concerning herself.

"I can't even begin to tell you how much I wanted to dislike you! I resented that Ted had made me give him that promise. I was prepared to find fault with you in every way. But all my plans and ideas were ruined from the first moment I saw you up there on that platform!" Jason told her with a soft chuckle, hugging her to him as his lips gently brushed her forehead. "You were so damned pretty, so young and determined. I guess I never even had a chance against you, did I?" he asked her in fond amusement, glancing down at her with a loving twinkle in his blue eyes.

"Never!" Hannah shook her head. "I wasn't prepared for you, either, Jason Caldwell. You were the handsomest man I had ever seen, and yet you were so cold and forbidding. There were times when I nearly despaired, nearly lost all hope of your loving me," she recalled with a tiny sigh as she trailed a finger up and down his muscular chest. The sunlight was streaming in through the lone window, but the two of them lost all track of time as they talked. They were startled when the knock sounded at the door. Hannah abruptly drew away from Jason and clutched the covers to her bosom instinctively, while Jason climbed swiftly from the bed, his handsome face wearing a fierce frown as he pulled on his trousers.

"I suppose your friends have returned," he remarked, obviously quite annoyed at the interruption.

"I'm only glad they didn't return before now!" Hannah whispered in response, stifling a giggle as she watched Jason wrestle with his clothing.

"Just a moment!" she called out, bouncing off the bed and dressing as quickly as possible. It wasn't long until she opened the door to admit Molly and an obviously impatient Rob.

"What the devil took you so long?" he asked, striding into the room, his arms laden with Molly's things. He came to an abrupt halt, his face wearing an almost ludicrous expression of astonishment when he spied a darkly scowling Jason standing near the bed.

"I want to have a word with you, Clancy!" Jason glared across at the other man. Molly eyed the handsome stranger fearfully, while Hannah hurried to explain.

"Molly, this is my husband, Jason. Jason, I'd like you to meet Molly Braden." She glanced from Jason to Rob and back with a worried look.

Hannah was relieved when Jason turned to Molly and responded politely, "I'm very pleased to make your acquaintance. But I'm afraid you two ladies will have to excuse Mr. Clancy and myself. We have a few things to discuss."

"Jason—" Hannah pleaded, throwing him an anxious glance.

"I'm sure our discussion can wait a bit longer," Rob remarked, returning to Molly's side nonchalantly.

"No!" Jason shouted, striving to keep his temper under control. He jerked his head toward the doorway. Rob shrugged as he put Molly's belongings on the floor, deciding evidently to bow to the inevitable as he preceded Jason from the room. "This won't take long," Jason reassured his wife on his way out. She merely nodded slowly in response, realizing it was useless to try and argue with him.

"Hannah, what is your husband doing here? And why is he so angry with Mr. Clancy?" Molly rushed to ask as the door closed behind the two men.

"He came after me, Molly. He came to tell me that he loves me!" Hannah replied with a bright smile. Not even her concern over what was happening between Jason and Rob could dampen the joy she was feeling.

"Then, if everything has worked out between you, why in heaven's name is he still apparently so furious with Rob?" Molly demanded, a worried frown on her attractive features.

"I'm not really sure, but it's something they'll have to settle between themselves. All we can do is wait for them to return. Come, let's sit down and I'll tell you more about what's happened between myself and Jason." She noticed that Molly's eyes shifted to the door on more than one occasion as she spoke, and she was herself much relieved when the two men returned less than half an hour later. She gave silent thanks when she noted that neither Rob's nor Jason's face bore any visible signs of a battle between them.

"We'll be leaving for home at dawn tomorrow morning," Jason announced casually as Hannah moved to his side. She was anxious to learn precisely what had occurred between Jason and Rob, but realized she would have to be patient.

"Are you all right?" Molly quietly asked Rob as she went to him.

"Fine, just fine," he replied lightly, grinning down at her. His eyes moved to Hannah's, and she gave him a questioning look. But her attention returned to Jason when he suggested that the four of them get something to eat, after which they would begin making preparations for the journey ahead—a journey the four of them were looking forward to for various reasons of their own.

Twenty

Jason, Hannah, Rob, and Molly stopped to make camp in the late afternoon of their first day out from Seattle. The skies were gray and overcast, the air cool and humid as they dismounted and gratefully stretched their legs after spending so much time in the saddle. Fortunately they had made very good time, pausing only briefly a few times throughout the day to rest and water the horses. There hadn't been much time for idle conversation, since Jason had set the brisk pace.

Hannah glanced at her husband as she swung down from the saddle, giving him a warm smile. She had not been afforded an opportunity to speak with him alone again since the previous day. He had spent the night at the same bunkhouse where Rob slept, while Molly had shared Hannah's room. But, she now mused as she attempted to shake some of the dust from her skirts, she had slept better than she had in quite a number of days, her dreams blissfully filled with visions of the happy life ahead for herself and Jason.

Within a matter of minutes, Rob started building the fire, while Molly was seated on the ground near him. Hannah watched as Jason carried their packs forward, setting them down on the ground near the fire, then suggesting, "Hannah and I will fetch more wood for the fire." He didn't wait for a reply from either Rob or Molly; he simply grasped his wife's hand and tugged her along with him as he proceeded to lead the two of them farther into the thick shelter of trees, some distance away from the camp.

"I thought we were supposed to be fetching more firewood," Hannah said in mock protest as Jason suddenly turned and pulled her up hard against him, his muscular arms surrounding her as he slowly lowered his head toward hers.

"We will, but first things first," he murmured seductively against her ear, his lips gently nuzzling at the slender column of her neck. "I've been wanting to hold you like this all day. Surely you wouldn't think of denying me this golden opportunity, would you?" he asked with a teasing grin and a gleam in his eyes.

"But what will Molly and Rob think? They'll worry if we're not back soon," Hannah pointed out, though her resistance was swiftly melting away as his hand moved down her back to cup her rounded buttocks and bring her even closer against his masculine hardness.

"Then let them," Jason replied a bit impatiently, his fingers working at the buttons on her bodice. "You can rest assured that Rob will have a pretty good idea of what detained us. Besides, this won't take long."

"Oh, that's very reassuring!" Hannah retorted with playful sarcasm. "But Jason, speaking of Rob"—her breath quickened as his fingers continued with their skillful action—"just exactly what did happen between the two of you yesterday?"

"Nothing of much importance. I merely tried to make

a few things clearer to him. Let's just say he and I have called a truce of sorts, though an uneasy one. But I don't want to talk about that now. I didn't bring you out here to talk about Rob Clancy!" He began to lower Hannah to the ground below.

She came to rest on a blanket of leaves, but sat upright again as she remarked mischievously, "You once told me it wasn't safe to go wandering about in the woods, remember? What if someone sees us?" She had to admit to herself that she wanted him as much as he did her, and she gasped aloud with pleasure as his warm lips descended to the white flesh of her bosom which was now bared to his searing touch.

"I'll look after you," Jason murmured. Soon there was no further need for talk between them, as they gave themselves up to their overwhelming passions.

It was some time later before the two of them returned to the camp, their arms laden with firewood. Rob threw them a quick glance, a knowing expression in his eyes, while Molly asked innocently, "What took you so long, Hannah? I was beginning to get worried about you." She was puzzled by the flush of color that suddenly rose to Hannah's cheeks, by the schooled expression on Jason's face. Suddenly she widened her eyes in realization, looking swiftly back toward the fire, her eyes meeting Rob's. She felt an unfamiliar weakness descend upon her as he stared across at her, and she hastily averted her gaze in confusion.

"This ought to be enough wood for the rest of the night," Jason said casually, setting his load on the ground before turning to do the same with Hannah's. "We'd best be getting on with the meal. I want us to get an early start in the morning." He busied himself with drawing supplies from one of the packs, while the two women set about putting the coffee on to boil and moving the iron skillet near the fire to heat.

Later, when they retired for the night, Hannah and Jason lay fully clothed together beneath a single blanket on one side of the fire, while Rob and Molly lay a few feet apart on the other side of the crackling flames. Jason positioned the rifle within an arm's length as he hugged his wife to him and closed his eyes.

"Jason," Hannah whispered suddenly, glancing up at his face in the shadowy firelight.

"Hmmm?" he mumbled, his eyes still closed.

"I was just thinking how very different this trip is from that first one we made together. The first time we made this particular journey, you barely spoke a word to me, remember?"

"I remember," he answered quietly, a faint smile on his lips. "I remember how scared you looked on that first night out, too."

"I had good reason to be frightened!" she retorted in a low voice. "You behaved as if you hated the very sight of me! I was wondering why I had ever been foolish enough to sign on for the voyage, how I was going to cope with a husband who obviously wanted nothing to do with me!" She prodded him sharply in the ribs. His eyes flew open and a deep frown appeared on his handsome face.

"You don't know how damned hard it was to keep from taking you that first night," he admitted, his eyes glancing downward to meet her gaze. "I'd have had to be made of stone to keep from wanting you, but I was bound and determined not to fall into that trap."

"Trap? But, I wasn't out to trap you," Hannah whispered. "I simply wanted you to acknowledge my existence, that's all!"

"I'm going to do a lot more than acknowledge your existence if you don't shut up and let me get some sleep!" he threatened with a mock scowl, his eyes shutting again. Several moments of silence passed before Hannah once more spoke.

"Jason?" She looked up toward his face, but he refused to open his eyes.

"Go to sleep!"

"I just thought you might be interested to know that I've decided I'd like for us to have a child," she whispered, then settled back down beside him and closed her own eyes.

She smiled to herself in satisfaction when he pulled her up against him, his eyes boring into hers as he demanded anxiously, "You're not already with child, are you?"

"No, of course not. But, I'd like to be, Jason. I'd like for us to get started on a family right away," she replied in earnest, her eyes shining up into his. "You do want children, don't you?"

"Yes, I do. But I'm not convinced that now is the right time to start a family."

"Why not?"

"Well, it might be better if we waited a while—at least until you and I have had some time to ourselves. I don't think I'm ready to share you with anything or anyone just yet!"

"All right," Hannah agreed with a sigh, snuggling against him. "But you never can tell—nature might just take its course and hurry things along a bit," she commented with a smile as she finally closed her eyes and soon drifted off into sleep.

They rode into Red Creek two days later, very tired and yet relieved to reach home once more. Tying the horses to the hitching post in front of Maggie's house, they trudged up the front steps. Rob raised a fist and pounded noisily on the door, startling his mother inside, who flung open the door a few seconds later, her face wearing an expression of extreme displeasure.

"There's no reason to be breaking down—" she started to scold, then broke off with an exclamation of joyful surprise when her eyes beheld the quartet on her doorstep. "Merciful heavens! Come in, come in!" They all stepped inside, and Maggie hugged Hannah immediately.

"Hannah, child! You don't know how relieved I am to see you again!"

"Oh, Maggie, you were so right," Hannah said, beaming. "You were right about everything, and I can promise you that I'll never run away like that again!"

"And so I see you do indeed still have the sense the good Lord gave you, after all!" Maggie rounded on Jason. She gave him a quick hug, then shook her son's arm fondly. Then she turned to face Molly with a questioning look on her smiling face. "And who might this pretty young thing be?"

"This is Molly Braden," Rob announced, stepping forward to make the introductions. "Molly, this is my mother, Maggie." He gave Molly a reassuring grin, but was pushed aside unceremoniously by his mother.

"I'm pleased to meet you, Molly! It's about time there were more young women around here. I suppose you'll be needing a room?"

"Maggie," Hannah explained, "Molly is a friend of

mine from the ship. Perhaps you'll remember my mentioning her a while back. We persuaded her to come along with us, and we thought you could use her help here."

"I most certainly can!" Maggie emphatically replied, putting an arm about Molly's shoulders and leading her toward the parlor. "And you're more than welcome here." Molly cast her a grateful look, then sank down onto the sofa in the parlor beside Maggie while Hannah took a seat in the chair across from them. The two men returned outside to see to the horses, leaving the women to get on with their talk.

"I would have thought a pretty young woman such as yourself would have been married by now," Maggie remarked as she turned to Molly again.

"I'm a widow, Mrs. Clancy. I wasn't as fortunate as Hannah when it comes to husbands."

"A widow, already?" Maggie clucked in sympathy. "I'm sorry to hear that. But still, I'm glad you've come. We'll have a grand old time, we will. And you're to call me Maggie, all right? I'd say that, judging from the way my rascal of a son was hovering about you, you won't be remaining a widow much longer!" She regretted the playful comment when she spied the telltale color rising to the younger woman's face.

Hannah wisely decided to change the subject, saying, "Jason has agreed to bring me back down to town in about a week to see how Molly's settling in here. I wish that we could stay a bit longer today, but we need to be getting back up to the cabin. Jason's been away from his logging camp long enough as it is."

"I understand. The two of you need to be alone in your

271

own home again. You needn't worry about Molly here," Maggie said, reaching out to pat Molly's hand with a reassuring smile. "She'll be just fine with me." The conversation focused on telling Molly more about Red Creek, about what sort of life she could expect.

Jason returned to fetch his wife a few minutes later. After taking their leave of Maggie, Rob, and Molly, he and Hannah began the ride up to their cabin. Hannah disliked having to leave her friend after only just arriving in town, but she knew she was leaving her in the best of care. And, besides, she reflected as she rode beside Jason toward the mountain, she was anxious to get home, to be alone with her husband, just as Maggie had said. It seemed so long since the two of them had been alone in the seclusion of their cabin, and she was looking forward with eager anticipation to starting their new life together.

They reached the cabin at dusk, but Hannah was still able to see the cabin outlined against the towering trees in the background. She slid from the saddle without waiting for assistance and hurried to open the cabin door, stepping inside to light a lamp as Jason took care of the horses. She was relieved to see that everything appeared much the way she had left it, and she turned to Jason with a bright smile as he stepped inside.

"Oh, Jason, it's so good to be home again!" she declared happily, laughing as he caught her up in his arms. When he put her down again, she watched as he set about building a fire in the fireplace. "Where's Thor?" she thought suddenly to ask, taking off her cloak and removing the pins from her hair.

"Tom's been looking after him up at the camp. I'm sure he'll bring him down as soon as he knows we're back." He was satisfied when the kindling sparked and caught fire, and he stood to his feet once more as he stared across at his wife. "You could use a bath, Mrs. Caldwell," he remarked as he viewed the dust on her clothing.

"And so could you, Mr. Caldwell," Hannah retorted with a toss of her head. "But it is getting late and—"

"It will help to take away the soreness from riding. I'll bring in the tub while you start heating the water," he insisted, moving past her and out the door. Soon the tub was sitting before the blazing fire, filled nearly to the rim with steaming water.

"Maybe you'd best go first," Hannah said, eyeing the tub wistfully as she faced Jason. "I'll make us something to eat. I'm sure you're very hungry."

"I am. But I have a better idea. You and Molly did all the cooking these past few days, so I'll fix supper tonight. I know you're just about worn out, so you go ahead and take your bath first." His kindness prompted Hannah to rush forward and bestow a quick kiss on him in gratitude. She was in truth very tired and her body ached all over, so she allowed him to cook the meal while she quickly undressed and eased her body into the soothing warmth of the water. She scrubbed herself all over until she was glowing pink, then washed her thick tresses. She was just putting on a clean nightgown and wrapper when Jason called out to say that their supper was ready.

"But what about your bath? The water will get cold. We can wait until you're through," she insisted as Jason carried the plate of food to the table.

"Don't worry about me. It's been my habit to wash up in mountain streams and rivers, and they're not exactly

273

what you'd call warm," he smiled. The two of them took their seats at the table and soon finished off the meal. Hannah sat sipping her coffee when Jason stood and announced that he would now take his bath. She began clearing away the dishes, smiling to herself when she heard a loud splash—followed by a muttered curse—as she entered the kitchen.

"Hannah!" Jason called out a few moments later.

"Yes, what is it?" She couldn't help noticing the way the drops of water glistened on his tanned, muscular form as he sat only half-immersed in the tub before the flickering light of the fire.

"Come here and scrub my back," he commanded in a low, vibrant voice. Hannah hesitated a moment, then crossed the floor with slow and steady steps. She knelt behind him, reaching out to take the cake of soap he held up to her, her eyes drawn to the wet, curling hair on his broad chest, and lower . . .

"There," she said, having soaped his back and rinsed it as well. She started to rise again, but his hand reached out to grip her wrist before she could move away.

"Now, how about the rest of me?" he asked with a bantering lightness to his voice, his eyes gleaming mischievously. Hannah smiled down at him uncertainly, not exactly sure how to respond to this unfamiliar Jason, but she had no further time to contemplate. Suddenly he stood up in the tub, the water splashing about them.

"Jason, what are you doing?" Hannah asked with a laugh, then gasped as he drew her against him. "You're getting my gown and wrapper soaked!" she squealed in protest, struggling ineffectually as he merely chuckled quietly, his arms holding her captive with ease.

274

"Then we'll have to make sure they stay dry," he responded, his eyes staring meaningfully into hers as he slowly began untying the sash at her waist. She yielded readily to him as he proceeded to draw off her wrapper, then her nightgown, until she was as naked as he. A shiver ran the length of her spine, and she stood there before him, unashamed, her bright curls fanning out across her shoulders, waiting for him to touch her again, waiting for him to claim her as his own. She melted willingly against him when he finally reached out for her, and he lifted her high in his arms as he carried her into the darkened bedroom and lowered her gently to the downy softness of their bed.

There was no longer a teasing lightness about Jason as he lowered his body on top of hers, as his lips captured hers in a tender kiss that swiftly grew more demanding. They both realized that there was no need to hurry this time, that they had the entire night to spend in their own private world together. They gave to each other out of love, each eager to please the other, each concentrating on the other's pleasure.

"It feels like ages since I've been able to make love to you the way I wanted to," Jason murmured against her ear, his lips trailing a path of fire downward to her firm breasts.

"I know," Hannah whispered in response, rendered nearly breathless as his warm tongue lazily circled her nipples. Moments later, he made it clear that he was intent upon kissing every inch of her soft white flesh. She trembled beneath his lips, a soft moan escaping her as his lips traveled the length of her body. She moved restlessly beneath his passionate mouth as he kissed her neck, her slender back, her rounded buttocks, her legs. He began stroking her gently between her parted thighs, and her head sank farther into the pillow as she felt the rapturous fire building to a consuming blaze deep within her. Her hands reached out to stroke Jason's muscular back, his arms, his throbbing maleness, before her fingers feverishly grasped his thick hair as his lips descended upon hers again. His hardness entered her welcoming softness, and he moved slowly, tantalizingly, then more and more rapidly, until the two of them reached the bursting pinnacle of fulfillment.

"Jason, I love you so very much," Hannah whispered softly as they lay entwined upon the bed a few minutes later.

"I love you, too," Jason murmured quietly, his lips tenderly brushing her damp forehead.

"I never knew it could be like this between us," Hannah remarked in wonderment, her fingers moving gently across his broad chest.

"It will be like this from now on," Jason replied, hugging her to him, a contented sigh escaping his lips. "I never knew there was a woman as magnificent as you, Hannah. I never thought I'd find such happiness with any woman."

"You're the one who's magnificent." Hannah nudged his arm playfully. "But I, too, never really believed I'd be fortunate enough to marry someone like you. To think how anxious I was all those months on board the ship, wondering what sort of man I'd find waiting for me in Seattle. If only I could have known it would be you!"

"I'm not perfect, Hannah." Jason glanced down at her. "I'm not promising that I'll always be the best husband, but I'll try. I've still got a lot to learn about loving and trusting. But, I do love you. I love you more than I ever dreamed I could."

"That's all that really matters, then, isn't it?" Hannah replied softly. She was satisfied when he kissed her again, stoking the fires of passion once more. Neither of them slept much for the remainder of the night, but neither of them cared.

Twenty-One

The following days were relatively peaceful and certainly blissful ones for Jason and Hannah. He returned to his work at the logging camp while she remained busy with her numerous chores at the cabin, even starting a summer garden. She would be waiting at the door to welcome him home with open arms at the end of each day, and their evenings were spent in getting to know one another better, their intimate discussions more often than not culminating in a passionate tumble in their bed. Hannah was constantly amazed to discover that she still had so much to learn about her husband, and she was taken to dizzying new heights by his skillful, tempestuous lovemaking.

The only thought that served occasionally to cloud her happiness was of Molly. She was concerned about her friend because she felt responsible for Molly's decision to leave Seattle and come to Red Creek. She was curious to know how Molly was getting along down at Maggie's, but she was also reluctant to leave the security and contentment she had found at home. Nevertheless, Hannah finally decided that she'd have to pay a call on her friend without further delay.

"Jason," she spoke softly one night as they lay together in the bed, the silvery moonlight filtering through the curtains at the window, "I'd like to ask you something."

"What is it?" he mumbled drowsily, half-asleep as he cradled her in his strong arms.

"It's been nearly two weeks since we came home. I feel it's time I paid a visit to Molly."

"You know good and well that Maggie's looking after her just fine," he replied, settling farther beneath the covers with a faint sigh.

"I'm sure she is, but I need to go and see for myself. I think Molly is probably beginning to wonder if I'm ever going to come. I care about her, and I want to make certain she knows it. Would you please take me to Red Creek, perhaps tomorrow?" she persisted, leaning upward to brush his chin lightly with her lips.

"Oh, all right," he surrendered easily. "But mind you—by the time we get down there and allow time to return home again, you won't be left with much time for visiting. I need to be getting a load of supplies while we're there, too."

"Thank you," Hannah murmured sweetly with a satisfied smile, rewarding him with a slow, tantalizing kiss on his unsuspecting lips. She started to move away again, crying out in surprise when his arm clamped her tightly against him and he rolled her swiftly onto her back. "Jason, surely you aren't—" she protested, though not very vigorously.

"You didn't really think I was going to let it end with one kiss, did you?" he cut her off with a wolfish grin, then proceeded to end all talk between them once more.

The two of them headed down to Red Creek just after dawn the following morning, traveling in the wagon instead of by horseback. Hannah enjoyed the trip, for the skies were unusually blue and clear, the air refreshingly fragrant and cool against her skin. When they arrived at the town, Jason dropped her off at Maggie's, telling her that he'd return there himself just as soon as he saw to the supplies. She smiled and blew him an affectionate kiss as he drove away, then turned and quickly climbed the front steps of Maggie's house.

"Hannah! Oh, Hannah, I've been hoping you would come!" Molly exclaimed with a glad smile of welcome as she opened the door. The two young women embraced and kissed one another, then strolled companionably into the parlor.

"Where is Maggie?" Hannah asked, glancing about as she drew off her cloak and straightened her dress.

"She's out at the moment. She said she had to fetch something from the general store. Oh, Hannah, it seems like ages since I saw you last!" Molly remarked with unbridled excitement, her eyes sparkling.

"Well, I don't suppose there's any need to ask how you're getting along," Hannah teasingly retorted, sinking down onto the sofa beside her friend. "You're looking very well."

"I never knew there were such good people like Maggie and her son. I've found more of a home here than I've ever had before in my whole life," Molly confessed, her young face looking almost radiant.

"I'm so glad. I'm sorry I didn't get down sooner, but—"

"There's no need to explain," Molly interrupted quickly with another smile. "It's plain to see that things are going well with you and Jason. I've just been wanting to see you, to talk to you again."

"And I've been wondering about you as well. By the way, you mentioned Rob a moment ago. Is he still here in town then?"

"He manages to come down every few days or so," Molly answered, her face coloring as she averted her gaze.

"Then he certainly can't be getting much work done at his logging camp," Hannah commented with a soft chuckle. She grew serious again and asked, "Molly, I don't mean to pry, but, well, is something going on between you and Rob Clancy?"

"I don't know what you mean," Molly replied evasively, still not looking her friend directly in the eye.

"Molly," Hannah said, taking hold of the other woman's shoulders and forcing her to face her squarely, "I'm not blind, you know. I saw the way you looked at Rob when we were in Seattle, the way you stayed close to him during the journey here. Are you by any chance in love with him?"

"In love with Rob Clancy?" Molly repeated, appearing quite flustered for a moment, obviously reluctant to answer. She rose to her feet and walked slowly to the other side of the room, before turning and finally saying, "Yes, I suppose I am." She sighed. "But it isn't all that simple."

"What do you mean? There's nothing so very complicated about being in love, is there?" Hannah remarked, then was forced to smile at her own words.

281

Complicated? she mused. Until recently, it had always been complicated between Jason and herself!

"You don't understand," Molly sighed again, moving back to take a seat beside Hannah once more. "I don't know how Rob feels about me."

"Well, has he said anything to you?"

"No, not exactly. Actually, not at all, I suppose. Well, you know how Rob is," she explained, her attractive young face wearing an expression of perplexity. "It's difficult to tell when he's serious or simply having fun."

"Yes, I know how Rob can be," Hannah stated a bit cryptically, half to herself.

"I mean, he flirts and laughs with me, but I try not to flatter myself enough to think that he means anything serious by it. After all, I *am* the only young woman in town, except for those at the saloons. I suppose it's only natural for a handsome, charming man such as Rob Clancy to be inclined to carry on a bit with the only eligible female in town."

"Have you talked to Maggie about this?" Hannah asked, her green eyes mirroring her growing concern. She realized that Molly was extremely serious about the situation, and she tried to think of some way she could help. She was tempted to talk to Rob herself, but was reluctant to interfere.

"Yes, a little. She seems to think he cares for me, but she can't say for certain, of course."

"I see," Hannah murmured, her face growing thoughtful. "One thing I do know, and that is that Rob Clancy has never been in love before."

"And how do you know that?" Molly asked in surprise.

"He told me so himself."

"You know, he talks about you an awful lot." Molly glanced at Hannah with slightly narrowed eyes.

"About me?" Hannah responded innocently.

"Yes, all the time, in fact. Sometimes I think he's quite taken with you."

"Don't be silly!" Hannah admonished. "Rob and I are very good friends, and that's all. You've no reason to think of being jealous of that. Jason's already made that particular mistake, remember?" she reminded Molly with a soft laugh.

"What am I going to do?" Molly demanded impatiently, rising to her feet again and moving restlessly about the room. "Sometimes I'm happy that he pays so much attention to me. And other times, I get worried that he's just toying with me, that nothing will come of it. I've never been in love before either," she admitted with a rueful little smile. "All those men in Seattle who wanted to marry me after Jack died, and I turned every one of them away because I swore to myself that I would marry for love the next time out. And now I find myself in this predicament!"

"I'm not really sure what to advise," Hannah said, standing and placing a consoling arm about Molly's shoulders. "I suppose you'll simply have to bide your time. I know Rob can be quite exasperating at times, but if you truly love him, you'll learn to be patient with him." In truth, Hannah was more than a little concerned about the situation. She knew that Rob was a charming rogue, and she well knew about his flirtatious manner. She was concerned that her friend would be deeply hurt, and she wondered if Rob was just enjoying himself at Molly's expense. After all, she mused, it wasn't so very long ago that he had asked her to marry him herself!

"I'm sorry if I sound childish and selfish—" Molly began, only to fall silent abruptly as the two of them heard the front door open and close. Maggie appeared in the doorway, her face lighting up with a warm smile.

"Hannah!" she cried with pleasure, rushing forward to greet her friend. "What brings you to town today? We've been hoping you would come down before now."

"We've been rather busy up at the cabin, but Jason agreed to bring me today because he needed to get some supplies. What do you have there?" Hannah asked, nodding at the bundle in Maggie's arms.

"Just some flour and sugar and the like."

"Did you get everything you needed?" Molly inquired conversationally, her own smiling self once more.

"Everything but the salt. I walked right out of the store and all the way back here before I happened to remember it," Maggie declared with a shake of her head.

"Hannah and I will be happy to fetch it for you," Molly offered, glancing toward her friend with a faintly pleading look in her eyes.

"Of course," agreed Hannah. "I'm not expecting Jason back here for some time yet."

"I'd surely appreciate it," Maggie thanked them, heading off toward the kitchen with her purchases. "But try not to be too long. I'd like for the three of us to have a nice long visit before Hannah has to leave," she called over her shoulder, then disappeared into the other room.

"I hope you don't mind my offering to go," Molly remarked as she and Hannah stepped outside. "I don't get out much, and I would like for us to spend some more time together alone."

"I don't mind at all." They began talking of Rob once more as they directed their steps toward the general store, unaware of the many admiring glances they received as they walked, the unusual sight of two lovely young women drawing the gaze of nearly every man in town. When they passed by Colette's saloon, Hannah was unable to resist the temptation of taking a quick look inside, disappointed when she was unable to see much in the semidarkness of the interior. They reached the general store, crossing inside while still chattering amiably together, and Hannah did not immediately notice the presence of the other woman standing nearby.

Quickly purchasing the salt for Maggie, they turned to leave, but suddenly their path was blocked. Hannah looked up to see Colette standing there, a decidedly ugly expression on her painted face.

"Please move aside," Hannah said frostily, dismayed to feel her cheeks flaming, still disturbed by the memory of the last time she had seen the hateful vixen.

"It will happen again," Colette smirked maliciously, tossing her head. "Jason will come to me again."

"I asked you to move aside!" Hannah repeated angrily, wanting to avoid a public confrontation, yet unable to keep a rising jealousy from plaguing her.

"I wonder how you can be the wife of a man who does not want you, a man who wants only to be with someone else!" Colette remarked derisively, her eyes flashing. "I tell you this; your husband will not stay away from me for long! He finds great pleasure with me, much more than he could ever hope to find with a foolish girl like you!"

"Hannah," Molly whispered urgently, her eyes wide in

285

her small face, "let's just leave! Don't even talk to her!"

"My husband and I are very happy together!" Hannah declared heatedly, no longer able to control her temper, unable to heed Molly's advice. "He loves me. Jason Caldwell loves me! There is nothing more you can do to us, Colette. Nothing more you can say to me that I will ever again be tempted to believe. I made the mistake of listening to you once, but never again! You are a jealous, spiteful woman, and I will not allow you to cause trouble between Jason and me!" she stated emphatically, her green eyes flashing in response.

"There is nothing you can do if your husband would rather be with me!" Colette retorted belligerently, taking up a threatening pose as she stood before Hannah, her hands on her hips and her mouth twisting into a sneer.

"We're going now, Molly!" Hannah announced loudly, reaching out to remove Colette forcibly from their path. However, Colette lunged forward in that instant, her fingers trying to claw at Hannah's bright curls. Molly gasped aloud, standing helplessly by, shocked and visibly frightened. Hannah managed to catch Colette's hands before they could inflict any damage, and she twisted the smaller woman about and sent her flying across to the other corner of the store with one violent push. She watched with immense satisfaction as Colette landed heavily against a barrel, then slid to the floor, unharmed except for her considerably wounded pride.

"If you ever dare to try and lay a hand on me again, I'll snatch you bald-headed!" Hannah told her in a low voice, her eyes narrowing as she glared toward a momentarily speechless Colette. She grabbed Molly quickly by the hand and started to make her exit, wanting nothing more than to put as much distance as she could between herself and the object of her fury.

"I'll make you pay for this!" she heard Colette threaten behind them, the woman's voice rising to a shrill screech. She hurled several vile invectives after Hannah, but Hannah was no longer listening. Instead, she marched swiftly down the boardwalk, pulling Molly along behind her.

"I certainly don't blame you for getting so angry," Molly said breathlessly as she scurried to keep pace with Hannah's longer strides. "But I'm afraid that a woman such as that will only try to make more trouble for you and Jason. There's no telling what she's capable of doing!"

"I know I shouldn't have allowed her to provoke me like that," Hannah murmured with an expressive grimace. "I shouldn't have let her anger me so. I should have simply walked past her and ignored her completely, just as you suggested." Finally she slowed her steps to a more sedate pace. "I suppose everyone in town will hear about our little skirmish. I don't know what Jason will think of me!"

"You know you need have no worries on that score," Molly insisted with a faint smile. "I guessed her identity easily, you know," she remarked as they reached the steps of the boardinghouse again. "I can understand why you were so distressed to find her and Jason together in her saloon that night!"

"Nevertheless, I shouldn't have lowered myself to her level," Hannah concluded, heaving a sigh as she and Molly stepped inside the house. Maggie came out of the kitchen to meet them, and the three of them passed the next hour in friendly conversation. They were seated together in the kitchen when Rob put in an appearance, his attractive face lighting up with pleasure when he spotted Hannah.

"Hannah! I was wondering when you were going to grace us with your charming presence once more!" he said grinning and moving forward to take her hand in greeting, then raising it dramatically upward to his lips.

"Stop that!" Hannah chided, removing her hand abruptly from his grasp as she fixed him with a stern eye. She glanced over at Molly, dismayed to see the pained look in her friend's eyes. The situation did not pass unnoticed by Maggie, either, but Rob seemed completely oblivious to the anxiety hanging in the air—the anxiety he himself was responsible for creating.

"And where is the fair lady's husband today?" Rob queried sarcastically, his brogue more pronounced than usual. He nodded briefly in Maggie's and Molly's direction, a disarming smile on his face, then returned his gaze to Hannah.

"He should be here shortly. In fact, I don't know what can be keeping him so long. He was going to get a load of supplies." She looked at Molly again, wishing there was some way to relieve her friend's distress. She began to grow quite angry with Rob—angry because of the way he was almost totally ignoring Molly, angry because she knew he could very well simply be flirting with a young woman who was hopelessly in love with him.

"I've come down to get some supplies myself. But I thought I'd pay a social call on two of my best girls while I was in town," he declared teasingly, grinning unabashedly at his mother and Molly. But his grin faded a bit when Molly fixed him with a strangely intense look in her eyes, and he grew uncomfortable, covering his discomfort by flirting even more shamelessly with Hannah. By the time Jason arrived to pay his respects and collect his wife, the situation was quite tense, and Hannah drew Molly aside before leaving.

"Molly, please don't let his behavior upset you," she urged her friend.

"He's made it a point to ignore me, Hannah, and, what's more, he's done nothing but make it perfectly clear for the last hour that he prefers your company to mine!" Molly whispered miserably, fighting back her tears.

"He's . . . well, I don't know what he's doing, but—" Hannah began, but had no further time to discuss the matter as Jason moved to her side and insisted that they would have to be on their way if they were to reach the cabin before nightfall. Hannah gave Molly one last encouraging smile, then left with her husband.

"What's worrying you?" Jason asked her once they were on their way, the wagon bouncing along over the trail through the woods.

"It's Molly," Hannah answered with a faint sigh.

"What the matter with Molly?" He focused his attention on guiding the horses through a particularly narrow stretch.

"She's in love with Rob Clancy, that's what's the matter!"

"With Rob?" he asked in amazement. "Damn! Of all the men your friend could have chosen from, she had to go and set her sights on that one!"

"A woman certainly can't help whom she falls in love with," Hannah retorted softly. Then, snuggling up against him on the wagon seat, she added softly, "Remember?" She laughed in delight as he jostled her playfully, and she soon put aside all thought of Molly and Rob as she and her husband rode homeward, the shelter of tall trees about them as the sun began to set.

Twenty-Two

Hannah and Jason settled back into their contented routine, each finding more joy and happiness than ever before. Hannah was increasingly hopeful that they would be able to lead such an idyllic life forever, but in truth she was becoming fearful that something might occur to destroy the happiness she and Jason had found together. They were getting along so well, had discovered more and more to share with one another, and she knew that Jason's painful, bitter past was finally being put to rest. All in all, Jason Caldwell was a decidedly wonderful husband, she told herself with a little smile as she prepared to till her garden one bright morning, some three days since they had returned from their visit to Red Creek.

The day had dawned clear and pleasantly cool, the morning sunshine brilliantly illuminating the colorful meadow surrounding the cabin. Thor was engrossed in investigating the butterflies and bees above the bright flowers, running gleefully from one plant to another. Hannah raised her face gratefully toward the sun's soothing warmth, startled when she heard Thor barking. She turned to see a lone rider approaching, and she shaded her eyes against the brightness, gazing curiously forward, relieved when the rider she spotted proved to be familiar to her.

"Morning, Mrs. Caldwell. Hello, there, Thor, you rascal," Doc Sam said as he swung down from the saddle.

"Why, good morning," Hannah responded with a warm smile of welcome. "What brings you up this way?" She set aside her task, raising a hand instinctively to her thick hair to tuck into place a few stray curls. Her cheeks glowed a healthy pink, the sun's rays already lightly coloring her skin, for she had neglected to bring a bonnet outside with her.

"Had to look in on some of my patients up at your husband's camp. I like to keep a check on things. I've got a message here for you from Molly Braden. Soon as she found out I was coming up here on my rounds, she insisted I bring it to you," he told her, reaching into his coat pocket and withdrawing a folded piece of paper.

Hannah took it from him with another smile, then offered, "Come on inside and I'll make us a fresh pot of coffee. Or I'll be more than happy to make you a late breakfast if you're hungry."

"No, thanks just the same. I've got other camps to visit before heading back to town. But, Molly told me to make certain you read that right away," he remarked, nodding briskly toward the paper Hannah still clutched in one hand. "She also said I was to wait until you'd read it," he added with a puzzled frown creasing his brow. He maintained his hold on the reins, obviously impatient to be off again, so Hannah unfolded the paper and quickly scanned its contents.

"Hannah," Molly wrote in a rather childish hand, "I need to speak with you as soon as possible. It concerns a most urgent matter, one that you and I spoke of the other day, and I would greatly value your advice at this time. Please try to come. Your friend, Molly Braden.'' Hannah sighed faintly, then glanced up to meet the doctor's curious eyes.

"I hope it's not bad news," he commented gruffly, though he appeared concerned.

"No, not exactly," Hannah murmured in response. "I hope you don't mind my asking, but could you possibly take me along with you when you return to Red Creek today?" she asked him unexpectedly.

"Well," he replied, his expression growing thoughtful, "I don't see why not. I'll be coming back this way later, just as soon as I finish my rounds."

"I'll have to check with my husband first, but I'm sure he'll agree to let me go. I would appreciate your escort. I'll arrange for Jason to come and fetch me home," she told him, forming a plan as she spoke.

"All right with me, then," he answered with a shrug, then mounted up once more. "I should be back here this afternoon, though I can't say exactly when. Just be ready to go, since we'll need to get back to town before it gets too late."

"I will. And, thank you." Hannah smiled gratefully, then watched as he rode away. She reflected that she certainly didn't want to travel to Red Creek again just yet, didn't want to leave Jason—even for a day—but she told herself that surely Molly wouldn't have sent such a plea for help if she didn't feel a bit desperate. "Rob Clancy," she muttered aloud, "I could wring your neck!"

Calling to Thor, Hannah turned about and marched resolutely inside the cabin, taking off her apron and flinging her cloak about her shoulders. Leaving the big dog inside the cabin, Hannah headed toward the trail that led up to the logging camp. She realized that Jason didn't approve of her visiting the logging camp, but she considered the matter important enough to risk any displeasure from him. Because Hannah knew that Molly's past life had been so miserable and unhappy, she wanted to do everything she could to help her friend. Molly needed her, and she must go. Jason would surely understand and consent to her plan. Such thoughts raced through her mind as she determinedly made her way along the narrow trail through the woods.

Hannah reached the logging camp within minutes, halting abruptly in bewilderment when she noticed that there was no one about, and she stepped farther into the large clearing. She glanced about in growing confusion, musing that such a thing was surely unusual, but then decided to go in search of Jason. Stepping carefully across the limb-strewn clearing, past the new bunkhouse, she walked farther and farther away from the trail, still quite puzzled and beginning to grow a little alarmed. Finally, as she was heading down the narrow path through the trees on the other side of the mountaintop, she was relieved to hear the sound of men's voices, shouting something she was unable to understand. She drew closer, anxiously searching the wooded landscape for any sign of Jason.

"Jason!" she called out, drawing her cloak about her more closely as she turned slowly about to scan the surrounding timber. Suddenly she heard the unmistakable sound of wood cracking, and she looked up in stunned horror to see a huge tree starting to sway perilously above her.

"Hannah!" Jason thundered from some distance

behind her. "Hannah, get out of the way! Run!" She heard him, but her feet refused to obey, feeling suddenly as though they were frozen to the ground. She was unable to do anything more than open her mouth to scream as the tree began falling toward her. She could hear men shouting in frantic warning, but she didn't know where to run. At that moment, Jason appeared, clutching her about the waist and pulling her violently aside with him, out of the tree's crushing path as it crashed noisily to the ground below, the trunk and heavy limbs missing them narrowly.

Hannah and Jason lay stunned and breathless, almost completely covered with small limbs and leaves as Jason's men came running to free them. Hannah felt scratched and bruised all over, and she could make out Jason's face enough in the dim light to see that he, too, bore the marks of the tree's descent.

"Are you all right?" he asked her in a voice that was not quite steady, his steely eyes searching her face as he knocked aside some branches impatiently.

"I—I think so," she answered him in a shaken voice, surprised when she felt the branches being lifted off them as the men worked feverishly to find them. She felt herself being pulled upward gently, and she raised her eyes to meet the worried gazes of the men about her, then turned to see Jason freed as well. His handsome face was indeed scratched and dirty in several places, and she realized vaguely that she must appear equally battered. Nonetheless, she attempted to smile gratefully at the men who stared anxiously at her, and she opened her mouth to thank them for their swift assistance, but her words were abruptly cut off by her husband, who now rounded on her with a visible fury boiling up inside of him. "What the hell are you doing up here?" he demanded, already satisfied that she was relatively unharmed. His temper was rising dangerously, though he could not say for certain why he was feeling such a rage.

"I—I came to find you," Hannah faltered, shocked at his wrathful words, glancing uneasily at the others who still stood around them. "You weren't at the clearing where I expected you to be, and I thought I might perhaps be able to find you—" she attempted to explain, her voice trailing off into space as he glared savagely down at her. The men now moved a few feet away, obviously uncomfortable at the scene they were witnessing.

"Haven't I made it clear enough to you that you're never to come up to the camp?" he roared, taking hold of her arm in a bruising grasp and administering a few brisk shakes. "Damn it, woman, why can't you ever listen to me!"

"Jason, please, can't we talk about this at the cabin?" she pleaded quietly, distressed to feel her face coloring hotly as she perceived the men still watching them. She attempted to pull herself free from his large hand, but he refused to release her.

"We'll talk about it now!" he growled in response, his own features suffused with a dull color, his eyes gleaming. "I've warned you to stay away, haven't I? It's just for such a reason as this that I've told you not to come near this place! Damn it, Hannah, you might have been killed!"

"Well, I wasn't, though, was I?" she retorted with spirit, her own temper rising beneath the onslaught of his anger. "I told you, I was simply coming to try and find you, to talk to you about something important. How on earth could I know that I might be in danger? If you had ever told me anything about your work, if you had ever allowed me to become familiar with it, then I might indeed have known better!"

"You should have known better, all right! You should have known better than to disobey me again!" He seemed totally oblivious to the curious onlookers, but Hannah certainly was not. She felt the hot tears stinging her eyes, could feel the pain and hurt building in her heart. She could not know that the men who worked for her husband were actually feeling sympathy for her—were convinced that Jason was being much too harsh with his beautiful young wife—for they remained totally silent.

"I'm truly sorry if I've made you angry, but I didn't know this was going to happen," she attempted to soothe him, but to no avail. She hardly recognized the fierce stranger before her, for he certainly didn't seem like the loving, attentive husband she had known for the past few weeks. She was at a loss as to why he was behaving so irrationally, and she didn't know how to deal with him.

"Don't you have any better sense than to walk right into the path of a tree we're cutting? Damn it, couldn't you even hear us yelling?" he lashed out, apparently beyond all reason now. Something inside of him had snapped when he had picked himself up off the ground a few moments ago, though he couldn't say what was driving him to such emotional violence.

"I didn't know what any of you were yelling! And how could I possibly have known that you were cutting the tree right near where I was standing?" Hannah retorted defiantly, jerking her arm free of his grasp now. She turned her back on him and started back up toward the clearing, clutching her bedraggled skirts as she marched.

She gasped as Jason suddenly grasped her arm again, as he began pulling her quite forcefully along with him, continuing in the same direction. She glanced back over her shoulder to see the men still watching, and she felt totally humiliated at his unwarranted treatment of her. She twisted and squirmed, endeavoring to make him release her, but he held her arm in a firm grip, not even bothering to stop when she stumbled on a rock and nearly lost her balance. She cried out as they neared the bunkhouse up at the logging camp.

"Jason, let go of me! You're hurting me!" However, he ignored her completely, pulling her roughly along with him, treating her as if she were a naughty child to be dealt with for some mischievous prank. She grew more and more angry herself as they moved along the trail, and, by the time they had reached the cabin, she was near to seething with fury. She gasped again as he kicked open the door and flung her inside. Thor bounded out past her, obviously overjoyed to see his master, but the dog beat a hasty retreat around the corner when he encountered Jason's blazing eyes.

"You'll not ever come near the logging camp again, do you understand?" Jason spoke from tightly clenched teeth, slamming the door resoundingly behind him as he advanced upon Hannah with a menacing scowl on his handsome face.

"Jason Caldwell," she fumed, her bosom heaving with indignation, "how dare you treat me that way, especially in front of all those men!" Her green eyes flashed fire at him, her chin lifting in further defiance as he halted to tower above her.

"You deserve to be treated a hell of a lot worse for disobeying me like that!"

"I didn't do it to disobey you!" she exclaimed in absolute exasperation. "I came looking for you because I needed to talk to you about something! I never dreamed that such a simple thing would turn out to be so disastrous! I never believed you could be so cruel!" she cried, her anger only serving to heighten her beauty as she faced him courageously.

"Cruel?" he repeated with a snort of sarcastic laughter. "Cruel because I don't want you hurt, because I don't want you leered at by men who are used to spending their time with the whores down in town?"

"So that's it!" Hannah cried triumphantly, her eyes sparkling with anger. "It's because of your ridiculous jealousy that you're so angry, isn't it? Because you still can't trust your own wife!"

"That's not it at all!" he responded with a growl, whirling away from her and slamming his fist violently downward onto the wooden mantel above the fireplace. "I love you, Hannah, but I expect you to obey me in all things!" he ordered tightly.

"And I love you, but I refuse to be treated like a child every time I display the fact that I have a mind of my own!" she replied, crossing her arms over her chest. "I do have a mind of my own, and I fully intend to use it! I'll do what you say, Jason, I'll obey you when I can, but I'm not going to allow you to run roughshod over me! We are partners in this marriage, and I am a grown woman!"

"Then why the hell don't you act like one!" he roared, turning back to glare icily down into her upturned face again. "You will obey me, damn it!" His hands reached out to grasp her shoulders, but she had apparently decided that she'd endured enough of his manhandling, and, without pausing to think further about it, she raised her hand and dealt him a stinging blow across one tanned cheek.

Hannah stared up at him speechlessly, waiting breathlessly for him to react, but he stood perfectly still and quiet for several long, agonizing moments, only his narrowed eyes giving evidence of his rage. Then a single muscle twitched in his reddened cheek, and his hands shot out and grabbed her, catching her off guard. She tried to escape him, tried to flee from the purposeful gleam in his steely blue eyes, but her struggles were entirely useless. Before she quite knew what was happening, he had taken a seat in one of the chairs before the fireplace and had jerked her abruptly across his bended knee, her cheeks flaming as she found herself face down across his lap, her bright hair spilling out of its pins to trail across the floor below. Then, with a single abrupt movement, he had tossed her skirts and petticoat above her head and yanked down her drawers.

"What do you think you're doing? Jason Caldwell, you let go of me! Let me go!" Hannah stormed, only to cry out again in shocked and painful surprise a second later when his large hand descended upon the unprotected softness of her bare bottom. "Stop it!" she demanded tearfully, but he ignored her squeals of protest and proceeded to spank her several more times, his palm stinging painfully against her rounded flesh, before standing and lifting her high in his muscular arms. He strode with his squirming burden into the bedroom and dumped her onto the bed. The wooden slats of the bed came very close to breaking as Hannah landed hard upon the mattress, and she raised her wrathful, tear-streaked face to Jason's impassive one, so angry she could not speak.

"I've got work to do," he announced in a low, even

300

voice, then turned upon his booted heel and stalked from the bedroom and out of the cabin, leaving a stunned and totally infuriated Hannah in his wake.

"Oh!" she cried aloud, putting a hand to her burning derrière and then beating viciously at the pillow. How could he behave so monstrously, so hatefully? she asked herself. She had never been so humiliated in all her life, had never felt such an uncontrollable urge to react so violently herself.

What had happened? Hannah wondered wretchedly. How could things have gone so completely and utterly wrong in so short a time?

She was convinced that she could never forgive Jason, that things could never again be right between them, and the thought caused her to burst into tears as she lay upon the bed, now feeling emotionally drained over the unpleasant episode. She wept for quite some time, tempted to pack her things and leave, yet too exhausted to act. She was still fuming over her husband's treatment of her later that day when she heard a knock at the cabin door. Hannah answered it, then stood with an expression of dawning dismay on her face to discover that it was the doctor. She had completely forgotten that he had promised to return for her and take her to town with him.

"Are you ready to leave?" he asked, making it apparent that he was in a hurry to be off. It was already late in the afternoon and would be dark before he could reach home again.

"Oh, I . . . I'm sorry," Hannah faltered in embarrassment. "I'm afraid I won't be able to go along with you after all." She was still sorely tempted to do so, to run away from Jason, to make him worry and fret about her and wonder if she had left him for good, but something deep inside of her caused her to decide to remain. "I would appreciate it if you would tell Molly Braden that I'll come and see her as soon as I can. And," she added with an apologetic smile, "I'm sorry if I inconvenienced you." She wondered vaguely whether he would be able to tell that she had been weeping, but she tried to behave as normally as possible.

"I'll give her your message," Doc Sam replied briskly, then mounted up and rode away. Hannah closed the door again and wandered aimlessly into the kitchen, staring with unseeing eyes out the single window as if in a trance. What am I going to do? she sighed desperately. How on earth was it ever going to be right again between herself and Jason?

Twenty-Three

When Jason returned to the cabin much later that evening, Hannah served him his supper dutifully, but she did so in obstinate silence, eyeing her husband occasionally with an expression of her green eyes that displayed ample evidence of her wounded pride and resentment. Jason, however, seemed equally disinclined to discuss the quarrel between them, and, by the time the two of them were preparing to retire for the night, the silence was beginning to weigh heavily between them.

Jason soon began to find the tense atmosphere extremely annoying. "Hannah," he spoke quietly, turning his head toward her once they were in bed. She was reclining as far away from him as she possibly could, perched on the very edge of the bed, the mountain of covers hiding all but the very top of her bright hair from his view. Receiving no response from her, he decided to persist nonetheless. "Hannah, turn over. I want to talk to you."

"I'll have nothing to say to you until you're prepared to apologize for the way you treated me," she replied stiffly, still lying rigid beside him, refusing to so much as turn her head in his direction. In truth, she was very heartsore at what had occurred, and she desperately wanted them to mend their differences, but she also wanted to ensure that her husband would never again treat her like a mindless idiot. It still hurt her immensely to think of his humiliating actions, his words that had stung her so.

"I wouldn't have been forced to treat you that way if you had only obeyed me the way you're supposed to do!"

"You had no right to behave the way you did, and you know it!" Hannah's voice answered from beneath the covers.

"And you sure as hell had no right to disobey me again!" he countered angrily, telling himself that he'd had just about enough of her willful defiance of him. He had been ready to try and talk things out, and just look at what he was getting for his efforts! "Now, come on, turn over and look at me, and let's try to talk things over!" he commanded rather gruffly, giving it another try. He became further irritated when she merely snuggled deeper beneath the covers. He reached out impatiently and forced her to turn over upon her back, thereby prompting her to respond by jumping up from the bed furiously, clutching her pillow and one of the blankets in her arms before her like a shield.

"I won't have anything to discuss with you until you're ready to apologize. And I refuse to stay here and let you bully me any longer!" Hannah informed him with sparkling eyes, her face flushed. She marched rapidly from the bedroom and out into the other room, throwing her pillow and the blanket down to the bare wooden floor before the dying fire, then stretching out uncomfortably upon the floor herself as she drew the single blanket up over her trembling form.

"Just what do you think you're doing out here?" Jason demanded in a deep voice, towering over her with an expression of extreme displeasure on his handsome features.

"Exactly what it looks like! I am going to sleep here tonight!" Hannah answered defiantly, then rolled upon her side and closed her eyes resolutely. She cried out when she felt herself being lifted in Jason's strong arms. "What are you doing? Don't you think you've done enough harm for one day! I suppose you're going to resort to physical violence again!" she snapped, glaring furiously down into his scowling face as he held her there before the fire.

"You're coming back to bed where you belong!" he said masterfully, carrying her back into the bedroom. "Whatever else might happen between us, you are going to share my bed as my wife!" he added, placing her upon the bed none too gently and then imprisoning her shoulders in a firm grip.

"I will not!" Hannah declared tearfully. "I don't want to—to sleep with a man who doesn't trust me, who treats me like a stupid little schoolgirl!" she pronounced, pushing against him as her luxuriant hair tumbled riotously about her face. "Leave me alone, Jason Caldwell! Just leave me alone!"

"All right, I will!" he acquiesced unexpectedly, causing her to abruptly cease her struggles and stare up at him in amazement. "In fact, I give you my word that I won't lay another hand on you until you ask me to!" he roared, his eyes smoldering. He stood up, glaring down at her a moment longer, then spun about and stalked around the room, seizing up his clothes and slamming the bedroom door behind him as he left.

Hannah lay quiet and still in the bed, much shaken by yet another emotional battle with the man she loved. She wondered where he had gone, whether he would return, where he would sleep if he did not. And though she was still furious with him, she began to experience a growing remorse for the way she herself had behaved. She drew the covers up over her as she waited there alone miserably, in the darkness, her thoughts a confusing jumble in her head. It wasn't always wonderful to love someone, she reflected with a sigh. But love him she did, and the longer she lay in the bed wondering whether he would return, the more she began to wish that he would indeed return so that she could try to talk to him, to tell him that, no matter what happened, she would always love him with all her heart.

But Jason did not return to the cabin that night. In fact, he didn't arrive until late in the following evening, entering the cabin with an inscrutable look on his face, a dull light in his steely eyes. Hannah was seated in a chair before the blazing fire, her attention focused on the sewing in her lap. When she heard the cabin door opening, she turned about abruptly and gazed up at Jason with a questioning look in her own bright eyes. She was looking quite lovely that evening, her beautiful hair unbound to cascade freely about her shoulders, her admirable figure encased in a simple but flattering dress.

Neither of them appeared to want to be the first to speak. Jason moved slowly across the room, and, with Hannah's eyes fastened intently upon him, took a seat in the chair beside her, still not directly meeting her gaze. He stared unblinkingly into the dancing flames while Hannah waited almost breathlessly for him to say something, anything at all. Finally, when she was preparing to make the first move herself, he spoke.

"Hannah, I've been doing a lot of thinking. About what happened between us yesterday, and last night as well." He still didn't look at her, his gaze drifting from the fire to his hands as he leaned forward in the chair, his elbows resting upon his muscular thighs. "I shouldn't have exploded like I did last night." He waited another moment, visibly uneasy, then added, "And, I'd like you to know that I'm also sorry for the way I acted up at the camp yesterday."

"Oh, Jason," Hannah murmured gratefully, "I—I suppose it did seem as if I was willfully defying you. But that was truly not my intent."

"I realize that now. But, you've got to understand something. I do trust you," he said in a low voice, gazing across at her now with an earnest look in his gleaming blue eyes. "It's not because I don't trust you that I don't want you up there. It's because I don't totally trust my men. You don't know what it's been like around these parts without decent womenfolk. You're young and beautiful, and I want to protect you from what I'm afraid they might be tempted to do. You're mine, damn it, and I don't intend to let anyone forget it!"

"But," Hannah reasoned, her own voice soft, "you can't simply isolate me from the rest of the world. I want to be a part of every area of your life, including your work. I want to learn about what you do. I want to learn everything you can teach me."

"I know," Jason replied with a heavy sigh. "But I can't bear the thought of anything happening to you—not when I've really just found you. I nearly went wild when

307

I saw that tree crashing down toward you yesterday! I don't think I've ever experienced such overwhelming terror before. Then, after I saw you were all right, I guess I went a little crazy. All I could think about was that you were nearly killed, that I had nearly lost you, and I was absolutely furious with you for putting me through such hell!"

"I'm sorry," Hannah murmured in apology, "but I really didn't think about anything like that happening. I was merely trying to find you, to ask you about something I thought to be important at the time."

"What was it?"

"It doesn't seem very important now," Hannah admitted with a soft chuckle. "I received a message from Molly, wanting me to come to town. She said she needed to talk to me about something quite urgent."

"Rob?" A sardonic half-smile played about his mouth as he looked back toward the fire.

"Yes," Hannah answered with another smile, feeling suddenly as if a very heavy weight had been lifted from her shoulders. It was so good to be talking with Jason like this again. "I gather that things aren't going that well between them. I suppose Molly wanted my advice on how to proceed in her pursuit of that maddening man!"

"That's one thing you certainly don't need to be telling her." There was another moment of silence, until he suddenly rose slowly to his full height, his hands reaching downward to draw his wife up gently before him. "Hannah, my love, can you ever forgive me for being such a damned fool?" he asked, his expression quite solemn.

"I suppose so," she answered, gazing up at him with

adoring eyes. "But Jason, there is something else we need to get settled," she added with a tiny frown, her fingers tracing a repetitive path along the front of his flannel shirt.

"What do you mean?" he demanded, his arms tightening about her waist.

"I don't want to be treated like a child," she insisted. "I am a grown woman, your wife. I want you to treat me as such."

"I'll be more than happy to," he commented with a twinkle of loving amusement.

"Seriously, Jason," she said, the familiar weakness descending upon her as he continued to smile down at her in that same disturbing manner, his eyes gleaming with humor—and something else. "You treated me like a naughty child last night, remember? I don't want that to happen again."

"It won't," Jason replied with a maddening grin, his head lowering toward hers now. "Unless I think you need it," he added, silencing her indignant protest with his warm, seductive lips on hers. A few seconds later, neither of them gave any more thought to what had served to separate them for a time.

They did, however, speak of it again the next morning while on their way down the mountain to Red Creek. Jason had generously offered to escort his wife to town, realizing that she was still concerned about Molly. While riding beside her on horseback, he decided to tell her what had happened the night he had left her alone at the cabin following their disagreement.

"As you probably guessed, I spent the night up at the camp, in the bunkhouse with the others. I hadn't been there more than five minutes when Tom started in on me about how rough I had been on you. Needless to say," he admitted with a wry grin on his tanned face as he glanced sideways at her, "I was in no mood to hear any lectures on how to treat my own wife!"

"What did you do?" Hannah asked, attempting to hide a smile.

"You probably already know the answer to that, too," he remarked with another grin. "It was all I could do to restrain myself from planting my fist in his face when he kept on; but before I quite knew what was going on, some of the other men had joined in with him. It seems, Mrs. Caldwell, that you have acquired quite a number of gallant defenders among the ranks of my employees!"

"Well, I hope it shows you once and for all that you have nothing to fear on my account from your men!" Hannah remarked as her delighted laughter rang out, unable to contain her mirth any longer.

The journey continued in such a happy, teasing vein, and they rode into town just after noon on the cool, cloudy day. Once they had arrived at Maggie's and been greeted by both Maggie and Molly, Jason announced that he had business to attend to and immediately took himself off. Maggie wisely decided to leave the two younger women alone together in the parlor, and she went on with her chores in the kitchen while Molly seemed ready to burst with excitement as she drew Hannah along with her.

"Molly, I'm sorry I was unable to come when you asked me to," Hannah started to explain, only to be interrupted by a laughing, beaming Molly.

"Oh, Hannah!" she cried, hugging her friend. "It

turns out that I didn't need your help after all!" she remarked, perching on the edge of the sofa. She laughed aloud at the look of confusion on her friend's face, and she hurried to enlighten Hannah. "Rob Clancy and I are to be married!"

"Married!" Hannah exclaimed in profound astonishment, sinking down onto the sofa with a look of utter disbelief on her face.

"Yes, isn't it wonderful!" Molly replied, unable to contain her joy as she hugged her friend again.

"But how on earth did all this happen? Why, you sent me that message only two days ago!" Hannah pointed out in bewilderment.

"It happened that same day! I suppose it actually worked out for the best that you didn't come, you see."

"Tell me exactly how it came about!" Hannah insisted with an answering laugh, still not quite able to fathom that Rob Clancy had proposed marriage to Molly.

"Well," Molly began, clutching her friend's hand as she talked, "you're well aware of the fact that I've been in love with Rob for a while, actually from the first moment I saw him. You're also aware that he has kept me confused and upset, never knowing how he truly felt about me in return. I decided that I had endured enough of such torture, which is why I sent you that message. You see, Rob had laughed and flirted with me a lot when I first came here; but then, for some unknown reason, he suddenly began acting rather aloof toward me. I was so distressed by his behavior that I felt I had to talk to someone about the situation right away, and you were my natural choice. I didn't know what I was going to do until something entirely unforeseen happened."

"And what was that?" Hannah asked in growing confusion.

"Well, Rob came here that same day. I was alone out in the kitchen. Maggie had gone out for some reason or another, though I don't remember exactly what it was. Anyway, Rob came into the kitchen, apparently expecting to find his mother there, but finding me instead . . ."

"Molly!" Rob spoke in surprise, halting just inside the doorway. He smiled charmingly at her as she rose hastily from her seat at the small table. She had been peeling a bowl of potatoes, and she put aside her task hurriedly and smoothed her apron.

"Good day, Mr. Clancy," she responded rather formally, her own face remaining impassive.

"Mr. Clancy!" he repeated with an amused chuckle, smiling at her again.

"Are you by any chance looking for your mother?" Molly asked coolly, ignoring the bantering note she detected in his voice.

"Yes," he replied, his smile fading a bit. "Where is she?" He leaned negligently against the doorframe, his gaze drawn back to Molly's slightly flushed face. She suddenly began fidgeting nervously with her apron strings, attempting to loosen the knot she had tied accidentally.

"I don't know, but I'm sure she'll return soon." She continued trying to untie the strings, but remained unsuccessful. Rob took note of her predicament and moved forward to offer assistance.

"Here, let me do that," he said, spinning her about and moving his hands to the strings at her waist. Her back was to him, the top of her head barely coming up to his chin, and he stared downward at her shining mass of dark hair, inhaling the fresh scent of lavender that clung to her skin. His look grew warm, his eyes softening, but she could not see his burning gaze.

"That's quite all right. I'll take care of it later," Molly declared, growing very uncomfortable with his closeness. She attempted to move away, but he merely held fast to the apron strings and she was thereby forced to remain.

"Hold still!" he commanded good-naturedly. "I'll have this undone in just a moment." His fingers worked at the knot, but he soon perceived that he would also meet with failure, though he pretended to continue trying as he stared down at Molly again, his gaze moving slowly downward from her hair to her small, slender back, then lower to the alluring curve of her hips beneath her gathered skirts. His silent appraisal was interrupted as Molly sought to escape him once more.

"Really, it doesn't matter!" she insisted, her voice rising. She pulled at the strings with her hands, surprised when Rob still refused to release them, and even more surprised, as well as quite shocked, when he suddenly bestowed a light slap upon her bottom. She whirled about to face him with a look of indignation, and she drew in her breath sharply as she viewed the expression in Rob's eyes. She gasped in wondrous amazement when he suddenly pulled her up hard against him, his arms encircling her as his head lowered and his lips captured hers in a searing kiss.

When he finally released her again, they were both visibly shaken by the unexpectedly passionate encounter, and Molly could merely stand and watch in dazed silence, her eyes very wide in her lovely face, as Rob threw her an unfathomable look, his face now unsmiling, and turned to stride swiftly from the room.

Rob had never even touched her before! Molly told herself dumbfoundedly. She began to grow hopeful again, although cautiously so, praying that his kiss signaled something far deeper than a mere flirtation, an act of momentary madness on his part. But she was sorely disappointed when she encountered him again that evening at the supper table. He spoke very little to her, and she was suffering from a visible loss of appetite as she sought valiantly to hide the dejection she felt. She was at least grateful that all but one of the boarders had decided not to take the evening meal there that night.

As the meal was drawing to a close, Rob remarked to his mother, "I heard the good doctor mention that he stopped by the Caldwell place earlier today." He glanced surreptitiously toward Molly, but she pretended disinterest and picked distractedly at the food on her plate.

"Oh?" Maggie replied. "And how are Hannah and Jason getting along, as if I didn't already know?" she added with a broad smile, passing the bowl of potatoes to the man at the other end of the table.

"Actually, he did say that Hannah seemed a bit preoccupied about something. I think there's every distinct possibility that Jason's causing the poor girl some worry again." He pushed his plate away, then leaned casually back in his chair and folded his arms across his chest.

"Well, it's certainly no business of yours whether that's the case or not, now, is it?" Maggie reminded him emphatically.

"Ah, but I think it is," he answered with a sardonic grin. "After all, Hannah and I have been through a lot together, and it's only natural that I'd be concerned about her well-being."

"And it's probably also natural that you'll be thinking of causing trouble between them again, is that it?" his mother demanded sternly, her eyes narrowing as she stared at her son.

Molly suddenly decided that she had heard enough, and she rose to her feet with a hastily murmured excuse, then rapidly fled the dining room, seeking refuge in the parlor. Hannah! she fumed silently. Rob Clancy seemed always to be talking of her friend Hannah! If he paid only half as much attention to her as he seemed to want to pay to Jason Caldwell's wife . . .

"Molly?" Rob's voice behind her startled her, causing her to spin about to face him, her bosom heaving beneath her fitted bodice.

"Yes?" she replied shakily, endeavoring to sound much calmer than she actually felt. Why had he come after her?

"Are you feeling unwell?" he inquired with a look of genuine concern, his eyes searching her face. She could feel her cheeks flaming beneath his gaze, and she could suddenly no longer contain the misery welling up deep within her.

"Unwell? What on earth makes you think that?" she sarcastically retorted, presenting her back to him again as she stepped to the far side of the parlor. The room was cloaked in half-darkness.

"Something's wrong, isn't it?" he demanded with a deepening frown on his usually smiling features. He

315

started to move toward her, then stopped to light the lamp on the small oak table beside the sofa. "Now," he said, approaching her as she still refused to face him, "what is this all about?"

"Nothing," Molly replied mulishly. "Nothing at all."

"It isn't like you to act so moody."

"And I suppose it isn't like Hannah, either, is it?" she demanded, whirling about, her eyes flashing up at him. This was a new and unfamiliar Molly, and Rob's expression grew increasingly confused.

"Hannah? What are you talking about? What does she have to do with the way you're acting?"

"Nothing," Molly repeated stubbornly, her heart aching as she attempted to brush past him. "If you'll please excuse me, I need to go upstairs to my room and freshen up a bit. I have a caller coming this evening." It was a bold-faced lie, but she was feeling quite desperate and wanted him to feel just as miserable as she. That is, she told herself with an inner sob, if he even cared enough to feel jealous!

"A caller? I didn't know you were seeing anyone here in town." His voice was low. "Now, who is it?"

"It's really none of your business, Rob Clancy!" Molly cried angrily, hot tears starting to her eyes. She gasped aloud as his hands moved to her shoulders; he had been correct in assuming that she was poised for flight. "Let go of me! It's none of your concern who I see or what I do!"

"It damned sure is!" he responded, his usual good nature giving way to bitter pangs of jealousy. The sensation was quite new to him, and he was surprised at the consuming rage he felt toward Molly's unknown admirer.

316

"And just why is it?" Molly tearfully demanded, twisting futilely in his grasp.

But Rob didn't answer her. He stood there with his hands still gripping her shoulders, his eyes gazing deeply into hers. The realization hit him full force at that precise moment. He knew that he had been fighting against it all along, had refused to admit it, even to himself. He had been falling in love with Molly Braden almost from the very first moment he set eyes on her. The kiss they had shared today should have proven it to him, but he hadn't wanted to believe it. He was truly in love! What he had felt for Hannah was just a strong physical attraction, a fierce infatuation. Now he was hopelessly in love with a spirited young widow he had met only a few short weeks ago!

"Please, Rob," Molly sadly murmured, interpreting his silence to mean that he truly did not care, "let me go."

"Molly, I—" he began, only to break off as he searched for the right words to tell her how he felt.

"There's nothing more to say," she insisted rather forlornly, wanting nothing more at that moment than to be alone up in her room where she could surrender to the overwhelming urge to cry for hours as she felt her heart breaking.

"You're not going to entertain your caller tonight, Molly Braden," Rob commanded, causing Molly to gaze up at him in breathless surprise. Her heart was beating frantically in her breast as she met his meaningful gaze. "In fact, you won't be entertaining any more callers— not ever again—at least, not of the opposite gender."

"And just why is that?" she asked, the anticipation

317

almost too much for her.

"Because you're going to be spending all your time with me," he answered, flashing her one of his totally disarming grins. "I love you, Molly. I love you with all my heart and I'm asking you to be my wife."

"Are—are you serious?" Molly faltered in disbelief.

"Quite serious. More serious than I've ever been in my life. I love you. I only just now realized how much. Dare I hope that you return my regard?" he asked teasingly, though he inwardly held his breath for her answer.

A sudden elation descended upon him as she exclaimed, "Oh, Rob, of course I do!" Her face was beaming now with rapturous delight. "I have loved you from the very first!"

He reached out to draw her to him and she came quite willingly, surrendering against him and returning his embrace with passionate fervor, delighting him with her response. They remained in the parlor alone together for quite some time longer, and Maggie made certain that they were undisturbed.

"So you see, Hannah," Molly remarked as she finished her tale, "all my worrying and fretting was for naught!"

"I'm so very glad." Then Hannah's smile turned into a thoughtful little frown. "But I hope you understand that there was never any reason for you to be jealous of me."

"I know that. Rob and I settled quite a few things between us, you see, including his infatuation with you. I honestly don't mind the way he felt about you, for he didn't really know what it was to truly love someone."

"Well, I'm quite certain he knows now!" stated Hannah emphatically as she affectionately hugged her friend once more. Maggie finally appeared in the doorway and joined in their happy conversation. Jason, too, added his sincere congratulations when he returned to the boardinghouse, and he agreed to wait a bit longer than usual before starting the trip homeward. He sat and watched with an indulgent look on his handsome face as the three women proceeded to talk of the plans for Molly's wedding.

Twenty-Four

After promising Maggie and Molly to return within the week, Hannah and Jason took their leave and mounted up to begin the ride homeward. They had not traveled far from town before hearing the distant sound of thunder in the darkening sky above, signifying that there would most likely be rain before they were able to reach the shelter of the cabin. Jason therefore quickened the pace, and Hannah endeavored to ride uncomplainingly beside him.

"Jason," she finally spoke as they entered a particularly dense patch of forest, the trail winding narrowly through the thick brush and trees, "I'm sorry to ask, but do you suppose we might stop for a moment? My poor horse appears to be having great difficulty in keeping up with yours, and I must admit that I'm tiring as well!"

"All right," he agreed, pulling on the reins of his horse and slowing the animal to a gradual halt. "We'll take a minute or two to rest, but no more. We've got to keep going if we're going to try and make it home before the storm breaks," he cautioned, gazing upward toward the threatening clouds with a look of concern.

"A minute or two will be enough," Hannah murmured

with a grateful smile, allowing him to assist her down from the saddle. "I seem to be tiring a bit more easily these days. Just let me catch my breath, and I'll be ready to ride again." There was a small stream just off to one side of the trail, and Hannah watched as Jason led the horses to the water. She followed after him, careful to keep her full skirts from entangling in the brush. "You know, it's still unbelievable to think that Rob Clancy and Molly are to be married!" she remarked with another smile as Jason turned back to her. "Why, it seems like only yesterday that we were all in Seattle and—"

"Shhh!" Jason commanded, startling her as he held up a hand and signaled for her to be silent. He motioned for her to remain still as well, while he appeared to be listening intently. Hannah was tempted to ask what he had heard—what had caused his sudden, unexpected alarm—but she dared not speak. Finally, she, too, heard what his woodsman's ears had detected first; the sound of several riders approaching behind them on the trail, heading straight in their direction.

Hannah's eyes widened in growing anxiety, and she stared breathlessly at Jason, waiting for him to either move or speak. He suddenly grabbed her by the hand and pulled her urgently along with him, the horses following closely behind as they emerged from the brush and made their way back to the trail.

Jason turned and lifted Hannah in his arms, tossing her easily up to the saddle, then whispering, "I don't know exactly who they are or what they want, but I have a feeling they mean trouble for us. Now, ride as fast as you can, keep on the trail, and head for the cabin. I'll come on after you, just as soon as I get a look at who's following us."

"But, Jason," Hannah frantically whispered in response, fearful for him, "don't you think we should both get out of here before they come? I mean, if you think there's danger—"

"No!" he whispered, his blue eyes flashing to indicate that he would brook no resistance. "Now, get out of here!" he sharply ordered in a low voice, raising a hand and administering a hard slap upon the horse's rump. The frightened animal lurched forward, and Hannah was forced to clutch at the saddle horn to keep from losing her balance as Jason stood watching until she was out of sight on the winding trail ahead.

Hannah told herself that Jason had a rifle, that he was well able to take care of himself, to defend himself if the need arose, but she also realized that she couldn't merely ride away and leave him in possible trouble. She tugged at the reins with all her strength, causing the wildly galloping horse to slow to a canter, then a complete halt. Maneuvering quickly about, she headed back the way she had come, convinced that she was doing the right thing in making certain that her beloved husband was safe. She knew that he'd be absolutely livid with fury for the way she had so blatantly disobeyed him again, but her concern for him outweighed any fear of his temper as she rode.

She was startled by the loud report of a single gunshot ringing out in the stillness of the cool air, and she was further astonished to see Jason riding toward her now at a breakneck pace. He yelled something in her direction—a warning, perhaps—but she had no time to think about what was happening, for in the next instant both she and Jason were overtaken by half a dozen riders, all wearing hoods over their heads to conceal their identities.

Hannah raised terror-stricken eyes to Jason as they were both roughly dragged from their saddles by the unknown assailants.

She screamed loudly in frantic protest, "Let go of me! Who are you?" She fought valiantly against the men who grappled with her, but to no avail.

"Get your hands off her!" Jason demanded courageously, a savage look on his handsome face as he sought to protect her. She screamed in stunned horror as she saw one of the men who was struggling to subdue her violently resisting husband suddenly raise an arm and bring the butt of his pistol cracking down upon the back of Jason's head.

"Jason!" Hannah screamed again, her voice rising hysterically as she renewed her fight against the hands that held her, trying desperately to get to her unconscious husband. She didn't know if he was alive or dead, and she wasn't allowed to find out. She was lifted up in front of one of the horsemen, a man who had never dismounted with the others. The remaining men also swiftly mounted, but they galloped away in the opposite direction, leaving Hannah alone with the stranger who clamped an arm about her waist as she continued to twist and squirm.

"Let go of me!" she cried. "Please, let me see to my husband!" She found it difficult to breathe when his arm tightened about her cruelly like a band of iron, and she was unable to speak any longer as the man kicked his horse and they rode with furious speed away from the spot where Jason lay so still upon the ground. Within minutes, Hannah slumped forward in mingled shock and despair.

They stopped once, some time later, and she was

dragged down from the tiring horse, only to have her hands tied before her and a hood placed upon her own head. Before she could either protest or ask what was happening to her, she was again being lifted up on horseback, the man mounting behind her again. She noted vaguely that the thunder was beginning to rumble with greater intensity as they began to ride again, but she could only collapse miserably back against her abductor, the stranger who held her close to him when the drenching, chilling rain started to fall.

Hannah had no idea how long they rode. She lost all sense of time as she endured the exhausting journey, and she lapsed into a semiconscious state sometime after nightfall. When she awakened fully again, she was once more being lifted down from the horse and placed into another man's waiting arms, a man who held her as if she were no heavier than a babe, then carried a short distance into some sort of shelter. A cabin near the river perhaps, she thought, since she could hear the sound of water lapping against wood. When she was finally set upon her feet, however, she realized that she was aboard a ship, and she swayed slightly as she felt the vessel moving back and forth with the motion she remembered so well. The paralyzing numbness that had overtaken her soon began to wear off, and her mind worked feverishly. She began to wonder what she was going to do, how she was going to manage to escape. She thought of Jason again, and tears began to gather in her burning eyes as she prayed that he was still alive, that he would somehow be able to find her.

Hannah gasped in alarm as the hood was suddenly and unexpectedly snatched from her head, and she stood with eyes very wide in her pale face, her thick, damp hair streaming about her shoulders as she faced the large, burly man towering above her in a small, airless cabin.

"Who . . . who are you? Why was I brought here?" Hannah demanded with as much bravado as she could muster, her voice sounding strained and foreign to her ears. She realized that her hands were still bound as she stood defenseless before the man, and her eyes moved furtively about the cabin, seeking any possible avenue of escape. The cabin was dimly lit by a single lamp, and she saw that the man was forced to stoop below the ceiling.

"It won't do you no good to be asking me anything," the man growled, his ugly face made even uglier by the huge expanse of untrimmed black beard, his brown eyes narrowing as if to intimidate. His manners, clothing, and features were very coarse. "You just keep your mouth shut and you won't be hurt." He glared menacingly down at her once more, before turning about and clumping noisily from the cabin, slamming the door forcefully behind him. He returned a few seconds later, withdrawing a gleaming knife from his belt and advancing upon Hannah.

"No, don't!" she screamed in terror, only to nearly faint with relief when he merely used the knife to cut loose the rope that bound her hands. He left her alone again, and she sighed heavily, sinking onto the narrow bunk hanging on one wall of the tiny cabin as she rubbed at her chafed wrists. There was a single porthole, but it was so dark outside she knew she'd be unable to see anything. She had no idea where she was, or even who had taken her or what purpose her abduction could possibly be serving. She was so very weary, could still only think of Jason, could still clearly see the horrible way he had crumpled almost lifelessly to the ground when the man had hit him. Oh, Jason, she silently pleaded, please be alive! Please, my darling, please be alive!

He must be alive, she now sought to reason with herself. If they had meant to kill him, it surely would have been much simpler to have shot him outright. They must have intended to knock him unconscious, she insisted to herself. Yes, he was alive. She knew, deep in her heart, that he was alive, that he would try and find a way to rescue her. She knew that no woman could love a man as much as she loved Jason and not know when he was dead. She held fast to that thought.

Hannah came awake with a start when the ship began to move. She hadn't meant to fall asleep, and she flew across to the porthole and peered outward into the blackness, then moved to stand before the lamp on the rough-hewn wooden table, the only piece of furniture in the cabin aside from the bunk. She was sore and aching all over, but she vowed to remain awake and alert, to try and think of some way to escape whenever the ugly, scowling man returned. She began to pace restlessly about the small room, whirling about in renewed alarm when she heard the key turn in the lock. She waited breathlessly as the door slowly swung open, and her eyes widened in profound shock as she came face to face with Lewis Harland again.

"You!" she gasped in disbelief.

"Were you expecting someone else?" Harland sneered in response, closing the door and stepping farther into the cabin. Hannah remembered all too well his dark features, his raven-black hair, and his strange golden eyes. He smiled at her, flashing white teeth as his eyes moved boldly and insultingly up and down her trembling curves. "My, my," he remarked mockingly as he took note of her disheveled appearance, "we'll have to do something about those clothes of yours, won't we?"

"Why did you do this? What do you want with me?" Hannah demanded, refusing to let him see how frightened she really was. She squared her shoulders and lifted her chin proudly, unaware as she did so that it only served to make her even more desirable in the man's eyes.

"All in good time," he replied evasively, waving a hand airily in her direction. He was dressed in the same flashy manner she recalled, and he moved closer to her now, his steps slow and measured as she shrank back against the wall. "It won't do you any good to try and run away from me, Hannah. We are quite some distance from shore by now. There's no way you'll be able to escape me this time."

"Where are you taking me?" Hannah asked, stalling desperately for time, hoping to avoid what she knew he intended. She realized that if he touched her at all, she would become hysterical, would claw and scratch and bite at him like some wild thing. Dear God, she prayed silently, help me! She was further alarmed by the naked desire she saw in his golden eyes, and she was dismayed when she realized that she could move no farther in the small room.

"There will be time for all the explanations later," Harland answered with another leering grin, his eyes fastening lustfully on the curve of her breasts beneath her wet, clinging bodice. "For now, I suggest that we get to know one another better. It's going to be a long journey, and, you must admit, I've been very patient." His hands reached out for her, but she knocked them aside, then bolted past him for the door. He caught her

327

easily, grasping her by one arm and pulling her roughly back against him, then twisting the arm painfully behind her back as she continued to resist. "I told you it won't do you any good to try and run away! There are men above who would dearly love to have the opportunity to sample your delectable white flesh, to have a taste of your womanly charms. Would you perhaps prefer that I let them have you, my dear?" he asked with a soft, derisive laugh.

Hannah's eyes swept closed in despair, and her struggles ceased. She knew, however, that she could never willingly submit to him, could never allow him to touch her intimately as only Jason had. She cried out softly as he twisted her arm again, and she fought back the tears that stung her eyelids as he pulled her back toward the bunk.

Just then a loud knock sounded at the door. Harland muttered a savage curse and Hannah found herself momentarily released. She scurried back toward the porthole on the opposite side of the cabin, while Harland swung open the door impatiently, a frown of immense displeasure at the interruption marring his face.

"What the hell do you want? Didn't I make my instructions clear enough?" he shouted. It was the large black-bearded man who stood on the other side of the doorway, and he pulled thoughtfully at his beard as he hastened to explain.

"I know you said you didn't want to be disturbed, but the captain wants to see you right away."

"What for? I've already settled everything with him!" Harland snapped irritably, already beginning to close the heavy wooden door again.

"He said it concerns a certain sum of money you owe

him," the larger man persisted, his huge foot moving to intercept the door.

"I've already paid him well for his troubles!" Harland replied angrily. But it soon became obvious to him that he'd have to see the captain and square away the matter himself, and he finally reluctantly agreed to do so, turning to Hannah, muttering, "I won't be long. Then we'll take up where we left off!" With another malicious laugh, he was gone, leaving her alone with her turbulent thoughts once more.

When Harland returned less than half an hour later, he opened the door with an expectant, wolfish look on his face—a look that quickly turned into a puzzled frown as his eyes quickly scanned the interior of the cabin and found no evidence of his prisoner. He then smiled to himself, stepping across the threshold. But, instead of entering the cabin straightaway, he sidestepped a bit, and was satisfied when he kicked the door resoundingly shut with his foot to find Hannah hiding on the other side of the doorway, her hands clutching one of the table's legs as she stood in obvious readiness to attack.

"It's a good thing I had enough foresight to anticipate what you would do, isn't it, Mrs. Caldwell?" he remarked mockingly as he advanced upon her again, a menacing light in his narrowed golden eyes. Hannah still clutched the piece of splintered wood in her hands, and she knew that she would fight with the very last ounce of her strength before she would ever let herself be taken by him.

"I'll kill you if you try to touch me again!" Hannah threatened bravely, moving backward as he continued to step toward her. She found herself wedged into a corner of the cabin with no place to run, and she raised her arms as she prepared to do battle.

"Do you honestly believe I'd let you stop me if I really wanted to take you?" Harland's eyes gleamed with cruel amusement at her resistance. "Rest assured, Mrs. Caldwell, much as I would enjoy taking you here and now, hearing you beg me for mercy, it wouldn't be quite the perfect revenge I've dreamed of and plotted for so long."

"What are you talking about? Why do you want revenge on Jason?" Hannah demanded in an unsteady voice. She was afraid that he was merely toying with her, enjoying a cruel game; although the naked desire she had viewed in his eyes a short while earlier had now been replaced by a light of determination—determination to carry out his plan for revenge.

"I'll tell you," he replied finally after appearing to ponder her questions for a moment. "After all, I think it's about time you learned what sort of man your husband really is. He's nothing more than a common murderer!" he declared with an especially vicious expression on his dark features.

"That's a lie!"

"He murdered someone very dear to me a few years ago. That's precisely the reason I can't rest until I have attained my revenge. And that's the reason I brought you here, why I'm taking you to San Francisco with me. It's rather ironic that we're journeying to the same city where your husband murdered my sister six years ago, isn't it!"

"San Francisco?" Hannah repeated in bewilderment, then fell silent as the pieces began to fall into place in her mind. Elizabeth! The woman who had betrayed Jason was Lewis Harland's sister!

"Don't you think I've worked out the perfect plan for revenge?" He gloated, a twisted smile on his face now. "I'll make Jason Caldwell pay as I should have done years ago. I tried to before, only I must admit that I didn't plan it well enough then. That day I took you from your cabin—well, let's just say that it was an unfortunate impulse. But not this time. No, this time I've got everything worked out in advance, right down to the last detail."

"But Jason didn't murder Elizabeth!" Hannah sought frantically to reason with him. "He told me about it himself. She was killed accidentally when a gun went off during his struggle with another man. He never meant for her to be killed!"

"I'd expect him to tell you a lie such as that! Do you really expect him to admit to his own wife what sort of murdering bastard he really is? I know as well as anyone that Elizabeth was no saint, but she was the only one in my life who ever really loved me, and I can't let her death go unavenged! Your husband killed her. I heard it from a man who was there—a man who actually witnessed my sister's death. After I was released from a prison back East, I went to San Francisco looking for Elizabeth, only to learn of her murder. It was a long time before I could track him down, but I finally found him. And now—now he's going to pay, to suffer the same agony I've been through for years. I'm going to take you to San Francisco with me and force you to become my mistress. I'm going to pour my seed into Jason Caldwell's wife! I'll ruin his precious wife for him!" he announced with a lurid smile of anticipation.

"You—you can't do this!" Hannah protested, fear gripping her heart as she realized the man was beyond all reason where Jason was concerned. "Jason will come after me! He'll kill you if you—"

"Precisely what I expect him to try and do! You see, I left him alive for a reason. I want him to suffer, to be tormented by the thought that his beloved little wife is the mistress of a man who has sworn revenge on him. In fact, I plan to send him a ransom note just as soon as we arrive in San Francisco. Either way, he'll have to meet with me sooner or later, and then I'll kill him—that is, once he knows what I've done to you."

"What if he's already dead?" Hannah asked bitterly, knowing that he was not. She would have to think of some way to escape, to make her way back to Jason before Lewis Harland's evil plan was put into action!

"I'll simply enjoy you for a while and then sell you to some of the white slavers who are always eager to pay top prices for beautiful young women such as you. Who knows? If you're as good in bed as I expect you to be, if there is truly fire and passion beneath that cool exterior of yours, then I might keep you with me for a long time. Either way, I'll accomplish everything I want with this particular plan," Harland stated triumphantly, much pleased with himself as he smiled at her. "I'll have some time to enjoy bedding you, and I'll finally have the revenge I have sought for so long."

"You're insane! You can't possibly be sane and be planning such a thing!" Hannah remarked fearfully, a feeling of heavy dread settling upon her as she gazed into his golden eyes.

"Insane?" he repeated, then laughed aloud. "Perhaps. But, sane or not, once we reach San Francisco, you'll become my mistress. I'll allow you the remainder of the voyage, which should last only a few more days, to decide whether or not you'll come willingly. It will be much easier on you if you do, you know. I can be quite cruel if I choose to be," he threatened casually, his eyes narrowing imperceptibly. "But I want to make sure we are afforded complete and uninterrupted privacy when I finally take you, Hannah Caldwell." Hannah watched in wide-eyed fear as he made her a mocking bow, then turned and left her alone in the cabin.

Hannah waited a few moments, then sank wearily down upon the bunk, the piece of wood in her hands clattering unheeded to the floor. What am I going to do? she asked herself again and again. Jason, oh, Jason! her heart cried out to him as she buried her face in her hands and finally allowed the tears to flow. Surely their love for one another wouldn't meet with such a tragic end!

Twenty-Five

Hours after Hannah had been taken, Jason awakened to the cold raindrops splashing and dancing across his face. Hannah! he exclaimed silently, lying there alone in the darkness of the woods. He quickly eased himself up into a sitting position, wincing with the sharp pain that shot through his head where the pistol had connected with his skull. His eyes, focusing slowly, searched the surrounding darkness frantically for any sign of his wife. She was gone, he realized dully. Someone had taken her—had apparently planned that ambush in order to abduct her.

Hannah! his mind repeated, his eyes shutting once more in heartfelt anguish. He knew he couldn't bear to lose her, couldn't imagine his life without her. He would find her! he vowed to himself as he staggered to his feet, striving to keep his balance as a wave of dizziness threatened to overcome him. If those bastards, whoever they were, had harmed so much as one hair on her head, he'd kill them with his bare hands!

Raising a hand to his head, he withdrew it and saw that his wound was still bleeding, though fortunately not as much as he had expected. He was relieved to discover that he was still able to walk, even though his legs were unsteady and his head ached terribly. He began making his way back down the trail, a fierce look of determination on his face, intent upon only one thing as the pouring rain continued to drench his already soaked clothing. He shivered as the night air swept across the leaf-strewn trail, but he merely closed his jacket and continued on his way.

He would find her—would find out who had taken her and where they had gone, he repeated to himself again and again. His heart twisted painfully at the thought of the immense fear she must be experiencing, of what might happen to her, but he resolutely forced himself to remain calm and level-headed as he tramped back toward the town. He knew he could make it—would have to make it—in time to save Hannah.

Jason arrived on Maggie's doorstep just before dawn, cold and wet and extremely tired, yet still rigidly determined. He raised a fist and pounded noisily at the door, relieved when he saw that it was Rob who answered.

"Jason! What is it, man? What's happened?" Rob demanded with an expression of genuine concern, immediately ushering the taller man inside.

"Someone's taken Hannah!" Jason's face was lined and weary, his eyes glowing with a savage light. "I don't know who they are, or why they've done it, but they ambushed us on the way home yesterday."

"Hannah!" Rob repeated in disbelief, then added, "Damn it, Jason, we've got to find her!"

"I intend to do just that," Jason declared grimly.

Rob noticed the trickle of blood running down Jason's neck, and said quickly, "We've got to see to that head of yours."

"I don't have time for that now!" Jason growled impatiently, already turning about toward the door once more. "I've got to get after them, find out where they're headed. I'll need a horse and some provisions—"

"You'll have to make time if you expect to be able to find your wife!" Rob harshly countered. "You sure as hell won't be any good to her if you bleed to death!" He was satisfied when Jason finally agreed to spare a few moments, and the two of them stepped across the entrance foyer and into the kitchen. Rob set about fetching towels and a bowl of warm water.

"I was knocked unconscious by one of the cowards! I didn't even get a look at their faces. They were all wearing hoods. The last thing I remember was Hannah's screaming—" Jason remarked in a voice barely audible, his features tightening and his eyes narrowing. "Damn it, Rob, why didn't she just do as I said! If she hadn't seen fit to disobey me again, if she hadn't ridden back—"

"Hold still while I see to this!" Rob snapped, applying a piece of the clean toweling to Jason's wound, his own features scowling. Hannah was very dear to him as well, was a good friend, and he knew that he'd never rest until she had been recovered. "You're certain you don't have any idea who might have done it?" he asked as he began bandaging Jason's head.

"It could have been anyone. Anyone who might bear me a grudge, might want to use Hannah to get at me. It might have been someone who simply wanted her for himself—" He broke off, then abruptly rose to his feet. "I've got to get going. I'll try and find out if anyone here in town might have seen anything, might be able to give me any clues." He headed for the doorway, but Rob

336

detained him with a hand on his arm.

"I'm coming with you," he insisted quietly.

"I'll work better alone," Jason replied stubbornly, his eyes meeting Rob's.

"I'm coming with you," Rob repeated with a determined scowl of his own. Jason was much too tired and sick at heart to argue with him further. He had to admit that Rob's assistance might result in their finding Hannah even sooner, so he nodded curtly at the other man in silent understanding. The two of them were almost out the front door when Maggie and Molly appeared at the foot of the staircase.

"Rob! Jason! What's going on?" Maggie demanded. She was still attired in her nightgown and wrapper, as was the younger woman beside her. Molly immediately rushed to Rob's side and eyed Jason with concern.

"A group of men wearing hoods ambushed Jason and Hannah on their way home yesterday," Rob hurried to explain. Both Molly and Maggie gasped aloud at his statement. "Jason was knocked unconscious and the ambushers took off with Hannah," he finished, his arm tightening about Molly's trembling shoulders.

"Hannah's been kidnapped?" Molly asked in stunned disbelief, her eyes moving swiftly from Rob to Jason and back.

"What are you going to do?" Maggie asked, her voice remaining calm, though her heart was pounding in her breast. Her eyes were already filling with tears at the thought of her young friend's plight. "Do you know who might have taken her?"

"No, but we're planning to start asking questions here in town first," Rob assured them.

"Oh, Jason, I'm so sorry," Maggie murmured in

sympathy, unable to hold the tears back now. "Who on earth would ever want to do such a thing?"

"I don't know," Jason mumbled, wrenching open the front door once more as he made it apparent that he was impatient to be on his way. "But I'm sure as hell going to find out! I'm going to find her!" he vowed, striding outside and down the steps.

"We'll find her. I'll let you know as soon as we discover anything," Rob promised his mother. He gave Molly a quick, encouraging kiss, then hurried to catch up with Jason.

The two women stood together in the doorway and watched as Rob and Jason headed toward the other buildings in the town. As Maggie closed the door slowly, she and Molly glanced at one another, their eyes revealing their mutual worry and sadness for a brief moment, before they began slowly moving into the kitchen in silence. Each prayed for Hannah's safety, for Rob and Jason to find her soon. They then sat down to wait for any news Rob might bring them, the minutes passing very slowly.

Jason had insisted that he and Rob split up and concentrate on opposite sides of the town. His boots clumped noisily on the muddy boardwalk as he strode in the direction of the general store, believing someone there might be able to enlighten him about something concerning Hannah's abductors, anything at all that would prove helpful. The rain had ceased momentarily, though the sky remained dark and threatening, its blackness matching Jason's mood. The sun was just beginning to rise above the horizon, the town now beginning to stir as dawn arrived.

Jason was so totally preoccupied with thoughts of

Hannah and the men who had taken her that he didn't realize for a second that his path was being blocked—until he suddenly collided with the person who stood defiantly before him. He glared downward to see that it was Colette, who had stepped out from the doorway to her saloon, facing him with an oddly triumphant smile on her painted features.

"What is your hurry, Jason?" she asked in a deep, throaty voice as she pressed even closer against him, her breasts brushing seductively against his muscular chest. "It is still so early in the day—much too early to be wasting your time looking so grim."

"I haven't got the time for any of your games right now, Colette!" Jason angrily muttered, his large hands clasping her arms in a bruising grip as he easily moved her aside and out of his way. He was already several feet ahead on the boardwalk when he heard her voice behind him.

"It's too bad about your dear little wife. I guess you'll be very lonely now that she is gone, won't you? Perhaps you will be a bit more friendly to me now!" The scornful little smile on her face vanished as Jason rounded on her furiously, closing the distance between them as he seized her arms once more. Colette grew fearful as she viewed the brutal light in his steely eyes, the almost murderous expression on his handsome face.

"What do you know about it?" he demanded, causing her to cry out as his hands tightened on her soft flesh.

"Stop it! You're hurting me, Jason!" Colette lashed out, her own features turning ugly as she struggled to escape him. Her fear increased as she realized that she had just stupidly given herself away, had revealed that she knew of Hannah's disappearance.

"How did you know about Hannah?" Jason asked her harshly, his suspicions already aroused by Colette's defiant attitude.

"I heard some talk about her!" Colette cried, gasping as Jason abruptly yanked her closer, his head lowering so that his face, a mask of grim fury now, was mere inches from her own.

"Talk? I don't see how that's possible, since I was the only one who could have known about it until a few minutes ago!"

"I heard some talk about it, I tell you!"

"You know something, don't you? What is it? You're going to tell me all you know, even if I have to beat it out of you!" he threatened, almost beyond all reason now. He could think only of Hannah, about the fact that Colette apparently knew something about her abduction and was refusing to tell him.

Rob prevented him from reacting with unrestrained violence when he appeared suddenly at Jason's side and declared breathlessly, "Jason! Jason, I've got some news!" Then he noticed Jason's menacing expression and Colette's eyes filled with mingled hostility and fear. "What's going on here?" he demanded of Jason.

"She knows something about Hannah," Jason answered evenly, though he was trembling with the force of his fury. Colette merely glared up at him with flashing eyes, her chin lifting in further defiance as she deemed herself safe once more.

"What do you know about it, Colette?" Rob demanded quietly, his eyes narrowing as he stared at her.

"I know nothing!" she lied easily.

"It doesn't matter!" Rob hurried to say as he watched

Jason's face grow savage again. "I think I discovered something that might refresh her memory. Lewis Harland was seen around here again."

"Harland!" Jason roared, his voice holding barely controlled violence. Of course! he told himself. Who else would hate him enough, was vengeful enough toward him to do such a thing? He should have killed him that day he had taken Hannah from the cabin! He shouldn't have listened to her pleas for mercy, should have killed the bastard there and then!

"Why should that have anything to do with me?" Colette demanded spitefully, still squirming in Jason's harsh grip.

"Harland was seen spending a lot of time coming and going from your saloon," Rob remarked in growing suspicion.

"So?" Colette defiantly countered, feigning indifference. "Many men come to my saloon."

"Where is he?" Jason thundered, administering a hard, bone-rattling shake that snapped her head forward and back. "Where has he taken Hannah?" He was convinced that she must have helped Harland plan that ambush, and he was growing extremely impatient with her reluctance to talk.

"I'm not going to tell you anything!" Colette cried, struggling so violently now that she actually succeeded in freeing herself for a brief instant. She began scurrying back inside her saloon, but Jason caught her again easily and pulled her forcibly along with him toward the back room she used for storage. Rob followed after them, glancing about to make certain that there would be no interference from the handful of men still inside the

341

smoke-filled building.

One young, bearded fellow was gallant enough to block Rob's path for a moment to protest their rough handling of Colette, but Rob shoved him aside, saying harshly, "This is a private matter." The younger man scowled darkly, but made no further moves to rescue the loudly cursing woman. Jason pulled Colette into the room and threw her into a chair. Rob entered after them and closed the door, then stood and watched as Jason towered menacingly above Colette and spoke between tightly clenched teeth,

"Now, you're going to tell us everything you know— do you understand?"

"And what will you do if I decide not to?" Colette answered spitefully, straightening her red satin skirts and adjusting the low-cut bodice that revealed a great deal of her creamy flesh.

"You're going to tell me what you know!" Jason growled, his hands closing on her shoulders, his handsome face suffused with a dull color. "You're going to tell me because I'll kill you if you don't!" he threatened brutally.

Rob glanced sharply at him.

"Your threats do not frighten me!" Colette exclaimed with a malicious laugh. Why not tell him? she suddenly asked herself. Why not tell him what Lewis Harland was planning for his dear little wife? There was nothing he could do about it now, since Lewis and his prisoner were already well on their way. Yes, she told herself, a smug, malevolent look on her face now. She would tell Jason Caldwell and watch him squirm in agony, would make him pay for his shabby treatment of her!

"Colette, tell us the truth," Rob insisted, feeling quite anxious now at what Jason might be tempted to do.

"I think I *will* tell you!" she announced gleefully, smiling slyly at their visible surprise. "In fact, it will give me great pleasure to tell you!" she added with a triumphant smirk. "Yes, it was Lewis Harland who arranged for your wife to be taken. Only it will not do you any good to know that now. They are on their way to San Francisco at this very moment!"

"San Francisco!" Jason repeated harshly, then scowled ferociously. "Why did he take her?" he demanded, then realized with a sinking feeling of dread in the pit of his stomach that he already knew.

"He took her for reasons you're already aware of, dearest Jason! It had to do with a certain lady named Elizabeth, did it not?" Colette taunted him cruelly, satisfied as she viewed the sudden shadow of pain that crossed Jason's face, glad that Lewis had enlightened her before carrying out his plan.

"Elizabeth!" Rob exclaimed in astonishment. "Jason, what's she talking about?"

"Lewis Harland is Elizabeth's brother," Jason answered dully. "He thinks I killed her and he swore to kill me. I refused to take him seriously, though I should have known better. I should have realized that he hadn't actually gone for good—not after what he had already tried to do once before!" he said grimly.

"What did you have to do with all this?" Rob demanded as he rounded on Colette, moving swiftly closer to where she was lounging negligently in the chair.

"I? Why, nothing," she purred, smiling almost seductively up at the two men. "But I did know what he

343

was planning to do!" she announced, sitting upright in the chair now as she faced them belligerently. "I'm glad he took her away, glad she's gone! She'll be getting exactly what she deserves!"

"What is he planning to do with her?" Jason's face was impassive as he gazed down at her with cold, steely eyes.

"What do you think?" Colette countered sarcastically. "He's going to ruin her for you, Jason Caldwell! He's going to see to it that you'll never want to touch her again!" she told him with obvious relish.

Rob managed to restrain Jason as he lunged for Colette, and he pulled his friend from the woman who now appeared quite terrified. Jason glared at Rob for an instant before jerking away and flinging open the door.

Jason gazed back at Colette with an intense light in his steely eyes, warning in a voice that was vibrant with emotion, "You'll answer for your part in this!" He stared at her a moment longer before striding swiftly out of the room. Rob hurried after him, leaving Colette alone in the dim light of the small, cluttered room.

Rob was forced to run in order to catch up with Jason as the taller man stalked back toward Maggie's. He finally halted when he reached the front steps of the house and turned to Rob, his handsome face a mask of inner rage, the savage violence he was feeling barely contained.

"I need that horse and those provisions," Jason said tightly.

"What are you planning to do?"

"Damn it, I've got to go after her!" Jason bellowed, clenching his fists at his side. "I've got to find her before—" His voice trailed off, his jaw tightening as he gazed unseeingly toward the gray sky.

344

"He's already got a pretty good head start by now," Rob reminded him, his own expression turning pensive.

"I've wasted enough time talking!" Jason replied sharply, striding purposefully toward the back of the house where the stable was located. Rob watched him go, then swiftly climbed the steps and went inside the house to fetch the provisions they would need for their journey. Molly and his mother were still waiting in the kitchen, and the two of them jumped up and began plying him with anxious questions.

"I haven't got time to explain everything right now," Rob cut them off. "We'll need some food," he said to his mother, who immediately set about gathering the things she judged they would need. Rob drew Molly close to him as he briefly told them what he knew. "Lewis Harland, an old enemy of Jason's, was the one responsible for Hannah's abduction. He's taking her to San Francisco. I guess we'll go on to Seattle and catch a ship there, then head on down to San Francisco ourselves."

"But, Rob," Molly asked, raising swollen eyes to his face, "how can you possibly hope to find her?"

"I don't know," he admitted with a long sigh. "But you can rest assured that Jason will find a way. If anyone can find her, he can." He took the stuffed bag Maggie handed him, then walked with Molly and the older woman to the back door leading out to the stable. "I don't know how long we'll be gone."

"Send us word whenever you can," Maggie instructed, her face lined with worry. She clasped her son tightly to her bosom for a moment, whispering in his ear, "And may the good Lord keep watch over you," before turning abruptly away and disappearing into the kitchen, leaving

345

the two young people alone together.

"I'm sorry I have to leave you," Rob murmured as he drew Molly into his arms and buried his face in her soft, fragrant hair.

"I know," she answered quietly, savoring the feel of his strong arms about her, realizing that it might be some time before she would be with him again. "But Rob," she said, raising her face to his, "I understand. Hannah is my friend, too. I only pray that you will all return safely!" she added as she reached upward and drew his head down to hers, her lips pressing against his.

Rob left the house a few moments later, his arms laden with the provisions as he stepped across the yard to the stable. Jason had already saddled a horse and was waiting impatiently. He took the bag of food from Rob without a word.

Rob gazed at him in disbelief. "Don't tell me you're planning to go alone!"

"I don't have time to stand here arguing with you about it," Jason muttered, throwing the bag behind the saddle and tying it securely.

"There's no need for arguing," Rob replied with a shrug of his shoulders, striding past Jason and beginning to saddle a mount for himself.

"What the hell do you think you're doing?"

"I'm going with you, of course. You know there's no way you can prevent me from going, either, so you might as well get used to the fact that you're going to have to endure my company all the way to San Francisco and back!" He ignored Jason's narrowing eyes and finished with his task, then swung up into the saddle as Jason did the same wordlessly. Jason kicked his mount into a gallop, anxious to be after Hannah, yet dreading what he

346

would find. He began praying that she would remain unharmed somehow, that Lewis Harland wouldn't be able to carry out his dastardly plan. He remained silent and grim-faced beside an equally subdued Rob as the two of them soon left Red Creek behind, a slight drizzle beginning to fall from the rumbling sky above.

Twenty-Six

Hannah was later to wonder how she managed to endure the voyage to San Francisco as Lewis Harland's prisoner. Although he did not attempt to touch her again, he did force his decidedly unpleasant presence upon her several times throughout those days at sea, usually late in the evenings after the large black-bearded fellow had brought her a plate of unappetizing food and a cup of bitter ale. She constantly wondered how Jason was doing, where he was, grateful that Harland was set upon waiting until they docked in San Francisco to carry out his evil scheme. She was thankful that she was merely forced to listen to his vile threats and brutal remarks concerning herself and Jason on those dreaded occasions he visited her. Not once was she allowed to leave the confines of the stifling cabin, and she was convinced that she might very well have cracked beneath the mental and emotional strain if she hadn't been able to force herself to concentrate solely on plotting her escape, on comforting thoughts of Jason following to rescue her in time. Knowing that he loved her and would surely find her gave her the strength to remain calm and rational, and yet she grew anxiously impatient for them to reach San

Francisco so that she might discover the means of escape before Harland changed his mind and decided to try and force his repulsive attentions on her before their arrival.

Thus Hannah was relieved when her captor stepped inside her cabin one morning and brusquely announced that they had finally sighted their destination. Frantic thoughts of fleeing, of screaming for help immediately entered her mind, but she remained silent as Harland led her up on deck. She raised her face gratefully toward the soothing warmth of the sun's bright rays, breathing deeply of the cool, salty air as she gazed ahead toward the city as the ship pulled into port.

Hannah had glimpsed San Francisco from a short distance away once before, when their ship had paused briefly in order to load cargo on the brides' voyage to Seattle. Then the bustling port city had represented excitement and anticipation, for the young women had realized that they would soon be meeting the men who would become their husbands, beginning their new lives. Now, however, she could only peer at the waterfront as they drew closer, the many buildings erected upon the steep hills, with trepidation and fear. She was still able to notice that the glistening blue waters of the bay and the outlying landscape were really quite beautiful. She glanced about to see that there were ships loaded with lumber everywhere along the docks—many just arriving, as was the one on which she had been kept captive these past few days. Men were unloading cargo all along the crowded waterfront, and Hannah told herself that she would simply have to bide her time for only a short period longer as the captain maneuvered their vessel closer. She suddenly turned to find Harland gazing at her with a strange, unfathomable expression on his dark hawkish features.

"I can easily guess what you've been thinking," he stated, his golden eyes narrowing as if he could indeed read her thoughts. "I warn you, Hannah, don't even think of trying to escape me!"

"You'll never be able to keep me a prisoner here once we go ashore!" she retorted defiantly, her green eyes blazing with renewed spirit. "There will be too many people who will be willing to help me!" she remarked bravely, hoping she sounded much more confident than she actually felt.

Harland laughed deep in his throat, a scornful and derisive rumble of amusement. The other men on deck glanced their way curiously, but they had been warned to keep their distance and their eyes from the man and his female companion, so they returned their attention to their work again as the ship slowly made its way toward an empty dock.

"Your naïveté amazes me!" Harland sneered as his hand tightened cruelly upon the flesh of her upper arm. "In case you haven't heard, San Francisco isn't anything like that little hole in the ground you're used to! This is the infamous Barbary Coast, my dear, a safe and very willing haven for outlaws, gamblers, prostitutes and other degenerates. Do you honestly believe anyone such as I've mentioned is going to lift a finger to help you? No one will even notice, even if I *did* allow you to scream for help."

"There are some decent people here as well!" Hannah insisted, her chin lifting. "I'll find some way to escape you. Jason will be coming after me, and he'll kill you when he finds us!" She gasped aloud at the end of her proud statement, for he had suddenly withdrawn a small pistol from the pocket of his coat and was pressing it threateningly against her side.

"Keep quiet now!" he cautioned menacingly, moving closer to her so that it appeared he was merely placing an affectionate arm about her waist as he held the weapon in his hand, the barrel still pressing against her. "You're not going to give me any trouble, do you understand?" he muttered closer to her ear as the ship finally dropped anchor and shuddered to a halt. "Believe me, I'd hate to have to kill you and forego the pleasures of your tempting charms, but my purposes would still be served if I were forced to do so. After all, as you've said before, your precious Jason will be coming after us. It won't really make much difference whether you're alive or dead, will it?" His arm nearly cut off her breath as it tightened about her waist, and he now began pulling her along with him toward the gangplank.

"You'll never get away with this!" Hannah whispered fervently, nevertheless forced to go along with him. The waterfront area was noisy, music and raucous laughter drifting on the swirling wind as Harland drew her away from the ship and past the scores of saloons and other such establishments. Harland passed them without notice, frantically trying to think of some way to get away from her captor as they walked. She was tempted several times to call out to the men and women she saw, some of them bumping rudely against her as she and Harland made their way quickly toward an unpainted, two-story building with a gaudy, illegible sign hanging out front. Harland rushed her up the steps and inside the building, and Hannah's widening eyes hastily scanned the room in

351

which Harland now removed his arm from about her waist.

"Rather colorful, wouldn't you say?" he remarked sarcastically as he saw her eyes taking in the threadbare, stained red carpet, the equally shabby furnishings. Red and gold were predominant throughout the room that obviously served as some sort of parlor, and Hannah raised fearfully questioning eyes to Harland.

"Where are we? What is this place?" she demanded, noticing that the gun was still clasped in his hand.

"All in good time," he murmured evasively. He took her arm again and began pulling her up the curved staircase with him. Hannah was shocked when she viewed the crude paintings which lined the walls along the staircase—paintings which depicted unclothed men and women engaged in decidedly lusty pursuits. She suddenly felt nauseous as realization dawned upon her, and Lewis Harland laughed again at the look on her lovely young face as she hung back.

"I can see that you're enlightened now," he said, obviously enjoying her fear and distaste. "Actually, it's been inhabited by its present tenants only for a couple of years now. Before that, it was an almost respectable rooming house—the same rooming house where your beloved husband murdered my sister six years ago!" His face had turned ugly now, and Hannah trembled involuntarily as he finally opened a door at the far end of the landing, thrust her roughly inside, then slammed the door resoundingly behind them.

"You're—you're insane!" Hannah cried, backing away from him.

"Insane? No, not insane, my dear, merely determined.

Determined to make Jason Caldwell pay for his crime." Harland turned unexpectedly and wrenched the door open again, announcing calmly, "I'll leave you alone for a while now. But rest assured that I will return. Oh," he added, flashing her an ugly grin, "I've arranged for you to be attired in more fitting clothing when I return this evening. Don't forget, you're going to be playing the part of my mistress for as long as I choose. You must therefore look the part!" With that, he turned and was gone. Hannah heard the sound of the door being locked from the outside as she stood numbly in the center of the room.

She turned about slowly, taking in the sight of the same gaudy, worn furnishings as she had seen downstairs. There were a couple of the lewd paintings on the walls, a simple washstand and small wardrobe, and a rather ornate iron bedstead covered with a dirty red throw. There was a single window in the room, and she hurried over to it, dismayed when she discovered that she was unable to raise it. Hannah was contemplating the notion of using something in the room to break the glass when she heard the door being unlocked again. She whirled about to face the woman who sauntered inside.

"He didn't tell me you were young and pretty!" the woman commented acidly, eyeing Hannah with an openly hostile look. "Here!" She moved forward and shoved a pile of clothing at Hannah. "You're to give me that dress you're wearing and put these things on instead." She was several years older than Hannah, her pockmarked face heavily lined and ravaged beneath her thick makeup. Her bright red hair was piled in a comically elaborate style atop her head, making her appear several

353

inches taller than Hannah. She was wearing a low-cut blue satin dress with an immodestly short hemline, the entire, rather worn frock trimmed in shiny silver lace. The woman noticed that Hannah was staring at her, and she snapped irritably, "What do you think you're looking at? Haven't you ever seen one of my 'kind' before?"

"Who are you? Don't you realize that I'm being kept up here against my will, that Lewis Harland has made me his prisoner?" Hannah rushed to say.

"Prisoner?" the other woman repeated in apparent disbelief, then cackled aloud in pure amusement. "That's a rich one! Why, any one of us girls would give our eyeteeth to be Harland's woman, and here you stand expecting me to believe that you're unwilling!"

"Please, you've got to believe me!" Hannah pleaded desperately, tossing the clothing on the bed and turning to the woman with an earnest expression in her sparkling green eyes. "Lewis Harland kidnapped me from my husband! He brought me here as part of his revenge for something he believes my husband did. You've got to help me escape at once!"

"Look," the woman responded with an unpleasant look on her painted face, "I don't give a damn whether you're his prisoner or not! As far as I'm concerned, you can play any kind of games you want to play. All I know is that I have my instructions from Harland, and I'm being paid damn well to keep my mouth shut. You're to change into those things I brought you and be ready for Harland when he gets back. I'm not supposed to let you out of this room, so it's not going to do you any good to try and talk me into anything!"

"But," Hannah insisted desperately, "doesn't that prove to you what I've been trying to tell you? If I'm not allowed to leave this room, doesn't that prove to you that I am indeed his prisoner?"

"It doesn't prove a thing!" the woman muttered in an ill humor, stepping forward and grasping Hannah's arm suddenly. "All I know is, I'm to make sure you take that dress of yours off and put on those things I brought you." When Hannah resisted, the woman's expression turned even uglier, and she threatened, "I can easily call in some of the other girls to help me, you know! Is that what you'd like me to do? I don't have all day to stand here playing nursemaid to some crazy little idiot!"

Hannah detested having to give in, but she was forced to admit that she couldn't bear the humiliation the woman was suggesting. She turned her back and pulled off her dress angrily. She let it fall in a heap on the floor at her feet, and she watched with at least some small measure of satisfaction as the woman was forced to reach down and retrieve the discarded dress. She snatched it up off the floor and leveled a blistering curse to Hannah's ears, then wheeled about and slammed from the room, locking Hannah in once more.

Hannah eyed the bright yellow dress on the bed with considerable distaste. But, she told herself with an expressive grimace, it was better than being forced to encounter Harland again in nothing more than her undergarments, so she proceeded to dress herself in the hated new costume. Afterward, she was unable to resist the temptation to view herself in the mirror hanging above the washstand, and she surveyed the image scornfully, unable to believe it was her own reflection that stared back at her. The dress molded her curves, its low-cut bodice revealing a great deal of her full white bosom. She realized that she now looked no better than the coarse creature who had brought her the dress. Of course, she told herself, this was exactly the humiliation Lewis Harland intended for her.

There was nothing for her to do but sit upon the bed and await Harland's return. She thought about screaming for help, but knew no one would be able to hear her on the streets below. She thought again of breaking the window and attempting her escape that way, but realized that the noise of the glass shattering would only alert the others in the house to her scheme. Therefore, she sat and waited and thought about Jason—about what was going to happen to the two of them if she didn't manage to get away somehow. Finally she began praying, her eyes closing as she stretched out upon the bed and drew the red throw over her scantily clad form.

Hannah awoke with a start, frightened to discover that she had drifted off to sleep. The room was now bathed in darkness, and she wondered sleepily what had startled her awake. She heard a sound outside her door, heard the key rattling in the lock, then watched breathlessly as a dark shadow entered the room and stumbled noisily across the floor toward the bed.

"Very well, my dearest Hannah," she heard the hated voice, his words oddly slurred, "I think it's time we get to know one another better." He placed his knee on the bed and reached down for her, but she rolled away and bounced off the bed, scurrying toward the door and trying desperately to turn the knob. Harland caught up with her and pulled her back into his arms, laughing in enjoyment at the uneven contest. He's drunk! Hannah realized. Although she considered him quite dangerous when sober, she knew that there might possibly be a way to escape him now. She struggled free from his grip and flew to the opposite corner of the room.

"It won't do you any good to run from me," he spoke with a soft triumphant laugh. "I'm going to enjoy making you cry for mercy tonight! I'm going to enjoy taking what is Jason Caldwell's and putting my brand on it!"

Hannah remained perfectly still and quiet as he stumbled about in the dark, searching for her, and she made another move toward the door. She cried aloud in frustration as Harland suddenly lit the lamp beside the bed, illuminating his way as he caught her again before she could escape. She screamed and kicked at him with fury.

"Let go of me!" she cried, violently striking out at him, oblivious to the fact that her blows were inflicting little damage.

"I'm going to enjoy taming you," Harland whispered evilly. "I'm going to take you and break your spirit, Hannah! I promise you that you'll want everything I give you before I'm through with you! Oh, yes, you'll be begging me for it!"

"Never!" Hannah spat defiantly at him, screaming deep in her throat as his head lowered, his dark face moving closer and closer to hers. His lips finally succeeded in capturing hers in a bruising, punishing kiss, and she felt herself growing faint, still desperately twisting, squirming, and kicking out at him. Her arms were pinned helplessly at her sides as his lips traveled across her face, downward to her slender neck, then

357

lower still to the white flesh of her rounded breasts displayed above the scant bodice of the yellow dress. Suddenly Hannah pulled one of her arms free and her nails raked savagely across the side of Harland's face, causing him to momentarily leap away from her. She took advantage of the brief opportunity and bolted toward the door, actually managing to open it before Harland caught her again.

"Help! Someone help me!" Hannah shrieked in despair, knowing that she would eventually be overpowered by him if she didn't think of something. "Please, someone help me!" She could hear Harland's cruel laughter ringing in her ears, and she lunged forward frantically, causing Harland to fall on top of her as they both landed hard upon the bare wooden floor outside the room.

"Damn!" she heard him softly curse. Hannah was already scrambling from beneath him before he staggered to his feet again, and she eluded his grasp as she hurried away, flying down the curved staircase and wrenching open the front door to the house, past all the unsuspecting, laughing people gathered in the parlor, disappearing outside into the friendly darkness. She glanced anxiously behind her a few times, relieved when she didn't spot Harland giving chase, her steps flying along the street. She was intent only upon escaping, desperate to find a safe place to hide before he could find her again. She was oblivious to the sights and sounds about her as she ran for her very life, past the bright lights of the gambling houses and saloons along the waterfront. She was forced to halt, however, when she abruptly collided with someone—a man whose arms instinctively reached out to steady her.

"Well, well, what have we here!" he exclaimed, his bloodshot eyes moving appreciatively up and down her well-displayed form.

"Please, there's—there's someone after me!" Hannah gasped, breathless from both fear and her running. She tried to free her arm from the man's grasp—a man who appeared very large and ominously looming in the semidarkness where they were standing—but he held fast.

"What's your hurry? My money's just as good, ain't it?" he insinuated crudely.

"What?" she repeated in stunned astonishment, then realized what he must mean. "You don't understand! I don't have time to explain, but I have to get away—" The man cut her off and started pulling her down the street with him, back in the direction from which she had come.

"No!" she cried, twisting frantically in his grip. "No, you don't understand! I need help!" she tried to explain, the other people around them ignoring her completely as the man pulled her relentlessly along.

"And I still say my money's as good as anyone else's!" the man growled in irritation. He became enraged when Hannah continued to resist, and he raised an arm to strike her when she broke loose and ran. He hesitated only a moment, then took off after her. Hannah's panic increased as she looked back to view his pursuit. She didn't know which way to run, didn't know what she was to do. Suddenly her dilemma was solved as she was pulled inside one of the noisy, crowded saloons on the waterfront. She gazed up to see that two young men, their faces not unkind, were now arguing rather good-naturedly over which one was to buy her a drink and enjoy her company.

"I saw her first!" one of the young men insisted, reaching out to fling a proprietary arm about Hannah's shoulders. His companion, however, disagreed loudly, and Hannah finally forced them to listen to her protests as she raised her voice to be heard above the loud music and boisterous laughter surrounding them.

"I'm not what you think I am!" she cried, nearly at the breaking point now. She was feeling very sick and tired and was still terrified that Harland would find her. Her face grew alarmingly pale in the harsh lighting of the saloon, and she was unaware that a woman across the crowded room had seen her being pulled inside, could see that Hannah was an unfamiliar newcomer. The woman, possibly twenty years or so older than Hannah, started making her way across the saloon. She was greeted and hugged by several of the customers as she passed them, her bright yellow hair and dark green dress making her appear quite striking. She was a tall woman, with a full, curving frame to match, and she frowned as she drew closer to where Hannah was now swaying wearily between the two young men. Just as the woman reached Hannah's side, Hannah suddenly closed her eyes and fainted.

When she awakened some time later, her eyes fluttered open and she experienced a rising panic as she viewed the unfamiliar surroundings. She immediately sat upright in the bed upon which she had been sleeping, her eyes hastily scanning the room for any sign of another person. She was startled as she glanced downward to see that she was clad in a clean white cotton nightgown, her bright hair unbound and streaming freely about her shoulders. The room was small, but appeared clean and cheerful, and soft sunlight was streaming in from the curtained window.

Hannah was alarmed when she heard the door opening, and her widened eyes were full of fear as she waited breathlessly for the person to enter. She was confused when she perceived the strange woman crossing into the room, certain that she had never set eyes on her before.

"Who are you? And where am I?" she demanded, drawing the covers up to her chin.

"You're in my room. My name's Sal. You gave us quite a scare, you know, swooning like that," the woman remarked soothingly. She was carrying a tray in her hands, and Hannah was thankful to see that the woman had brought her food and drink. "Here, get this down you. You'll feel a mite better when you get something in your stomach." She gazed curiously at Hannah, her features unsmiling, but Hannah could see that the woman's eyes were kind.

"I—I don't know how I came to be here in your room, but I want you to know I'm certainly grateful for your help. The last thing I remember was standing inside a saloon, surrounded on either side by two men who were arguing over me—" she murmured with a heavy sigh, leaning wearily back against the pillow. She sat bolt upright again as she stared upward at Sal and demanded anxiously, "Lewis Harland didn't find me, did he? You're not working for him, are you?"

"Lewis Harland? Can't say I ever heard the name before." Sal set the tray in front of Hannah, then took a seat on a chair beside the bed. She appeared much plainer in the daylight, her hair pulled severely away from her face, her face devoid of the heavy makeup she affected in the evening hours. She was also dressed in a simple cotton frock, and Hannah couldn't help thinking that there was a certain motherly air about the older woman. "Now," Sal said, gazing at Hannah with a searching look in her brown eyes, "maybe you'll tell me how you came to be in my place last night."

"Your place?" Hannah repeated in surprise. "You own the saloon? Is that where I am now?" she asked.

"That's where you are. I don't usually like for other girls to come in, you know. I only took pity on you because, well, because you looked different somehow, and I could see right away that you weren't feeling too well." She paused for an instant, then questioned, "Where do you usually work?"

"I don't work anyplace here!" Hannah said tearfully, feeling a sudden wave of dizziness and nausea. She composed herself enough to continue, relieved when the weakness passed. "My name is Hannah Caldwell. A man named Lewis Harland abducted me and brought me here to San Francisco. My husband, Jason Caldwell, owns a logging camp east of Seattle," she explained patiently.

"Seattle?" Sal repeated, then grew silent as her expression became thoughtful. "But, you were dressed just like the other women who work here along the waterfront," she pointed out, her eyes narrowing as she stared at Hannah's flushed face.

"I know. Harland forced me to wear those awful clothes. He was planning to keep me a prisoner here to—to make me his mistress. He was then planning to kill my husband when he came after us."

"And just why was this man going to do all that?"

"Because he believes Jason murdered his sister several years ago, here in San Francisco. But he didn't!"

Sal made no reply at first, still appearing to digest all that Hannah had told her. When she did speak again, she was already rising to her feet and crossing toward the doorway.

"Eat your breakfast before it gets cold. I'll be back in a while, and then you can tell me more about this Lewis Harland and Jason Caldwell and yourself." Hannah stared after her a moment, then started eating, suddenly feeling quite ravenous. Afterward, she dozed off to sleep again peacefully, awakening just after noon. The terrible ordeal she had endured had taken its toll on her, and she was dismayed to discover how weak she felt as she attempted to climb from the bed and dress herself. She made it as far as the foot of the brass bed, then was forced to hold onto the bedpost for support. She was standing there, her senses reeling, when Sal stepped inside the room again.

"What do you think you're doing out of bed?" the woman demanded, immediately at Hannah's side and offering her strong shoulder for support.

"I've got to leave, Sal. I've got to get away before Lewis Harland finds me again!"

"You're certainly in no condition to be going anywhere! Why, just look at yourself. You're as weak as a newborn kitten. Just how far do you think you'd get? Besides," she said, helping Hannah beneath the covers again, "you're perfectly safe here for the time being."

"I don't know why I'm so weak," Hannah murmured,

obviously puzzled as she leaned back with a sigh. "I'm usually never ill. And I've certainly never fainted before!"

"You'll feel all right in a couple of days," Sal assured her, then grew quite serious as she took a seat beside the bed again. "Hannah, I want you to know you're welcome to stay here as long as you like. I promise you that Harland won't be able to find you here. And, since I've sort of taken a liking to you, I've already starting trying to figure out a way to get you back home to that husband of yours."

"So you do believe me!" Hannah responded gratefully.

"I believe you. It's plain to see you must be who and what you say you are."

"Oh, Sal," Hannah replied softly, her eyes brimming with tears, "I never believed I'd find help! After I ran away from Harland last night, I didn't know where to turn, didn't think anyone was going to be willing to help me. But if you'll allow me to stay here for a while, at least until Jason comes for me, I'll work for you, I'll earn my keep. Of course, I'll never be able to repay you for the kindness you've shown me."

"We'll talk about that later," Sal declared, waving away her gratitude. "For now, if you think you're feeling up to it, I'd like to hear more about this Harland bastard, and about that husband of yours. It isn't often I get the chance to talk to someone like you, Hannah Caldwell. You remind me so much of myself when I was your age—" she remarked in a very quiet voice, her words trailing off.

Hannah told her all she could, talked for quite some time about Jason and their life together, about Harland

and his thirst for revenge. Sal listened intently, then, surrendering to Hannah's insistent pleas for information about herself, told the younger woman a bit about her own life—a life filled with ill fortune and heartbreak.

Afterward, as Sal was preparing to leave the room again, Hannah commented, "Sal, you're so very different from the others, aren't you?"

"Different? I don't know about that. What makes you say that?"

"Well, there's a woman back in Red Creek. She owns a saloon, too, but she isn't anything at all like you."

"Get some more rest now," Sal ordered hastily, then closed the door briskly on her way out. She grew thoughtful again as she stood alone in the narrow hallway, the music and laughter from downstairs drifting upward. She had been very much like Hannah once, she mused to herself. Perhaps if she had been fortunate enough to find a man who loved her as much as Hannah's Jason loved his young wife, well . . . She shook off such maudlin thoughts and marched resolutely down the hallway and down the staircase, already wearing her bright, colorful dress and her painted face as she forced a smile to her lips and began mingling with the increasing number of customers.

Meanwhile, Hannah lay alone in the room upstairs, the soft sunlight filling the room as she closed her eyes. She dreamed of Jason, of the love they shared, of what they had planned for their future together. She dreamed that Jason was searching for her, that he was calling her name aloud, while a strange mist swirled about him. But she was unable to answer him, unable to tell him where to find her. When she awakened some time later, she felt as if the dream had been real. She began praying fervently that Harland would never capture her again, that she could somehow manage to work her way back to Jason, that he would find her soon. She whispered his name over and over again, as if by doing so she could will him to come to her.

Twenty-Seven

Jason Caldwell stood alone on the pitching deck of the masted lumber ship, his hands clenching the smoothly worn wooden rail as the wind and salty spray swirled about him. A week, he told himself, his handsome face grim in the gray light of the morning. It had been one week since he had last seen Hannah, a week filled with tortured visions and unbearable fears for her safety. Though they were drawing closer to San Francisco each moment, the vessel slicing rapidly through the white-capped seas, the speed was not nearly fast enough for him. He could think only of his beloved wife, could see her beautiful face before his eyes at all times. Dear God, he thought, his fingers grasping the rail so hard that his knuckles turned white, please let me find her. Don't let Harland harm her.

"Jason," Rob's voice spoke nearby. "Captain Dean says it shouldn't be too difficult to discover which ship Harland took—at least not as long as we're willing to pay well for the information." Rob stood beside the taller man, his own hands reaching hastily out toward the rail for support. "We'll find her, you know," he added softly, worry creasing his brow as he glanced at Jason. He told himself that he hadn't seen his old friend looking so grim since all those years ago when Elizabeth had betrayed him so cruelly. Elizabeth, he thought, his mouth twisting bitterly. She was still causing Jason heartache, even though she'd been dead for six years now.

"I'm going to kill him, Rob," Jason muttered, his eyes glowing dangerously as they stared out toward the deep blue waters. "And if he's laid a hand on her—"

"There's no reason to be torturing yourself this way, man! Hannah might even have managed to get away from him. Nevertheless, you can't keep dwelling on what might be happening. Let's concentrate on how we're going to start trying to find her once we get there. We need to have some sort of plan."

"You're right," Jason replied, taking Rob's advice, at least for the moment, drawing his thoughts away from his fears for Hannah. "We'll get the information about the ship first; then we'll go from there. There must be someone who will recall seeing Hannah, someone who will loosen his tongue for what I'll pay him."

"We'll find her," Rob declared reassuringly, then fell silent. He knew that Jason was being driven nearly wild with worry, and he only hoped that his old friend would be able to remain calm once they arrived and began their search. He knew they'd progress a hell of a lot faster if Jason managed to contain his damnable temper when dealing with the sort of people they'd be seeking out. Once again, he was glad that he had insisted on accompanying the man beside him to San Francisco. Though Jason was in no disposition to admit it, he'd be needing Rob Clancy's help before they were through.

Their ship docked at the waterfront on a relatively warm, mostly sunny afternoon a few days later. And, just as the captain had predicted, they were soon able to make successful inquiries regarding the ship Harland had used to transport his prisoner to San Francisco. They were also able to find a man who admitted seeing a beautiful young woman accompanying Lewis Harland from the ship—a young woman who fit Hannah's description. But the man was unable to give them any clues as to where Harland had taken her. After more than two days of nothing but false leads, Rob and Jason finally decided to separate and each search on his own.

"If you find anything—anything at all—get word back to Captain Dean. I'll make it a point to check back at the ship every night," Jason commanded tersely as he and Rob stood on the waterfront that night. Jason was looking quite drawn and weary, driven to exhaustion by days of futile searching and no sleep. He seemed totally unaware of the many sights and sounds about him, still intent upon only one thing, his mind able to focus only on finding his wife.

"But we've got to get some rest," Rob protested, almost ready to drop himself. "I don't know about you, but I have to have sleep in order to keep going this way. Why don't the two of us return to the ship and then start again first thing in the morning?"

"You go on. Just be sure to pass the word through Captain Dean if you hear anything." With that, Jason turned and strode away, leaving Rob to stare after him with a perplexed expression on his attractive face. The music and laughter drifted on the wind about Rob as he made his way back toward the ship, grateful that Captain Dean had chosen to remain in the city for a few days before heading back to Seattle.

Throughout the following days, Rob and Jason

questioned scores of people along the docks, and Jason finally decided to begin concentrating on the saloons and other disreputable establishments. Instinct told him that Hannah was still somewhere along the waterfront, that Harland hadn't taken her far from the ship. But, he sighed, there were still so many places to search, so many people to be questioned. It seemed like an impossible task that faced him, but he was determined to succeed. He was able to keep going by thinking of his wife, by maintaining his cherished hopes for a future with Hannah.

Finally Jason arrived on the doorstep of a vaguely familiar house. It was mere seconds until he realized that the house was the same one where he had found Elizabeth and her lover together all those years before, the house where Elizabeth had died. He cursed himself for not thinking of the place sooner, and he quickly climbed the broken steps and pounded forcefully on the unpainted front door. It was opened by a woman who was attired in a sleazy satin dress, her face heavily rouged, her pale skin glowing in the harsh light of the noisy interior of the house.

"Well, come in, come in!" the woman exclaimed with a brazenly seductive smile, moving forward and grasping Jason's arm as her body pressed suggestively against his. "My name's Flora." Jason glimpsed other men and women inside the house, and his gaze returned to Flora as he smiled and played along.

"Well, now, Flora, why don't you and I go upstairs and have a little talk?" Flora laughed gaily in response, drawing him inside and up the stairs with her, past the crowded parlor where other women were entertaining their male admirers in various stages of undress. Flora led Jason along the landing and then flung open the door to a room which was lit dimly by a single lamp burning beside an unmade bed. She closed the door behind her and smiled at Jason again, her fingers already moving impatiently to the buttons on his shirt as he stood in silence and watched her, his eyes narrowing a bit. Suddenly his large hand shot out and grasped her wrist, causing her to complain loudly as she raised angrily questioning eyes to his handsome face.

"What the hell's the matter?"

"I told you that I want to have a little talk with you," Jason remarked somberly, releasing her wrist and staring down at her. "I need some information, and I'm willing to pay you well for your time." He drew several bills from his coat pocket and noticed the way Flora's eyes lit up at the sight.

"Just what is it you want to know?" she demanded, eager to be paid, yet disappointed that the tall, muscular stranger only wanted information and nothing else.

"I'm looking for a man named Lewis Harland."

"Harland? Never heard of him," she lied. She gasped in fear as Jason seized her wrist again and pulled her closer. His steely eyes gazed deep into her frightened ones.

"Yes, you do. I don't have time to play games with you, Flora. I told you, I'll pay you well for anything you tell me, but it damn sure better be the truth," he told her in a deep, resonant voice. He released her again, and she rubbed her wrist where his hand had left red marks upon her white flesh.

"All right," she said, deciding to tell him what she knew. After all, Harland might have paid her to keep her mouth shut, but he still owed her some of what he had promised. He certainly hadn't given her enough to

371

ensure her silence in the face of an even greater payment, such as the one she intended to get out of the man before her.

"So you do know him!" Jason responded, smiling faintly in triumph. "Where is he now?"

"I don't know," Flora answered truthfully. "He was here, all right, but he hasn't been back for days now."

"Was there a woman with him?" Jason quietly demanded. "A young woman with golden hair and green eyes?"

"Yeah, but she hasn't been back, either." Flora's eyes widened greedily when she viewed the amount of money Jason now proceeded to place in her waiting hand, delighted with what she had received for so little effort on her part. "That gal expected me to believe she was some kind of prisoner or something," she added, her mouth twisting scornfully at the memory, "but I didn't fall for that act for one minute. She was here only for that one day. I don't know exactly what happened to her after that." She paused for a second, then said, "Oh, yes, one other thing. Harland made her change into a yellow dress, if that helps any."

"You're sure that's all you can tell me? You're certain you're not hiding anything, perhaps protecting Harland?" Jason demanded curtly, his handsome features suffused with a ruddy, angry color.

"That's it," Flora declared with an emphatic nod. As Jason opened the door, she couldn't refrain from asking, her curiosity aroused, "Just why are you so interested in Lewis Harland and that strange gal of his?"

"The woman is my wife!" And Jason stalked from the room. Flora stared at him a minute, then shrugged her shoulders and stuffed the money into the scanty bodice of her satin dress as she returned downstairs.

Jason berated himself repeatedly for not thinking of the house sooner as he strode away. I should have remembered, he told himself as he paused for a moment and stared outward at the glistening blue waters of the bay. I should have expected Harland to take her there. It angered him almost beyond reason that Hannah had been kept in a place like that—even for a day—but he tried not to think about that as he continued his search resolutely. He was finally forced to abandon his efforts when he could barely stand for lack of sleep, and he returned to the ship and fell into a deep sleep as soon as his head hit the pillow. However, he was up at dawn the following morning and on his way once more, more than ever certain that he would eventually find his wife.

It was three more days before Jason walked into Sal's saloon. He and Rob had both been checking all along the waterfront for more than a week, neither of them finding any further clues. It was nearly midnight when Jason strode into Sal's place that night, immediately catching the eye of none other than the owner herself, who was always one to appreciate a man of Jason's rugged good looks.

"Hello there, stranger," Sal greeted him with a broad, saucy smile and a certain glimmer in her eye. She told herself that this particular customer was the best thing she'd seen inside her place for a long time, and suddenly she found herself wishing that she were at least ten years younger. Jason nodded at her as he passed by, stepping forward across the crowded room to the bar. Sal watched him exchange a few words with the bartender, pleased when he returned his gaze to her, and even more pleased when he walked back in her direction.

"The bartender tells me you own this place," he said, his handsome face unsmiling and his eyes a trifle bloodshot.

"That's right. What can I do for you?" Sal asked with another smile, raising her voice a bit to be heard above the loud music and booming voices about them.

"I'm looking for someone. I thought maybe you might have seen her."

"Why don't we go sit down? You can buy me a drink, and we'll talk about it," Sal suggested, leading the way to an empty table. She motioned for one of her girls to bring a bottle and two glasses, then looked at Jason again. "Now, just who is it you're looking for?" She took the bottle of whiskey and the glasses the girl brought, pouring herself and Jason a drink. She was raising the glass to her painted lips when Jason's words caused her to pause suddenly in surprise.

"I'm looking for a young woman named Hannah Caldwell." He watched the woman across from him, his eyes scrutinizing her every expression quite carefully. "I heard she was wearing a yellow dress when seen last."

"Hannah Caldwell?" Sal repeated as if thinking over the name. "No, can't say I've ever heard of her."

"Have you heard of a man by the name of Lewis Harland?"

"No, not that I recall." Damn! cursed Sal in silence. Hannah had warned her that Harland would be looking for her. This deceptively handsome fellow here must be Lewis Harland himself! She reminded herself to remain cool and nonchalant, though she was feeling inwardly disappointed that he had turned out to be the evil man who had tried to harm her friend Hannah.

"You might have seen them around, though,"

Jason persisted, still staring across at Sal as he downed the drink in his own glass. "Hannah's a beautiful woman, one that you'd most likely remember if you'd ever seen her."

"I see a lot of pretty girls in here, mister," Sal replied airily with an expressive wave of her hand.

"Hannah isn't like the others," he stated quietly, raising his steely blue eyes to the woman's face again.

"Why don't you just tell me what it is you want with her and that fellow you mentioned?"

"Hannah Caldwell is my wife. Lewis Harland abducted her and brought her here."

"What makes you think I might have seen her? This isn't a very small city, you know. She and that Harland could be anywhere."

"I'm questioning everyone along the waterfront," Jason told her, taking another drink as his eyes moved about the saloon.

"Well, why don't you just tell me what she looks like, and I'll be sure to keep an eye out for her," Sal offered generously, though she was tempted to have some of her men take the no-account scoundrel outside and beat him to a pulp. After all that Hannah had told her about Lewis Harland, it was all she could do to sit here and talk to him in such polite terms.

"She stands above average height, has golden hair and very pretty features. She's not like the others you're used to seeing down here," he repeated. He could still see her clearly in his mind's eye, could still see the terror written on her beautiful young face that day she had been torn from his side.

"I'll sure enough keep an eye out for her," Sal said, rising to her feet by way of dismissal. "By the way," she added, turning back to him, "what did you say your name was?"

"Jason Caldwell."

"Well, Jason Caldwell," she remarked, hiding her distaste of the man, "I'll put the word out if I see a golden-haired beauty with green eyes in a yellow dress anywhere." She forced herself to smile down at him a second longer, before turning about to mingle with the other men in the saloon. She told herself that she would have to caution Hannah about Harland's search first thing in the morning.

Jason stared at Sal long and hard, his gaze returning to her several times as he left the saloon. His steps had only taken him a short distance before he had decided upon his next course of action, and he turned back toward the rear of the saloon.

The woman knew something! It was the first solid lead he'd had in days, and he was determined to discover why Sal had been lying to him. He had been suspicious about her from the very first, and when she'd mentioned that last little bit about Hannah's green eyes, he had known for certain that she was hiding something. Now, he had to get inside the saloon and search the place, had to find out if someone else there might be able to tell him something about Hannah's whereabouts.

It was just possible that Sal was in league with Lewis Harland, he thought as he gazed upward toward the second-floor windows, his tall form casting a long shadow as he stood just around the corner of the building, the bright lights from within shining forth. It was also just possible that Hannah was being kept a prisoner inside the saloon at this very moment, he told himself with a scowl. Whatever the case, he was certain that Sal knew much more than she was willing to tell, and he would either find Hannah inside, or he'd confront Sal again—only under much less friendly circumstances!

Jason muttered a curse when he heard women's laughter nearby as he approached the back entrance to the saloon. He looked up to see two women advancing toward him at that moment, but there was no place for him to hide. He stood his ground and smiled disarmingly at them as they drew closer, their painted faces illuminated by the pale light glowing from the windows above.

"Evening, ladies," Jason drawled lazily, pushing his hat farther back upon his head.

"What are you doing around here?" one of the women asked, her gaze moving openly and appreciatively up and down Jason's tall, muscular form. "You men aren't supposed to come around back, you know. Sal's orders."

"Are you waiting for someone in particular?" the other woman purred, moving closer to Jason and touching him lightly on the arm. She was fairly young and attractive, though she was wearing a great deal of powder and rouge, her brassy blond hair piled high atop her head. The other woman was attired in the same sort of gaudy low-cut dress, and the two of them smiled at Jason in a decidedly brazen fashion. "If not, I'll be more than happy to show you a good time."

"I saw him first!" the younger of the two insisted, laying her hand possessively on Jason's arm.

"We both saw him at the same time!" the other one snapped, her hand clutching at Jason's other arm.

"You do owe me a favor, don't you remember, Dixie?" the younger woman sarcastically reminded her friend. Dixie opened her mouth to protest, but Jason began moving away from them, toward the back door.

Dixie declared, "All right, all right! But, you get this straight, Lacy. I won't owe you a damn thing after this!" She glared at the other woman for a second, then spun about and flounced away, leaving Jason alone with the eager young woman named Lacy.

"Come on, let's you and me get on upstairs where we can have some privacy," Lacy said, taking his arm and pulling him impatiently up the steps and through the darkened doorway. Jason allowed her to lead the way up the back staircase, and the two of them were standing out in the hallway when a door opened at the opposite end and a young woman stepped out.

She was wearing a faded cotton dress and an apron, her golden curls hidden beneath a kerchief. She had apparently been cleaning the room she had just left, for she still held a dustcloth in her hand. It wasn't her usual custom to be working so late at night, but she had been unable to sleep and had therefore decided to continue with some of her chores, believing all of Sal's girls would be occupied with the customers in the saloon downstairs. Though Sal had insisted she rest more, Hannah was determined to repay the good woman for her kindness and generosity. As she now turned about to walk down the hallway to the room where she slept, she halted abruptly when she noticed a man and woman going inside one of the rooms. She recognized the woman as Lacy, but she managed to catch only a glimpse of the man—a very disturbing glimpse, for he had looked very much like her Jason.

I must be going quite mad! Hannah told herself as she shook her head. She reached up to draw the kerchief from her head, her luxurious tresses tumbling down about her shoulders as she trod wearily toward her own room. But, once again, she detected something familiar about the man when she heard the faint sound of his deep voice, and she paused quietly before the door to Lacy's room.

Her heart pounded frantically in her breast when she heard the man's voice again. It sounded so very much like Jason's voice, Hannah reflected, telling herself that she was merely tired and terribly lonely for her husband. But, as she forced herself away once more, the door swung open suddenly and Lacy swept angrily from the room, muttering something about fetching Sal. She had left the door wide open, and Hannah, literally holding her breath, stepped forward and peered cautiously inside. She gasped aloud when her eyes beheld the room's lone occupant.

"Jason!" she whispered, her eyes very wide in her face, her mouth open in stunned astonishment. She stood totally speechless and unable to move as he spun around and saw her as well.

"Hannah! Dear God, Hannah!" Jason's voice rang out, his face exuberant as he crossed the space between them in long strides and gathered her close, clasping her so tightly against him that she could barely breathe.

"Oh, Jason, I can't believe you're finally here!" Hannah cried, her eyes filling with tears of profound happiness. She buried her face in his broad chest, savoring the feel of his warm, muscular arms about her, feeling faint with mingled relief and joy.

"Are you all right?" he demanded anxiously. "Harland—where is he?" he asked in a rush, his lips now

379

roaming hungrily across her upturned, smiling face. "I thought I had lost you, was afraid I'd never find you again!"

"Jason," Hannah breathed, her arms entwining about his neck as her lips eagerly sought his. "I'm fine—I'm fine now that you're here!" Their lips touched, their senses reeling as they shared the passionate embrace that followed.

Finally Jason raised his head and asked harshly again, "Harland?"

"I don't know where he is. I was able to get away from him the first night we arrived in the city," she explained, her arms tightening about him as if she were drowning. "Don't ever let me go, my darling. Don't ever let go of me again!"

"I don't intend to," he replied softly. "But you are all right, aren't you? Harland didn't hurt you, did he?" he anxiously queried, his blue eyes gazing deeply into her shining green ones.

"No, he didn't hurt me. But Jason," she asked tearfully, "would you still want me if he had—"

"Of course I'd still want you!" he interjected with a stern frown, followed by another kiss. "I was only concerned about you because I love you. I love you more than life itself! Nothing—absolutely nothing—can ever change that!" he assured her in a voice charged with emotion, before capturing her waiting lips in a searing kiss once more.

At that precise moment, Sal arrived on the scene, three of her men accompanying her. She was shocked to see her young friend engaged in such impassioned activity, and she was further startled when she noticed the man who was holding her young charge so intimately in his arms. Meanwhile, Hannah happened to look up and see the surprised faces of the four, and she hastened to reassure Sal as she blushed and drew away from her husband, keeping a hand on his arm.

"Oh, Sal, this is Jason! He's come for me, just as I always knew he would!"

"Jason?" Sal repeated in obvious confusion. Jason's eyes met her gaze, and he smiled faintly at her. Realizing her mistake, Sal hurried forward to clasp Hannah to her as she said, "Oh, Hannah, I'm very happy for you! I know you never gave up hope that he'd find you, though I must admit I never thought he'd be able to do it." She was naturally quite pleased for her friend, and yet she'd be sorry to see Hannah leave. It had been such a long time since she had felt close to anyone, and she had come to think of Hannah as a daughter of sorts. But she realized as she observed the love and joy written on the faces of the two young people, it was for the best. After all, she had a business to run, and it didn't pay to be getting too sentimental about anyone or anything, not in her particular line of work. She had chosen her way of life and would have to live with the consequences.

Soon Jason and Hannah were left alone together in the privacy of her room above the saloon. Hannah proceeded to inform her husband of everything that had happened since that terrible afternoon she had been abducted. He listened to her in grim silence, his arms tightening about her as he held her lovingly upon his lap. Afterward, Hannah insisted on knowing how Jason had come to find her, and she finally couldn't resist demanding, "And just what were you doing, Jason Caldwell, coming upstairs with Lacy that way?"

"Now who's the one being jealous?" Jason retorted

with a teasing smile. "Actually, I had to think of some way to get into this blasted place!" He chuckled softly at the severe expression on her lovely face as she eyed him.

Following another long, ardent kiss, Hannah raised her head and said, "By the way, there's something you ought to know. Something very important."

"What's that?" he asked, cradling her head upon his shoulder.

"I should have known that night I fainted. I'd never fainted before in my life! And then, I thought it was just the emotional strain that caused my weakness and nausea—"

"What are you talking about?" Jason demanded impatiently, shaking her slightly.

"Can't you guess?" she asked with a secretive little smile, drawing away a bit and gazing down at him with all her love glowing in her eyes. When he merely frowned at her in bewilderment, she hurried to enlighten him. "Oh, Jason, we're going to have a baby!"

"A baby?" he repeated, his frown deepening. Suddenly, as her words sank in, he stood with Hannah in his arms and twirled her about happily, then proceeded to kiss her soundly. "When?" he demanded, laughing aloud with immense pleasure. "When will it be?"

"Oh, I'd say in about seven months or so," she answered, then laughed as well as he sat back down in the chair with her abruptly and demanded to know if she was feeling all right.

"Of course I'm all right! In fact, I can assure you that I've never felt better than I do at this very moment!" She was rewarded by yet another kiss, and she murmured softly in protest when Jason stood and resolutely put her away from him.

"We've got to be getting back to the ship. I don't want to take any chances of losing you again. Besides," he told her as he drew her firmly from the room with him and headed toward the stairs, "I'm not sure I like the idea of my wife living in a saloon!"

Hannah bid good-bye to Sal and thanked her again for all her help, as did Jason. Sal apologized to Jason for not trusting him, but he waved away her apologies, saying that he understood her motives and suspicions. Jason and Hannah then strode hand in hand from the brightly lit saloon and out into the chilling wind that swept off the waters of the bay. Neither of them noticed the man standing off to one side of the building, a man who stared at the two of them with golden eyes, his dark, hawkish features twisted into an ugly smile.

Twenty-Eight

As Jason and Hannah moved farther away from the glaring lights of the saloons and gambling houses, their path was illuminated by what little pale moonlight shone through the partial cover of clouds in the darkened sky above. The dock where Captain Dean's ship was anchored appeared to be totally deserted, and Jason was puzzled when there was also no sight of anyone in the surrounding waterfront area as they approached the vessel. He chose not to communicate his growing concern to Hannah, instead casually explaining to her that the captain was an old friend, and that Rob Clancy was most likely asleep on board at the moment. However, his eyes continued to scan the darkness as they walked.

Hannah was profoundly grateful for Rob's assistance, realizing that his good-natured presence had probably helped Jason a great deal during the ordeal of the past few weeks. She was naturally anxious to offer her gratitude in person, but she wanted nothing more at that moment than to be alone with her husband, to feel safe from Lewis Harland and leave all thought of him far behind.

Suddenly five men appeared seemingly out of nowhere and blocked Jason's and Hannah's way. Her breath caught, and she could make out the faces of the men who confronted them, but only one of them was familiar to her. Her green eyes widened in renewed terror when she gazed across at the man who stood apart from the others now.

"Lewis Harland!" she breathed, her eyes flying to Jason's face.

"You sorry no-account bastard!" Jason shouted, flinging Hannah protectively behind him. "I was hoping to have the chance to meet you face to face before leaving!"

"You won't be leaving," Harland replied with a contemptuous sneer on his dark features. "I'd say my plan worked quite well, wouldn't you?"

"It isn't over with yet!" Jason muttered furiously, his eyes searching the shadowy darkness of the ship's deck. He was trying to think of some way to ensure Hannah's safety, and he hoped desperately that someone was indeed on board the ship below and would be able to hear them. Rage was boiling inside of him as he encountered the man who had dared to treat Hannah so badly, the man who had sworn insane revenge for something Jason had not done.

"You're right," Harland agreed with an ugly grin, his golden eyes moving to rest upon Hannah's frightened face. "It isn't over with yet. I'll be settling the score with your wife in just a while. But first, your time has come, Jason Caldwell. I'm finally going to make you pay for what you did to my sister all those years ago."

"I've told you. I didn't kill her," Jason countered quietly, stalling for time. He reached behind him and pressed Hannah's arm for reassurance, then began pushing her slowly away from him.

"You're lying!" Harland cried savagely. "And you're going to pay for what you did! It won't be a quick death for you. Oh, no, it's going to be very slow and quite painful, just as you deserve." His strange eyes took on an even more fanatical light, his features becoming even more twisted. "After you're dead, after you've been beaten beyond recognition and your carcass thrown into the bay as bait for the waiting sharks, then I'll have all the time in the world to enjoy your wife's soft body, to—"

"Run, Hannah! Run!" Jason commanded suddenly, pushing Hannah violently away from him. She did as he ordered and turned and ran as fast as she could, her feet flying across the dock and back toward the crowded saloons, her voice screaming frantically for help.

"It won't do her any good!" Harland spat furiously at Jason, motioning curtly for his men to proceed with their vile work. He wheeled about and started giving chase after Hannah himself. Jason was sick at heart when he heard his wife's cries as Harland apparently caught up with her. Meanwhile, the four men advanced upon him with evil intent written on their coarse features. Jason was preparing to do battle with all four of them when Rob suddenly appeared behind the men.

"What's going on here? Jason! Was that Hannah I heard screaming?" Rob demanded. He had just returned from one of the saloons, and it didn't take him long to size up the explosive situation. He charged ahead with a bloodcurdling yell as he and Jason fought outnumbered against Harland's bullies.

The four attackers were as large as Jason, yet none of them were quite as fast nor as skilled in fighting as he and Rob. One of the four lunged forward and attempted to pin Jason's arms behind his back, while another came at him and started to plant his fist into Jason's midsection. However, Jason buckled suddenly at the waist, tossing the man behind him over his head, the fellow landing heavily on the hard wooden planks of the dock. The other man managed to catch Jason on the chin, causing Jason to stagger backward from the force of the blow, but he came forward again, this time successfully knocking the man down with a well-aimed punch to the man's bearded jaw.

Meanwhile, Rob was encountering considerable difficulty with the other two, and he was at the moment pinned beneath one of them while the other was preparing to kick him in the ribs. It was then that they heard someone shouting, and Jason glanced up to see Captain Dean and several members of his crew hurrying toward them.

"Hey, it's a fight!" one of the crew yelled enthusiastically as he and his companions charged ahead. Rob and Jason allowed Captain Dean's men to take care of Harland's four henchmen, and Jason started running toward the other end of the dock.

"Was that Hannah's voice I heard?" Rob gasped, still breathing heavily, blood pouring from his nose as he hurried to keep pace with Jason. "Where is she?"

"Harland's got her!" Jason answered savagely, his own handsome face bearing visible marks of the brief contest. He and Rob took off in the direction Jason had last seen his wife heading, and they had begun searching along the other docks for any sign of Harland and his captive when they suddenly heard Hannah scream. They flew toward that scream when they heard another, and they finally discovered Harland holding Hannah at the end of one of the other docks, the pale moonlight filtering through the clouds above as it shone upon the man who was now using his prisoner's body as a shield. He had drawn a gun and was holding it cocked against Hannah's trembling form.

"Don't come any closer or I'll kill her!" Harland threatened.

"Let her go!" Jason demanded fiercely, still advancing slowly upon them.

"And I said I'd kill her if you don't stop now!" Harland repeated brutally, pressing the gun even closer against Hannah's side.

She stared helplessly toward her husband, then cried desperately, "Jason, go back or he'll kill you!" She was fearful that Harland wouldn't hesitate to shoot her husband, since she knew that's what he had wanted all along. She feverishly tried to think of some way she could prevent it, when an idea suddenly occurred to her—an idea borne from a recent incident.

"You're nothing but a damned coward, Harland! A coward hiding behind a woman's skirts!" Jason muttered furiously, he and Rob halting abruptly now. Before either of them could think of anything, Hannah acted. She suddenly pretended to faint, her entire body going completely limp, catching Harland off guard as her full weight sagged against his arm. Jason took advantage of her ploy and lunged forward, knocking the gun from Harland's grasp and kicking it harmlessly out of the way. Rob rushed forward and helped Hannah to her feet, pulling her back to safety a short distance away.

"Now let's see how brave you are!" Jason's voice came out between clenched teeth, his fist smashing against Harland's chin. Harland stumbled backward, but his eyes narrowed into mere slits, his face flushed with uncontrolled fury as he suddenly drew a knife from his belt. He stepped menacingly toward Jason, brandishing the glistening steel in one hand, causing Hannah to cry out in alarm.

"Jason, watch out!" She screamed as the knife slashed across Jason's muscular chest, leaving a trail of bright red blood. She would have rushed forward if it hadn't been for Rob's hands detaining her, and she watched in breathless terror as Harland came at Jason again, the knife still held high in his hand.

"What's the matter, Caldwell? Don't tell me you're afraid of a little thing like this!" Harland sneered, slashing back and forth as Jason managed to dodge the blade each time. "Was my sister afraid when you murdered her? Did she beg you for mercy? Did you kill her in cold blood, without any remorse, the way I'm going to kill you now?"

"I didn't kill her," Jason muttered in a low, deadly voice, trying to get to Harland without being cut again. "I've told you before; that gun went off accidentally. Your sister and her lover intended for *me* to be the one killed!"

"You're still lying!" Lewis Harland cried in a rage, advancing on him again. "I'm only sorry I was forced to wait so long to avenge her death. But now—now you're going to pay for what you did to her!" Hannah screamed again as the blade nearly made contact with the flesh of Jason's upper left arm. Then an idea occurred to Jason— an idea that he hoped would somehow enable him to get to Harland. Suddenly he moved to a stack of large wooden crates and tugged forcefully at the heavy ropes which bound them together. It was too late by the time Harland realized what Jason was about, and he stood with his mouth gaping in horrified surprise as the crates came crashing upon him.

"Jason!" Hannah cried out in alarm, relieved when she saw that he had managed to move out of the way of the heavy crates. Harland was hidden from view by the debris, and she watched as Jason hurried toward the man, impatiently knocking aside the pieces of wood and the bags of sugar they had contained. She watched her husband's face, afraid that Harland would be waiting to jump him again, but she realized that something was wrong when Jason merely stood staring downward. She pulled away from Rob and rushed forward to her husband's side, puzzled when he put out a hand to stop her.

"It's best if you don't see it, Hannah," he ordered quietly. She was about to ask him what he meant when she glimpsed, out of the corner of her eye, Lewis Harland's face, his features frozen grotesquely in death. He had been knocked down by the crashing weight of the loaded crates, and had apparently fallen on his own knife. The blade was buried to the hilt in his chest, and he had attempted to rise once before falling dead upon his side.

"Oh, Jason, are you all right?" Hannah asked anxiously, shuddering as she turned away from the hideous sight. She was obviously concerned about the wounds Jason had sustained, though he insisted they were nothing.

"I guess you could say it's for the best it ended this way," he murmured as he put his arm around Hannah's shoulders. "Elizabeth's ghost haunted me for so long. But no longer. Never again."

"What do you want to do about the body?" Rob asked quietly, nodding toward the dead man.

"Nothing. They'll just believe he died in a brawl out here on the docks. I don't want Hannah involved in any more of this. She's been through enough." He hugged his wife close to him, unable to keep from wincing a bit at the sharp pain the movement caused. Hannah reached down and tore off a piece of her apron, then pressed it gently but firmly to the cuts on his chest.

"Then we can go home now?" she asked, her bright hair streaming in disarray about her face and shoulders, her dress torn and bloody. She had never appeared more beautiful to Jason as they walked along the waterfront and back toward the ship that would carry them home again.

"Yes, Hannah," he told her with a loving smile, his gaze catching hers and holding it, "we're going home."

They sailed for Seattle the very next day, having persuaded Captain Dean to depart the sinful city sooner than he had originally planned. He had been persuaded easily enough, however, when Hannah pleaded with him sweetly to take them home. She and Jason were even afforded the luxury of a private cabin on the trip homeward, and they passed most of the voyage shut away alone in the confines of the small room.

They spoke of their dreams and plans for their future together, of their hopes for the child Hannah was carrying, a child that had been conceived in deepest love. Jason held his wife close in his arms, almost afraid to touch her for fear of harming her in some way, until she quickly assured him that there was no need for such overly cautious treatment, demanding that he behave much the same toward her as he had done before she had been abducted. They were both glowing from the force of their renewed love by the time they reached Red Creek again.

Rob was understandably quite anxious to be with his own love once more, and he bounded impatiently up the steps of his mother's boardinghouse once they arrived. Hannah and Jason smiled knowingly at one another, then followed after him.

"The saints be praised!" Maggie cried, flying to clasp Hannah tightly in her arms as she wept with joy for the fact that her dear friend had been returned to them safe and sound. Molly soon appeared in the doorway to the parlor, her face flushed and happy as Rob stood with an arm about her, and she, too, rushed forward to welcome her friend. It wasn't long until Jason insisted on taking his wife home with him, and Hannah paused long enough to tell her two friends the good news of her pregnancy. After receiving further hugs and congratulations, she and Jason headed up toward their cabin, promising to return to town the following week for Rob and Molly's wedding.

Hannah nearly cried for joy herself when Thor came bounding exuberantly down the trail from the timber camp. She patted his head and spoke lovingly to him, then laughed in delight when Jason suddenly lifted her high in his strong arms and started inside the cabin.

"Jason, what are you doing?" she demanded with another soft laugh as he carried her through the doorway.

"What do you think I'm doing? I'm carrying my bride across the threshold," he answered with a mischievous grin and a certain, irresistible twinkle in his blue eyes.

"But, I'm no longer a bride!" she reminded him,

392

though she smiled into his own adoring gaze. She was so glad to be home, to be completely alone with the man she loved. She glanced quickly about the cabin, pleasantly surprised to see that everything appeared exactly the same as when she had last seen it.

"You'll always be my bride," Jason promised her in a voice full of meaning as he carried her into their bedroom and placed her gently upon the bed. She smiled invitingly up at him, her arms instinctively reaching upward for him as he lay down beside her, and it wasn't long at all before the two of them were undressed and beneath the covers.

Hannah's eyes swept closed in dizzying ecstasy as Jason's strong, knowing hands sought out the most sensitive, intimate places on her trembling body, and she trailed her fingers sensuously up and down his muscular back, her hands gripping him harder as their flesh mingled, as the two of them soared to rapturous heights, becoming one in every way.

"Have I ever told you how very much I love you, Mrs. Caldwell?" Jason asked quietly with a contented smile on his handsome face, cradling his wife in his arms, their skin warm and glowing in the tender aftermath of their impassioned lovemaking.

"Yes, but I should like to hear you say it again and again, Mr. Caldwell!" Hannah lovingly responded, nestling against him with a happy sigh, pressing her soft curves to his lean, muscular hardness. She knew that she and Jason would always share a very special love that few people seemed destined to find in their lifetimes. She was convinced that the two of them had been brought together for a purpose, that they would never be parted again. What had begun all those months ago as a desperate means of escape from her unhappy life back in the East had culminated in her finding the one man on earth who could make her feel the way she felt now, and she gave silent thanks as she closed her eyes and drifted off into a restful sleep beside her husband.

Epilogue

Hannah Caldwell sat contentedly before the blazing fire, a golden-haired, blue-eyed, happily gurgling baby on her lap as the two of them took a much-needed rest from the day's routine. A knock sounded unexpectedly at the door and Hannah hurried to answer it, causing her young son to grin in delight at the speed with which his mother moved. Hannah opened the door to reveal another young woman—a woman who was quite obviously expecting a child of her own.

"Molly!" Hannah cried with pleasure. "I didn't know you and Rob would be coming by today. I thought we wouldn't see you again until the church meeting next week." She ushered her friend inside, then handed Molly little Patrick while she set about putting a fresh pot of coffee on the stove.

"Rob had some business matters to discuss with Jason, so I insisted that he bring me along as well," Molly explained. She chuckled softly as she added, "He's beginning to treat me like a fragile little doll or something! The doctor said it was perfectly all right for me to ride, just as long as we took things a bit slower. She rocked the baby to and fro in her arms, humming a soothing little tune, suddenly very impatient to have a child of her own to love and care for.

"I know how you feel," Hannah remarked as she stood in the doorway and watched her friend enjoying little Patrick's squeals and gurgles. "But I promise you, it will be over with soon enough! After all, you and Rob have been married only a little more than a year. It's good that you had some time together first." She brought the coffeepot and two cups to the table, then sank down in the chair across from her friend. "I must admit, though, a child seems to draw you even closer together." She reached out for Patrick, who was returned to his mother's lap and promptly became engrossed in teething on a piece of toweling while the two women talked.

It had been more than a year since Hannah and Jason had returned from San Francisco and settled down on their mountain. In that time, quite a number of surprising things had happened. Rob and Jason had finally mended all their past differences and actually formed a partnership. Rob and Molly were married and built a cabin not far from the one where Jason and Hannah lived. The town of Red Creek was changing rapidly, what with more families venturing forth into the territory. In fact, the town was proud to boast of two general stores, as well as a new church meeting house for the twice-monthly services. Colette had left town before Jason's and Hannah's return, and no one had heard of her whereabouts since. Maggie Clancy was being courted by the proprietor of the newest general store, an attractive widower from the East who was making it quite obvious to everyone that he found Maggie's company totally delightful. Maggie had given no indication whether she was going to accept the gentleman's proposal of marriage, but Hannah believed she would say yes, for she knew her friend to be increasingly lonely and missing companionship since Rob and Molly had moved away from town.

"Hannah," Molly remarked suddenly, her expression growing quite solemn as she gazed across at her friend, "did you ever really think things would turn out this way? I mean, all those months we were on that ship, did you ever really believe we would end up being so happy?"

"I had no idea," Hannah admitted with a slight shake of her head as she hugged Patrick close to her. "All of my dreams have been surpassed by having Jason and Patrick in my life." Suddenly the door swung open and Jason and Rob strode inside. Patrick's round little face lit up at the sight of his tall father, and Jason took hold of his son and lifted him high in the air, rewarded by the baby's delighted laughter. Rob paused a moment to tickle little Patrick and smile at the baby, before moving to his wife's side and placing an affectionate hand on her shoulder, while Hannah sat and surveyed the happy scene with a sense of wonderment.

No, she mused as she found herself surprisingly close to tears, she could never have imagined such a life for herself! She was married to a man who loved and cherished her, a man whom she loved so deeply she could never feel complete unless she was with him. And Patrick, she thought, her eyes moving to his happy little face. There were simply no words to describe the warmth and contentment she felt because of him.

Later that same evening, after Hannah had placed little Patrick in his cradle for the night, she and Jason sat together before the red glow cast by the crackling fire. Jason suddenly reached over and drew his wife from her chair and onto his lap, his strong arms going about her to hold her close. Thor lay dozing, curled up on the floor beside the hearth, his eyes blinking open every now and then as Jason and Hannah talked.

"Have I told you lately that I love you, Mrs. Caldwell?" Jason asked quietly, his lips brushing her cheek tenderly as she snuggled against him.

"Yes, but please tell me again, Mr. Caldwell," Hannah responded lovingly, her face lifting for his kiss as his lips captured hers.